On The Banks Of The Amazon

by

William Henry Giles Kingston

Double9
BOOKS

On The Banks Of The Amazon
by William Henry Giles Kingston

ISBN: 978-93-64284-32-5

Published by

DOUBLE 9 BOOKS
2/13-B, Ansari Road
Daryaganj, New Delhi – 110002
info@double9books.com
www.double9books.com
Tel. 011-40042856

ABOUT THE AUTHOR

William Henry Giles Kingston (1814-1880) was a prolific English writer, best known for his adventure novels aimed at younger readers. His works, often set in exotic locations and filled with thrilling escapades, have captivated generations of readers and remain influential in the genre of children's adventure literature. Kingston's first book, "The Circassian Chief," was published in 1844, but it was his adventure novels for young readers that brought him widespread recognition and success. He wrote over 130 books, many of which were serialized in magazines before being published in book form. His stories often featured young protagonists embarking on voyages, exploring new lands, and overcoming various challenges. Some of his most famous works include "Peter the Whaler" (1851), "The Three Midshipmen" (1862), "The Three Lieutenants" (1870), and "The Three Admirals" (1878). Kingston's writing style is characterized by its vivid descriptions, moral lessons, and emphasis on courage, loyalty, and perseverance. ingston's adventure novels have left a lasting impact on children's literature, inspiring many young readers to develop an interest in geography, history, and exploration. His works have been translated into several languages and have remained in print for many years, a testament to their enduring popularity and appeal. Kingston died on August 5, 1880, in Willesden, Middlesex, leaving behind a rich legacy of adventure stories that continue to entertain and educate readers around the world.

CONTENTS

Chapter One
My school-boy days and friends

I might find an excuse for being proud, if I were so,—not because my ancestors were of exalted rank or title, or celebrated for noble deeds or unbounded wealth, or, indeed, on account of any ordinary reasons,— but because I was born in one of the highest cities in the world. I saw the light in Quito, the capital of Ecuador, then forming the northern part of the Spanish province of Peru. The first objects I remember beyond the courtyard of our house in which I used to play, with its fountain and flower-bed in the centre, and surrounding arches of sun-burned bricks, were lofty mountains towering up into the sky. From one of them, called Pichincha, which looked quite close through the clear atmosphere of that region, I remember seeing flames of fire and dark masses of smoke, intermingled with dust and ashes, spouting forth. Now and then, when the wind blew from it, thick showers of dust fell down over us, causing great consternation; for many thought that stones and rocks might follow and overwhelm the city. All day long a lofty column of smoke rose up towards the sky, and at night a vast mass of fire was seen ascending from the summit; but no harm was done to the city, so that we could gaze calmly at the spectacle without apprehension. Pichincha is, indeed, only one of several mountains in the neighbourhood from the tops of which bonfires occasionally blaze forth. Further off, but rising still higher, is the glittering cone of Cotopaxi, which, like a tyrant, has made its power felt by the devastation it has often caused in the plains which surround its base: while near it rise the peaks of Corazon and Rumiñagui. Far more dreaded than their fires is the quaking and heaving and tumbling about of the earth, shaking down as it does human habitations and mountain-tops, towers and steeples, and uprooting trees, and opening wide chasms, turning streams from their courses, and overwhelming towns and villages, and destroying in other ways the works of men's hands, and human beings themselves, in its wild commotion.

These burning mountains, in spite of their fire and smoke, appear but insignificant pigmies compared to that mighty mountain which rises in their neighbourhood—the majestic Chimborazo. We could see far off its snow-white dome, free of clouds, towering into the deep blue sky, many thousand feet above the ocean; while on the other side its brother, Tunguragua, shoots up above the surrounding heights, but, in spite of its ambitious efforts, has failed to reach the same altitude I might speak of Antisana, and many other lofty heights with hard names? but I fancy that a fair idea may be formed of that wonderful region of giant mountains from the description I have already given.

I used often to think that I should like to get to the top of Chimborazo, the way up looked so easy at a distance; but no one has ever reached its summit, though several valiant philosophers and others have made the attempt.

The mountain range I have described, of which Chimborazo was long considered the highest point, till Aconcagua in Chili was found to be higher, rises from the ocean in the far-off southern end of America, and runs up along its western shore, ever proud and grand, with snow-topped heights rising tens of thousands of feet above the ocean, till it sinks once more towards the northern extremity of the southern half of the continent, running along the Isthmus of Panama, through Mexico at a less elevation, again to rise in the almost unbroken range of the Rocky Mountains, not to sink till it reaches the snow-covered plains of the Arctic region.

But I am becoming too scientific and geographical; and I must confess that it was not till many years after the time of which I am speaking that I knew anything about the matter. My father, Don Martin Fiel, had been for some years settled in Quito as a merchant. His mother was Spanish, or partly so, born in Peru—I believe that she had some of the blood of the Incas in her veins, a matter of which she was not a little proud, I have been told—but his father was an Englishman, and our proper family name was Faithful. My father, having lived for many years in the Spanish South American provinces, had obtained the rights and privileges of a Spaniard. He had, however, been sent over to England for his education, and was a thorough Englishman at heart. He had made during his younger days several visits to England for mercantile purposes, and during one of them had married my mother. He was, though really a Protestant—I am sorry to have to make the confession—nominally a Roman Catholic; for he, being a Spanish subject, could not otherwise at that time have resided in any part of the territories of Spain and carried on his business with freedom: but I feel now that no person has a right to conceal their true faith, and to pretend to believe what is false, for the sake of any worldly advantage. My mother, however, had stipulated that all her children should be brought up as Protestants. To this he had agreed, though he found when he had sons that he was in consequence subjected to considerable annoyance from the priests, who threatened to denounce him as a heretic. To avoid this, he had to send his children to England at an early age for their education; indeed, had we remained at Quito we could only have obtained a very poor one at any public school or college. It will be understood from what I have said, that though we were really English, and I have always felt like an Englishman, we had both Spanish and native connections, which will account for some of the circumstances which afterwards occurred to us.

My father, though he himself resided at Quito, had also a house of business at Guayaquil, which imported European manufactured goods, and exported in return Peruvian bark and other articles, of which I shall by-and-by have to speak. He was greatly respected by his fellow-citizens, although they might have been somewhat jealous of him for succeeding in his business through his energy and perseverance, while they themselves, sitting idle all the day smoking their cigarettes without attempting to exert their minds, were left behind. My dear mother lived very much alone, for the society of the ladies of Quito, though they are very charming in manner, afforded her but little satisfaction, from their utter want of education.

I remember the joy which the arrival of my eldest sister, Fanny—or Doña Francisca, as the Spaniards called her—who had gone to school in England, and Aunt Martha, who brought her back, caused in the family. I had another sister, Ellen, much younger; a sweet, dear little girl, of whom I was very fond. She was indeed the pet of the family. My elder brother, John, was at school in England. I remember thinking Aunt Martha, who was my mother's elder sister, very stiff and formal; and I was not at all pleased when she expressed her intention of teaching me and keeping me in order. My mother's health had been delicate, and I had been left very much to the care of old Domingos, a negro servant of my father's, who had been with him since his boyhood, and with my grandfather before him. He was the butler, or major-domo, the head over all the other servants, and, I believe, deservedly trusted. Among them I remember best little Maria, a young negro slave girl who attended especially on Ellen; and Antonio, a Gallego from the north of Spain, a worthy, honest fellow, who had been in the family from his boyhood, and was much attached to us all. I soon learned to like Aunt Martha better than I had expected, for though I thought her looks very terrible at first—and she was certainly firm—she was really kind and gentle. Under her instruction I gained the first knowledge of the letters of the alphabet, of which I was before profoundly ignorant. Of course she was very gentle with Ellen, as everybody was, and Fanny seemed to be very fond of her. She was courageous, too, as I before long had evidence. I remember one night being suddenly lifted in her arms, and carried out by her into the patio of courtyard. There was a strange rumbling noise underneath our feet, and I could see the stout walls of our house rocking to and fro; and yet, though the earth was tumbling about, she did not tremble in the least, but I heard her telling the servants not to shriek out or to pray to the saints, who could not help them, but to put their trust in God, who made the world, and who would save them from danger if it was his good will. It was a very fearful night, however, and though I believe the earthquake did not last long, it tumbled down, during the few minutes of its duration, a number of buildings, and many of the inhabitants were buried beneath the ruins. Our house, however, which was on the outskirts of the city, and had no upper story, although some of the walls were cracked, escaped without further injury; and before morning we were in our beds again, and I, for my part, was sleeping soundly.

A short time after this I found that some great event was about to take place, and I saw trunks being packed; and my mother, who had been ill for some time, was very busy, and looked, I often thought, somewhat sad; and then I heard that she and Ellen and I were going to England, to be accompanied by Domingos and Maria, and that we were to remain there some time, and that I was to go to school, and then, if my father did not join us, that John and Ellen and I were to come back together with our mother, unless she returned before that time. Aunt Martha and Fanny were to stay and take care of my father. Of course I was highly delighted when I heard this, and began packing a box with my playthings, and all sorts of articles, and was very indignant when Maria told me that they were not to go. I do not remember much about the journey, except that my father came with us, and that the party rode on mules; that Domingos carried me before him; that we went up and down mountains and into deep valleys; and that sometimes it was very hot, and sometimes very cold; and that we stopped at very uncivilised-looking resting-places at night; and that at last we reached a large town, close to the sea, which was, I have since learned, Guayaquil. I remember seeing some magnificent fruits—pine-apples, oranges, lemons, limes, alligator-pears, melons, and many others—and eating some of them, or probably I should not have recollected the circumstance. The place was very busy, and far more people were moving about than I had been accustomed to see at Quito; and in the harbour were a number of vessels— large ships and small ones, and curious rafts, on which the natives were sailing or paddling about, called *balsas*. They were made of light balsa wood, which is very buoyant. They were of all sizes, and some had come in from a considerable distance along the coast. Then my father accompanied us on board a big ship, and took an affectionate leave of my mother and sister and me; and we all cried very much at parting, at least Ellen and I did, though I was so well pleased with all the sights I witnessed that I soon forgot my sorrow. Then the sails of the *Pizarro*—that was the name of our ship—

were set, and we glided out of the harbour, while the boat containing my father returned to the shore. The *Pizarro* was, I should say, a Spanish ship, commanded by Captain Lopez, a very worthy man, in whom my father had great confidence, or he would not have committed our mother and us to his charge. At that time Spanish vessels alone were allowed by the Spaniards to trade to the ports of their colonies, which contributed with many other causes greatly to retard their progress. I, however, knew nothing about such matters at that time. I remember the compass in the binnacle placed before a big wheel, at which a man was always standing steering the ship, and I was told that we were sailing south. I thought the ocean, which was blue, and calm, and glittering in the sunshine, must be very wide, and wondered where it could end, or whether it had an end towards the west. On the east was the coast of Peru, and I could see the lofty snow-capped mountains rising up out of the plain, looking as if they were intended to bear up the sky should it come down towards the earth. Day after day we glided on. There they were as high as ever, apparently quite close to us, though I heard the captain tell my mother that they were fifty miles off or more. I scarcely believed him, though I did not think so big and grave a man could tell a story. I did not understand at that time to what a distance objects can be seen in that pure, clear atmosphere. We after that stood off the coast for many hours, and yet they appeared almost as high as ever. The mountains I saw were the Andes or the Cordilleras, among which I had lived so long without having a clear idea of their extent.

We were not idle during the voyage, for our mother set to work the second day we were at sea to give us our lessons. She had made a point of teaching us English as soon as we could utter a word; but though Ellen spoke it very well from being always with her, I spoke Spanish mixed with Quichua, the native Indian tongue, much more readily. We now, however, learned all our lessons in English, and read a great deal, so that I got on rapidly.

The weather at length began to grow unusually cold, and the sky was covered with clouds. We put on warm clothes, and kept much oftener than usual in the cabin. The ship too began to tumble about, and I thought sometimes would be sent right over. I remember inquiring seriously if a *waterquake* were taking place; for I had hitherto seen the ocean so calm, that I fancied it would always remain so, and that it was only the earth which was given to shaking and tumbling about. The wind whistled and roared, and the spray flew over the deck, and the sailors went out on the yards and reefed the sails; but no one seemed to mind what was happening, so I was soon content, and thought all was right; and when I looked on the waves, it struck me that they were not a quarter as high as the mountains I had been accustomed to see, and wondered how they were able to tumble the great big ship about in the way they did. Still on we went day after day, and I discovered that we were sailing in an opposite direction to that we had before steered. I could not make it out, till the captain showed me a chart, and gave me my first lesson in geography on a grand scale; and I then saw that we had come down the west coast of South America, and were now sailing northward along its eastern coast.

I was very glad when I could go on deck again without greatcoat, and the sun shone forth as brightly almost as it does at Quito. Then in a little time the weather got very hot again, and there was no wind, and the ship lay on the glassy sea, her white sails flapping against the masts. There we lay day after day, and I began to think that at that rate we should never get to England; but Captain Lopez told me that I need not trouble myself about the matter, as the wind was sure to come some day or other, and that then we should glide along as fast as ever. I found that he was right, though we were becalmed several times after that.

At length we saw the crew very busy in polishing up the ship, and ranging the cables along the deck, as getting them ready for anchoring in called; and men were aloft all day looking out ahead; and then came the shout of "Terra! terra!—España!" and I found that we were approaching the coast of Spain. The next morning when I went on deck the ship was at anchor, surrounded by land, with a large city on one side, and other towns or villages scattered about on the other. This was the beautiful Bay of Cadiz. Near us lay a large ship with the English flag flying at her peak. Captain Lopez went on board her, and then hurried on shore with certain papers in his hand; and when he returned, we all went on board the English ship. Soon after, the anchor was hove up, the sails let fall, and away we sailed out of the harbour. Thus we did not even set foot on Spanish soil. I asked my mother the reason of this: she replied, that finding the ship on the point of sailing, she did not like to lose the opportunity of going to England in her; that the ship was called the *Inca*, commanded by Captain Byles, with whom she and my father were acquainted.

I remember that Captain Byles was very kind and attentive, that the cabin was very neat and clean—a quality for which that of the *Pizarro* was not remarkable—while the English crew, many of whom were old men-of-war's-men, paid off at the end of the war, were far more orderly than the Spaniards. There was a black cook, Sam by name, and a white goat. With the former we soon struck up a friendship, for he was good-natured and kind to us, and a most intelligent fellow; the latter used to chase us round and round the deck, and several times tumbled me head over heels when I jumped before her to prevent her from butting at Ellen. Of Sam I shall have to speak more by-and-by. I do not remember many more incidents of the voyage till one day I saw the men heaving the lead, and I found that we were in the chops of the Channel; and then I heard the shout of "Land! land!" from one of the crew at the mast-head, and I was told that England was in sight; and after a time I saw a light-blue line away over the bow on the left side, and heard that it was the Lizard, which I explained to Ellen was not a creature, but a point of land at the west end of England. With a fine breeze, studdingsails on either side, the colours flying, the sky bright and the sea blue, the big ship, her canvas glittering in the sunlight glided proudly up Channel. Even the gruffest old seaman began to smile, and every one seemed in good spirits. At last a little one-masted vessel came dancing over the small waves towards us, our sails were brailed up, a boat put off from her, and a big man with huge whiskers, and rough greatcoat, and broad-brimmed hat climbed up the side, and shook hands with the captain; and I heard that the pilot had come on board, and that we were sailing into the Downs. I went below, and on returning on deck I looked up and saw, instead of the broad sheets of white canvas which had so long been spread, the long yards above my head with the sails closely furled. The ship was at anchor. In a short time the boat came alongside, and my mother and sister and I, with our attendants, were lowered into her. We rowed on shore, and went to a big house, where all the people were wonderfully polite. I asked if this was to be our future home, but my mother told me it was an inn—very unlike the resting-places we had stopped at on our journey from Quito.

The next day we were all seated inside a yellow carriage, with Domingos and Maria on the outside, and rolling away over the smooth road at a great rate. We went on and on, changing horses every now and then, through a country dotted about with houses which looked very large and grand, and green trees which looked very small after those I had been accustomed to see. At length the houses became thicker and thicker, and we were driving through long streets with numberless carriages dashing here and there, and carts, and vans, and vehicles of all sorts; and my mother told me we were in London. We drove on, and I thought we should soon be on the other side; but I found that we had not got nearly into the centre of it. I had thought Quito a large city, but this, I guessed, must be ten times larger. All the houses, too, looked wonderfully high, and I thought if an earthquake were to occur, how quickly they would all topple down. I asked my mother how people could venture to build such tall houses. She laughed, and said that happily in England there were no earthquakes; and that, in another city in the north, there were houses ten stories high.

We stopped at last before a house in a long, dull-looking street, and a gentleman came to the door and handed us all out, and kissed my mother and Ellen and me, and welcomed us to England; and I found that he was Uncle James, my mother's brother; and there was our aunt, his wife, and a number of cousins, boys and girls; and we were all soon quite at home and happy, though I did not exactly know what to do with myself.

A few days after that, Uncle James and my mother and I drove out in a carriage, and there was a box on the top of it full of my clothes, and several other things; and then I found that I was going to school. I was rather pleased than otherwise; not that I wished to leave my mother and Ellen, but I wanted to know what sort of a place school was. We went some distance away from London, and stopped before a house with an iron gate, and a huge stone lion on each side of it. We got out, and were shown into a drawing-room, and there we sat, till a tall gentleman dressed in black, with a very white head, made his appearance, and my mother and Uncle James talked to him for some time; then he called me up, patted me on the head, and told me he hoped that I should be a good boy, and learn my lessons well. I did not feel quite comfortable when my mother got up and kissed me again and again, and looked somewhat sad; and then Uncle James wished me good-bye; and out they went, while the tall gentleman kept me by the hand.

"Now, Harry Faithful," he said, "I will introduce you to your school-fellows;" and he conducted me through a passage, at the end of which was a door which opened out into a large open space covered with gravel, with high walls on either side. A big tree stood in the centre, and a vast number of boys of all ages were running about. Some had hoops, others were jumping over long ropes, and others, with reins fastened to their arms held by bigger boys, were scampering round and round, playing at horses. Some were leaping over each other's backs, and others were hopping about with their arms folded charging at each other. I thought it very good fun, and hoped that was the way they were always employed.

The tall gentleman, after waiting a minute or two, called out, "Antony Nyass, come here. Here is the son of an old friend of your father's. I expect you to look after him."

Then he turned round to me, and said, "When the bell rings, you will come in with the rest, and we will lose no time in placing you."

"And so you are the new boy," said my companion. "What is your name?" I told him. "Well, I am very glad you are come," he observed, "for I want a chum. We will have all sorts of fun together. Will you have a hoop? I have got a prime one which beats all those of the fellows in my class; or will you go shares in a pair of leather reins?" I told him that I should be very glad to do what he liked, and that I had plenty of money, though I could not say how much, as I was not accustomed to English coin, and could not remember what it was called. "Oh, I will soon put you up to that," he said, laughing; "but do not show it now. We will see by-and-by what you can do with it."

While we were speaking, a number of other boys collected round us, and began to ask me all sorts of questions—who I was, who my friends were, where I had come from, how old I was, and if I had ever been to another school.

"Do not tell them," whispered Nyass.

"What is that you are saying, Master Tony!" exclaimed one of the boys. "You are putting him up to some of your own tricks."

"I will tell you all by-and-by," I answered, taking my new friend's hint.

"Can you run?" asked Tony. "Tell them that you will race any one of them," he whispered.

"I do not know, but I will try," I replied.

"Who is for a race?" exclaimed Tony. "He will run you down to the bottom of the play-ground and back again, and if he does not beat all the fellows of his own size I shall be surprised."

I was light and active, and though I had never before run a race, having no companions to run with, I did my best to follow out Tony's suggestion. At the word, off I set as hard as I could tear; five or six other fellows besides Tony ran also. He kept up with me, though we distanced the rest. He touched the wall at the bottom, and I followed his example.

"Now, back again as hard as you can go! I am the best runner of my size in the school," he cried out, as he kept close to me; "if you beat me, your fame is established, and the fellows will treat you with respect after that."

I felt, however, very doubtful whether I could beat Tony; but I did my best, and as we neared the point we started from I found myself drawing ahead of him. "That is it!" he shouted; "keep on, and you will do it." I suspected that he was letting me get ahead of him on purpose, and I reached the starting-point four or five paces before him. I felt, however, that I could not have run another minute if my life had depended on it; while he came in without the slightest panting. The other fellows followed mostly together, a short distance behind.

It is curious how slight a thing gives a boy a position at once in a school. Thanks to Tony, I gained one at once, and ever afterwards kept it. I do not intend to give an account of my school-life and adventures, as I have more interesting matter to describe. I was placed in the lowest class, as might have been expected. Although I knew nothing of Latin, I was up to several things which my class-mates were not, and as I did my best to learn, I soon caught up a number of them. My friend Tony was in the class above me, and he was always ready to give me any help. Though not quarrelsome, I had several battles to fight, and got into scrapes now and then, but not often, and altogether I believed I was getting on pretty well. Tony, my first acquaintance, remained my firm friend. Although now and then we had quarrels, we quickly made them up again. He used to listen with eager ears to the accounts I gave him of my voyage, and the wonders of my native land. He never laughed at my foreign accent, though the other boys did; but I very soon got rid of it. I used to try to teach him Spanish, and the Indian language, which I had learned from the servants; but I soon forgot them myself, and had difficulty even in recalling a few words of the tongue which I once spoke with ease.

"I say, Harry, I should so like to go out with you to that country," said Tony to me one day. "When you go back I must try and get my father to let me accompany you."

I, of course, was well pleased at the proposal, and we talked for days together of what we should do when we got out there. At last we began to think that it was very hard we should have to wait till we had grown big fellows like those at the head of the school, and Tony proposed that we should start away by ourselves. We looked at the map, and considered how we could best accomplish our object. We observed the mighty river Amazon rising at no great distance—so it seemed on paper—from Quito itself, and running right across the continent into the Atlantic.

"Will it not be fun paddling up by ourselves in a canoe!" exclaimed Tony. "We will have guns to go on shore and shoot birds and beasts; and when we grow tired of paddling we will sail along before the wind; and we will have a tent, and sleep in it at night, and light a fire in front of it to cook our suppers and keep off the wild beasts; and then, when we arrive at the upper end of the river, we will sell our canoe to the Indians, and trudge away on foot with knapsacks on our backs up the mountains, till we reach your father's house; and will not he be astonished to see us!"

I agreed with him in his last idea certainly, but I was puzzled to think how we were to reach the mouth of the Amazon, and when we were there how we were to procure canoe. All the rest appeared pretty easy in the way Tony proposed it, and, after all, even on a big map, the river did not look so very long.

"Well, my idea is," said Tony, "that we should save up all our pocket-money, and then, some day when we have got very hard lessons to do, or anything disagreeable takes place, run off, and get aboard a ship sailing to South America. I should not mind being cabin-boy for a short time; and as you know Spanish and Indian, you could tell the captain you would interpret for him, and of course he would be very glad to have you; and then, you know, we should soon learn to be sailors; and it will be much pleasanter climbing about the rigging and up the masts and along the yards than sitting at our desks all day bothering our heads with Caesar and Ovid and sums and history and geography, and all that sort of thing."

"But I have not got Caesar and Ovid to do yet," I observed; "and I want to have a little more schooling; for Uncle James says I shall not be fit for anything until I do. Do not you think we had better wait till I get into your class, or rather higher still?"

Tony said he was much disappointed at my drawing back, which he argued I was doing when I made these remarks. However, I spoke in perfect sincerity, and fully believed that I should enjoy the adventure he proposed just as much as he would. I had my doubts, however, whether we should receive so favourable a reception at the end of our journey as he supposed. However, he continued talking and talking about the matter, till I agreed to consider what could be done during another half.

I spent my first holidays in London at Uncle James's, and my brother John came there, and I was surprised to find what a big fellow he was. We were very good friends, and he took me out to see a number of the sights of London. We went, among other places, to Exeter Change, where there were all sorts of wild beasts. I had no idea until then that there were so many in the world. I was highly interested, and learned the names of nearly all of them; and John told me where they had come from, and all about their habits. Then Uncle James gave me a book of natural history, which I read with great delight. I found by the book that the beasts I had seen at Exeter Change were only a very small number of those which exist in different parts of the world. I liked that book of natural history better than any I had ever read; except, perhaps, "Robinson Crusoe," which Tony had lent me, and which he said was the best book that ever was written. I thus gained a very considerable knowledge of the quadrupeds and the feathered tribes of the animal kingdom, and Uncle James said he thought some day I should become a first-rate naturalist, if I had opportunities of studying the creatures in their native wild. I resolved the next summer holidays, which were to be spent in the country, to catch as many of the creatures as I could, and form a menagerie of my own. I should say I had not told John of the plan Tony and I had in contemplation—of exploring the Amazon by ourselves. I thought, from some of his remarks, that he possibly might not approve of it.

I soon got tired of London, after I had seen the usual sights, though I was glad to be with my mother and Ellen and my cousins. John also was very kind, but he was such a big fellow that I stood in as much awe of him as I did of my uncle. I was not sorry, therefore, to find myself at school with companions of my own age. As the weather was very cold, Tony and I agreed that we would put off our expedition till the summer, and in the meantime we talked of the menagerie I proposed making, and other subjects of equal importance, which prevented us thinking about the former matter.

I had a good many friends among my school-fellows. Arthur Mallet, next to Tony, was my chief friend. He was by several months my junior—a delicate, gentle boy, amiable, sensible, and clever. He was liked by the masters as well as by the boys, and that is saying much in his favour. Poor fellow, notwithstanding this he was frequently out of spirits. I asked him one day why he looked so sad. He was silent for some minutes. "I will tell you, Harry," he said at length. "I am thinking of my mother. She is dying. I know it, for she told me so. She never deceived me. When she has gone I shall have no one to care for me—and—and—Harry, I shall have to depend on the charity of strangers for support. She urged me to work hard, that I might be independent; but it will be a long time before I can become so. For myself I do not so much mind, but it troubles my mother greatly; and then to have her die—though I know she is going to heaven—I cannot bear the thought." He said more in the same style. "And then, should my father come back—oh, what will he do!" he added.

"I thought from what you said that you had no father," I remarked. "Where is he then, Arthur?"

"That is what I do not know," he answered. "Do not speak about it to any one, Harry. He went away a long time ago, on account of something that had happened. He could not bear to stay in England. But he was not to blame. That is all I know. He could not take her with him; and my grandmother and aunts with whom she was left died, and their fortune was lost; and what she has now got is only for her life, and that troubles her also greatly."

I tried as well as I could to comfort Arthur, and after this felt more than ever anxious to stand by him an a friend. "I may some day be able to help him," I thought—but I did not tell him so. Our friendship had been disinterested, and thus I wished it to remain.

I said that I had many friends at school, but there were some few whom I looked upon in a contrary light; especially one big boy, Houlston, of whom all the little ones were dreadfully afraid. He used to make us do anything that seized his fancy, and if we ventured to refuse, often thrashed us. Poor

Arthur Mallet frequently came in for his ill-treatment, and bore it, we all thought, with far too much patience. At last Tony and I and a few other fellows agreed that we would stand it no longer. One day Houlston and one of the upper form boys, who was younger than himself, had a dispute. We thought that he was going to thrash the other fellow; but the latter standing up in his own defence, Houlston walked off, not venturing, as we supposed, to encounter him. This, of course, gave us courage. A few day afterwards Tony was reading, when Houlston, coming by, seized his book, saying he wanted it. Tony watched his opportunity, and snatching it up, made off out of the school-room, through the play-ground into a yard on one side, which, not being overlooked by any of the windows from the house, was the usual place for pugilistic encounters. Houlston followed. I saw Arthur Mallet and several of those who had promised to side with us standing near. Arthur joined us, though somewhat unwillingly. We made chase. Tony, who had fled to the yard, was at length overtaken by his pursuer, who began hitting him over the head and shoulders. I signed to my companions, and making a spring, jumped on Houlston's back and began belabouring him with might and main. I shouted to the others to come on and attack him on either side. He was furious, and struck out right and left at them; but I, clinging pertinaciously to his back, prevented his blows having due effect. My companions on this closed in, and two of them seizing him by the legs, down he came, with me still clinging to his back. The rest now threw themselves upon him. Handkerchiefs were brought out, and in spite of his struggles they managed to tie his arms behind him, while I kept him down. Though he kicked out furiously, by jumping on his body we succeeded in securing his legs, and we thus had him in our power. It was in the evening of a half-holiday. On one side of the yard was a wood-shed. Into this we dragged him. Astonishment and the efforts he made to free himself had prevented him from shouting for help. Before he had uttered a cry, Rawlings, one of the biggest of our party, running up, shoved a handkerchief into his mouth, which completely gagged him. We then all ran away, leaving him without compunction in the dark and cold. Assembling again in the school-room, we agreed to leave him till somebody coming by might release him. Tea-time came, and Houlston did not make his appearance. I began to grow anxious, and communicated my fears to Arthur, who sat next to me. Still he did not come. Tea was over. At last Arthur entreated that we would go and ascertain what was the matter. It was now quite dark. I remember quite well the uncomfortable feeling I had, as, stealing out, we groped our way in the dark to the yard. On approaching the wood-house we heard a groan. Could it proceed from Houlston? My heart beat more tranquilly, though, for the groan showed that he was alive. We crept in. He was where we had left him; but his hands were icy cold. I bethought me first of withdrawing the handkerchief from his mouth. Some of the fellows proposed leaving him again.

"Oh no, no; pray don't do that!" exclaimed Arthur. "Perhaps he will promise to give up bullying if we agree to cast him loose."

"You hear that, Houlston?" said Tony. "Will you become a good fellow and treat the little chaps properly, or will you spend the night out here?"

Houlston only grumbled out some words which we could not understand. At last we heard him say, "What is it you want?" It was evident from his tone that he was greatly humbled. That is not surprising, for he must have been very cold and very hungry, and Tony repeated the question.

"He will not promise. We must put the gag in again," said two or three of the other fellows.

"Will you promise?" asked Tony again.

"Oh, do let him go!" again exclaimed Arthur, whose kind heart was moved by the pitiable condition of our captive. "He will promise—I know he will; and I do not mind if he bullies me ever so much. We should think any one very cruel who kept us out in the cold as we have kept him. I am sure that he will promise what we ask—won't you, Houlston?"

"No, he will not," said another boy. "He will have a couple of hours to wait till the names are called over, and perhaps somebody will then come and look for him. He will be much colder by that time."

"Oh yes, I will promise!" cried Houlston. "Let me go, and I will not bully you little fellows any more. Just try me. And I will remember what Mallet said—he has more feeling than any of you; I did not expect him to have spoken as he has, for I treated him always worse than any of you."

"You promise, on your word of honour," said Tony; "and you will not go and complain of us? You must promise that too."

Houlston was completely humbled. He promised all we demanded.

"We may trust to his word. I am sure we may!" exclaimed Arthur. "Oh, do let us loose him!"

"Thank you, Mallet. Thank you, Faithful. I am much obliged to you," whispered Houlston, as Arthur undid the handkerchief which bound his wrists. The others were in the meantime casting off those round his legs. We lifted him up, for he was so numbed and chilled that he could not walk. Arthur had brought a slice of bread and butter doubled up in his pocket. He offered it to Houlston, who took it gratefully. His clothes, I felt, were covered with chips of wood and dust. We brushed him with our hands as well as we could in the dark, and then led him back into the playroom, where the boys were collecting after tea. I watched him narrowly, fearing mat he might tell some of the big fellows what had happened; but he went to his box without speaking to any one, and then taking up his books, proceeded to the school-room to learn his lessons for the next day. We kept our counsel, and were convinced that Houlston wisely kept his, for not a word did he utter to any of his companions of what had occurred. From that day forward he was generally kind and good-natured, and especially so to Arthur Mallet. He helped him in his lessons, and was constantly making him presents of such things as boys prize, though older people may not set much value on them. Though he might lose his temper with others, he never did so with Arthur, and always seemed anxious to show his friendly feeling in a variety of ways. I have seldom seen a fellow so greatly changed for the better as Houlston became, owing, I believe, greatly to the way Arthur had pleaded his cause when the rest of us seemed inclined to revenge ourselves still further than we had already done.

I should not have mentioned the circumstance, except for the sake of the moral it taught me. There is an old saying, that when a bull runs at you the best way of escaping him is to seize him by the horns; and from the manner we overcame Houlston, I am convinced of the wisdom of the advice. Ever since, when a difficulty has occurred, I have seized it boldly, grappled with it as we grappled with Houlston, summoned up all my courage, resolution, and strength, just as Tony and I called our companions to our assistance, and dragged it, metaphorically speaking, to the ground, gagged it as we gagged the bully, and not let it loose again till I have been convinced that it would no longer trouble me. Again, when I have had any difficult thing to do, I have done it at once, or tried my best to do it. I have never put off a disagreeable thing which I may have had to do till another day. I have got it over as soon as possible, whatever it may have been. I have generally found that the anticipation is worse than the reality. I cannot understand what made Houlston take to bullying; and I must say after this he showed much good feeling, and became a firm friend both to Tony and me, not appearing to harbour any ill-feeling for the way we had treated him.

I must hurry over my school-boy days. I was not able to carry out my plan of the menagerie the next summer. My uncle, instead of going to his country house, took us all to the sea-side. I, however, on that occasion picked up a good deal of knowledge about vessels and boats, and fish, and marine animals; and instead of a menagerie we had an aquarium, into which we used to put the small fish and other creatures we caught in the pools on the rocks. I was making an important step in the study of natural history—

gaining the custom of observing the habits of creatures. The following year I carried out my long-intended plan, having induced one of my cousins to join me in it. We made several cages and boxes; and among our captives we numbered a couple of rabbits, a weasel, hedgehog, ferret, and stoat, with a number of pigeons and other birds, and, I may add, three or four snakes. We caught a viper—or, as it is frequently called, an adder—the only venomous creature which exist in England; but my uncle objected to our keeping it alive, though he consented to its being turned into a bottle of spirits. We killed another, and cut off its head to observe its poisonous fangs. On dissecting the head, we found that the fangs exist on either side of the upper jaw, in which they lie down flat towards the throat. They are on hinges, the roots connected with little bags of poison. When the creature is irritated and about to bite, these fangs rise up. They are hollow, with small orifices at their points. When biting, the roots of the fangs are pressed against the bags of poison, which thus exudes through the orifices and enters the wound they make. All venomous serpents are provided with fangs, but in the jaws of some species the fangs, instead of lying down, are always erect, ready for action. The nature of the poison varies in different species. The poison of some produces paralysis; that of others causes the body when bitten to swell and become putrid. The venom of some is so powerful that it rapidly courses through the veins and destroys life in a few minutes; that of others makes much slower progress. The English viper, or adder, has but a small quantity of poison in its bag, and its bite rarely produces death. Some of the smallest snakes, in tropical climes, are the most venomous. However, I shall by-and-by have a good deal to say on the subject.

From what I have mentioned, it will be understood that I had already got a taste for and some insight into natural history, and when I returned to school I was able to discourse very learnedly on the subject. This made Tony more anxious to carry out our long-projected undertaking. Still, as we were very well treated at school, we had no excuse for running away, and put it off from day to day. At length, in truth, we began to grow wiser, and look at it in a different light. Tony, indeed, one day confided his plan to Houlston.

"Well, when you make up your mind to go, just tell me," said Houlston.

"What I would you go with us?" exclaimed Tony. "That would be capital. With a big fellow like you we should be able to make our way anywhere."

"Not exactly that," was the answer. "I'll tell you what I should do, Nyass. As soon as I found that you had started, I should make chase after you and bring you back. Depend upon it, it would be the best mark of friendship I could show you! Time enough by-and-by—when you have gone through school and been at college, and got a little more knowledge than you now possess in your heads—to start on such an expedition. I have a great notion that I should like to do something of the sort myself; so, if you ever start on an expedition to South America or any other part of the world, find me out if you can, and let me know, and then perhaps I shall be ready to accompany you."

These sensible remarks of Houlston put Tony completely off his purpose, and we finally agreed to follow the advice of our school-fellow, and wait patiently till we had finished our studies.

In the meantime I should say that my mother had rejoined my father at Quito. When I first came to England I thought that the time when I should leave school was a very long way off. It seemed like a dream when I found myself at last a big fellow of sixteen at the commencement of the summer holidays. There was Ellen, almost a grown-up young lady—in my eyes, at all events—and John, who had been in Uncle James's counting-house in London, a man with big whiskers.

"Well, Harry," said Uncle James, "would you like to go back to school, or accompany John and Ellen to South America? Your father wishes to have John's assistance, and perhaps you also can make yourself useful."

Although by this time I found school a far pleasanter place than when I was a little boy, yet, as may be supposed, I did not take long to decide.

"I will accompany John," I said without hesitation.

"We shall have to part with you soon, then, I am sorry to say," observed my uncle; "for Captain Byles, who still commands the *Inca*, is about to sail for Guayaquil. In consequence of the emancipation of the Spanish South American provinces from the iron yoke of the mother country, their ports are now free, and ships of all nations can trade to them, which was not the case when you came home. Captain Byles has twice before been to the Pacific, and we have resolved to send the *Inca* there again. He will be very glad to have you as passenger. You must lose no time, therefore, in getting ready."

I replied very honestly that I was sorry to leave him and aunt and cousins; but, at the same time, I could not help feeling delighted at the thought of again seeing my father and mother and Fanny, and revisiting the magnificent scenes which had made so deep an impression upon my mind, besides being able to indulge on a large scale in the study of the natural history of that wonderful region. I did not forget my friends, Tony and Arthur Mallet, and as soon as I had time I sat down and wrote to them both. At the end of a week I received the following reply from Tony:—

"Dear Harry,—Your letter threw me into a state of wild commotion. You to be actually starting for the country we have so often talked about, while, as far as I could see, I was destined to stick quietly at a desk in my father's counting-house. After thinking the matter over, however, and recollecting how kind and considerate he has always been, I determined to show him your letter, and tell him frankly of my long-cherished wish to go abroad. He talked to me a good deal to ascertain whether I was in earnest. 'I did not wish to send you from me,' he said at last; 'but I will now tell you that a few months ago I received a letter from a cousin of mine who has lately established a house of business at Para in Brazil, requesting me to send out two steady lads as clerks, adding that he should be very glad to receive a son of mine if I could spare him.' I jumped at the idea; for though I should have liked to have gone out with you, Harry, yet, as I have no means of doing that, I am delighted to go to Para, because, as it is at the mouth of the Amazon, it is the very place of all others I should have chosen. It is where we proposed going to when we used to talk of our expedition up the mighty river, and perhaps, after all, we may be able somehow or other to realise those wild fancies of our early days. To be sure, when I come to measure off the distance on the map, which we did not then think of doing, I find that Quito and Para are a tremendous long way apart. Still, perhaps some day or other we may be able to accomplish a meeting. At all events, I told my father that I was willing to accept our cousin's offer, and at the same time I put in a word for Houlston, from whom I had heard a few days before, telling me that he was looking about for something to do, and ready to do anything or go anywhere. He has no parents, or brothers or sisters, or any tie to keep him in England. I showed his letter to my father, and told him that he was a big, strong fellow, and that though I did not much like him when I was a little fellow, he was greatly improved. My father on this said he would send for him, and should he possess the necessary qualifications, he should be very glad to recommend him for the appointment. Houlston came, and as he writes well, and is a good hand at arithmetic, and has a fair amount of knowledge on other matters, my father told me that he would recommend him for the appointment. The long and short of the matter is, that Houlston and I are to go up to London with my father in a few days, to get our outfits, and to secure a passage by the first vessel sailing for Para or the nearest port to it in Brazil. We shall meet, Harry, and we will then talk matters over, and, I hope, strike out some plan by which we may be able to carry out our early designs, although perhaps not in the same way we formerly proposed. Houlston sends his kind regards to you, and says he shall be very happy to meet you again *Adeos, meu amigo*—that is, Good-bye, my friend. I have lost no time in beginning to learn Portuguese, which is the language the Brazilians speak, and I intend to work hard at it on the voyage, so as to be able to talk away in a fashion when I land. — Your sincere old friend, Antony Nyass."

I was very glad to get this letter, but was much disappointed at not hearing from Arthur. Another day's post, however, brought me a letter from him. I should have said that he had left school three months before, and that I had not since heard from him. His letter was a very sad one. I gathered from it that what he had dreaded had come to pass. His mother was dead, and he was left almost destitute, though he tried to hide from me as much as possible the fact of his poverty.

I at once made up my mind what to do. I took the letter to my uncle, told him all about Arthur, and entreated that he might be sent out with us in the *Inca*. "I will answer for it that he will amply repay all the kindness he may receive," I added. Uncle James said that he would consider the matter, and in the course of the day told me, to my great satisfaction, that I might write to Mallet and invite him to come up to town. Arthur lost no time in obeying the summons. My uncle was much pleased with him, and Arthur gratefully accepted the proposal that he should accompany us to Quito.

Two days afterwards Tony and Houlston arrived in London. A ship for Para was on the point of sailing. They had therefore to hurry on their preparations. They spent the evening with us at my uncle's, and John told me that he liked Houlston very well, and hoped some day to see him again. Tony he thought a capital fellow — so enthusiastic and warm-hearted, yet not wanting in sense; but Arthur, as I knew he would, he liked better than either. Tony brought with him a beautiful black cocker spaniel. "Here, Harry, I want you to accept this fellow as a keepsake from me," he said, leading the dog up to me. "Pat him on the head, call him True, and tell him you are going to be his master, and he will understand you. He can do everything but talk; but though he does not often give tongue, he is as brave as a lion."

I warmly thanked Tony for his gift as I patted True, who jumped up and licked my hand. "But you want a dog for yourself. I scarcely like to take him from you," I said.

"Set your mind at rest; I have his brother — whom I left at our lodgings — his equal in most respects, if not quite so great a beauty," he answered. "You will excuse me, I know. I have called my dog 'Faithful,' after you. As I cannot have you with me, I wanted something to remind me of you; and faithful I am sure he will prove to me, as yours will prove true to you."

I thanked Tony for his kind feeling for me, and assured him that I considered it a compliment that he had called his dog after me.

True was indeed a beauty—a Welsh cocker—somewhat larger than usual perhaps. He came up in his moral qualities to all Tony had said about him. He took to me at once, and a true friend he ever proved. We accompanied our friends aboard their ship, which was a Portuguese, called the *Vasco da Gama*. She was a fine large vessel. The crew were small and swarthy, but active-looking fellows, most of them wearing long red caps on their heads, and blue or pink-striped shirts, with knives stuck in their girdles. They jabbered and shouted tremendously as they got under weigh. Tony and Houlston stood on the poop bidding us farewell. "We shall meet, Harry! we shall meet!" Tony cried out. "Good-bye, Harry; good-bye, Arthur; good-bye, old fellows!"

"Perhaps we shall overtake you on the voyage!" shouted John.

"Not much fear of that," answered Houlston.

We were soon too far off to exchange further words, though we could hear the voices of the crew even when we had got to a considerable distance from the ship.

Chapter Two
Outward bound

Nearly a week after this we were on board the *Inca*, silently gliding down the Thames, the only voices heard on board being that of the pilot or the officers who repeated his orders. We had a quick run down Channel, and Captain Byles said he should not be surprised if, after all, we should reach the Equator before the Portuguese ship. I found that several of the crew had been on board when I came to England, Sam the black cook among the number. He was the only one, however, who remembered Ellen and me. I inquired after my old friend the goat.

"What! you remember her, Massa Harry!" exclaimed Sam. "Dat good. Goat gone to live on shore; eat fresh grass instead of hay!"

He was well pleased to find that I had remembered the dumb animal, and still more so that I had not forgotten him. Sam told me that he had become a Christian since I had seen him. I told him I thought that he was so then.

"Berry different, Massa Harry, between what is called Christian and real Christian. One night I was on shore, and not knowing where I go, I turn into small chapel where a man talk to de people, and I heard him say, 'God lubs you!' He lubs bad man and bad woman, and black man, and brown man, and white man all de same. Him pure, holy God, and no bad, impure, unholy person dwell wid him; and all men ever born unholy, impure, and so dey must all be punished. But he say he let One be punished for de oders, and so him sent his Son into de world to suffer for dem, and dat ebery one who trust dat Son, and lub him, go free, and come and live wid him for ever and ever. You ask how dat is. Hear God's words: 'God so loved de world dat he gave his only-begotten Son, dat whosoever believeth in him should not perish, but have eternal life.' Oh, he is a kind, good, merciful God! Him hear de prayers of all who come unto him. Him no want any one to say prayers for dem; but dey may come boldly t'rough Jesus Christ, and he hear black man pray, and brown man pray, and leetle child pray, just as well as learned white man; and so when I hear dis I say, 'Dat just de God for me;' and so I go to de minister—dat is de man who was preaching—and he tell me a great deal more; and I go ebery day I was ashore, and now I bery happy, because I know dat when I die dere is One who has taken my sins upon himself, who was punished instead of me who paid de great debt I owed to God."

I have tried to give Sam's remarks as nearly as I can in his words. They made a great impression on me; for before I must own that I did not understand God's simple plan of salvation. Sam had a Bible, which he was constantly reading, and delighted to explain to the crew. He had gained considerable influence with them, and though many were careless, and did not listen to him, all treated him with respect. Captain Byles spoke in very high terms of Sam, who had, I found, been the means of bringing home the truth to him. He had prayers every day, when the weather permitted, in his cabin, and a service on the Sunday for the whale of the crew, while I never heard a harsh or wrong expression escape his lips.

"You t'ink, Massa Harry, perhaps, I go into dat chapel by chance," observed Sam to me one day; "now I t'ink dere is no such t'ing as chance. God orders everyt'ing. He sees us all day and all night long, and orders all for de best."

I agreed with Sam, and I may say that I never forgot the lessons I received from him. I found great pleasure in listening to him while he read the Bible and explained it in his own somewhat curious way, as far as language was concerned. I had before been accustomed to read the Bible as a task, but I now took to reading it with satisfaction and profit. From others of the crew I learned a good deal of seamanship, especially how to knot and splice,—an art which I found afterwards very useful.

We had been several weeks from England, and had thus far carried the fine weather with us, when clouds appeared in the horizon which soon began to rush in dense masses over the sky. The sea, hitherto so calm, tossed and foamed, and the wind howled and shrieked through the rigging. I asked the captain if he thought we were going to have a severe gale.

"It looks very like it," he answered, "but we must do our best and trust in God. Once I used to think that while I was doing my best, God was fighting against me, but now, Harry, I see it the other way. It is a great thing to feel that the All-Powerful who rules the world is with us. It makes a man far happier and more courageous."

The crew had gone aloft to furl the sails, and the ship was soon under her three closely-reefed topsails. Still the wind increased, and the seas rose up on either side as if they would overwhelm her. The night was coming on. The captain held a consultation with his mates. The first mate and one of the best hands went to the helm. The main and mizzen-topsails were furled, the helm was put up, and the ship was kept away before the wind. The huge seas followed close astern, roaring and hissing after us. Arthur and I had remained on deck.

"I must beg you to go below," said the captain; "for if one of these seas was to break on board, you might be swept off, and no one could save you." Still, I was very unwilling to obey. John, however, coming on deck, saw the danger we were in, and pulled us down the hatchway. We found Ellen in the cabin kneeling at the table with Maria at her side. She had the Bible open, though it was a difficult matter to read by the flickering light of the lamp, which swung backwards and forwards. Still, every now and then, by keeping her finger on a verse, she was able to catch a few words; while Maria, with her large eyes wide open fixed on her young mistress, was listening eagerly to what she said. So engaged were they, that neither of them observed our entrance. Now Ellen stopped, and I heard her lifting up her voice in prayer for the safety of the ship and all on board. John and I, making our way to the other side of the table, knelt down likewise. Though she saw us she did not stop. We remained thus for some time, when a shout from the deck reached us. I could not help rushing up again. John followed me. During the few minutes we had been below the darkness had increased, but at that instant a vivid flash of lightning bursting from the sky, showed a large ship ahead of us. We were running on towards her. Again all was darkness, and I expected to hear the fearful crash of the two ships meeting. Again another flash, followed by a fearful peal of thunder, lighted up the atmosphere. The ship was no longer there, but an object floating on the foaming waves. It was a boat full of people. It seemed impossible that she could live many moments in so fearful a sea. Presently I saw our crew running with ropes to the side. Already the stern of the boat was sinking beneath the waves. There was a thundering sound, as if a big gun had been fired. Our foresail had burst from the bolt-ropes. We rushed on close to the boat. John, Arthur, and I sprang to the side. Several persons were clinging to the ropes which had been thrown over to them. We assisted in hauling them up. A sea struck us at that moment, and two were washed away. Three others clung on, and were partly hauled and partly washed on board; while a dog which was swimming near them was lifted up by a wave and let directly down on the deck. We and they had to cling to the bulwarks to save ourselves from being carried off to leeward. One of our men, who had let go his hold while assisting the strangers, was carried off by the rush of water across the deck, and before any one could help him, he was seen struggling amid the foaming billows astern. On flew the *Inca* over the spot where the ship had just before been seen. We managed to drag the strangers to the companion hatch, and, with the assistance of Sam, carried them below, followed by the dog which had been so curiously saved with them. True, when he entered the cabin, instead of barking, ran up to him wagging his tail and showing every sign of pleasure. I observed how like the two animals were to each other. The mystery was soon solved. The officers and crew remained on deck to bend another sail. As the light of the lamp fell on the features of the first person we got into the cabin, what was my astonishment to recognise my old friend Tony Nyass. His surprise at seeing me was equally great.

Several persons were clinging to the ropes.

"Is Houlston saved?" were the first words he uttered. "He was close to me!"

"Yes, all right!" exclaimed a young man, who, helped by Sam, tottered into the cabin. It was Houlston himself, though I should not have known him, so pale and scared did he look. The third was one of the mates of the Portuguese ship.

"And Faithful, too," cried Tony, kneeling down and embracing his dog. "My old fellow, I am indeed very glad you have escaped." Faithful seemed as well pleased as his master; and True knew him at once, and welcomed him by leaping up to lick his face, though as he did so the ship gave a tremendous roll, and over he tumbled to the other side of the cabin.

I need not say how thankful we were that the lives of our old school-fellows had been preserved. They were shivering with cold, so, taking them into our cabin, we got off their wet clothes and put them to bed. Tony then told me that after the commencement of the gale, the ship had sprung a leak, and that though the crew had behaved very well, and stood manfully to the pumps, the water could not be got under. When it was found that the ship must go down, the boats were prepared. He and Houlston, with the second mate and several of the crew, had got into one of them, and shoved clear of the ship just as she sank; but the other, he was afraid, had been immediately overwhelmed; indeed, it seemed scarcely possible that any boat could have lived many minutes in the heavy sea then running. It was wonderful that the boat he was in had remained long enough afloat to allow our ship to get near her.

During the whole of that night the hurricane blew as hard as ever, we continuing to run before it. Every moment I expected to hear that the ship had sprung a leak, and that we should have to share the fate of the unfortunate *Vasco da Gama*. We were dreadfully knocked about. Our bulwarks were stove in, and two of our boats carried away. We lost our topmasts, and received other damage; but the stout old ship still battled bravely with the seas. As the morning broke the wind began to abate. By noon the sun was shining brightly, and the sea had gone much down.

"Perhaps, after all," observed Tony, "we shall go round the Cape with you to Quito, and then have to find our way down the Amazon to Para, as I suppose that will then be the shortest road there."

"I am afraid, young gentleman, you would find that a very long road," observed Captain Byles. "As the ship requires repairs, I must run into Rio de Janeiro, and from thence you will more easily get to Para, though I should have been very happy to have had your company round Cape Horn."

Tony was much disappointed on hearing this. We had still a long run before us, and the prospect of Tony and Houlston's company on board for many days. The Portuguese mate, Mr Lima, had friends at Para, and he undertook to assist Houlston and Tony in getting there. He was a very well-mannered, amiable man, and as he spoke a little English, we were able to converse together. He gave me much information regarding the Brazils, which is by far the largest country in South America. Although a very small portion only is cultivated, it is also the richest both in vegetable and mineral wealth. He told me of its magnificent forests, its plantations of coffee and tobacco, and certain of its valleys, in some of which gold in abundance is found, and in others diamonds of extraordinary value.

"What do you say, Harry—shall we go and hunt for them?" exclaimed Tony when he heard this.

Mr Lima laughed. "The Government are too wide-awake to allow you to do that," he observed. "No one is allowed to go into that part of the country except those employed in collecting the diamonds; but I will tell you one thing, it is the poorest part of the Brazils. If the same number of people who are engaged in collecting the diamonds were employed in cultivating the waste ground, the country would, I believe, be far richer. However, perhaps my friends here may obtain permission to visit the mines, and if so, I dare say they will some day give you an account of them."

Of course Tony said he would do so. If he was fortunate enough to get there.

When the weather grew fine we passed our time very pleasantly, for we had a number of interesting books, especially of natural history, in which we old school-fellows fortunately took great delight. Houlston and Tony had agreed to make collections of objects of natural history when they were settled at Para, and as they had lost all their own books, I gave them some of mine, as there was little prospect of their getting any at Rio de Janeiro—so the captain told us. At length one morning, just at sunrise, when I went on deck to enjoy the cool air, I heard the shout of "Land!" and looking out, I saw a line of blue mountains rising out of the water. The breeze carried us quickly towards them, and in a short time we could distinguish a lofty height, shaped like a sugar-loaf, which stands at the south side of the entrance into the harbour of Rio. A little to the left rose three peaks, which Mr Lima, the Portuguese mate, called the *Tres Irmaos*, or the "Three Brothers," with the lofty peak of Corcovado a little further south. On the right of the entrance we could distinguish the white walls of the fortress of Santa Cruz, which commands it, with another range of mountains rising above it, and terminating in a bold, lofty promontory, known as Cape Frio, while far beyond towered up the blue outline of the distant Organ Mountains. We sailed on, passing between the lofty heights I have described, being hailed, as we glided under the frowning guns of Santa Cruz, by a stentorian voice, with various questions as to who we were, whence we came, our object in entering the port, to all of which Captain Byles replied through his speaking-trumpet. It would be difficult to describe the beautiful scene in which we now found ourselves,—curious-shaped canoes and boats of all rigs, manned by half-naked blacks, sailing about, and a number of vessels at anchor in the vast harbour; numerous white forts, backed by picturesque hills rising above them, covered with the richest verdure, and villages peeping forth here and there in beautiful little bays; while higher up the bay the vast city appeared, extending for miles along its irregular shore, and running back almost to the foot of the Tijuca Mountains, with hills and heights in every direction. In the midst of this scene we dropped our anchor under the frowning fortress of Villegagnon, the first castle erected by Europeans in that region.

I cannot hope to convey by words a correct idea of the beauty of the scenery or the magnificence of the harbour. All visitors agree that it is one of the finest in the world. We went on shore, and were very kindly received by an English merchant—the correspondent of the house to which the *Inca* belonged. John and I were anxious to help Tony and Houlston as far as we had the power, but our new friend undertook to supply their wants, and to enable them to reach Para by the first vessel sailing for that port.

I will not attempt to describe Rio fully. It is a large city, with heights rising about in various parts, covered with buildings. Most of the streets are very narrow, the architecture very unlike anything I had seen in England. Numbers of priests; gangs of slaves, carrying loads; ladies in black hoods reaching to the feet, called mantilhas; gentlemen in cloaks; soldiers on foot and on horseback, were moving about in all directions. We made a few interesting excursions in the neighbourhood of the city, and several expeditions about the bay.

Captain Byles was, of course, anxious to proceed on his voyage, and therefore used all expedition in getting the ship ready for sea. We, however, had time to make one long excursion with our new friend to the Organ Mountains, which we could see from the bay in the far distance. I was sorry that Ellen could not go, as it was considered that the trip would be too fatiguing for her. We sailed up to the head of the bay for many miles in a pleasure-vessel belonging to our friend, sleeping on board the first night. Early the next morning we started on mules towards the mountains. The air was most delicious, pure, though warm, and the scenery very beautiful, as we made our way among heights covered with a great variety of tropical trees and creepers bearing magnificent flowers. Among them were the tall, gently-curved palmetto, elegant tree ferns, unsurpassed by any of their neighbours in beauty, fuchsias in their native glory, passion-flowers, and wild vines, hanging in graceful festoons, and orchids with their brilliant red spikes. As we passed through the valley we saw directly before us the mountains we were about to visit, and from their shape we agreed that they were well called the Organ Mountains; for as we then saw them, the centre height especially wore the appearance of a huge organ. "A grand instrument that," said Tony, "such as I suppose an angel might choose to sound forth the music of the spheres."

We wound our way up amid the tame beautiful and wild scenery till we reached the summit, whence we enjoyed a magnificent view over the surrounding country, with Rio and the blue ocean in the far distance. We had not come without provisions, nor had the scenery taken away our appetites. We had also brought our guns, and led by our friend, we started off on foot in search of game. We had gone some distance, when, as we were approaching one of the numerous pools of dear water which are found even in the higher parts of the Organ Mountains, our friend stopped us and pointed towards a large tree, beneath the shade of whose wide-spreading boughs lay a creature apparently asleep. At first I thought he was a large horse or hornless cow, but as we crept closer to it, and could see the shape of its head, I discovered that it was a very different animal. "That is a tapir—the largest wild animal we have in South America," whispered our friend. As we approached the animal got up and looked about. We remained perfectly quiet, to examine it at leisure. It appeared to be nearly four feet in height, and perhaps six in length, the colour a deep brown, almost black. It had a stiff mane, and a very short stumpy tail, while its body appeared destitute of hair. It was not so, however, as I afterwards found; but the hair could not be perceived in consequence of being closely depressed to the surface. Its legs were short and thick, and its feet of great size. The head was unlike that of any other animal I had ever seen. It was very long, and the upper lip or snout was lengthened into a kind of proboscis, which looked as if it might grow up into the trunk of an elephant. We were to leeward of the animal, but it quickly discovered us, and began to move off, when Faithful and True rushed forward, barking vehemently. Houlston fired, but the shot bounded off the tapir's thick shield-like hide, and away it went dashing through the dense underwood with a force which broke down the shrubs opposing its progress. We had great difficulty in getting back our brave little dogs. They returned at length, panting with their exertions. Fortunately the tapir was frightened, or they would have found him more than a match for them. Our friend told us that it has four toes on its front feet, and three on the hinder ones, cased with horn. It manages with its flexible upper lip to tear away the leaves and to pick up the water-melons and gourds which it finds when it goes forth at night in search of food. However, it is in no way particular, being almost as omnivorous as the hog. Its senses of smell and hearing are very acute. Its eyes, though, are small and its ears short. Its voice is a shrill kind of whistle, such as one would not expect to proceed from an animal of such massive bulk. It is extremely fond of the water, and delights in floundering about in the mud. It can swim and dive also admirably, and will often remain underneath the surface for many minutes together, and then rising for a fresh supply of air, plunge down again. It indeed appears to be almost as amphibious as the hippopotamus, and has consequently been called *Hippopotamus terrestris*.

We all laughed at Houlston's ill success. It was the first attempt, I believe, he had ever made at shooting.

"The aim was not bad though," observed Tony, "and if the hide had been soft, the shot would have gone into it."

"It was a good large object, however, to aim at," said John. "A bullet would have been more effectual in bringing the creature to the ground."

"I am not quite so certain of that," observed our friend, "for its tough hide is almost bullet-proof."

Houlston stood our bantering very good-naturedly, and managed in the course of the day to bring down a couple of birds. "You see, I improve by practice," he observed; "and one of these days I may turn out a dead-shot."

I have described the tapir here as it was the first I met, but I afterwards had better opportunities of observing the animal. As soon as our mules had rested we commenced our return, as our friend could not be long absent from Rio. We were at length once more on board the *Inca*.

Tony and Houlston expected to start with the Portuguese mate for the north in the course of two or three days, and they promised to send me an account of their adventures as soon as possible on their arrival at Para. The *Inca* appeared once more in fit trim to encounter any storm we might meet with in our passage round Cape Horn. At first the weather was very lovely; but as we were running down the coast of Patagonia a heavy gale sprang up from the southward, which threatened to drive us back again. Fortunately a sheltering bay was near at hand. Running into it, the ship was brought to an anchor, and we there lay as calmly as if no storm was raging without. The country, however, was wild and desolate in appearance. I should have thought no human beings would have been found on it, but on looking through our glasses we observed a number moving about, some on horseback, others on foot, apparently watching us. "Are you inclined to go on bore, gentlemen?" said the captain to us. Of course we replied Yes. Ellen begged that she might go likewise. We objected, fearing that she might be exposed to danger. "She will be perfectly safe," answered Captain Byles; "for though the people on shore are not very prepossessing, I have always found them perfectly harmless. We will, however, carry our muskets, and the crew shall be armed likewise."

We were soon on shore, proceeding over the rough ground towards the natives. They seeing Ellen and Maria in our midst, advanced without fear. They halted, however, at a little distance from us, when we put out our hands and walked towards them. They were big, stout men of a brown complexion, with long black hair hanging down their necks. Their only dress consisted of skins fastened across their shoulders, leaving bare their enormous limbs. When we put out our hands they put out theirs.

"Good day, my friends," said Captain Byles.

"Good day," exclaimed the savages in almost the same tone.

"Hillo! what, do you speak English?" cried Arthur.

"Hillo! what, do you speak English?" echoed the Patagonians.

"Of course I do," answered Arthur.

"Of course I do," said the natives.

Indeed, whatever words we uttered they repeated. We on this burst into fits of laughter, our new acquaintances doing the same, as if we had uttered a capital joke. They beat us, however, at that, for though we stopped, they continued laughing—ay right heartily. At all events they knew what that meant. Friendship was thus speedily established. Pointing to their skin tents at no great distance, supported on poles, and in shape like those of gipsies, but rather larger, they seemed to invite us to them. We accordingly accompanied them. In front of the tents sat a number of women. They differed somewhat from the men, by having more ample robes of skin, and their hair bound by fillets round their heads. They were, however, very unprepossessing-looking ladies. They all seemed to regard Ellen with looks of astonishment now gazing at her, now at her black attendant, and were evidently discussing among themselves how it was that they were of such different colours. We saw a number of horses scattered about the plain, and several of the men were riding backwards and forwards armed with bows, and having at their backs large quivers full of arrows, and small round shields. The women were broiling meat at fires before the tents. They offered us some, and from the bones and feathers scattered about, we concluded that it was the flesh of the ostrich, which bird inhabits in large numbers the vast plains of Patagonia. Savage as they looked, they evidently wished to treat us civilly, for they spread some skins on the ground inside one of their tents, and signed to us to take our seats on them. To please them we ate a little of the food they set before us, although I must say their style of cookery was not attractive. After we had sat for some time, they continuing to imitate everything we said or did, we took a stroll round the encampment. We had not gone far when a large grey bird with a long neck and long legs, having three toes on its feet, stalked up to us, and putting out its head, grunted in our faces. Arthur and I took off our hats and made it a bow in return, greatly to the amusement of the Patagonians, who burst into loud fits of laughter at the joke. We recognised the bird at once as the *Rhea Americana*, or American ostrich. As we did not retreat, it uttered a sharp hiss, and then poised itself as if it was about to attack us, and so I think it would have done, had not the natives driven it away. It was about five feet high, the neck completely feathered, the back of a dark hue, with the plumes of the wings white. It is said that the male bird takes care of the eggs which several hens lay scattered about on the sand. He sweeps them together with his feet into a hollow, which serves as a nest, sits to hatch them, and accompanies the young till they are able to look after themselves. On such occasions he will attack a man on horseback who approaches his charges, and will leap up and try to kick him.

Captain Byles now told us it was time to return on board. We accordingly shook hands and made our way towards the boat. The people, however, began to assemble round us in considerable numbers. The captain therefore ordered us all to keep together and to hurry on, without, however, showing any signs of fear. I was very thankful, for Ellen's sake, when at last we reached the boat in safety. Whether the natives had thought of attempting to stop us or not, I do not know. Perhaps they only purposed to do us honour by thus accompanying us to the beach. We agreed that though the men at first looked gigantic, yet this was owing probably to their style of dress; and the captain was of opinion that very few of them were much above six feet. He told me that they live chiefly on flesh—that of horses, or emus, or guanacoes (a species of llama), and any other animal they can catch. We did not venture on shore again; and after waiting a few days, once more put to sea. I thought that these natives were about as savage in appearance as any people could be. I discovered, however, shortly afterwards, that there are other people sunk still lower in the scale of humanity.

Captain Byles purposed running through the Straits of Magellan. Just, however, as we were entering them, a strong south westerly gale sprang up, which prevented us from making the attempt. We accordingly stood into a sheltered bay in Terra del Fuego. The shore looked very inhospitable—dark rocks rose up at a little distance from the water and seemed to form a barrier between the sea and the interior. There were a few trees, all stunted and bending one way as if forced thus by the wind. Still, John and Arthur and I had a fancy for visiting the shore, in the hope of obtaining some wild fowl. Having landed with one of the mates and True, we took our way along the shores of the bay till we arrived at some high rocks. Over these we climbed. On descending, we found ourselves on the side of an inlet. We had reached the shore, when heavy showers of snow began to fall, driven against our faces by the sharp wind. We were about, therefore, to turn back, when we saw several figures moving at a little distance. Curious to see the natives, which we concluded these were, in spite of the snow we pushed on. We advanced cautiously, keeping a much as possible behind the rocks till we were at a short distance from them. We were thus able to observe them before we were discovered. They were wild-looking savages. Their colour was that of mahogany or rusty iron; their dresses, skins loosely wrapped round them and very scanty. One fellow was seated on the side of a canoe with a couple of dogs near him; while a woman, perhaps his wife, sat at a little distance, crouching on the ground, covered by her skin robe. As soon as they discovered us, instead of approaching as the Patagonians had done, they sat stupidly gazing at us, lost apparently in astonishment. They did not, however, exhibit any sign of alarm as we walked up to them. At length they got up, shouting out some words and patting their breasts, which we concluded was a sign of friendship. Their dogs snarled at True and he barked in return, and I had to hold him tight to prevent his flying at them. Perhaps they understood each other better than we did the ill-favoured curs' masters or their masters did us. Still the greeting did not sound amicable. The natives were small, thin, and dirty in the extreme. Their weapons were bows and arrows. The only habitations we could see were wretched lean-tos, just capable of sheltering them from the wind. Having an old clasp-knife in my pocket, I presented it to the chief, who received it with evident signs of satisfaction. As there was no inducement to hold further intercourse with him, we returned by the way we had come, without having seen a single bird near enough to shoot.

"Yet, Harry, those people have souls, destined to live for ever," said Arthur, in answer to a remark I made that they were little better than brutes. "Don't you think if the gospel were taken to them it would have its never-failing effect? I will speak to Captain Byles on the subject when we get on board."

He did so. Long since then several noble Christian missionaries visited that benighted region. Some perished, but others are still labouring to make known the glad tidings of salvation to the rude inhabitants of Patagonia and Terra del Fuego.

Finding it impossible to pass through the Straits, we had to go round Cape Horn. A couple of weeks, however, elapsed before we were clear into the Pacific. After this we had a quick run, and once more the lofty summits of the Cordilleras greeted our eyes. Though I was but a young child when I had last seen them, so deep was the impression they had made on me that I recognised them at once.

Chapter Three
A Journey across the Cordilleras

At length the *Inca* was at anchor off the city of Guayaquil. I had a faint recollection of its appearance, with Chimborazo's snow-capped dome towering up in the distance. Ellen, who had forgotten all about being there, was delighted with the scenery. Guayaquil is situated at the mouth of the river Guayas—the largest on the Pacific coast. On going on shore, however, we were somewhat disappointed, as the buildings, though grand at a distance, have a tumbledown appearance, partly owing to the earthquakes to which they are subjected, and partly to the carelessness of the inhabitants in repairing them. We had great hopes of meeting our father, but his correspondents in the city had not heard from him for some time. The country, we found, was in a very unsettled state, owing to which, probably, he had not come down from Quito. We bade farewell to our kind captain and the crew of the *Inca*.

Some time before, Peru, Chili, and the other Spanish provinces of South America had thrown off their allegiance to the mother country, forming themselves into republics. Their government, however, especially in the northern provinces, had been as yet far from well established. Disturbances were continually occurring, preventing the progress of the country. First one party took up arms to overthrow another in authority, and in a short time those who had been superseded played the same trick to those who had stepped into their places.

We lost no time in making preparations for our journey, the first part of which was to be performed on board a boat,—seventy miles up the river to Bodegas. We were there to engage mules to proceed over the mountains to Quito, of the difficulties of which journey I had some slight recollection.

We spent two days at Guayaquil. Had we not been anxious about our father and the rest of our family, we should have been well amused. From the balcony of our house we had a magnificent view of the towering range of the Andes seen from the east of us, and extending like a mighty wall north and south. Far away on the left, and fully a hundred miles off, appeared the mighty Chimborazo, whose snow-capped summit, rising far above its fellows, formed a superb background to the range of lesser mountains and grand forests which cover the intermediate space. I have before mentioned the delicious fruits that may be found in abundance in the city; and I described the curious balsas, on board of which the natives navigate the coasts and rivers. We all supplied ourselves with straw hats, such as are shipped in great numbers from this place under the name of Panama hats. They are made from the leaves of an arborescent plant about five feet high, resembling the palm called *toquilla*. The leaf grows on a three-cornered stalk, and is about a yard long. It is slit into shreds, and after being immersed in boiling water is bleached in the sun. The plaiting is very fine, and the hat is so flexible that it can be turned inside out, or rolled up and put into the pocket. It is impenetrable to rain and very durable. The chief export from the place are chinchona, tobacco, orchilla weed, hides, cotton, coffee, and cacao.

Our friends, we found, were anxious about the difficulties we might encounter on our journey, on account of the disturbed state of the country. They advised us, indeed, to postpone our departure till our father's arrival, or till we should hear from him. The thought, however, that he and our mother and sister might be exposed to danger made us the more desirous of proceeding; and at length our friends—against their better judgment, they assured us—concluded the arrangements for our journey. We were seated taking coffee the evening before we were to start, with the magnificent scene I have described before us, when a stranger was ushered into the room. He wore over his shoulders a gay-coloured poncho, and held a broad-brimmed hat in his hand. His breeches were of dark cloth, open at the knee, and he had on embroidered gaiters, and huge spurs, with rowels the size of a crown-piece. His jet-black hair, which hung over his shoulders, his reddish-olive complexion, dark eyes, and somewhat broad face, though his features were in other respects regular and handsome, told us at once that he was a native Peruvian. Our friends saluted him as Don José. He addressed us in a kind tone, and told us that, having heard we were about to proceed to Quito, as he was also going in that direction, and might be of service, he should be happy to accompany us. Our friends at once replied that we would thankfully accept his offer, and all arrangements were quickly made. We were glad to obtain so intelligent a companion. His kind and gentle manner at once gained our confidence, and though his dress and appearance were those of ordinary Indians of the upper class, he looked like one accustomed to receive the respect of his fellow-men. That he was no common person we were sure. Why he took the interest in us which he evinced we could not tell. John and I talked the matter over, and at length, recollecting that our father's mother was of Indian descent, we came to the conclusion that besides being a friend of our father, he was connected by the ties of blood with our family. Still, from the way our friend spoke, there appeared to be some mystery about him; but they did not offer to enlighten us, nor could we with propriety ask them, he also was evidently not inclined to be communicative about himself.

Next morning at daylight we went on board our boat. In the centre was an awning, or *toldo*, which served as a cabin. The crew, consisting of eight native Indians, urged her on with long broad-bladed oars when the wind was contrary, while their chief or captain stood astern and steered with another. When the wind was favourable a large sail was hoisted, and we glided rapidly up the river. The banks are beautifully green, and covered with an exuberant growth of many varieties of trees; indeed, the plains on either side vie in richness of vegetation with any other spot between the tropics. Several times we cut off bends of the river by narrow canals, the branches of the trees, interwoven by numberless creepers, which hung down in festoons covered with brilliant blossoms, forming a dense canopy over our heads. Although the stream is sluggish, we were unable to reach Bodegas that night. We stopped therefore at the house of a gentleman engaged in the cultivation of cacao. The tree on which it grows somewhat resembles a lilac in size and shape. The fruit is yellowish-red, and oblong in shape, and the seeds are enveloped in a mass of white pulp. It is from the seeds that chocolate is prepared. The flowers and fruits grow directly out of the trunk and branches. Cacao—or, as we call it, cocoa—was used by the Mexicans before the arrival of the Spaniards. It was called by them *chocolatt*, from whence we derive the name of the compound of which it is the chief ingredient—chocolate. So highly was it esteemed, that Linnaeus thought it worthy of the name of *theobroma*—"food for gods." The tree is raised from seed, and seldom rises higher than from twenty to thirty feet; the leaves are large, oblong, and pointed. It is an evergreen, and bears fruits and blossoms all the year round. The fruits are pointed oval pods, six inches long, and contain in five compartments from twenty-five to thirty seeds or kernels, enveloped in a white pithy pulp with a sweet taste. These seeds when dried form the cocoa of commerce, from which the beverage is made and chocolate is manufactured. There are three harvests in the year, when the pods are pulled from the trees and gathered into baskets. They are then thrown into pits and covered with sand, where they remain three or four days to get rid of, by fermentation, a strong bitter flavour they possess. They are then carefully cleaned and dried in large flat trays in the sun. After this they are packed in sacks for the market. Our friend in the morning showed us some blossoms which had burst forth from the roots during the night, which happened to be somewhat damp and warm—an example of the expansive powers of vegetable life in that region. An oil is extracted from another species of cacao, the nut of which is small and white. It is called cacao-butter, and is used by the natives for burns and sores and cutaneous diseases. A large quantity of cacao for the manufacture of chocolate is exported to Spain. Among the trees were numbers of the broad-leaved plantain and banana, which had been planted to protect the young cacao trees from the heat of the sun. The fruit of the banana, one of the most useful productions of the Tropics, is eaten raw, roasted, boiled, and fried. It grows in large bunches, weighing from sixty to seventy pounds each.

Continuing our voyage the next day, we passed amid groves of oranges and lemons, whose rich perfume was wafted across the water to us. Here also the mango, bearing a golden fruit, spread around its splendid foliage; while, above all, the beautiful cocoanut palm lifted its superb head. Now and then we saw monkeys gambolling among the trees, as well as many birds of brilliant plumage. Among others, a beautiful bird got up from a bed of reeds we were passing, spreading wide its wings and broad tail directly before us. John shot it, and the small canoe we sent to pick it up. It was about the size of a partridge, with a crane-like bill, a slender neck, and shorter legs than ordinary waders, though a wader it was. The plumage was shaded curiously in bands and lines with brown, fawn-colour, red, grey, and black, which Ellen said reminded her of a superb moth she had seen. It was the caurale, or sun-bird (*Scolopax Helios*), our books told us, found also in Demerara. Less attractive in appearance were the gallinazos, or vultures, the scavengers of those regions; while frequently on the mud banks we caught sight of alligators basking in the hot sun, often fast asleep, with their mouths wide open.

We reached Bodegas early in the day. It is a large village, built on a flat. In the rainy season it is so completely flooded that the people have to take refuge in the upper stories of their houses. Thanks to our friend Don José, and the exertions of his chief attendant, Isoro, mules were quickly procured; and as the attractions of Bodegas were not great, we immediately set off towards the mountains. John called Isoro Don José's henchman. He was, like his master, of pure Indian blood, but of not so high a type. Still, he was good-looking, active, and intelligent. His dress differed only from that of Don José in being of coarser materials. We were at once struck with the respect and devotion with which Isoro treated his master, and with the confidence Don José evidently reposed in him. We had a journey before us of two hundred miles, which would occupy eight or ten days. The first village we passed through was built high up off the ground on stilts, for in the rainy season the whole country is completely flooded. After passing the green plain, we entered a dense forest. Road, I should say, there was none. Nothing, it seemed to me, could surpass the rich luxuriance of the vegetation. On either side were numerous species of palms, their light and feathery foliage rising among the other trees; bananas, with their long, glossy, green leaves; and here and there groves of the slender and graceful bamboo, shooting upwards for many feet straight as arrows, their light leaves curling over towards their summits; while orchids of various sorts, many bearing rich-coloured flowers, entwined themselves like snakes round the trunks and branches. Don José told us that in the rainy season this road is flooded, and that then the canoe takes the place of mules.

We put up the first night at a *tambo*, or road-side inn, a bamboo hut of two stories, thatched with plantain leaves. As the lower part was occupied by four-footed animals, we had to climb into the upper story by means of a couple of stout bamboos with notches cut in them. We here hung up our hammocks, and screened off a part for Ellen and Maria. Next day we began to ascend the mountains by the most rugged of paths. Sometimes we had to wind up the precipice on a narrow ledge, scarcely affording footing to the mules. It was trying to the nerves, for while on one side rose a perpendicular wall of rock, on the other the precipice went sheer down for several hundred feet, with a roaring torrent at the bottom. Wild rocks were before and above us, trees and shrubs, however, growing out of every crevice and on each spot where soil could rest, while behind spread out a wide extent of forest, amid which we could distinguish the river winding its way to the Pacific. Few birds or beasts were to be seen—the monkeys and parrots we had left below us; gallinazos, or black vultures, were, however, still met with, as they are everywhere throughout the continent, performing their graceful evolutions in the air, wheeling round and round without closing their wings, in large flocks, above the watery region we had left. The black vulture (*Cathartes atratus*), which closely resembles the well-known turkey buzzard in habits and appearance, performs, like it, the duty of scavenger, and is protected therefore by the inhabitants of all parts of the country. It may be distinguished from the latter by the form of the feathers on the neck, which descend from the back of the head towards the throat in a sloping direction; whereas the turkey buzzard has a frill of them completely round the throat. The head and part of the neck of the black vulture are destitute of feathers, and are covered with a black wrinkled skin, on which a few hairs only grow. "See, what grand fellows are these!" exclaimed Arthur. I gazed up. On a rock close above us stood a couple of large birds, which were unmistakably vultures.

"Dreadful-looking creatures," cried Ellen. "They make me shudder. They seem as if preparing to pounce down on some little innocent lambs to carry them off."

"It would prefer a dead mule, I suspect," observed John. "Like other vultures, it is not nice as to the nature of its food. It is called the King of the Vultures (*Sarcoramphus papa*), properly so, for it is the strongest and bravest of the vulture tribe though inferior in size to the condor. Observe its head and neck, brilliantly coloured with scarlet and yellow to make amends for the want of feathers. On the crown of its head, too, is a rich scarlet patch. Close to the eye there is a silvery blue mark, and above it part of the skin is blue and part scarlet. The bill is orange and black, and those curious lumps or carbuncles on its forehead are rich orange. At the lower part of the neck it wears a black ruff. The wing feathers and tail are black, and the lower part of the body white, and the rest a fine grey satin colour."

While John was speaking, the birds, spreading out their huge wings, glided off the rock, and then by an imperceptible movement of them soared upwards, and, hovering for a few seconds in the air, they darted downwards into the plain, and were lost to sight.

"You need not be afraid of their attacking any living creature, Señora Ellen," observed Don José. "They have no relish for meat till it has gained a higher flavour than we should like, and dead lizards and snakes are much to their taste. Even those they discover, I believe, rather by sight than by scent."

We had been proceeding along a somewhat broader part of the road than usual, though, as it was very steep, we climbed but slowly. Now rounding a sharp point, we came to a spot which made me wonder if those ahead could possibly have got by; and I could not help gazing anxiously downwards, almost expecting to find that some one had fallen over the precipice. Ellen kept up her courage admirably, and never hesitated to follow where others led. I could not help asking once if she did not feel afraid. "No," she answered. "I always look upwards when I come to a difficult place, and so pass without alarm." Ellen's plan is the right one, metaphorically speaking, to adopt in all the difficulties and trials of life: look upwards, and we shall be carried safely through them. On we went till we found ourselves among a chaos of mountains, separated by ravines so deep that the eye could scarcely distinguish the rapid streams which found their way below. On one side rose into the clear blue sky the majestic summit of Chimborazo, while other peaked and round-topped mountains reared their heads proudly around. At length the summit of the sierra was reached, and our mules commenced a descent into the valley, drawing their legs together and sliding down with fearful velocity. I had bean anxious before, I was doubly so now; but the animals with wonderful sagacity kept the centre of the path, and in time I lost all sensation of fear, and could admire the beautiful scenery.

The tambos, or road-side inns, we stopped at were mostly huts of the rudest kind, with mud walls and floors, kept by Indians, and dirty in the extreme. The entertainment provided for us was boiled chicken and potato-soup, called in the mountains *locro*. Wooden spoons were served to enable us to ladle up the soup, but our fingers had to be used for the chicken, instead of knives and forks.

We seldom had an opportunity while on mule-back of exchanging thoughts except at the top of our voices, as in most places we were compelled to travel in Indian file, one following the other. We were once more ascending the steep side of the mountain, when, on rounding a point, we saw coming towards us a single traveller. As he caught sight of us he stopped his mule, and made signs for us to come on toward the spot where the greater width of the road would allow us to pass him. As we got up to him I saw that he was a negro, dressed in the usual poncho and broad-brimmed hat of the traveller in the Andes. Don José, John, and Arthur had ridden by, when the stranger's eye fell on Maria.

"It must be, after all!" I heard him exclaim in Spanish. "Maria! yes, it is you! Si, *si*, and I rejoice greatly."

"And you are Domingos; I am sure you are," exclaimed Maria.

"Yes, that is true," answered the old man. "I have come expressly to find you. I have brought bad news; but it might be worse, so be not alarmed."

"What is it?" I asked eagerly. "Are my father, or mother, or sister ill?"

"No; they are all well," said Domingos; "but sad events have occurred at Quito. There has been a great disturbance—a revolution—no new thing unhappily; and your father's house has been burned down, and they have had to fly, and try to escape from the country. They are safe by this time, I hope. I came on to conduct you to them. I have been riding fast to try and meet you to prevent you taking the direct road to Quito. A body of troops are marching along the road, and if you were to fall into their hands you would be ill-treated. We will descend some distance by the way you have come, and take shelter in yonder forest which clothes the side of the mountain. We shall be safe there, and I doubt not obtain shelter in one of the huts of the chinchona gatherers."

Domingos had given me this account in a few hurried words. I instantly called to the rest of our party who were ahead, and we were all soon collected in a nook in the side of the mountain, where we held a consultation as to what should be done. We quickly agreed to follow the advice of Domingos. Don José was greatly agitated at hearing what had occurred.

"They would treat me with but scant ceremony, were I to fall into their hands," he observed; "and I am afraid that you would suffer also were I to be found in your company. However, we may easily escape in the forest should any search be made for us, and therefore let us lose no time in seeking its shelter."

While he was speaking, I caught sight of some figures high up the mountain, at a point round which the path wound its way. I pointed them out to Domingos.

"They are the soldiers," he exclaimed; "I see the glitter of their arms! We have no time to lose. Move on, my friends, move on! If we were overtaken it would fare hard with us."

Don José, who had also been looking towards the point, made us a sign to follow, and rapidly led the way down the side of the mountain, our native muleteers being evidently as anxious to avoid the soldiers as we were. The Indians had, it appeared, taken an active part in the insurrection which had just broken out, and our guides knew, therefore, that, should they be caught, the party in power would very likely wreak their vengeance on their heads.

We descended for a considerable distance along the path by which we had come. Occasionally looking back, I caught sight of the troops as they wound their way in a thin column down the mountain. We, however, appeared to be keeping well ahead of them; and I hoped that our small party might have escaped observation. At length Don José stopped, and getting off his mule, surveyed the side of the hill which sloped away below us. Coming back, he took the bridle of his mule, and made it leap off the path on one side on to what appeared a mere ledge of rock. "Come on," he shouted; "I will show you the way; but you must all dismount and follow the mules on foot." We accordingly got off our animals, which were made to leap down to the ledge below us, and willingly followed the first mule, which Don José was leading. John and I took charge of Ellen, while Domingos helped Maria along. The path was very narrow and steep, but where the mules had gone we had little doubt that we could follow. In a short time we found ourselves descending by a zig-zag path among trees which grew out of the side of the mountain, here and there huge blocks of rock projecting among them. Thus we went on for a considerable distance. Once when we stopped I looked upwards, and caught sight of the head of the column of troops just as they were reaching the very place we had left. At length we reached the bottom of the valley, through which a stream went foaming and roaring downwards over a rocky bed. The mountains rose up on either side, completely surrounding us. "This stream will be a safe guide," observed

Don José; "and if we proceed along its banks, we shall reach a spot where we can remain concealed even should a whole regiment come in search of us." We proceeded on foot some distance, the active mules leaping from rock to rock, while we scrambled on after them. Sometimes we could with difficulty get round the rugged points at the foot of which the stream forced its way, while the cliffs towered up high above our heads. Here and there we caught sight of the snowy pinnacles of the mountains rising towards the sky. At length we emerged into a more open valley, and were once more able to mount our mules. We now entered the forest. Don José led the way by a path which was scarcely perceptible. I observed here and there notches on the barks of the trees, which I concluded served to guide him. Through an opening in the trees I saw the sun setting towards the valley below us; and had I not possessed great confidence in our conductor, I should have been afraid that we were about to be benighted. Directly afterwards we entered a thicker part of the forest. Often it was with difficulty we could see our way amid the dense foliage. Don José, however, did not hesitate. After proceeding for some distance, the sound of a woodman's axe reached our ears, and we saw through an opening ahead several persons engaged cutting away at the vines which had prevented the tall tree they had just hewn down from reaching the ground. A little way beyond was a hut, and in its neighbourhood several persons were at work. "These are my friends," said Don José, "and they will willingly afford us shelter for the night, and protect us to the best of their power."

While he was speaking, the man who appeared to be the director of the party came forward and greeted him. A short conversation ensued.

"We will remain here for to-night," said Don José, "but it may be more prudent to proceed further into the depths of the forest to-morrow. It is possible that our enemies may discover the road we have taken and come here to search for us, and, besides the risk we ourselves should run, we should bring trouble on our friends."

Riding up to the hut, our mules were unloaded, and our hammocks and the packages were taken inside. It was a large shed, far better built than many of the tambos we had stopped at, with thick walls and roof to protect the bark from the effects of the weather. It was already about half full of bundles of this valuable commodity. Each bundle was tightly done up, and weighed as much as a man could carry up the steep mountain's side.

We as usual set to work to form a separate chamber for Ellen and her attendant: this we did with bundles of the bark, leaving a door and window for ventilation. Ellen thanked us for our trouble, saying that she had not had so comfortable a room since the commencement of our journey. John,

Arthur, and I slung our hammocks in the building, while the rest of the party were accommodated in the huts of the bark-gatherers. A rough table was soon formed within the large shed, and benches were brought in, and a substantial repast made ready. The chief dishes were the usual potato-soup and some roast meat. We could not at first make out whether it was venison or mutton, but found on inquiry that it was the flesh of a vicuña, which had been shot by the sportsman of the party in the morning. It is an animal resembling the llama, the well-known beast of burden of the ancient Peruvians. Don José and his friend sat down to table with us, and Domingos waited.

"But of what use is this bark!" asked Ellen, looking up at the huge bundles piled up on either side. "Is it for tanning?"

"Oh no," answered John. "This is the celebrated Peruvian bark, to which the name of chinchona has been given. It was bestowed on it in consequence of the wife of the Viceroy of Peru, the Countess of Chinchona, having been cured of a tertian ague in the year 1638. The count and his wife, on returning to Spain, took with them a quantity of the healing bark; and they were thus the first persons to introduce this valuable medicine into Europe, where it was for some time known as the countess's bark or powder, and was named by the celebrated naturalist Linnaeus chinchona, in memory of the great service the countess had rendered to the human race. The Jesuits were great promoters also of the introduction of the bark into Europe. Some Jesuit missionaries in 1670 sent parcels of the powder or bark to Rome, whence it was distributed throughout Europe by the Cardinal de Lugo, and used for the cure of agues with great success. Hence, also, it was often called Jesuit's bark, and cardinal's bark."

"Yes, I have heard of that," observed Don José, laughing; "and I am told that for some time it was in consequence opposed by the Protestants, and especially favoured by the Roman Catholics."

"Yes," said John, "I believe that for a very long time a very strong prejudice existed against it; and even physicians opposed its use, considering it at best a dangerous medicine. It is now, however, acknowledged to be a sovereign remedy for ague of all descriptions. I believe the French astronomer De la Condamine, who went to Quito in the year 1735 to measure an arc of a degree, and thus to determine the shape of the earth, was the first person who sent home a full account of the tree."

"We call it quinquina," (bark of barks), observed Don José. "Some of its virtues, if not all, were known to the Peruvians long before they were discovered by Europeans."

"Ah! that is the reason it is called quinine by the English," observed John. "I did not before know the derivation of the word."

"Since its use became general in Europe, the export trade of the quinquina has been very considerable," observed Don José. "Forests containing groves of these trees are found in various regions throughout the northern parts of the Cordilleras. My friend here has been engaged since his boyhood in collecting the bark, as was his father before him. When searching for new districts, it is the custom for the cascarilleros, or bark-collectors, to set forth in parties of a dozen or more men, with supplies of food and tools. They make their way into the unknown forest, where they suppose, from its elevation above the sea and its general appearance, that the chinchona trees will be found. They are always accompanied by an experienced searcher, called the *cateador*. He climbs the highest tree in the neighbourhood, and searches about till he discovers the *manchas*, or clumps, of the chinchona trees by their dark colour, and the peculiar reflection of the light from their leaves, which can be distinguished even in the midst of a wide expanse of forest. He then, descending, conducts the party through the tangled brushwood, often for hours together, marking his way with his wood-knife, till he reaches the clump. Here they build rough huts, such as you see around us, and commence their work. The first operation is to cut down a tree, when the bark is carefully stripped off, and kept as free as possible from dirt or moisture, as it easily becomes mouldy, and loses its colour. It is important to cut the tree as close down to the ground as possible, in order that fresh shoots may grow up. There are various species of the quinquina. One is known by the name of grey bark, another as the red bark, which is considered the most valuable. The bark which you see around you is of the latter species; and the men employed in collecting can each make from one to two dollars a day. In the more distant forests, however, they have to undergo great danger in the work. Sometimes they have been known to lose themselves in the forest and having exhausted their provisions, have died of hunger. They are compelled also to carry the load of bark on their own backs, and occasionally a man breaks down under the weight and can proceed no further, when, if he is separated from his companions, he has little hope of escaping with life. There are, besides the species I have mentioned, a vast number of chinchona, though the bark of some yields little or none of the valuable drug."

As soon as supper was over we retired to our hammocks, that we might be prepared to set out at an early hour to a more secure spot in the forest. John and I lay awake for some time, talking over our prospects. Of course we were very anxious about what might happen to our family; for though Domingos had evidently not wished to alarm us, we saw that he was uneasy about them. We also could not shut our eyes to the difficulties and dangers we should have to undergo; not that we cared much about them on our own account, but on Ellen's. Though she was a brave girl, we were afraid that she might suffer from the hardships she might have to endure in travelling over that mountain region. What our father had done to draw upon himself the hostility of the Government party we could not tell. He had, however, always shown an interest in the natives, and by his just and kind treatment of them had won their regard. We concluded, therefore, that he was in some way supposed to be implicated in the outbreak which had lately taken place. At length we dropped off to sleep.

The rest of the night passed quietly away. I awoke as the grey dawn was stealing into the hut, and at once turned out of my hammock. I stood contemplating the wild scene for some minutes, admiring the size and variety of the trees which rose up in the forest before me. Some had enormous buttress trunks, which sent down rope-like tendrils from their branches in every direction. There was the gigantic balsam-tree, the india-rubber-tree, and many others. Among them were numerous palms—one towering above the rest with its roots shooting out in every direction from eight feet above the ground, and another slender and beautiful; but the most remarkable of all was the *sayal*—so Don José called it—the monarch of the palms of these forests. It had rather a short, thick stem, the inner fibres of its stalk being like black wool; but its remarkable feature was its enormous leaves, which grew erect from the stem for forty feet in length. They must be the largest leaves, John and I agreed, in the whole vegetable kingdom. There were many bright and scarlet flowers, and numberless beautiful orchids hanging from the branches of the trees. Beyond the forest rose rugged cliffs, dark black rocks with lofty ranges of mountains towering above them. I was soon joined by my companions, and in a little time Ellen and Maria came forth. As it was almost dark when we reached the spot, we had formed no idea of the wonderful scenery surrounding us Domingos did not appear, and John inquired of Don José what had become of him.

"He has gone to ascertain in what direction the troops have marched," he answered. "We shall have to take our road accordingly. Besides the high road, there is another by which I can lead you, but it is still more steep and difficult yet, as we shall thus avoid the risk of meeting with enemies, it may be the safest for us."

A couple of hours passed away, during which we breakfasted on some delicious chocolate prepared by our host. Still Domingos had not returned. The mules, however, were got ready, that we might start, should it be necessary, immediately he appeared.

"I trust the honest man has not been taken prisoner," observed Don José; "it might fare ill with him. But I am sure he would endure any cruelty rather than betray us; and if he does not soon appear we will proceed on our journey, and my friend here will send a man to show him the road we have taken."

An hour passed, and as Domingos did not return, we mounted our mules and proceeded through the forest. Had we been on foot we might have followed some paths which the bark-collectors had cut; but many of them would only allow of a person proceeding in a stooping posture under the numberless creepers which were interwoven amid the branches of the trees. We had therefore to make a considerable circuit. At length we came to a less frequented part of the forest, and here we were compelled to use our knives and hatchets to clear away the art-work of creepers which impeded our progress. We all dismounted, and led the mules through the path we had thus formed. In several places we found, after an hour's toil, that we had not progressed more than half a mile.

"We shall reach more open country by-and-by," said Don José, "so we need not despair."

At length we came upon a small party of men engaged in stripping off the bark from a tree which they had lately cut down. Don José spoke to them. They saluted him with marks of respect, and one of them, throwing his arm over his shoulder, led us through the forest to a small hut concealed by the surrounding trees. Its interior was not very tempting, but it would afford us shelter from the night air should we be detained there. It was destitute of furniture, with the exception of several hammocks hung up at one end, and a few pots and other cooking apparatus in the corner. Our attendants, however, at once began to sweep it out, while Ellen and Maria sat down on a log outside.

"The night is likely to be fine, and our friends will gladly give you up their hut," said Don José.

"We will wait here till Domingos appears. I have made arrangements that we should have ample notice should any enemies come in pursuit of us. We are surrounded by friends, and I have no doubt we shall be able to escape."

Don José had secured a fresh supply of food, so that in a short time an ample meal was spread on the ground, round which we collected in picnic fashion. We had just concluded it when we heard footsteps approaching. As we looked out, Domingos appeared before us. His countenance exhibited anxiety, and taking Don José aside, he conversed with him for some minutes.

"We must proceed at early dawn by the road I have mentioned to you," said our friend, returning to us. "Domingos has had a narrow escape of being made prisoner. He tells me that the soldiers are pursuing the patriots and natives in every direction, and treating them with the greatest cruelty, shooting and hanging them whenever they are found. Although they would not venture probably to ill-treat you, you might be subjected to great inconvenience, and certainly detained and prevented from reaching your parents. However, I trust that we shall be able to avoid them, and to reach the eastern slopes of the Andes without interruption. Your father has ever proved my firmest friend, and I rejoice therefore to have the opportunity of showing my gratitude by being of service to his children. We shall be able to remain here during the night, and will recommence our journey by dawn, so as to reach the most difficult pass by mid-day, and I trust before evening to have gained a place of safety."

"You will do well, my dear masters, to trust our friend thoroughly," said Domingos to John and me, while Don José was at a little distance. "I know your father has a great regard for him, and whatever he promises he can perform. You are indeed fortunate in meeting with him. He is a cacique, whose fathers once had great power in the country; and though deprived of his lands, he is still looked up to with respect by the natives in all parts of the country."

"Then how comes he to be called Don José?" I asked.

"That is the name by which he is known to the whites, and it is the safest by which to speak of him," answered Domingos. "I know not if I ought to tell his real name; but you will be cautious, or he might be displeased with me."

"Yes; do tell me," I said; "I am curious to know more about him."

Domingos looked around. The person we were speaking of was still out of hearing.

"I will tell you, then," he replied. "His real name is Pumacagua. His father, who headed the last attempt of the Indians to gain their liberty before the revolution, when numerous tribes gathered to his standard, was defeated, made prisoner, and shot. Young José, our friend, after fighting bravely, escaped, and though sought for, was not discovered. Your father had concealed him at great hazard, and afforded him shelter till better times came round. He and I were the only persons in the secret. José Pumacagua has, therefore, reason to be grateful to your father, besides being connected with him by the ties of blood."

Just then Don José, as I will still call him, came up, and we were unable to ask further questions of Domingos. Ellen was much interested when we afterwards narrated to her what we had heard, and said that she should try and get Don José to tell us his adventures, as she was sure they must be very curious.

We were soon left quite alone; for the cascarilleros, having loaded themselves with the result of their labour, took their way through the forest. Our friend told us that they were carrying the bark to a village out of the forest, where it would be free from damp, and be exposed to the drying influence of the sun. When thoroughly dried it would be conveyed to the town of Guaranda, and then sent down by mules to Guayaquil. I should have mentioned that the chinchona trees surrounding us were very beautiful and graceful. They had large, broad, oval, deep green, shining leaves, with white and fragrant flowers, and the bark was of a red colour. The trees varied in height from forty to sixty feet. There were other trees in the neighbourhood which looked very like them, but Don José showed us the difference. The nature of the bark is known by its splintery, fibrous, or corky texture. The true bark is of the former character.

Having cleaned out the hut, we made our usual arrangements for passing the night. Don José and Domingos, I saw, were somewhat uneasy, and two of the men were sent out as scouts to watch the path by which we had reached the hut.

"It is well to take precautions against surprise," observed our friend. "However, our enemies, if they do follow us, will not travel during the night, so that we shall be able, by moving early, to have a good start of them."

At length, two hours after sunset, the Indians returned, reporting that they had seen no one. I was awaked by hearing Don José's voice—"Up, friends, up! We will be on the road, and not breakfast till we reach a spot where no foe is likely to follow us." He held a torch in his hand, by the light of which we got ready to mount. The Indians had meantime saddled the mules, which were brought round to the door of the hut. "Follow my example," he said, producing from a bag which he carried slung over his shoulder, under his poncho, some dried leaves. "This will enable you to travel on for many hours without hunger, and assist in preventing the damp air of the forest from having any ill effect." Sitting down on the trunk of a felled tree, he placed the bag before him, and put leaf after leaf into his mouth, till he had formed a small ball. He then took out from the bag a little cake, which I have since found was composed of carbonate of potash, prepared by burning the stalk of the quinoa plant, and mixing the ashes with lime and water. The cakes thus formed are called *llipta*. The coca-bag, which he called his *chuspa*, was made of llama cloth, dyed red and blue in patterns, with woollen tassels hanging from it. His attendants followed their master's example, as did John, Arthur, and I. Domingos, however, declined doing so, and speedily prepared some chocolate for Ellen, Maria, and himself. A little time was thus occupied, and mounting, we turned our mules' heads towards the east, just as the grey light of dawn appeared above the mountain-tops, the stars still shining with a calm light out of the deep blue sky above our heads, not glittering and twinkling as in northern climes. We were thus initiated by our friend in the use of the far-famed coca.

"How do you like it?" he asked.

"I find the smell of the leaf agreeable and aromatic, and now I am chewing it, it appears to give out a grateful fragrance," I answered. It caused, I found, a slight irritation, which somewhat excited the saliva.

"Ah! you will be enabled to go on if you wish till noon without eating, and then with a fresh supply continue on with active exercise till nightfall," he observed. "It is with this wonderful leaf that the running chasquis or messengers have from time immemorial been able to take their long journeys over the mountains and deserts. It must not be used to excess, or it might prove prejudicial to the health, yet in moderation it is both soothing and invigorating. It will prevent any difficulty of respiration also as you ascend the steep mountain-sides."

The coca-plant grows, I should say, at an elevation of about 6000 feet above the level of the sea. It is a shrub from four to six feet high, the branches straight and alternate, and the leaves, in form and size, like tea-leaves. They are gathered three times a year. They are then spread out in a drying-yard and carefully dried in the sun. The dried leaf is called coca. They are afterwards packed in sacks made of banana leaves. It is most important to keep them dry, as they otherwise quickly spoil.

Daylight at length enabled us to see our way along one of the wildest and most rugged paths on which I should think it is possible for animals to proceed. Up, up we went, with a roaring torrent on one side, and a glorious view beyond of mountain above mountain, some snow-covered, others running up into sharp peaks—others, again, considerably lower, clothed even to their summits with graceful palms, whose feathery tops stood out against the sky. Sometimes we had to cross narrow chasms on the fallen stems of trees; now we arrived at a wide one, to be crossed by means of a suspension bridge, which swung frightfully from side to side. It made me giddy as I watched those who first passed along it. It was composed of the tough fibres of the maguey, a sort of osier of great tenacity and strength, woven into cables. Several of these cables forming the roadway were stretched over buttresses of stone on either side of the bank, and secured to stout timbers driven into the ground beyond them. The roadway was covered with planks, and on either side was a railing of the same sort of rope as the rest of the bridge. Light as it appeared, the mules one by one were led over. We followed, not venturing to look down into the foaming torrent, rushing impetuously along a hundred feet or more below us. Soon after this a ladder of rocks appeared in front of us. We were here compelled to dismount, Don José and John helping up Ellen, Domingos assisting Maria, Arthur and I scrambling up by ourselves while the Indians, waiting till we had reached the summit, remained behind to drive on the mules. Every instant I expected to see one of them roll over; but they climbed up more like monkeys than quadrupeds, and at length joined us on a small level spot at the summit.

"A dozen bold men might hold this pass against a thousand enemies," observed our friend. "Few but our people know it, though. We will proceed yet higher, and cross the most elevated pass before we stop for breakfast, if your sister can endure hunger so long."

"Oh yes, yes!" exclaimed Ellen. "I would not have you delay on my account. The chocolate I took prevents me feeling any hunger, even though this pure air is calculated to give an appetite."

On and on we went, at as rapid a rate as our mules could move, upwards and upwards, the scenery if possible growing wilder and wilder at every step. Huge masses of rock rose above our heads, with snow-topped pinnacles peeping out at each break between them. We had gone on some way further, when at a short distance on our left I saw perched on the top of a rock a huge bird, its head bent forward as if about to pounce down upon us. Presently we saw its wings expand. It was of great size, with huge claws, a pointed, powerful beak, a neck destitute of feathers, and a huge comb on its forehead. The feathers were of a glossy black hue, with a white ruff at the base of the neck.

"Do you think he will attack us?" I said to Don José.

He laughed. "No; he is a coward! We can easily drive him off if he make the attempt."

He shouted loudly. At that instant the condor, for such was the bird near us, spreading out its huge wings, slowly glided into the air. At first the weight of its body seemed to keep it down, but gradually it rose, mounting higher and higher, until it appeared like a mere speck in the blue sky.

"He has gone off to the distant ocean," observed our companion; "or to seek for prey among the flocks on the plains below. He will not return till evening, when probably we shall see him, or some of his brothers, flying over our heads, and pitching on the lofty peaks amid which they dwell."

The highest point of the pass was at length reached. We all felt a difficulty in breathing, and even our hardy mules stood still and gasped for breath. We let them proceed slowly, while we had time to admire the magnificent spectacle which the mountain scenery afforded. Around us on every side rose up lofty peaks and rugged heights, prominent among which appeared the snow-capped, truncated peak of Cotopaxi, looking like a vast sugar-loaf. The rocks, too—huge masses of porphyry—were broken into all sorts of shapes, and were of every variety of colour, from dark brown to the brightest lilac, green, purple, and red, and others of a clear white, producing a very curious and beautiful effect, and at the same time showing us to what violent throes and upheavings that region has been subjected. Below our feet was spread out that gloomy plain which has been so frequently devastated by the lava and ashes which the mountain has cast forth.

Descending, we reached a sheltered spot, where grass was found for our tired mules. Our saddle-bags were unpacked, the fires lighted, and in a short time cups of boiling chocolate and a steaming stew, previously cooked, were arranged for us on the grass.

While wandering a little way from our temporary camp, I saw some large pale yellow flowers growing on a low shrub. Presently several small beautiful birds appeared hovering above them, in no way daunted by my presence. As they dipped their long bills into the flowers, I could observe their plumage, and was convinced, though found at so great an elevation, that they were humming-birds. After watching them for some time, I called Ellen and Arthur to look at them.

"Ah, yes, they are worthy of admiration," exclaimed our Inca friend. "The bird is the Chimborazian hill-star humming-bird. It is found 16,000 feet above the ocean, close to the region of snow, and seldom at a less elevation than 12,000 feet."

The head and throat of the little creature which had excited our admiration shone with the most brilliant tints, though the rest of the body was of a more sombre hue. The upper parts of the body were of a pale, dusky green, except the wings, which were of the purple-brown tint common to humming-birds in general. The head and throat were of the most resplendent hue, with an emerald green triangular patch on the throat, while a broad collar of velvety black divided the brilliant colours of the head from the sober ones of the body. The hen bird, which was mostly of a sombre olive-green, was flying about under the bushes, and almost escaped our notice.

Don José told us that a similar bird inhabits the sides of Pichincha, with different marks on its neck, and that neither at any time visits the other, each keeping to its own mountain, on which they find the food, flowers, and insects best suited to their respective tastes. It would have been barbarous to have shot the beautiful little birds; but even had we wished it, it would have been difficult to do so. So rapid was their flight, that it was only when they were hovering over a flower that we could have taken aim. Ellen wanted to have one caught to keep as a pet; but Don José assured her that it would not live in the low region of the Amazon, but that we should there find many still more beautiful species of the same family, some of which she might very likely be able to tame. After watching the birds for some time, we returned to the camp.

Domingos was the first to mount his mule, riding on ahead, that he might ascertain if the road was clear, while he promised to return and give us notice should any enemies appear, that we might have time to conceal ourselves. This we hoped to be able to do among the wild rocks which rose up in every direction. We rode on, however, without interruption for the remainder of the day, and stopped towards evening at a small mud hut, inhabited by a Quichua family, who willingly agreed with Don José to conceal and protect us with their lives. In the morning we proceeded in the same way as on the previous day. Thus for several days we travelled on, resting during the night at rude tambos, the inhabitants of which, directly Don José spoke to them, willingly undertook to give us accommodation. The weather was fine, the air pure, bracing, and exhilarating; and in spite of the fatigue we underwent, none of us suffered. Ellen and Maria bore the journey wonderfully. Although we were making our way towards the east, frequently we found ourselves riding round a mountain with our backs to the rising sun. Now we were ascending by the side of steep precipices, and now again descending into deep ravines. At length Don José gave us the satisfactory intelligence that we had left Quito behind us to the north-west, and that we might hope to escape falling in with hostile forces. "Still," he said privately to John and me, "I cannot promise that we are altogether safe. We must use great caution, and avoid as much as possible the beaten tracks. Parties may have been sent out to the east in search of fugitives; but we will hope for the best."

As we were ascending a mountain-side, we saw before us, winding downwards, a long line of animals. A couple of Indians walked at the head of the troop, while several other men came at intervals among them. Each animal carried a small pack on its back; and we soon knew them to be llamas, as they advanced carrying their long necks upright, with their large and brilliant eyes, their thick lips, and long and movable ears. They were of a brown colour, with the under parts whitish.

As we approached, in spite of the efforts of their conductors, they scattered away up and down the mountains, leaving the path open to us. The Indians, however, made no complaint; but as we gained a height above them, we saw them exerting themselves to re-collect their scattered cavalcade. They were going, Don José told us, to the coast, to bring back salt—an article without which human beings can but ill support life in any part of the world.

We soon after found ourselves travelling on a wide, lofty plain, bounded by still higher peaks. In several directions we saw herds of llamas, as also a smaller animal of the same species—the alpaca. It somewhat resembles the sheep, but its neck is longer, and its head more gracefully formed. The wool appeared very long, soft, fine, and of a silky lustre. Some of those we saw were quite white, others black, and others again variegated. There were vast herds of them, tended by Indians, as sheep are by their shepherds in other parts of the world.

The following day, descending from the plain and passing through a deep valley, we caught sight of a herd of similar creatures, which Don José told us were vicuñas. Their shape appeared slighter and more elegant than that of the alpaca, with a longer and more graceful neck. The colour of the upper part of the body was a reddish yellow, while the under side was of a light ochre. A peculiar shrill cry reached our ears as we approached, and the whole herd turned, advancing a few paces, and then suddenly wheeling round, off they went at a rapid rate. Don José told us that they are hunted with the bolas, as cattle are in the plains. There is another animal, the huanacu, which is larger than the llama, but resembles it greatly. It is considered by some naturalists to be a wild species of the llama. Huanacus live in small troops. Their disposition is very different from that of the llama. Though easily tamed when caught young, they can seldom be trained to carry burdens.

John reminded me of an account he had read of the llama, which is likened to the dromedary of the desert, the services it is called upon to perform being similar. Though it has not the ugly hump of the dromedary, it possesses the same callosities on the breast and knees; its hoof is divided in the same manner, and is of the same formation. Its internal construction, which enables it to go for a long time without drinking, is also similar. It will carry about one hundred pounds, and proceed at the rate of twelve or fourteen miles a day. When overloaded, however, it lies down, and nothing will induce it to rise till it has been relieved of part of its cargo.

Llamas were the only beasts of burden employed by the ancient Peruvians. Mules and horses were introduced by the Spaniards, and have now in many places superseded the llamas, as mules will carry a much greater weight, and are far more enduring and patient animals.

Chapter Four
Adventures among the Mountains

We had been travelling on for many days, yet had made but slow progress. This was not surprising, considering that we had to climb up steep mountains and to descend again into deep valleys, to cross rapid streams and wade through morasses, again to mount upwards and wind round and round numberless rugged heights, with perpendicular precipices, now on one side, now on the other, and gulfs below so profound that often our eyes, when we unwisely made the attempt, could scarcely fathom them. Still almost interminable ranges of mountains appeared to the east. As we looked back, we could see the lofty heights of Pichincha, Corazon, Rumiñagui, Cotopaxi, Antisana, and many others.

We had a mountain before us. Our patient mules slowly climbed up it. The summit reached, the ridge was so narrow that parts of the same rocks might have been hurled, the one down into the valley towards the setting sun, the other in the direction of the Atlantic. We there stood fifteen thousand feet at least above the ocean, our animals panting with the exertion, and we ourselves, though inured to the air of the mountains, breathing with difficulty. Still before us there was a scene of wild grandeur,—mountain rising beyond mountain, with deep valleys intervening, their bottoms and sides clothed with a dense unbroken mass of foliage.

"I fear beyond this we shall find no pathway for our mules," observed Don José, as we were descending the height; "but we will endeavour to procure bearers for the luggage, and will, in the meantime, encamp in some sheltered spot, and try and ascertain in which direction my friend, your father, and his party have gone."

We were nearly an hour descending, our mules carefully picking their way among the rocks and lofty trees, and along the edges of yawning chasms, which threatened to swallow us up. Sometimes we passed through wooded regions, where the giant trees, falling from age, remained suspended in the network of sipos or wild vines, which hung from the branches of their neighbours. Now we had to make our way round the trunks, now to pass beneath them. As I looked up, I could not help dreading that the cordage which held them might give way, and allow them to fall at that instant and crush us. At last we reached a level spot or terrace on the mountain-side, but still the bottom of the valley seemed far down below us.

"We will encamp here," said our friend, "and remain till we can ascertain the direction we must pursue to come up with our friends. We are here above the damp and close air of the valley. From yonder torrent we can obtain the water we require," (he pointed to a cascade which came rushing and foaming down, at a little distance, through a cleft in the mountain), "while the forest around will afford an ample supply of provision. We are at such a distance from the usual track, that we shall not, I hope, be discovered, should any of our enemies venture in this direction."

John at once agreed to our friend's proposal.

"Our mules," continued Don José, "are of no further use, for it would be almost impossible for them to make their way amid the tangled forest through which we must pass. We will therefore send them back to a solitary rancho or farm, the proprietor of which is my friend, where they will remain in safety till better times, when they can be forwarded to their owners."

This plan being agreed on, the animals were unloaded, and our native attendants set to work to build huts, which might afford us sufficient shelter for the night. We all helped; but we found that they were so much more expert, that they had erected three huts while we had not finished one. Long stakes were first cut down. Two of them were driven into the ground and joined at their top, and about twelve feet beyond them, other two were driven in, and connected by a long pole. Against this a number of stakes were arranged to serve as rafters. Meantime a quantity of large palm-leaves had been procured, which were attached to the rafters by thin sipos or vines, beginning at the bottom, so that they overlapped each other in the fashion of tiles. They were so neatly and securely fastened, that it was evident the heaviest shower would not penetrate them. In a short time we had seven or eight of these huts up, sufficient to accommodate the whole of the party. The natives then descending into the forest, brought back a quantity of wood, which they had cut from a tree which they called *sindicaspi*, which means the "wood that burns." We found it answer its character; for though it was perfectly green, and just brought out of the damp forest, no sooner was fire put to it than it blazed up as if it had been long dried in the sun.

We were still at a considerable elevation, where there was but little of animal life. Even here, however, beautiful humming-birds flew among the bushes. They seemed very like the hill-stars we had seen at Chimborazo—wonderful little feathered gems; but they flew so rapidly about that it was difficult to distinguish their appearance. Now a gleam of one bright colour caught the eye, now another. Now, as they passed, all their hues were blended into one.

"I should so like to have some of those beautiful little creatures as pets," said Ellen. "I wonder if they could be tamed!"

"No doubt about it," said Don José. "The difficulty is to catch them first. But, small as they are, they are in no degree timid; and if you could take some of them young, you would find that they would willingly feed off your hand; but, bold and brave, they love freedom, and will not consent to live in captivity. Perhaps Isoro may catch some for you. He knows all the birds and beasts of this region, and trees and herbs, as, at one time, did all the people of our race. The study of God's works is a truly noble one, and such the enlightened Incas considered it; and therefore it was the especial study of young chiefs in bygone days. But, alas! in these times of our degeneracy, in that, as in many other points, we are grievously deficient compared to our ancestors."

"Oh, thank you," said Ellen. "I shall indeed be obliged to Isoro if he can show me how to tame some of these beautiful little birds."

"I would rather have one of those fellows I see perched on yonder pinnacle," observed Arthur, pointing to a rock at some distance, whence a huge condor, with outspread wings, was about to take flight. "What a grand thing it would be to get on his back, and make him fly with one over the mountain-tops. He looks big and strong enough to do it."

"I am afraid that, with all his strength, he would find it a hard matter to lift a heavy youth like you from the ground," observed Don José. "Yet even a condor can be tamed, and if he is well fed, becomes satisfied with his lot. Large as he is, he is a mean creature, and a coward."

While Don José was speaking, the condor came flying by. Not a movement of his wings was perceptible. We hallooed and clapped our hands.

"He seems not to hear our voices," I observed.

"He is too far off for that," said our companion. "Though we see him clearly, he is at a greater distance than you suppose. In this pure atmosphere, objects appear much nearer than they really are; indeed, even with long practice, it is difficult to ascertain distances by the eye alone. See there, on yonder slope! It would take an active man an hour or more to reach the height over which these vicuñas are bounding, and yet they seem almost within reach of our rifles."

He pointed to a shoulder of the mountain which projected some distance into the valley, over which several animals were making their way, scrambling up rocks which I should have thought the most agile deer could scarcely have attempted to scale.

Isoro had received a hint from his master; and after being absent from the camp for some time, returned with a beautiful little live bird, which he presented, greatly to her delight, to Ellen. Though its bright, sharp specks of eyes were glancing about in every direction, it remained quietly in her hand, without attempting to escape. The greater portion of its body was light green, bronzed on the side of the neck and face, and the lower part of the back was of a deep crimson red. The wings were purple-brown, and the throat metallic green; but the tail was its most remarkable feature. That was very long, brown at the base, and the greater part of its length of the brightest fiery red, tipped with a velvety black band.

"Why, its tail is a perfect comet," exclaimed Ellen, who had been for some time admiring it.

She had given it the name by which it is chiefly known—the Sappho comet, or bar-tailed humming-bird. It is a migratory bird, seldom, however, found so far north. It is a native of Bolivia, where it is found in gardens, and near the abodes of men, of whom it seems to have no fear. In the winter it flies off to the warm regions of eastern Peru, so Isoro told us.

"I am afraid that it will not live in captivity," he remarked. "Shall I kill it for you, señora?"

"Oh no! no!" exclaimed Ellen. "On no account. If I cannot make a pet of it, I would not keep it even as an unwilling captive. Pray, let it go at once."

Isoro let the bird perch on his finger. It looked about for an instant, and then expanding its glossy wings, off it flew, its long tail gleaming like a flash of lightning in the air, and was in an instant lost to sight. Isoro had, I believe, caught the little creature by the bill, with a sort of bird-lime, placed in the lower part of a flower, where it was held captive long enough to enable him to seize it.

We did not fail to keep up a large fire in the centre of our camp during the night, lest any prowling puma might venture to pay us a visit. The warmth, also, which it afforded in that keen mountain air was grateful.

After Ellen and Maria had retired to their hut, which had been made as comfortable for them as circumstances would allow, we sat up discussing our plans. I found that Don José and John had become anxious at not finding our father. Our friend had sent out several Indians in different directions to search for him, with orders to come back to the spot where we were now encamped. I was surprised to find the influence he possessed among all the natives we had met.

As soon as we had encamped, Isoro and two other Indians set off to forage in the neighbourhood, as well as to obtain information. They came back late in the evening, driving before them three hogs, which they had purchased at a native hut some distance off. A pen was soon built, in which to confine the animals: one of them was destined to be turned into pork the following morning. The mules had already been sent away, and True and the pigs were the only four-footed animals in the camp.

Our whole party had been for some time asleep, when I was aroused by a horrible squeaking, followed by a loud bark from True, who was sleeping under my hammock. The squeaks and a few spasmodic grunts which succeeded them soon ceased. The voices of my companions outside the hut showed me that they were on the alert; and knowing that True would attack our visitor, whether puma or jaguar, I tied him to one of the posts of the hut before I went out—a proceeding of which he did not at all approve.

"Cuguacuara! cuguacuara!" I heard the Indians exclaiming.

"A puma has carried off one of the hogs," said John, who appeared with his gun ready for action.

"Where has it gone?" I asked.

"That is what we are going to ascertain," he answered.

We set out with Don José, Isoro, and several of the Indians, the latter armed only with their spears. There was a bright moon, so we had no great difficulty in seeing our way, though in that region of precipices it was necessary to be cautious. Isoro and the Indians led the way, tracing the puma by the blood which their keen sight discovered on the ground. We had not gone far when they stopped and signified that the beast was near. Turning a point of rock, we saw before us, in a hollow on the side of the mountain—a shallow cavern overgrown with shrubs, into which the moon shone brightly—not only one, but two huge pumas, the nearest with its paws on the hog it had just stolen. We had formed our camp close to their lair. The savage brutes, thus brought to bay, and unable to escape, snarled fiercely at us. No animal is more hated by the Indians than the puma, on account of the depredations it commits on their flocks and herds. They had little chance, therefore, of being allowed to escape. I expected, moreover, at any moment to see them spring at us.

Rising in the air he fell backwards.

"Do you take the nearest," said Don José, calmly, to John; "I will take the other. Reserve your fire, Harry, in case one of them should spring."

He and John fired. The nearest puma gave a tremendous spring forward. I had my weapon ready, and drew the trigger. The bullet struck him, and, first rising in the air, he fell backwards, and lay without moving. The Indians rushed forward, and, with shouts of triumph, soon knocked out any sparks of life which remained in the animals. They then, fastening some sipos round the bodies, dragged them and the hog to the camp.

I had just time to measure one of them, before they were skinned and cut up. It had a body four feet in length; and a tail two and a half feet long, black at the tip, but without the characteristic tuft of the lion. Its limbs were very thick and muscular, to enable it to climb trees and spring a great distance. Its coat was of a light tawny tint, and of a greyish-white below.

The Indians, delighted with their prize, sat up the rest of the night cooking and eating the flesh, and telling anecdotes about the creatures. The puma (*Leopardus concolor*) will seldom face a man when encountered boldly. It attacks his flocks, however; and hunts deer, vicuñas, llamas, and, indeed, all animals it meets with except its rival, the jaguar. It takes post on the branch of a tree, pressing itself so closely along it as scarcely to be distinguished; and from thence springs down on a passing deer or other animal, seizing it by the head, which it draws back till the neck is broken. I shall have by-and-by to recount another adventure with pumas of a far more terrific character; so will say no more about them at present, except that we found the flesh very white, and much like veal.

We spent three days at the encampment. At length one evening Don José declared his intention of setting forth himself with Isoro. I begged that I might accompany him, and John also seemed anxious to go.

"No, Señor John," said our friend; "it is your duty to remain and take care of your young sister. But I will consent to take Harry with me, and we will set forth to-morrow morning by daybreak. John, Arthur, and your servants will be sufficient to guard the camp; but do not move out beyond the point which intervenes between this and the pass, lest you may be perceived by any enemy travelling on it. And let me advise you also to be cautious how you receive any stranger who may perchance find his way here. At night be careful to keep a fire burning, and to set a watch. If you strictly follow my injunctions, I shall have no fear. I need not remind you of your young sister, whom it is your duty to watch over; and the consequences to her, as indeed to us all, would be sad through any carelessness."

John, though evidently disappointed, promised to follow our friend's advice. Next morning, even before the sun had risen above the tops of the eastern mountains, while the valley was concealed by a dense mist, which looked as if a sheet had been drawn across it, we were on foot, and had finished breakfast. Don José, Isoro, and I were each provided with long, stout staves. Our rifles were slung at our backs; wallets containing our provisions were hung over our shoulders; and our feet were shod with alpargates, which are sandals made of aloe fibres. They are invariably worn by the natives, as any ordinary boots would immediately be cut to pieces by the rocky ground. These, indeed, did not last more than three or four days. We had supplied ourselves, however, with a considerable number at one of the last places at which we had stopped, as well as with axes and wood-knives, and several other articles which we should require in our journey through the forest. We had obtained also two bales of cloth, some clasp-knives, glass beads, and trinkets, with which to pay the Indians for the services we might require of them.

Ellen came out of her hut just as we were ready to start. She seemed very anxious when she heard that I was to be one of the party. Don José, however, assured her that he would run into no unnecessary danger, and that our journey was absolutely necessary to ascertain whether our father had passed by that way, or was still in the mountains behind us. "I, too, am well acquainted with the country," he added; "and even should any of our enemies come in this direction, I shall easily be able to elude them."

I wished to take True with me; but Don José said that he would be of more use at the camp,—that he might possibly betray us where we were going, and insisted on his being left behind. Poor fellow, he gazed inquiringly into my face when I tied him up, to know why he was thus treated, and seemed to say, I thought, "You know I shall watch over you better than any one else, and you may be sorry you left me behind." Our friend was, however, so peremptory in the matter, that I was compelled to yield to his wishes.

Bidding farewell to our friends, we took our way for some little distance along the path we had come, and then, turning off, proceeded northward, by which we should intersect, Don José said, another passage across the mountains. Had I not been in active exercise every day for so long, I should have found great difficulty in scaling those mountain heights; but my nerves were firm, and from so frequently looking down precipices, I no longer felt any dizziness, even when standing on the edge of the deepest.

We travelled on for several days—sometimes through forests, at others along the bare mountain-sides, above the region of vegetation. Some nights were spent in huts, which we erected for ourselves, such as those I have just described. The natives, when we stopped at their abodes, always received our friend with great respect and attention. The accommodation they could afford, however, was but scanty. They were built of reeds thatched with palm, and consisted of but one room.

I have not yet described the natives of this region. They were of a bronzed colour, with a sad and serious expression of countenance. They were seldom five feet high, and the women were even shorter. They had somewhat broad foreheads; their heads covered with thick, straight, coarse, yet soft, jet-black hair, which hung down their backs. Their mouths were large, but their lips were not thicker than those of Europeans, and their teeth were invariably fine. They had large, well-formed chins; cheek-bones rounded; their eyes somewhat small, with black eyebrows; and little or no beard. They had broad chests and square shoulders, and well-made backs and legs, which showed the strength possessed by them. They were pleasant-looking people. The men wore a short kilt, with a poncho over their shoulders; the women, a petticoat of larger dimensions.

They offered us, on entering their huts, cups of the *guayusa* tea. It is an infusion of the large leaf of a tall shrub which grows wild in that region. We found it very refreshing: though not so powerful a stimulant as coca, it supports the strength, as do the leaves of that plant, and we found it enable us to go for a considerable time without food. The cleanest corner of the hut was assigned us for our sleeping-place at night, with mats and dried leaves in the place of mattresses. Our friend made inquiries as to whether any white people had passed in that direction; and, by his orders, the natives were sent out to gain information. I saw that he was uneasy, though he did not explain to me the reason.

One morning we were on the point of again setting forward, when a native, with a long mountain-staff in his hand, entered the hut. He exchanged a few words with Don José.

"We must hasten away, Harry," said our friend; "there is not a moment to be lost. The enemy have been tracking us, I find; but I trust that your father has escaped them, and will ere long gain the banks of the Napo, down which he may voyage to the Amazon. We shall be able to reach the same river by a longer route, along which there will be less fear of being followed."

He made these remarks as we were throwing our wallets over our backs. Taking our staves, he leading, we hurried from the hut, following a narrow path which led up the side of the mountain. We had approached the hut by a lower and more frequented path than we were now taking; but we were, I found, going in the direction from which we had come on the previous day. Don José went first, I followed, and Isoro brought up the rear. Though I exerted all my strength, I had some difficulty in keeping up with my friend. Anxious as I was to obtain more particulars of what had occurred, we could not exchange words at the rate we were going. Every now and then, as we were climbing the cliffs, whenever I happened to look back I saw Isoro turning an uneasy glance over his shoulder. It was evident that we were pursued. We reached the edge of a deep ravine, which appeared to bar our further progress. Don José, however, without making any remark, continued climbing on along it; and at length I saw what appeared to be a rope stretched across the chasm.

"Hasten, master! hasten!" I heard Isoro cry out: I knew enough of the Quichua language to understand him.

We continued on till we reached the end of the rope, fastened to the stump of a tree, and stretched across the chasm to the opposite side, where it was secured in the same manner, a platform being raised to the same elevation as the rock on which we stood.

"Harry," said my friend, turning to me for the first time, "I have seen your nerves thoroughly tried, and I know your muscles are well-knit, or I would not ask you to pass along this perilous bridge."

The rope was formed of the tough fibres of the maguey—an osier which grows in the moist ground of that region. It possesses a great degree of tenacity and strength.

"Master, let me go first," exclaimed Isoro, springing forward. "If it breaks with me it will matter little, and you will have still a chance for life."

Without waiting for Don José's answer, Isoro threw himself upon the rope, and, holding on by hands and feet, began to work himself along. I watched him anxiously. It was indeed a fearful mode of crossing that awful gulf; and yet I knew that I must pass as he was doing. I was thankful that the distance was not great, at all events. I breathed more freely when at length I saw him alight on the platform. I entreated Don José to go next. "It will give me more courage," I said. "As you wish," he replied. "Let me caution you, only before I go, to shut your eyes, and not to think of the gulf below you. You will then find the passage perfectly easy."

Saying this, he took hold of the rope, and began to work his way across. Scarcely, however, had he got into the centre, when I saw Isoro pointing in the direction we had come from.

"Hasten! hasten!" he shouted out.

I looked round, and caught sight of two enormous hounds approaching at full speed. I could hear their loud, baying voices as they came on panting up the mountain-side. I did not hesitate a moment, when urged by Isoro to cross at once. "The rope will bear you," he shouted out—"not a moment is to be lost!"

Seizing the rope, I shut my eyes and began the awful passage; for awful it was, as, in spite of my resolution, I could not help thinking of the deep chasm over which I was making my way. I should be unwilling again to attempt so fearful a passage; and yet, perhaps, once accustomed to it, I should have thought nothing of the undertaking. I was surprised when I felt my friend take my arm.

"You are safe," he said; "lower your feet;"—and I found myself standing on the platform.

On opening my eyes, and looking towards the cliff from which we had come, I saw two huge blood-hounds, with open mouths, baying at us. Isoro, I should have said, had taken my rifle as well as his own, and placed it against the tree.

"We must get rid of these animals," said Don José, "or they will betray the road we have taken."

Saying this, he levelled his piece, and one of the dogs, as it sprung forward on receiving the bullet, fell over the chasm into the depths below. Isoro followed his master's example. His bullet took effect; but the blood-hound, though wounded, was not killed outright, and retreated a few paces. I was afraid he would have escaped; but before he had gone far, he fell over, and after a few struggles, was dead.

"The animal must not remain there," observed Isoro, throwing himself upon the rope; and in a few minutes he had again crossed the chasm.

Seizing the dog by the legs, he drew it to the edge, and hurled it after its companion. Then, searching about in the crevices of the rocks for moss and lichens, he strewed them over the ground where the dog had fallen, so as to obliterate the traces of blood. He was some time thus occupied before he had performed the operation to his satisfaction; and then he once more crossed the chasm, with as much unconcern as if he had been passing along an ordinary road. I proposed letting go the rope to prevent our pursuers following.

"That is not necessary," said Don José. "It would cause trouble to our friends, and I doubt whether our enemies will venture to cross. At all events, the so doing would betray the route we have taken, and they may find the means of crossing some leagues further down the stream."

We accordingly proceeded as before. We now came to a track, which, had I been alone, I could not have followed, as it was generally, to my eyes, altogether undistinguishable; yet Don José and Isoro traced it without difficulty. It now led us along the edge of a precipice, where, it seemed to me, so narrow was the space between the cliff on one side and the fearful gulf on the other, that we could not possibly get by. Our leader, however, went on without hesitation. At length he appeared to reflect that my nerves might not be as firm as his.

"Here, Harry," he said, "take hold of the centre of my staff; Isoro will hold the other end, and you may pass without risk."

I did as he directed, keeping my eyes away from the gulf as much as possible. Now and then the path became somewhat wider; then again it narrowed, affording just space to support our feet. I leaned against the cliff, unwilling to throw more weight than I could possibly help on the staff. I breathed more freely when we were once more ascending the mountain-side. We were making our way round a rugged point of rock, and Don José's head had just risen above it, when he called to us to stop.

"I see some people coming this way," he observed. "They may be friends, but they may be foes. Harry, I am sorry to have exposed you to this danger; for it is me they seek, not you. However, they have not seen us, and we have yet time to conceal ourselves. Fortunately I know of a place near here where we shall be able to do so; and unless yonder band have these savage blood-hounds with them, we may yet escape capture."

Saying this, he began rapidly to ascend the mountain-side among the wild and rugged rocks with which it was covered. After climbing up for some distance, we saw before us a small opening in the rocks.

"This is the spot I was seeking," observed our friend; "and unless it is known to our pursuers, we shall here remain in security till they have passed by."

He leading the way, we all entered the cavern. It soon opened out into a large chamber with rugged sides. The passage to it also had several buttresses or projecting rocks, behind which we might take post, and could have fired down without being seen on any one approaching. From the entrance, also, we could watch the pathway by which we had come; and it was so small and overgrown with shrubs that it could not be perceived at any distance. Don José told me to climb up behind one of the rocks, while he and Isoro took post behind others. So completely were they concealed, that I could not discover where they were except by their voices. We waited anxiously, till at length a band of armed men was seen winding round the hill. Already they had passed under the cave.

"We might follow, and without difficulty hurl every one of those fellows into the abyss below," observed Don José. "But we will spare them; they obey but the orders of their superiors."

After waiting a little time longer, Don José emerged from the cavern, and looking about, told us that the road was clear. We accordingly descended, though it required great caution to avoid making a rapid descent into the deep ravine below us. For the greater part of the day we continued toiling on, supported by the coca with which we occasionally replenished our mouths. At length, towards evening, we made our way to a native hut, where we were received as usual. Here hammocks were slung for us between the pole on which the roof rested, our hosts undertaking to keep careful watch to prevent surprise.

I had become very anxious about the rest of our party, fearing that they might have been discovered. At the end of two more days I recognised the features of the spot where we had left them. No one was to be seen. My heart sank. Had they been seized and carried off to Quito, or had they made their escape? Great was my satisfaction when, on rounding a rocky point, I caught sight of the huts, and saw Arthur running towards us. "We are all well—very thankful to see you return!" he exclaimed, "for we began to fear that you might have been lost." Directly afterwards John and Ellen emerged from their huts, and now all the party were gathered round us. Poor dear Ellen welcomed me with tears in her eyes. Her spirits revived when Don José told her he had reason to believe that our parents were in safety. True could not restrain his joy, but kept leaping up and licking my hands and face, and jumping round and round me. Wherever I went he closely followed, determined not again to lose sight of me. At supper he sat by my side watching my face, nor would he leave me even though John and Arthur tried to tempt him away with offers of bits of pork or parrots' legs.

All the party were eager to set out at once, but it was necessary before we could do so to procure bearers to convey our luggage along the long and intricate path we had to take through the forest. This our friend undertook to do by the following day from a village at no great distance off.

The next morning a dozen stout natives—young, active men—made their appearance. They all had at their backs large baskets bound by withes passing across the forehead and chest. They were but lightly clothed. A small poncho covered their shoulders, and the usual cloth and kilt was worn round the loins, a wisp of leaves preventing their backs being chafed by their burdens. Each man also carried a long staff in his hand, and a bag of roasted corn as provision for the journey. The burdens were soon adjusted. One of them had a sort of chair at his back, which Don José had ordered to carry the señora, as Ellen was denominated. She insisted, however, that she was well able to walk, and not without difficulty we persuaded her to take advantage of the conveyance which had been provided.

We forthwith set out, and descending the mountain, were soon in the midst of the thick forest. Two of the Indians, who carried lighter burdens than the rest, went ahead with axes in their hands to clear the way. It was extraordinary with what rapidity they cut through the sipos, or hanging vines, which threw their serpent-like coils from tree to tree. So quick is their growth in that moist region, that other travellers following in a few weeks would have to perform the same operation, our friend told us. As we advanced the forest became thicker and thicker, the dark foliage forming a lofty vault through which no sunlight can ever enter. The air felt cool and excessively damp, compared to the exposed sides of the mountains. A constant mist seemed to hang on the branches. Not a sound was to be heard; scarcely a bird did we see in the swampy shades. The stillness and gloom, indeed, became almost painful. From the lofty trees hung down thousands of lianas, or air-roots, some forming thick festoons, others perfectly straight, of all lengths, many reaching almost down to our heads, others again touching the ground and taking root in the soft earth. Here and there some giant of the forest, decayed by age, had fallen, to remain suspended in the loops of the sipos. Thus we went on, following in Indian file. I kept near Ellen to cheer her up, while True followed close at my heels, every now and then licking my hands and jumping up, as if to ask me what I thought of the strange region we had entered. We found it rather difficult to converse. Sometimes we walked on for a considerable distance in silence.

We had thus been progressing for some time, the only sound heard being that of our footsteps on the rustling leaves, or that produced by the sharp axes of our pioneers, when suddenly our ears were startled by a loud crash, which, contrasted with the previous silence, made it seem as if the whole forest was coming down together. Ellen gave way to a slight cry of alarm. "Do not be afraid, my young friends!" shouted Don José. "It is only an ancient tree, weary of standing so long." In a short time the crashing sound ceased, and directly afterwards we came in sight of a vast trunk, which had fallen across the path we were about to pass along. We had to make a circuit therefore to avoid it. We could not but feel thankful that it had not delayed its fall till we were passing beneath, although we might possibly have had time to escape, in consequence of its being upheld for a few seconds by the sipos, till its vast weight had dragged them down.

Chapter Five
The River reached at last

We were not yet free of the mountains, for numerous spurs of the mighty Andes run eastward, between which the many streams proceeding from their snow-capped heights make their way towards the Amazon. Once more we were compelled to ascend a steep height, and then to proceed along the ridge for a considerable distance; then again we descended, to find at the bottom a roaring torrent. This had to be crossed.

The huge trunk of a tree had been placed by the natives over the deeper part, resting on the rocks on either side. The water hissed and bubbled round it, threatening every instant to carry it away. Isoro, however, urged us to cross without delay. He observed signs in the west, among the mountains, of a coming storm, he said, and should it break before we were safe on the other side, we should be prevented from crossing altogether. Still, as we looked at the frail bridge, John and I were very unwilling to expose Ellen to the risk she must run. At length Don José ordered the Indians to form a long rope of sipos, and to stretch it across the stream, that it might assist to steady the bearers on their passage. This caused some delay. "Hasten! hasten!" cried Isoro. "I hear a sound which tells me that the waters are coming down!"

Don José on this led the way. Arthur kept close to him. I followed with True in my arms, for I had taken him up for fear of his being carried away by the current. Ellen's bearer same next. John walked close behind her, to render her assistance should it be required. With one hand I grasped the long sipo, with the other I kept tight hold of True. The rest had the advantage of being able to steady themselves with their poles. Domingos assisted Maria. The water, even before we reached the trunk, came roaring and hissing down round our legs, and I had some difficulty in stemming the current. I was thankful when our leader reached the trunk, and began his passage over it. I found it, however, very slippery with the spray which broke over it. I dared not look back to see how it fared with Ellen. I heard her voice, however, as she cried out, "Do not be afraid, Harry; my bearer steps firmly, and I am looking up at the blue sky and the waving tops of the tall trees; I do not feel any alarm." Still there was a wide extent of bubbling water to be crossed beyond the end of the slippery trunk, and I could hear the loud roar of the waters which came down from the mountains through the ravine. I saw Don José hastening on, and more than once he turned and beckoned us to proceed more rapidly. The end of the bridge was reached. Arthur hesitated to leap into the boiling water. Don José turned round and seized his hand and led him on. I followed. It seemed that every instant the depth of the water was increasing. I trembled for Ellen's safety, and yet could not venture to look back to ascertain how it was faring with her. I thought too of John, Maria, Domingos, and our Indians. The danger for those who came last would be greatly increased. Had it not been for the sipo, I could scarcely have kept my footing. Now I was wading up to my middle, now climbing over a rock worn smooth by the never-resting waters. The water was here somewhat shallower. I looked round. Ellen's bearer was following with firm steps, and was close behind me. "On! on!" cried John. Our leader was already near the edge, and I hoped we should soon be in safety, when I heard Ellen utter a shriek of terror. I sprang on to the bank. Her bearer followed. She had not been alarmed on her own account; but now looking across the stream, I saw the bearers following closely on each other, pressing along the bridge. From above the water, in a vast foaming volume, was coming rushing down, roaring loudly. John turned round, and taking Maria's hand, assisted her up the bank. Domingos clambered after her. Our peons came close together behind. One man was still on the bridge, when the torrent, striking it with fearful force, lifted it off the rock, and away it went wheeling downwards. The peon kept his footing for an instant, then, as it began to turn over, he sprang off it towards the shore; but unable to disengage himself from his burden, he was borne downwards amid the tossing waters. The Indians ran down the bank to try and render him assistance. John and I followed, with Don José, who seemed unusually agitated. Now we saw the man clutching hold of a rock; soon again he was torn off, and went floating downwards. Still he struggled on bravely, making his way towards the shore. I expected every moment to see him give up the unequal contest, for the mighty waters seemed to have him in their grasp. Fortunately the bundle he carried was large, and though heavy out of the water, was light in it, and instead of sinking, assisted to float him.

John and I continued to make our way along the banks with the rest. We had got some distance down, when we saw what appeared to be an eddy or backwater in the river. Below it the stream rushed on with the same impetuosity as before. I called to John. "I think we may save him," I said; and signed to the Indians to cut some long sipos which hung down from the branches above us. Several flexible ones were speedily cut and fastened together. Both John and I were good swimmers. He secured one to his waist, as did I, signing to the Indians to hold the other ends. Then we dashed into the stream, swimming out towards the struggling Indian. In another moment he would have been carried by us. I reached him just as I was at the extreme end of the sipo. John seized his arm directly afterwards, and together we towed him towards the bank, calling to the Indians to haul the sipo gently in. Soon reaching the bank, we dragged up our nearly drowned companion. Not till then did we discover that he was Isoro, who, it appeared, had taken the load of a sick bearer unable to carry it.

Isoro, as soon as he had recovered sufficiently to speak, thanked us warmly for preserving his life. Don José, who had come up, also added his thanks. "I value him much," he observed, "and should have grieved deeply had he lost his life."

We had little time for talking, however, for we had to hurry back to where we had left our companions, as the storm which had been brewing in the mountains now threatened to break over our heads. Our party, therefore, piling up their loads, made haste to erect some sheds similar to those we had already several times built. A quantity of the *sindicaspi*, or "wood that burns," was speedily cut, and fires were lighted, at which we dried our drenched clothes. Scarcely had our preparations been made, when the threatening storm burst over us, the wind howling and whistling through the trees, which waved to and fro, making a loud rustling sound; while every now and then we could hear the crashing noise of some patriarch of the forest, as it sank beneath the blast. The rain came in torrents, and the river, surging and swelling, rapidly increased its breadth. We had indeed reason to be thankful that we had not delayed our crossing a moment longer. Our fires were soon put out, and water came rushing down on either side of us through the forest. We, however, had chosen a slightly elevated spot for our camp, which, though surrounded by water, had hitherto escaped destruction. The rain continuing to pour down in a perfect deluge, compelled us to remain in our camp. So secure, however, had the roofs been made, that we kept dry inside. Occasionally John, Arthur, and I ran into Ellen's hut to pay her a visit. We found her and Maria sitting very composedly, employing themselves with their work, which they produced from one of the bundles they had unpacked. Don José remained in his hut, attended by Isoro. He was much more out of spirits than we had yet seen him.

"My young friends," he said, "I must soon bid you farewell. I had resolved to accompany you till I could see you embarked on the river. We shall reach it, I hope, in three or four days at furthest, but I cannot be longer absent from my people in these troubled times. I hope that you will soon overtake your father and family, who, from the accounts I have received, intend to wait for you at the mouth of the river, where it joins the Amazon. Though I must return, Isoro has expressed a wish to accompany you. You will find his assistance of value, as he has been among the wild tribes you will encounter on your passage, and knows their habits and customs. They are very different from the people you have hitherto met, and may give you much annoyance, unless cautiously dealt with."

We were very sorry to hear of Don José's intention of leaving us, as we had hoped that he intended to accompany us till we could overtake our father, though we were greatly obliged to him for his proposal of allowing Isoro to remain with us.

Once more, the clouds clearing away, we proceeded on our journey. We made, however, but slow progress, as in many places the sipos which had overgrown the path had to be cut way to allow of our passage through the forest. I can scarcely attempt to convey in words an idea of the dense mass of foliage amid which we had to force our way. Vast roots like huge snakes ran out over the ground in all directions, their upper parts forming huge buttresses to the giant stems. Then large ferns shot upwards, while a thick network of vines hung festooned in every possible form above our heads, many hanging down straight to the ground, while numberless curious air-plants hung suspended from the branches. Now and then gaily-plumaged birds were seen flitting amid the thick shade; but we were surprised at the paucity of animal life which existed. Not a quadruped was to be seen. A few monkeys and parrots were occasionally heard, though rarely caught sight of. We had numerous streams to cross; often, indeed, the same stream to cross several times. Frequently the passage was almost as dangerous as that I have described. Sometimes we stopped at the huts of the natives, where we were as usual well received. They were built of bamboo, fastened together with lianas or sipos, the roofs covered with large palm-leaves. They willingly supplied us with such provisions as they possessed. The chief article was *yuca* flour, with which we made cakes. It is the beet-like root of a small tree about ten feet high. When not hunting, the men appeared to spend their time in idleness. The women, however, were occasionally employed in manufacturing a thread called *pita* from the leaves of the aloe, which they carry to Quito for sale. Occasionally the men collected vanilla. It is a graceful climber, belonging to the orchid family. The stalk, the thickness of a finger, bears at each joint a lanceolate and ribbed leaf a foot long and three inches broad. It has large star-like white flowers, intermixed with stripes of red and yellow, which fill the forest with delicious odours. They are succeeded by long slender pods, containing numerous seeds imbedded in a thick oily balsamic pulp. The seeds, which are highly esteemed, are used for flavouring chocolate and other purposes. Monkeys are very fond of them, and pick all they find, so that few are left on the wild plants for man's use. Vanilla is, however, cultivated in Mexico and other parts of the world. The Indians also collected copal. It is a gum which exudes from a lofty leguminous tree, having a bark like that of the oak.

However, I must hurry on with an account of our journey. When we met with no habitations on our way, we were compelled to build sheds in the driest and most open spots we could find. At length, through an arched opening in the forest, the bright sheen of water caught our eyes, and hurrying on, we found ourselves standing on the bank of a stream, which opened up to us a watery highway to the Atlantic.

Still, we were well aware that we had many dangers to encounter. For many hundred leagues we could not hope to meet with Europeans, and although the natives among whom we had hitherto travelled had been friendly, we knew that numerous tribes existed along the banks of the Amazon or its tributaries, who might prove hostile to strangers. Our chief anxiety, however, was about our father and mother. When we might once more meet, we could not tell. Still we felt sure that they would not willingly proceed till we had overtaken them.

We had arrived at a part of the river at a distance from any native village. We had therefore to depend on ourselves for the means of making our intended voyage. We were prepared, however, to build canoes of sufficient size for the accommodation of our reduced party. Accordingly we set to work to erect huts of a more substantial character than those we had hitherto built, in which we might live in some degree of comfort till the work was accomplished. With the assistance of our bearers, in a few hours we had a good-sized hut of bamboos put up, and strongly thatched with palm-leaves. One portion was walled in with a division forming two apartments. The larger was devoted to the accommodation of Ellen and her sable attendant. In the other, our goods were stored; while the rest of us slung our hammocks in a large open verandah, which formed, indeed, the greater part of the building. It was completed before nightfall. In front, between us and the river, a large fire was made up, which, fed by a peculiar kind of wood growing near, kept alight for many hours without being replenished.

We were seated at our evening meal, when we heard footsteps rapidly approaching, and an Indian appeared and saluted Don José. He was a stranger, and had evidently been travelling rapidly. Presenting a packet, he sank down on the ground with fatigue. A cup of *guayusa* tea soon revived him. Don José meantime opened his packet, and hastily read the contents.

"My young friends," he said, "I regret that I must immediately bid you farewell. I cannot longer be absent from my people. I know not what may occur; but if their leaders are away, they will have no hope of obtaining their freedom. Your father, however, was right to escape from the country. I am thankful to say that I can give you tidings of him. He has reached the mouth of the Napo in safety, and is there encamped, awaiting your arrival. Here, John, is a missive your father desires me to deliver to you."

Our friend handed my brother a note written hurriedly in pencil. It ran thus: "The messenger is about to leave, so I must be brief. We are all well, and purpose waiting your arrival on this healthy spot, near the mouth of the Napo. You will without difficulty find it, though we shall be on the watch for all canoes coming down the stream. Pass two rivers on your left hand, then a high bluff of red clay interspersed with stripes of orange, yellow, grey, and white. Proceed another league, till you pass, on a low point, a grove of bamboos. Rounding it, you will find a clear spot on a low hill overlooking the stream. It is there I have fixed our temporary abode."

"Oh, surely there will be no difficulty in finding them!" exclaimed Ellen. "I wish that the canoes were ready—or could we not set off by land?"

"I fear that you would have to encounter many difficulties," observed Don José, "if you were to make the attempt. I must counsel patience, the most difficult of all virtues. I wish that I could accompany you—or, at all events, remain till the canoes are ready; but you will find Isoro a skilful builder, and I will direct him to procure the assistance of some of the natives of this region, who will afterwards act as your crew, and navigate your canoes as far as they can venture down the river. After that, Isoro will return with them, as I am afraid that I could not induce him to remain away longer from me, though I would gladly let him accompany you if he would. Still I hope that you will have no great difficulty in accomplishing the short remainder of your voyage till you find your father and the rest of your family."

John and I thanked Don José again and again for the aid he had afforded us, and the sacrifices he had made on our account.

"Do not speak of them, my young friends," he replied. "I owe much to your father; and we are united by ties of which he, perhaps, will some day tell you."

We wished that our friend would explain himself more clearly, but he evidently did not intend to do so, and we therefore could not attempt to press the point. We sat up talking for some time before we turned into our hammocks.

Our hut was romantically situated. Before us flowed the rapid river; on either side rose the thick forest of palms and other trees, round the stems of which circled many a creeper, hanging in festoons from the branches overhead. In the far distance towered the outer range of those lofty mountains we were leaving, perhaps for ever; while round us were scattered the temporary wigwams which our attendants had put up for themselves. The never-ceasing murmur of the waters tended to lull us to sleep in spite of the strange sounds which ever and anon came from the forest, caused by tree-toads and crickets; while occasionally owls, goat-suckers, and frogs joined in the concert with their hooting, wailing, and hoarse croaks. My faithful dog True had taken up his usual place at night below my hammock. Suddenly I was awaked by hearing him utter a loud bark; and looking down, I saw by the fire, which was still burning brightly, a huge alligator poking his snout into the verandah, having evidently climbed up the bank with the intention of making a meal off the dog, or, perhaps, off one of the sleeping natives. True stood bravely at bay, barking furiously, and yet refusing to retreat. Leaping from my hammock, I seized a log, and dashed it in the huge saurian's face. All the party were speedily on foot. Isoro and Domingos came rushing forward with their long poles to attack the monster; while John, seizing his gun, fired at its head: The ball, however, glanced off its scaly coat. The reptile, finding itself disappointed of its expected feast, and that the odds were against it, retreated, and finally fell over with a loud plash into the stream. The incident warned us of the midnight visitors we might expect, and of the necessity of keeping a watch when sleeping near the river's bank. The fire was made up afresh. We were all soon again asleep, with the exception of one of the men, who was directed by Don José to keep watch for the remainder of the night.

The next morning our kind friend bade us farewell, and, accompanied by the bearers, took his way through the forest to the Andes. We saw him go with great regret. We remembered the dangers he would have to encounter, and we felt how probable it was that we should never again see him. Our party now consisted of Ellen, Maria, John, Arthur and I, Domingos and Isoro. John and I had our rifles; and Domingos a brace of long horse-pistols, which he took from his holsters when the mules were sent back; with a fair supply of ammunition. We had axes, and a few other tools for building our canoe; a stock of provisions, which had been carefully husbanded; and some bales of cotton and other articles with which to repay the natives for their services, or to purchase food. Isoro was armed with a long bow and spear, and Arthur was anxious to provide himself with similar weapons.

As soon as Don José had gone, Isoro set out according to his directions to find some natives. We were still, it will be remembered, within Peruvian territory; and although but slight communication was kept up with the natives of the scattered villages, yet the Spaniards had for some years past made their power felt, as the Incas had done in former ages, even in these remote districts. Isoro said he had therefore no fear of being ill-treated by any of the natives he might encounter.

As soon as breakfast was over, while John and Domingos remained at the hut, assisting Ellen and Maria to overhaul and re-arrange our goods, Arthur and I strolled out to try and shoot some birds. We had not gone far when we heard, at a little distance off, some loud, shrill, yelping cries. I was sure they were produced by birds, yet Arthur could scarcely believe it. The noises came, it seemed, from above our heads. Looking up, we at length caught sight of several large birds, perched on the higher branches above us, with enormous bills. We approached cautiously, hiding ourselves underneath some wide palm-leaves, between which we could observe the noisy assemblage. The birds seemed to be shouting out "To-o-cânó, to-o-cânó," and it is on this account that the Indians give them the name from which we derive that of toucans. One was perched above the rest, and he kept bending his neck downwards, and looking about in the most knowing way, as if to ascertain what sort of creatures we could be. The rest seemed to be employing themselves in picking some fruit, every now and then throwing up their huge beaks as if to let it slip down their throats. As we were anxious to procure some fresh food for dinner, I had been getting my gun ready as quietly as possible, and having selected the bird nearest to me, I raised it to my shoulder and fired. Down came the bird, fluttering among the branches, and we ran forward to secure our prize. On examining it, we found that its feet were like those of a parrot. It was of a black colour, with a gloss of green; about fifteen inches in length, with a long tail and short wings; the feathers at the bottom of the back being of a sulphur hue. The cheeks, throat, and fore part of the breast, were of the same tint, while across the lower part of the breast was a broad crimson bar; the under part being also crimson. The remainder of the flock having flown away, I was unable to obtain another shot. These birds we afterwards saw in great numbers. Their large beaks give them an awkward appearance when flying, yet when climbing about the trees they are evidently of great assistance, as also in picking fruit, or catching the insects they find among the bark.

We went some distance before I could get another shot. I then killed a green parrot, and soon after another. Arthur could scarcely believe that we should find them fit for eating. I was on the point of taking aim at a monkey which came peering out at us among the boughs, when he drew back my arm.

"You surely will not kill that creature!" he exclaimed. "I could never bring myself to eat it, if you do; and I am sure your sister would not."

I told him that monkeys form the principal food of many of the tribes in the country.

"Oh, but then they are no better than cannibals," he answered.

"Wait a little till we are pressed for want of food," I said. "Remember our stock of provisions is but small, and if we were to be over-particular, we should starve." The monkey, however, by his intervention escaped.

We went on for some time, gradually entering a denser part of the forest than we had yet reached. Sipos hung down from every bough, forming a curious tracery of living cordage above our heads, and more completely uniting the tall trees than even the masts of a ship are by the rigging, so that an active midshipman, or a still more agile monkey—I hope the former will pardon me for mentioning them together—could have no difficulty in progressing high up from the ground for miles together through the forest. Strange air-plants swung suspended from the branches, some like the crowns of huge pine-apples, others like parasols with fringes, or Chinese umbrellas—indeed, of all shapes and hues; while climbing plants of the most diverse and ornamental foliage possible wound their way upwards, and then formed graceful and elegant festoons, yet further to adorn this mighty sylvan palace. Such a scene, though often witnessed, seemed fresh and beautiful as at first. As I wished to get another shot or two, we crept slowly on, concealing ourselves as much as possible, lest any birds perched on the boughs might see us and fly away. There was little difficulty in doing so amongst the huge fern and palm-like foliage which surrounded us. In a short time we heard ahead of us a strange chattering and rustling in the trees, and moving cautiously on, we caught sight of a number of dark objects moving about at a rapid rate among the sipos. Stealing cautiously forward, we discovered them to be monkeys at their gambols; and curious gambols they were too. They had white faces, with black coats and thin bodies and limbs, and still longer tails, which kept whisking and twirling and whirling about in the most extraordinary style. Not for a moment were these tails of theirs at rest, except when they had hold of branches to allow their other limbs more freedom. I did not suppose that such muscular power could have existed in an animal's tail. They seemed to be playing each other all sorts of comical tricks. Now one would catch hold of a horizontal sipo, and swing vehemently backwards and forwards; now two or three would scramble up a perpendicular one, and a fourth would catch hold of the tail of the last and hang by it, whisking about his own tail meantime till it had found a branch of liana, when he would let go, and bring himself up again by that wonderful member of his, and skip away to a distance from his playmate, who might attempt to retaliate. If one happened for an instant to be sitting quietly on a sipo, or gently winging backwards and forwards, another was sure to come behind him and pull his tail, or give him a twitch on the ear, and then throw himself off the sipo out of the other's reach, holding on, however, firmly enough by his long appendage. One big fellow came creeping up thus behind another, and gave him a sly pinch on the neck. So funny was the face which the latter made as he turned round and lifted up his paw to give the other a box on the ear, that Arthur and I burst into fits of laughter. This startled the whole flock, who peered about them, skipping here and there, chattering to each other, as if to inquire the cause of the strange sounds which had reached their ears. At length one, bolder than the rest, creeping near, caught sight of us, when back he went to communicate the intelligence to his companions. A hurried consultation was evidently held by them, and then more came to look down at us, keeping wisely in the upper branches. We tried to be silent; but so extraordinary were the grimaces they made with their funny little white physiognomies, that we again burst into shouts of laughter, in which True joining with a loud bark, off scampered the monkeys, whisking their long tails, along the sipos and branches, till they were hid from sight, although we could still hear their chattering in the distance. I could not have had the heart to fire at such frolicsome creatures, even had we been more pressed for food than was the case.

"I wish that we could get one of them to tame," exclaimed Arthur. "It would make a delightful pet for your sister, and a capital playmate for True. They would become great friends, depend on it. He sadly wants a companion of his own amount of intellect, poor fellow."

"I doubt as to their having any intellect, and I don't think True would consider himself complimented by having them compared to him," I answered, laughing, though a little piqued that the sense of my favourite should be rated on an equality with that of a monkey. We discussed the matter as we went along. I was compelled to acknowledge at last that though True had sense, he might not even have reason, only instinct verging on it strongly developed.

"And what are those monkeys?" asked Arthur, who had not quite agreed with me, and wished to change the subject.

"I have no doubt that they are what the French call 'spider monkeys,'" I answered. "I found a description of them in my book, under the title of Ateles, or Coaita. The white-faced species is the *Ateles marginatus*. There are several species very similar in their appearance and habits."

I have more to say by-and-by about these spider monkeys.

We now found that it was time to begin our return to the river. As we were walking on we caught sight of some object moving among the tall grass. Arthur, True, and I followed at full speed. I had my gun ready to fire. It was a huge serpent. It seemed, however, more afraid of us than we were of it. On it went like a dark stream running amidst the verdure, moving almost in a straight line, with only the slightest perceptible bends, and it soon disappeared among the thick underwood. From its size it would have been an awkward creature to be surprised by unarmed; and True, I suspect, would have had little chance of escaping.

Shortly afterwards, looking up among the branches, we saw overhead a large flight of parrots. From their curious way of moving they seemed to be fighting in the air. Presently down one fell from among them, pitching into a soft clump of grass. I ran forward, expecting to find it dead; but scarcely had I taken it in my hand, than it revived, and I had no doubt it had been stunned by a blow on the head from one of its companions. It was of a bright green plumage, with a patch of scarlet beneath the wings. "I am sure your sister would like it for a pet," exclaimed Arthur; "do let us take it to her!" The parrot, however, seemed in no way disposed to submit to captivity, but struggled violently and bit at our fingers. I managed, however, to secure its beak, and we carried it in safety to the hut.

"Oh, what a beautiful little creature!" exclaimed Ellen as she saw it. "I have been so longing to have some pets, and I am much obliged to you for bringing it to me."

"I have tamed many birds," said Maria, "and I hope soon to make this one very amiable and happy."

Domingos, however, declared that the bird could not be kept without a cage. Some bamboos were growing at a short distance. He cut several small ones, and in a short time had constructed a good-sized cage, with the bars sufficiently close prevent the little stranger escaping. He then set to work to pluck the birds we had killed, and they were quickly roasting, spitted between forked sticks, before the fire. While we were engaged in preparing dinner we caught sight of several persons coming along the banks of the river. Isoro led the way; six natives followed. They were clad in somewhat scanty garments—a sort of kilt of matting, ornamented with feathers, round their waists, their cheeks and body painted with red and yellow. They were, however, pleasant-looking men. They had quivers at their backs, and long tubes, which I soon found to be blow-pipes, in their hands. True at first evidently did not approve of their presence, and went growling about, showing his teeth; but when he saw us treat them as friends, he became quiet, and went and lay down at the entrance to Ellen's room, eyeing them, however, as if not quite satisfied about the matter.

Isoro introduced the tallest of the party, whose kilt was rather more ornamented than those of his companions, as their chief—Naro by name. He had agreed to build us a couple of canoes, of sufficient size to convey us down the more dangerous parts of the river. After this we were to proceed in one, while he and his men returned in the other. We were to repay him with a dozen yards of cloth, a couple of knives, some beads, and other articles.

As soon as we had finished our roasted toucans and parrots, we set forth with our new allies in search of suitable trees for the shells of the boats. We hunted about for some time before they could fix on one. At length they pointed out one about fifteen feet in circumference. Some of the bark being cut off. I saw that the wood was of a yellow colour, and of a soft nature, which could be easily worked. The Indians, however, shook their heads, declaring that though the wood was good for a canoe, the tree was too large to be cut down. Isoro, in answer, told them that if they could make a canoe out of it, he would undertake to fell it. He soon showed his countrymen that he would make his words good, and wielding his sharp axe, he quickly cut a deep notch in the tree. Naro now seemed satisfied. While some of the party hewed at the trunk, others climbed the neighbouring trees to cut away the festoons of sipos and other creepers which might impede its fall. A road also had to be cleared to the river for the distance of nearly a quarter of a mile. All hands assisted in this work, and by evening we had made considerable progress.

The Indians camped round us at night. One of them had broken his blow-pipe, and was employed in taking it to pieces for the purpose of mending it. I had thus an opportunity of seeing how it was made. It was about ten feet long, and composed of two separate lengths of wood, each of which was scooped out so as to form one-half of the tube. Their tools appeared to be made of the teeth of some animal, which I afterwards found were those of the paca. These two pieces thus hollowed out are fastened together by winding round them long flat slips of the climbing palm-tree called the jacitara. The tube is then covered over with black bees'-wax. A mouth-piece made of wood is fastened to one end, which is broader than the other. From this it tapers away towards the muzzle. I was surprised to find how heavy the instrument was when I came to try and shoot from one. It is called by a variety of names—by the Spaniards, *zarabatana*; by some natives, the *samouran*; by others, the *tarbucan*; by the Portuguese, the *gravátana*. The arrows are made from thin strips of the hard rind of the leaf-stalks of palms, and are scraped at the end till they become as sharp as needles. Round the butt-end is wound a little mass from the silk-cotton tree, which exactly fits into the bore of the blow-pipe. The quivers were very neatly formed of the plaited strips of a plant growing wild, from which arrow-root is made. The upper part consisted of a rim of the red wood of the japura, highly polished; and it was secured over the shoulder by a belt ornamented with coloured fringes and tassels of cotton. We afterwards saw blow-pipes formed in a different way, two stems of small palms being selected, of different sizes, the smaller exactly to fit inside the larger. Thus any curve existing in the one is counteracted by that of the other. The arrows are tipped with the far-famed wourali poison, which quickly kills any animal they wound.

Next morning we returned to the tree, and worked away as before. Arthur and I undertook to cut down some smaller trees, to serve as rollers on which to drag the huge trunk to the side of the river, where it was to be hollowed out. We had, however, to supply ourselves with food, and two of our new friends prepared to go in search of game with their blow-pipes. Arthur and I begged to accompany them; but they made signs that we must not fire off our guns, as we should quickly put the game to flight, and that we must keep at a distance behind them.

"I wonder what they are going to shoot," asked Arthur.

"We shall soon see," I answered, as we followed our friends.

The noise of our operations in the forest had driven away most of its usual inhabitants from the neighbourhood. We therefore had to go some distance before we came in sight of any game. We kept, as we had promised, a little behind our friends. Suddenly one of them stopped, and raising his blow-pipe, a sound like that from a large pop-gun was heard, and we saw a bird, pierced by an arrow, fluttering among the branches. Gradually its wings ceased to move, and down fell a parrot. Advancing a little further, the Indian made us a sign to stop; and looking up among the branches, we caught sight of a troop of the same curious little monkeys with long tails which we had seen the day before. They kept frisking about, now climbing up the sipos, now throwing themselves down, hanging by their tails, and swinging backwards and forwards. Presently one of the natives lifted his blow-pipe, from which sped an arrow, piercing one of the poor little creatures. It hung for an instant by its tail round a branch, and then fell with a crash among the thick leaves. The others kept jumping about, apparently not aware of what had happened to their companion. Thus three or more were brought down before the rest discovered the enemy in their neighbourhood. They then all went off at a rapid rate, swinging themselves from branch to branch, but stopped again at a short distance to watch us.

"I would give anything to have one of those active little fellows alive!" exclaimed Arthur. "Don't you think, Harry, that we could make the Indians understand what we want?"

"We will try, at all events," I answered. "But I beg that you won't laugh at my pantomime."

Galling to the Indians, I took one of their arrows, and pointing it towards the monkeys, which were still to be seen a little way before us among the trees, eyeing us curiously, I shook my head violently, to show that I did not want it killed. Then I ran forward, and pretended to catch one, and to lead it along. "Now, Arthur, you must act the monkey," I exclaimed. On this he began frisking about, putting out his hand behind to represent a tail, while I pretended to be soothing him by stroking him on the head and back, and thus inducing him to accompany me.

The Indians watched us attentively, and then nodding their beads, began to talk together. They soon seemed to be agreed as to what we wanted, and signing to us to remain quiet, one of them again crept cautiously towards the monkeys, still frisking about within sight, while the other sat down with Arthur and me. We eagerly watched the Indian. He first selected an arrow, the point of which he scraped slightly and wetted. Presently he placed his blow-pipe within the loop of a sipo.

"Why, he's going to kill one of the poor creatures after all!" exclaimed Arthur.

"It looks very like it," I answered. "But we shall see."

The Indian waited for a few seconds, and then out flew his tiny dart with a loud pop. One of the monkeys was hit. "Oh dear! oh dear!" cried Arthur. "They could not have understood us." The monkey had been struck when hanging to one of the lower branches; it fell before it had time to save itself with its long tail, and the Indian instantly springing forward, caught it, and pulled out the dart. He then took something out of the bag hanging at his waist, and put it into its mouth, which he kept closed to prevent it from spluttering it out. The poor creature seemed so stunned or bewildered by its fall, and at finding itself suddenly in the grasp of a strange being twenty times its own size, that it made no resistance. The Indian brought it to us in his arms, much as a nurse carries a baby, and showed us that it was not much the worse for its wound. As we went along we observed that its eyes, which were at first dim, had quickly recovered their brightness, while its tail began to whisk about and coil itself round the native's arm. We were at a loss to account for the wonderful way in which it had so speedily recovered; nor did the Indians seem disposed to tell us their secret.

"I should so like to carry the little creature, it seems already so tame and gentle," said Arthur.

"You had better not take it from the Indian, or it may give you an ugly bite, and be off and up a tree in a twinkling," I answered. "It has no cause to love us as yet, at all events."

Arthur still insisting that he could carry the monkey, asked the Indian to let him have it. The native shook his head, and signified that the monkey would to a certainty escape if he did. At last, however, he and his companion stopped, and fastened the creature's tail tightly to its back, then they wound a quantity of fibre round its front paws, and finally put a muzzle over its mouth. "There; you may manage to carry him now," they seemed to say. "But take care, he may slip out of his bonds even yet, if you do not hold him fast."

The monkey glanced up at the countenance of Arthur, who looked down kindly at the creature, and carried it gently so as not to hurt it.

"I should like to give it a name," he said; "something appropriate."

"We will consult Ellen on that important matter," I answered. "When she sees how active it is, I think she will call it Nimble."

"Oh yes; that would be a capital name. Do let us call it Nimble," he exclaimed.

"You and Ellen shall choose its name, and I am sure that John will agree to whatever you decide," I replied.

This made Arthur perfectly contented, and he walked along stroking the monkey and talking gently to it, till the animal evidently began to feel confidence in him, and lay perfectly quiet in his arms.

The Indians did not as yet appear satisfied with the amount of game they had killed, and were on the look-out for more. I kept my gun in readiness for a shot. "Pray, Harry, do not kill another spider monkey," said Arthur; "it would make Nimble so unhappy, I am sure." I promised that I would not; indeed, I had not the heart to wish even to shoot one of the merry little creatures.

We soon afterwards, however, came in sight of several much larger monkeys, with stouter limbs, but excessively active, and furnished with long, strong, flexible tails. I recognised them as the species called by the Portuguese *Macaco barrigudo*, or the big-bellied monkey. The Indians shot one of them with their blow-pipes, the rest wisely swinging themselves off. The creature had a black and wrinkled face, with a low forehead and projecting eyebrows. The body was upwards of two feet in length, and the tail not much less. As the Indians held him up, Arthur and I agreed that he looked exactly like an old negro.

By the evening we had as many birds and monkeys as we could carry. Arthur offered to carry some of the birds in addition to Nimble, declaring that he could not bring himself to eat our four-handed game. "And that negro-looking old fellow, I would starve rather than touch him!" he exclaimed. "And as for Domingos, I should think him a cannibal if he were to eat him." Arthur, as we went along, kept trying to prevent his little charge from seeing its dead companions. "I am sure that it would make him unhappy," he observed; "for how can he tell that he is not going to be treated in the same way!"

So like was one part of the forest to another, that I had no idea we were near our huts when we came in sight of them True heard us approaching and came bounding forth to meet us, leaping up first to lick my hands and then sniffing up at poor little Nimble, who trembled at seeing him, and after vainly endeavouring to escape, clung tightly to Arthur for protection. "Do call off True; there's a good fellow!" exclaimed Arthur. "He will frighten poor little Nimble to death; but when they are better acquainted they will become very good friends, I dare say." I called True to me, and presently Ellen and Maria came running out of the hut towards us. Ellen was greatly pleased with Nimble, and thanked Arthur very much for having brought him. We carried Nimble into the hut, and Domingos found a leathern strap to fasten round his waist, by which he was secured to one of the beams in the roof. Here he could run from side to side of the hut, out of the reach of True. He kept looking down on us somewhat scared at first at his novel position, but in a short time took some nuts and fruit readily from Arthur's hand, and after examining and cautiously tasting them, to ascertain that they suited his palate, ate a hearty meal.

Ellen told us that she and Maria had been greatly alarmed during our absence by the appearance of a large creature—from their account a puma or a jaguar—which had come close to the hut. True had behaved nobly in standing on the defensive, while they had screamed and waved sticks to try to frighten it off. For some time, however, they were afraid that it would attack them, but at last it turned tail and retreated into the forest.

Domingos and our Indian friends lost no time in preparing the game which we had killed. Arthur and I watched them, when Domingos, without at all recognising the likeness which Arthur and I had discovered in the *macaco barrigudo* to himself, began without ceremony to skin it, and in a short time had it spitted and roasting before the fire. We had formed a rough table, and the first article of food which Domingos placed on it was a portion of the big monkey on a plantain leaf.

"Ah!" he said, "I have reserved this for you; for the meat is superior to that of either the other monkeys or the birds. Just try it, and you will agree with me."

Had he not talked about the monkey, probably no one would have objected to the meat, which did look very nice; but Ellen and Arthur both begged to have some of the birds, with the addition of some roasted plantains and farinha cakes. We made a very substantial meal, John and I agreeing that the big *macaco* was very nice food. Domingos thought so also, as he had claimed a joint as his own share.

I was awoke at night by hearing a strange rushing noise round my head, and raising it above the hammock I caught sight of numberless dark creatures with huge wings which kept sweeping round and round here and there through the verandah. Presently one of them pitched on the clew of my hammock. There was sufficient light from the bright stars to see its shape, and I beheld a creature with large ears standing out from the sides and top of its head, a spear-shaped appendage on the tip of its nose, while a pair of glittering black eyes and a grinning mouth gave it the appearance of a little imp. Presently it expanded its large wings and floated towards my head. I could stand this no longer, and singing out, dealt it a blow with my palm which sent it flying away. The cry awoke my companions, who jumped out of their hammocks, wondering what was the matter. We were quickly engaged in driving out the intruders, which we now discovered to be vampire bats. "Hillo!" cried Arthur, "what is the matter with my foot? There is blood flowing from it!" We found that one of the creatures had been sucking his too. John bound it up, and in a short time tranquillity was restored, and we were all soon in our hammocks. Hideous as these creatures appear, they are harmless, as the puncture they make is but slight, and the wound quickly heals. They showed their sense by selecting our hut for their night quarters, as they there found themselves more secure from the beasts which prey on them than in their abodes in the forest.

In the morning we examined several we had knocked down. They measured twenty-eight inches across the wings, which were of a leathery consistency, the bodies being covered with grey hair. We found their stomachs filled with the pulp and seeds of fruits, with the remains of a few insects only.

Our new friend Nimble soon became reconciled to his lot. Though he took food readily enough from Arthur, and by degrees let Ellen and Maria stroke his back, when any one else came near him he clambered up as high as he could reach into the roof. He soon discovered that True could not climb up to his perch, and in a short time he would swing himself off by his tail within a foot or two of the dog's nose, stretching out his paws as if he were going to catch him by the ear, taking good care to be ready to spring again far out of his reach should True show the slightest signs of leaping up.

"It won't be long before we see Master Nimble riding on True's back, and using his tail as a whip," said Arthur, who had been watching the two animals. He was right; and in a few days Nimble and True became very good friends.

Our boat-building proceeded well. A log of twenty feet in length having been cut off and placed on the rollers, we secured a number of tough lianas to it, and using them as traces, dragged it down to the river. We could, however, move it but slowly, and two whole days were thus consumed. The upper side being smoothed off, a slit was made down the whole length, which was opened slowly by wedges. Having cleared out a considerable portion of the inside, it was turned over and raised on trestles. Beneath it a fire was made along the whole length. Other pieces of hard wood were gradually driven in with wedges to increase the opening, the larger ones being in the centre, where the width was to be the greatest. In about eight hours the work was thus far completed. The bow and tern were made of hewn planks in a circular form, fastened with wooden pins. A plank on each side was next secured, and benches fixed in. The seams were caulked with gum collected from trees growing near, mixed with resin, which exuded from the trunks of others. We thus constructed a vessel, of sufficient size to make a voyage of upwards of one thousand miles down the mighty river, solely of materials found in the wilderness. Paddles were also quickly formed by the Indians of the tough wood of another tree, which they split into boards. They then wove some mats for sails, lianas of different thicknesses serving as cordage.

After this our native friends selected another tree, from which they proposed to form the second canoe. This was to be smaller, that they might be able to paddle it up against the stream. It was built in the same way as the first, but without mast or sails.

Chapter Six
Voyage on the River commenced

All was now ready for our departure from our first halting-place. Early in the morning, having carefully laden our two vessels, we embarked. John, Ellen, Maria, and Domingos went in the larger one, accompanied by Nimble and Poll, with Naro and two of his followers; while Isoro, Arthur, and I embarked in the smaller, with two of the other men. True, of course, went with us, his usual post being the bow, where he stood with his fore-feet on the gunwale, as if it were his especial duty to keep a look-out ahead. Isoro acted as captain, and Arthur and I and the two Indians, with paddles in our hands, formed the crew. Shoving off from the bank, we rapidly glided down the river, the current carrying us along at a great rate with little aid from our paddles. The large canoe took the lead, we following in her wake. The water whirled and eddied as we glided on. On either side rose the giant trees of the primeval forest—while, looking astern, we could see far away across the mighty mass of foliage the range of the Andes, with the beautiful cone of Cotopaxi standing out boldly above its fellows.

We soon, however, had something else to think of. Several dark rounded rocks rose up ahead of us, between which the water furiously rushed, dashing against their sides, and throwing up clouds of spray, while whirling, boiling eddies came bursting up from the bottom, as if some subaqueous explosion were taking place. Short cross waves curled up round us, with here and there smooth intervening spaces, the more treacherous for their apparent calmness; for as we passed through them we could with difficulty keep the head of our small canoe in the direction of our leader. The Indians plied their paddles with redoubled vigour, while the helmsman of John's canoe every now and then gave vent to loud, wild shrieks. Isoro sat calmly clenching his teeth, and looking out eagerly ahead. The large canoe went gliding on. And now we saw her passing between two rocks, over which the water dashing formed an arch of spray, almost concealing her from our sight. Presently we also were passing through the same channel. It seemed as if our small canoe would be swamped by the swelling waters. The clouds of spray which broke over her almost blinded us, the loud roaring, hissing sound of the waves as they rushed against the rocks deafened our ears, while the whirling current so confused our senses, that we could scarcely tell in what direction we were going.

"O Harry, what has become of the other canoe?" exclaimed Arthur.

A dark rock rose before us. No canoe was to be seen. A horror seized me. I feared that she had been engulfed. But presently, Isoro turning the head of our canoe, we shot past the rock, and to our joy again saw the other canoe rushing on with still greater speed towards another opening in the channel. We followed even faster than before. The current seemed to increase in rapidity as we advanced, pressed together by the narrower channel. Yet, fast as we went, we could scarcely keep pace with our leader. Now we glided on smoothly, now we pitched and tossed as the mimic waves rose up round us, and thus we went on, the navigation requiring the utmost watchfulness and exertion to escape destruction. We, perhaps, in our smaller canoe, were safer than those in the larger one; indeed, I thought more of them than ourselves. Should we meet with any accident, however, they could not return to help us, whereas we might push forward to their assistance. We followed the movements of the Indians. When they paddled fast, we also exerted ourselves; when they ceased, we also lifted our paddles out of the water. I was very glad that we were thus employed, as we, having plenty to do, thought less of the danger we were in.

After being thus tossed about for I cannot judge how long, every moment running the risk of being dashed on the rocks, now on one side, now on the other, we found the river again widening and the current flowing on more tranquilly. In a short time, however, we came to another rapid. Once more we were amid the wild tumult of waters. The current rushed on with fearful speed. Now we saw the stern of the leading canoe lifted up, and it appeared as if her bows were going under. I could not refrain from uttering a shriek of horror. Isoro and the Indians remained calm, just guiding our canoe. John's canoe disappeared. On we went, expecting the same fate which I dreaded had overtaken her. An instant afterwards we saw her again gliding on calmly. Downwards we slid over a watery hill, the Indians paddling with might and main, we following their example. We had descended a fall such as I should scarcely have supposed it possible so small a boat as ours could have passed over in safety. Our companions continued plying their paddles, sending out their breath in a low grunt, as if they had been holding it in for some minutes.

We now came up with the other canoe, which had been waiting for us.

"That was nervous work!" exclaimed John "I am thankful we are through the falls; they are the worst we shall meet with."

Paddling on till nearly dark, we landed on an island, where it was proposed we should pass the night. There were but few trees in the centre, the rest consisting of sand and rock. This spot had been selected to avoid the risk of being surprised by unfriendly natives or prowling jaguars. The canoes were hauled up, the goods landed, and fires were lighted, round which we were soon seated taking our evening meal. The Indians then cut a number of stout poles, which they drove into the ground, forming a square, the roof being thatched over with palm-leaves, extending some distance beyond the poles, so as to form deep eaves. To these poles were hung up our hammocks, a small part being, as usual, partitioned off for Ellen and Maria. This was our usual style of encampment. When the trees grew sufficiently wide apart, we sometimes secured our hammocks to them, with a roof such as I have mentioned above our heads. The fires were kept up all night, and a watch set to prevent surprise, should any unfriendly natives find us out, and come across the river in their canoes. Isoro advised us always to select an island for our night encampment. "Indeed," he observed, "it would be safer never to land on the banks, if you can avoid so doing."

Our Indians, besides their usual blow-pipes, had come provided with harpoons and lines for catching fish. Generally, at the end of our day's voyage, they would go out in the smaller canoe, and invariably come back with a good supply.

Arthur and I, with True, one day accompanied Naro and two of his men. While the Indians remained in the canoe, we landed and walked along the sandy shore of the island. True ran before us, shoving his nose into the tall reeds and rushes. Suddenly out he backed, barking furiously, but still retreating, and evidently less disposed than usual for battle. Fully expecting to see a huge anaconda come forth, Arthur and I retired to a safe distance, while I got my gun ready to fire at the serpent when he should appear. We stood watching the spot which True still faced, when the reeds were moved aside, and the oddest-looking monster I ever set eyes on came slowly forth, and for a moment looked about him. True actually turned tail, and fell back on us for support. He would have faced a lion, but the creature before him had not a vulnerable part on which he could lay hold. It meantime, regardless of him or us, made its way towards the water. It was as grotesque and unlike what we fancy a reality as those creatures which the wild imaginations of the painters of bygone days delighted in producing. How can I describe it? It was covered all over with armour—back, neck, and head. On its head it wore a curiously-shaped helmet, with a long tube in front serving as a snout, while its feet were webbed, and armed with sharp claws at the end of its thick and powerful legs. From the chin hung two fringe-like membranes, and the throat and neck were similarly ornamented.

Naro was not far off, and came paddling up at a great rate, crying out to us to turn the creature from the water. Its formidable appearance and size made us somewhat unwilling to get within reach of its head; for it was fully three feet long, and its covering would, it appeared, turn off a bullet. Arthur, however, bravely ran in front of it, and True kept barking round it, keeping wisely beyond its reach. We thus impeded its progress; but still it made way, and was just about to launch itself into the river when the canoe coming up, Naro's harpoon, struck it under the shield at the neck. It struggled to get free, but was hauled again on to the sand, and soon dispatched by the Indians. They seemed highly pleased at the capture, and signified that, in spite of its strange appearance, it was excellent for food.

"Why, after all, it is only a tortoise!" exclaimed Arthur, who had been examining it. A tortoise it was, though the strangest-looking of its tribe, but not at all uncommon.

The strange creature we had found was a matamata (*Chelys matamata*). It is found plentifully in Demerara, where its flesh is much esteemed. What we took to be a helmet, consisted of two membraneous prolongations of the skin, which projected out on either side from its broad and flattened head. The back was covered with a shield, with three distinct ridges or keels along it, and was broader before than behind. It had a stumpy pointed tail. I should add that it feeds only in the water, concealing itself among reeds by the bank, when it darts forward its long neck and seizes with its sharp beak any passing fish, reptile, or water-fowl—for it likes a variety of food—or it will swim after them at a great rate.

We carried the matamata to the camp, and on landing it drew it up with sipos, with its neck stretched out. Ellen could scarcely believe that it was a real creature.

"I am very glad that I did not meet it when by myself on the sands. I am sure that I should have run away, and dreamed about it for nights afterwards!" she exclaimed. "It was very brave, Harry, of you and Arthur to face it; and as for True, he is worthy to take rank with Saint George, for it must have appeared a perfect dragon to him."

"Barring the want of tail, my sister," observed John with a laugh. "True will find many more formidable antagonists than the matamata in these regions, and he must be taught to restrain his ardour, or he may some day, I fear, 'catch a Tartar.'"

Maria meantime stood behind us, lifting up her hands and uttering exclamations of astonishment, as she surveyed the creature at a respectful distance.

The next evening we again accompanied the Indians. It was very calm, and the water in a narrow channel through which we went smooth and clear, so that we could look down to a great depth and see the fish swimming about in vast numbers. Presently I caught sight of a huge black monster gliding silently up the channel just below the surface. It was, however, too far off for the harpoons of the Indians to reach it. We followed, they intimating that we should very likely come up with it. We had not gone far, when they ceased rowing and pointed ahead. There I saw, on the other side of a clump of bamboos which grew on a point projecting into the stream, a creature with a savage countenance and huge paws resting on the trunk of a tree overhanging the water. It was of a brownish-yellow colour, the upper parts of the body variegated with irregular oblong spots of black. It was so intently watching the stream that it did not appear to observe us. Had it not indeed been pointed out to me, I might not have discovered it, so much had it the appearance of the trunk on which it was resting. Presently we saw a huge black head projecting out of the stream. In an instant the jaguar, for such was the animal on the watch, sprang forward and seized its prey. The creature which had thus ventured within the grasp of the jaguar was a *manatee*, or sea-cow, the *peixe boi* of the Portuguese. A fearful struggle ensued, the manatee to escape, the jaguar to hold it fast. I lifted my gun to fire, but the Indians made a sign to me to desist. If I should kill the jaguar the manatee would escape, and their object was to allow the latter to be too exhausted to do so, and then to shoot the jaguar. Now it appeared as if the jaguar would drag the water-monster out of its native element, now that the former would be drawn into it. The sea-cow struggled bravely, but the beast of prey had got too firm a hold to let it escape. The surface of the water was lashed into foam. The jaguar's claws and teeth were firmly fixed in the thick hide of the sea-cow. Slowly it seemed to be drawn higher and higher out of its native element. So eager was the savage beast, that it did not even observe our approach, but continued with its sharp teeth gnawing into the back of its defenceless prey. We now paddled closer. It turned a look of savage rage towards us, seeming to doubt whether it should let go the manatee and stand on the defensive, or continue the strife. The way it held the sea-cow gave us a notion of its immense strength. Gradually the efforts of the manatee began to relax. It was very clear how the combat would have finished had we not been present. At a sign from the Indians I lifted my rifle and fired. The ball passed through the jaguar's neck. Though wounded, the fierce animal stood snarling savagely, with its fore-feet on the trunk of the tree, as if prepared to make a spring into the canoe. While I was reloading, the Indians raised their blow-pipes and sent two of their slender arrows quivering into its body. Still the jaguar stood at bay, apparently scarcely feeling the wound. Meantime the huge cow-fish was slipping off the bank.

Naro, on seeing this, ordered his men to paddle forward, while, harpoon in hand, he stood ready to dart it at the manatee. Every moment I expected to see the jaguar spring at us. Just as the manatee was disappearing under the water, the harpoon flew with unerring aim from Naro's hand, and was buried deeply in its body. Again we backed away from the bank, just in time, it seemed, for in another moment the jaguar would have sprung at us. Having got out of its reach, the Indians shot two more of their deadly arrows into its body. Still it stood, snarling and roaring with rage at being deprived of its prey. Gradually its cries of anger ceased, its glaring eyes grew dim, its legs seemed to refuse it support, and slowly it sank back among the mass of fern-like plants which bordered the bank.

Meantime, the Indians were engaged with the harpoon line, now hauling in on it, now slackening it out, a ruddy hue mixing with the current showing that the life-blood of the manatee was fast ebbing away. In a short time the struggles of the huge river monster ceased, and the Indians paddling towards the bank, towed it after them. I was all the while looking out for the jaguar. A movement in the shrubs among which it had fallen showed that it was still alive. I was sure that my shot had not injured it much, and I could scarcely suppose that those light needle-like darts could have done it much harm. I reminded Naro of the jaguar. He shook his head in reply. "He will no longer interfere with us," I understood him to say. The manatee was soon hauled on shore, and as it was too large to be taken bodily into the canoe, the Indians, having thoroughly knocked out any spark of life which might remain, began cutting it up.

The creature was between seven and eight feet long, and upwards of six in circumference in the thickest part. The body was perfectly smooth, and of a lead colour. It tapered off towards the tail, which was flat, horizontal, and semicircular, without any appearance of hind limbs. The head was not large, though the mouth was, with fleshy lips somewhat like those of a cow. There were stiff bristles on the lips, and a few hairs scattered over the body. Just behind the head were two powerful oval fins, having the breasts beneath them. The ears were minute holes, and the eyes very small. The skin of the back was fully an inch thick, and beneath it a layer of fat, also an inch or more thick. On examining the fins, or fore-limbs, as they should properly be called, we found bones exactly corresponding to those of the human arm, with five fingers at the extremity, every joint distinct, although completely encased in a stiff inflexible skin. The manatee feeds on the grass growing at the borders of the lakes and rivers. It swims at a rapid rate, moved on by the tail and paddles. The female produces generally only one at a birth, and clasps it, so Naro told us, in her paddles while giving it suck.

Having cut up the cow, with which we loaded the canoe, we paddled in towards where the jaguar had been seen. The chief and one of his followers without hesitation leaped on shore: Arthur and I followed, when to our surprise we saw the savage brute lying over on its side perfectly dead. It had been destroyed by the poison on the tip of the arrows, not by the wounds they or my bullet had produced. It was quickly skinned, cut up, and part of the meat added to our store, while the skin, which I thought was the most valuable part, was at my request taken on board.

On emerging from the inlet, we steered for the island, guided by the light of the camp-fire. We were welcomed with loud shouts by the generally impassive Indians, who were delighted with the supply of flesh which we had brought. No time was lost in cutting the meat into small pieces, each person fastening a dozen or more on long skewers. These were stuck in the ground, and slanted over the flames to roast. The meat tasted somewhat like pork, I thought, but John considered it more like beef.

We were one evening approaching a long island with a sand-bank extending from its side. Isoro told us that the Indians were unable to proceed further, and that after this we should find the navigation tolerably easy. The sand-bank, he said, was frequented by turtles, and they hoped to be able to supply us and themselves with a good store of eggs, and to catch also some turtles.

Having hauled up the canoes, and formed our sleeping-places as usual, leaving Domingos in charge of the camp, we all, including Ellen and Maria, set out to search for turtles' eggs, our Indians having in the meantime woven a number of baskets of reeds in which to carry them. Each of the Indians carried a long stick in his hand. We proceeded a short distance along the bank, till we came to a somewhat higher part. The sand felt quite hot to our feet. The Indians pointed out some slight marks in it, which they told us were made by the turtles. Going on, one of them stuck his stick into the sand. It sank easily down. Instantly he and his companions were on their knees digging with their hands, and soon cleared out a hole full of eggs. Upwards of one hundred were collected from that hole alone. In the meantime the rest were searching about, and we were soon all on our knees, busily engaged in picking up the eggs. The eggs were about an inch and a half in diameter, somewhat larger than an ordinary hen's egg. They have thin leathery shells, an oily yoke, and a white which does not coagulate. Having laden ourselves with as many as we could carry in our baskets, we returned to the camp. Domingos at once set to work to make cakes, mixing the eggs with flour. Others were roasted. The Indians, however, ate them raw.

While we sat round our camp-fire, Isoro excited our curiosity by an account of the way the turtles lay their eggs, and we agreed to start away the next morning before daybreak to watch the process. He called us about two hours before daybreak. We found that Naro and two of his men had already gone off to try and catch some of the animals. After walking a short distance, we discovered the Indians squatting down behind a shelter of branches, which they had put up to conceal themselves from the turtles. They told us to take our seats by them, and remain quiet. We had not been there long before we saw a number of dark objects moving over the light coloured sand. Two or three came close to us, when the Indians rushing out, quickly turned them on their backs, and again ran under shelter.

We waited for some time till the light of day enabled us to see more clearly, when, as far as our eyes could reach, we observed the upper part of the bank covered with turtles, all busily employed with their broad-webbed paws in excavating the sand, while others were apparently placing their eggs in the holes they had made. As the morning drew on, they began to waddle away towards the river. The margin of the upper bank was rather steep, and it was amusing to see them tumbling head foremost down the declivity, and then going on again till the leaders reached the water. We now all rushed forward, and were in time to catch several, turning them over on their backs, where they lay unable to move.

The first comer, Isoro told us, makes a hole about three feet deep. In this she lays her eggs, and then covers them up with sand. The next reaching the shore lays her eggs on the top of her predecessor's, and so on, several turtles will lay one above the others, till the pit, which holds about one hundred eggs, is full, when the last carefully sweeps the sand over the hole, so as to make it appear as if it had not been disturbed. It is only, indeed, from the tracks made by the turtles themselves as they are returning to the water that the nests can be traced. In the settled parts of the country great care is taken not to disturb these sand-banks till the whole body of turtles have laid their eggs. Sometimes they occupy fourteen days or more in the business. People are stationed at some elevated spot in the neighbourhood to warn off any one approaching the bank, and to take care that the timid turtles are in no way disturbed; otherwise it is supposed they would desert the ground altogether.

We had now a large supply of turtle and turtle eggs. Our Indian friends, well satisfied with their expedition, loaded their canoe almost to the water's edge. We also took on board as many as we could consume. Naro and his followers had behaved very well, but they were uninteresting people, and had done nothing particular to win our regard. John wrote a letter to Don José for Isoro to carry, and we all sent many messages, expressing our affectionate regard. Had it not been for Don José, we might have been subjected to much annoyance and trouble, and been prevented probably from following our family. We each of us presented Isoro also with a small remembrance. We parted from him with sincere regret; and I believe that had it not been for his devoted love to his master he would gladly have accompanied us. He and his companions waited till we had embarked in our own canoe, and cast off from the shore. A light breeze was blowing down the river. We hoisted our mat sail, and Domingos taking the steering oar, we recommenced our voyage down the river. The Indians then set forth on their toilsome one up the stream, having to paddle with might and main for many days against it.

Chapter Seven
Our Disappointment, Danger, and Anxiety

The tributary of the Amazon, down which we were proceeding, was in many places more than half a mile wide: what must be the width of the mighty river itself! This comparatively small stream was often tossed into waves, and we were thankful that we had the prospect of embarking in a larger vessel, with more experienced boatmen, for our further voyage. On either side of the river were clay banks, above which the lofty trees formed impenetrable walls; while here and there islands appeared, the soil of some raised but little above the river, while in others we could see evidences of the stream having separated them at no great distance of time from the mainland. We continued our custom of landing at night—indeed, whenever we had to put to shore—at one of these islands. They all supplied us with wood to light our fires, and poles for our huts: some were large enough to furnish game.

Thus several days passed away. We were, by our calculations, approaching the spot at which our father had led us to expect that we should find him. It may be supposed how eagerly we all looked out for the expected marks. At length the curiously-coloured bluff hill he had mentioned appeared in sight.

"There it is! there it is!" exclaimed Ellen. "I am sure it must be the spot papa speaks of."

We surveyed it with eager eyes, and agreed that there could be no mistake about the matter. With redoubled energy we paddled on, the breeze, though light, being in our favour. And now in a short time we came in sight of the expected group of bamboos. We quickly rounded it; and there, before us, appeared the hill. We looked out for the huts on its summit, but none were visible.

"Oh! perhaps papa thought it better to build them lower down, under the shade of that group of palms," said Ellen; and we agreed that she was probably right.

A small stream ran at the bottom of the hill, connected, probably, with one of the larger rivers we had passed. We paddled up it a short distance, hoping to find a convenient place for landing. Our hearts misgave us on finding no one come down to welcome us on shore.

"They probably do not observe us coming," observed Ellen. "Mamma and Fanny are in the house, and papa and the servants are out shooting."

I saw by the cheerful way she spoke she felt none of the apprehensions which John and I were experiencing. We soon found a clear spot, where the waters in the rainy season had carried away the trees and shrubs. Securing our canoe, we eagerly stepped on shore. The bank was somewhat steep; but we managed to climb up it, and, cutting our way through the intervening jungle, reached the foot of the hill. Even now I began to doubt whether, after all, this could be the spot our father spoke of. Not the slightest sound was heard, and there was no appearance of human habitations being near. True, as soon as we had got into the more open ground, went scampering along in high glee at finding himself on shore. John led the way, anxiously looking about on very side. We soon reached the top of the hill, gazing eagerly down towards the group of palm-trees Ellen had espied. No huts were to be seen.

"They cannot have been here!" exclaimed Ellen.

Just then John gave a start, and immediately hurried forward. We all followed. Before us we saw several posts standing upright, but they were blackened and charred, while several others lay scattered about. The grass around was burned, and the ground covered with ashes. It was too evident that a hut had stood there, which had been destroyed by fire; but whether it had been inhabited by our family or not, we in vain endeavoured to discover. No traces of them could we find. We looked at each other with anxious eyes. Ellen burst into tears, fully believing that something dreadful had happened. We wished to reassure her, but our own fears made this a hard matter. John stood silent for some time. Then again he walked over the spot, and examined narrowly the ground, looking among the neighbouring trees.

"Perhaps this was not their house," suggested Arthur; "or if it was, they may have escaped. Surely we should not give way to despair."

"I think the master is too cautious a man to have been taken by surprise," observed Domingos. "He is probably not far off, and we shall see him soon."

Maria did her best to comfort her young mistress.

"Do not cry, Doña Ellen; do not cry. We shall soon see them all," she said, putting her arms round her as she used to do when she was a child, and trying to comfort her.

Wishing to ascertain John's opinion, I went towards him.

"We must proceed further on," he said. "I am surprised that our father has not left any sign by which we might learn where he has gone."

"Perhaps he had to retreat in too great a hurry for that, yet he might have escaped in safety," observed Arthur.

"Do you think they were attacked by natives, and driven away?" I asked of John.

"About that I am doubtful," he answered, in a low voice, so that Ellen should not hear. "Yet had the hut simply been burned by accident, they would have rebuilt it. Our friend Naro gave the Indians of this part of the river a bad name. He called them *Majeronas*; and said that they are cannibals, and attack all strangers. I did not believe the account he gave of them; and had I done so, I would not have mentioned it, for fear of unnecessarily alarming Ellen. Still, Harry, I confess I am very, very anxious."

"So indeed am I, now you tell me about the *Majeronas*," I observed; "but still we must hope for the best. I cannot believe that anything so dreadful has happened as our fears suggest. Our poor mother, and sweet Fanny and Aunt Martha, to have been carried off and killed! Oh, I cannot think it true!"

"Don't you think it possible they got notice that they were about to be attacked, and made their escape in good time?" observed Arthur, in a more cheerful voice. "The natives, when they found that their prey had escaped them, would very naturally burn the house; and if they found any signals which Mr Faithful might have left, would have destroyed them also. I will ask Domingos; I think he will agree with me."

When we told Domingos what Arthur had said, he declared that he thought that was the most likely thing to have occurred. The suggestion raised our spirits. Domingos, however, advised as not to remain on the spot, lest the natives might discover us. Having made another search round, we accordingly took our way back to the canoe.

Shoving off, we went down the stream into the main river. As we paddled slowly along the shore, we examined it carefully, still in hopes of finding some signals which might direct us. We had gone on for some short distance, when Arthur, looking up at the hill, exclaimed, "See! who can those be?"

There we saw several figures with bows in their hands and high feathery plumes on their heads.

"They must be the *Majeronas*," exclaimed John. "We have indeed only just retreated in time."

"Oh, perhaps they will follow us!" cried Ellen.

"I do not think we need fear that," said Arthur, "as we have seen no canoes."

The Indians appeared only just to have discovered us. We saw them gesticulating to each other; and then they hurried down towards the river. We at once turned the canoe's head away from the bank, and paddled out into the centre of the stream, where we should be beyond the reach of their arrows.

By working away with our paddles we soon ran out of sight of them.

Having rested for some minutes to recover from our exertions, we continued on down the stream. As the day was drawing on, it was necessary to look out for an island on which to encamp, as we had received so strong a warning not to land on the main shore. We kept a bright look-out, but no signs of an island could we see. The wind, which had hitherto been light, now increased to a gentle breeze; and as it was in our favour, we hoisted our sail and stood on, glad to be relieved from the labour of paddling. Thus we continued our progress, hoping to get before night to a distance from our savage enemies.

The night came on, but there was still sufficient light to enable us to steer down the centre of the river. John proposed that we should form two watches; he and Arthur in one, Domingos and I in the other. This, of course, was agreed to. After some difficulty, we persuaded Ellen and Maria to lie down on the hammocks which were spread in the middle of the canoe under the awning. John and Arthur took the first watch; Domingos coiling himself away in the stern of the canoe, and I in the bows; to be ready for service should we be required.

Tired as I was, it was some time before I could manage to go to sleep. I lay looking up at the dark sky—out of which thousands of bright stars shone forth—and listening to the ripple of the water against the bows of the canoe. At length the sound lulled me to sleep, though I felt conscious that Arthur had covered me up with a piece of matting. It seemed but a moment afterwards that I heard his voice calling me to get up and take his place. I raised myself, and saw Domingos at the helm, and the sails still set. Arthur then lay down in the place I had occupied; and I did him the same service he had rendered me, by covering him carefully up so as to protect him from the night air.

It was the first time we had voyaged at night; and as we glided calmly on, I could not help regretting that we had not oftener sailed at the same hour, and thus escaped the heat of the day, the mosquitoes on shore, and enjoyed the cool breeze on the river. As I did not feel at all sleepy, I proposed to Domingos that we should allow John and Arthur to rest on, and continue ourselves on watch till daylight, when perhaps we might find some spot on which to land with safety.

We thus glided on for some hours, and were expecting to see the dawn break over the trees on our larboard bow, when the channel became even narrower than before. Had it not been that the current still ran with us, I should have supposed that we had entered some other stream; but the way the water ran showed that this could not be the case. We therefore continued on as before. A bright glow now appeared in the eastern sky. Rapidly it increased till the whole arch of heaven was suffused with a ruddy light. Suddenly John awoke, and uttered an exclamation of surprise on finding that it was daylight. His voice aroused the rest of the party. Just then the sun, like a mighty arch of fire, appeared above the trees; and directly afterwards we saw, running across the stream down which we were sailing, another and far broader river. The mighty Marañon, as the natives call the Upper Amazon—or the Solimoens, as it is named by the Portuguese—was before us, having flowed down for many hundred miles from the mountain lake of Lauricocha, in Peru, 12,500 feet above the sea-level.

As we gazed up and down the vast river, no object intervened till sky and water met, as on the ocean; while, on either side, the tall forest walls diminished in the perspective till they sank into thin lines. Even here, however, it is narrow, though already very deep, compared to the width it attains lower down. Our satisfaction at having escaped from the savages and arrived at the high road, along which we were to proceed, was counterbalanced by our anxiety for our family. We might, after all, have passed the spot where they were waiting for us; and yet it was not likely they would remain in the neighbourhood of such savages as the Majeronas had shown themselves. We agreed, therefore, at all risks, at once to row in towards the shore, and examine it carefully as we proceeded downwards.

We had not gone far, when we came in sight of a sand-bank, which offered a favourable spot for landing. We accordingly rowed in, looking carefully about for any signs of natives. As no huts or any human beings were to be seen, we landed.

While Domingos and Arthur were collecting wood for a fire, John and I, followed by True, with our guns, made our way through the forest, that we might survey the country, so as not to be taken by surprise. We had not gone far when I caught sight of three animals, which I should have taken for young hogs, from their brown colour, long coarse hair, and their general appearance, had they not been sitting up on their haunches, as no hog ever sat. They had large heads, and heavy blunt muzzles, and thick clumsy bodies without tails. They cast inquisitive looks at me, and would have sat on apparently till I had got close up to them, had not True dashed forward, when, uttering low sounds, between a grunt and a bark, they rushed towards the water. I fired at one of them, and knocked it over. The rest reached the river, though pursued by True, and instantly dived beneath the surface. John came up, and on examining the animal's mouth, we found it to be a rodent, and thus knew it to be a capybara, the largest of its order. When alarmed, it rushes to the water, swims as well as the otter, and takes its prey in a similar manner. It is, from its aquatic habits, often called the water-hog. It had short legs, and peculiarly long feet, partially webbed, which enable it to swim so well.

Directly afterwards, True turned a smaller animal out of a hollow trunk. It made off through the forest at great speed; but John shot it just as it was running behind a tree. It proved to be an agouti, also a rodent. It is in some respects like a hare or rabbit, with the coarse coat of a hog, but feeds itself like a squirrel. It is classed with the guinea-pig. It feeds on vegetables, and is very destructive to sugar-canes, which it rapidly gnaws through, and does not object to animal food.

While I carried our prizes down in triumph to Domingos, that he might prepare a portion of them for breakfast, John continued his search through the woods. I was on the point of joining him, when I heard him cry, "Look out!" and at the same instant another animal burst through the wood with True at his heels. I fired, and killed it. This also was a rodent; and John said that it was a paca, which lives always in the neighbourhood of water, to which it takes readily when chased. It has its habitation in burrows, which it forms a short distance only beneath the surface. The opening it conceals with dried leaves and small branches. Once in the water, it swims and dives so well that it generally escapes from the hunter. It was of a thick and somewhat clumsy form, about two feet in length and one in height. The hinder limbs were longer than the front ones, and considerably bent. The claws were thick and strong, fitted for digging. It had rigid whiskers, and the ears were nearly naked.

Presently I heard John cry out.

"Harry, I believe that I have been bitten by a snake on which I trod," he said, in his usual calm way. "I killed the creature, and I think it is poisonous; so go and call Domingos, for he will perhaps know what to do. But get him away if you can, so as not to frighten Ellen."

I ran off as fast as my legs could carry me, and was thankful to find that Ellen and Maria were sitting under the awning in the canoe, while Domingos was cooking at the fire, assisted by Arthur. In a breathless voice, my heart sinking with alarm, I told him what had happened.

"There is a bottle of agua ardente, and there is another thing we will try," he said, and rushed to the canoe.

I was afraid that he would tell Ellen; but he stepped on board with an unconcerned manner, as if he wanted something for a culinary purpose, and returned with two of the paddles, and a bottle and cup.

We found John seated on the bank, taking off his boot and sock.

"Here, Señor John, drink this," he said, giving him the cup full of liquid. "Señor Arthur will hold the bottle for you, while Señor Harry and I are making a grave for your leg. We must bury it. Don't despair, my dear master. The remedy is a wonderful one."

We were digging away, while he spoke, with the paddles, and in a few moments John's leg was buried deep in the earth, which was pressed down over it.

"Why, this is brandy," exclaimed John, as he swallowed the contents of a second cup which Arthur gave him.

"Of course, my dear master," answered Domingos, who, folding his arms, stood by, watching the effect of his treatment. "Some people think one remedy the best, some another. It is wise to try both. The brandy drives, the earth draws the poison forth."

Oh, how anxiously we watched John's countenance! No change took place.

Arthur and I went back, lest Ellen might be alarmed at our absence, leaving Domingos, who stood unmoved, in the same attitude as at first, watching his patient. At last Ellen put her head out from under the toldo, and asked when breakfast would be ready, as she and Maria were very hungry.

"What shall we tell her?" asked Arthur.

Just then I looked up, and saw Domingos coming towards us, waving the dead snake in his hand, and John following, walking as briskly as if nothing had been the matter with him.

"A wonderful cure has been wrought," he exclaimed, as he reached us. "But don't tell Domingos yet. Finding myself much as usual, I bethought me, as I sat with my leg in the hole, of looking into the reptile's mouth; and though it has a set of sharp teeth, I could discover no poisonous fangs. I am only sorry that so much good brandy was expended on me, which may be wanted on another occasion."

We now summoned Ellen, and told her in English what had occurred. Arthur and I having examined the head of the snake, to assure ourselves that John was right, cut it off and threw it into the river, while True breakfasted off the body, which we cooked for him. Domingos did not discover the truth till some time afterwards; and we heard him frequently boasting of the certain cure he knew for snake bites. I cannot, however, say that his remedy would not prove efficacious.

Having made a good breakfast on the agouti, we once more embarked, and glided down the stream.

I have not dwelt much on our anxiety, but, as may be supposed, we felt it greatly, and our conversation could not fail to be subdued and sad. Ellen, however, after her first grief had subdued, did her utmost, dear, good little sister that she was, to cheer our spirits. Often she kept repeating, "I am sure they have escaped! We shall before long find them. Depend on it, papa would not allow himself to be surprised! I have been praying for them ever since we commenced our journey, and I know my prayers will be heard."

Although I had felt great despondency, I could not help being influenced by Ellen's hopeful spirit. Still it seemed to me that the probability of our discovering them along the wide-extended banks of the river was but small indeed. They, too, how anxious they must be feeling on our account; for if they had been in danger, as we supposed, they must know we should be subjected to the same. However, I will not dwell longer on this subject, but only again repeat that our parents and our aunt and Fanny were never absent from our thoughts. A light breeze springing up, we hoisted our mat sail, and glided down the river. Nothing could be more delightful. The light air cooled us, and kept off the mosquitoes; and as the nights were bright, had we not been anxious to examine the shore, we agreed that we might have continued our voyage till it was necessary to land and procure food.

Suddenly, however, the wind again dropped. The sun, which had hitherto been casting his undimmed rays down on our heads, became obscured, as if a thick curtain had been drawn across it. The whole sky assumed a yellow tinge. Domingos looked anxiously round.

"I do not like the look of the weather," he observed. "It would be wise to lower the sail."

We had just got it down, when a low murmur was heard in the distant woods, increasing rapidly to a subdued roar. A white line appeared across the river. It came rapidly towards us. Now we could feel the wind blowing against our cheeks, and the whole surface of the water became suddenly rippled into wavelets, from which the white foam flew off in thick sheets. The sky had again changed to a greenish hue. The waves every moment increased in height.

"A hurricane is coming on," observed Domingos. "We cannot face it."

We put the canoe's head towards the shore.

"Paddle, my masters! paddle!" exclaimed Domingos. "We must reach the shore before the storm breaks with its full violence, or we may be lost!"

We had not paddled many strokes before we felt the canoe driven forward by the wind at a rapid rate. We exerted ourselves, running before the wind, and edging in at the same time towards the northern shore. Every instant the hurricane gained strength; and as we looked upward, the whole sky, we saw, had assumed a red and black appearance. A little ahead appeared a sand-bank, on which stood a number of tall-legged birds, cormorants, white cranes, and other waders, large and small. We might land on the island, and save our lives; but the wind setting directly on it, we might lose our canoe, or, at all events, the water would break into her and destroy our goods. Domingos steered the canoe admirably, while we made every effort to keep off the island. Presently down came the blast with greater fury than before. Some of the smaller birds were carried off their legs and borne away by the wind. Others, throwing themselves down, stuck their beaks into the sand, and clung on with their long claws, their feet extended. In spite of our danger, Arthur and I could not help laughing at the extraordinary appearance of the birds, as they thus lay in great numbers along the sand, looking as if they had been shot, and were lying dead till the sportsman could pick them up. On we drove, narrowly escaping being thrown upon the bank, on which the foaming seas broke with terrific force.

"Here it comes again!" cried Domingos. "Paddle bravely, and be not alarmed."

As he spoke, another blast, still more violent, struck us, and in an instant the covering of our canoe was torn away and lifted up. In vain we attempted to catch it. It was borne off by the wind towards the shore. So high were the waves which thus suddenly rose up, that we expected every moment to be overwhelmed; while we feared that unless we could manage to anchor we should be driven on the bank to leeward, where the canoe would be filled with water, and everything in her carried away. To resist the fury of the waves was impossible. In vain we strove to get under the lee of the island.

Destruction yawned before us, when we saw, amid the thick forest trees which lined the bank, a narrow opening. It was the entrance, we hoped, to an igarape,—one of those curious water-ways, or canoe paths, which form a network of canals many hundred miles in extent, on either bank of the Amazon. We exerted ourselves to the utmost to reach it, although the seas which struck the side of the canoe threatened every moment to upset her before we could do so. Ellen and Maria had got out their paddles, and laboured away with all their strength, Maria's stout arms indeed being a very efficient help. Domingos kept working away with his paddle, now on one side, now on another, now steering astern as he saw was requisite, twisting his features into a hundred different forms, and showing his white teeth as he shouted out in his eagerness. The tall trees were bending before the blast as if they were about to be torn from their roots and carried bodily inland. My fear was, on seeing them thus agitated, that should we get beneath them they might fall and crush us. Still we had no choice. It seemed doubtful whether we should reach the mouth of the igarape.

We redoubled our efforts, and just grazing by a point which projected from the shore, on which, had we been thrown, we should have been upset, we darted into the canal. Even there the water hissed and roared as it was forced into the narrow channel. As an arrow flies through the zarabatana, so we sped up the igarape. For a few seconds Domingos had to exert himself to steer the canoe in mid-channel, to prevent her being dashed against the roots of the tall trees which projected into it. At first the roar of the wind among the trunks and branches was almost deafening. Gradually it decreased, and in a short time we could hear only the distant murmur of the tempest on the outside of the woody boundary. We were not, however, to escape altogether from it, for down came the rain in a pelting shower, to which, from the loss of our awning, we were completely exposed. We quickly, however, rigged another with our sail, which afforded shelter to Ellen and Maria. Having secured the canoe, we all crept under it, and consulted what we should next do. What with the mantle of clouds across the sky, and the thick arch of boughs over our heads, so great was the darkness that we could scarcely persuade ourselves that night was not coming on. We sat patiently, hoping that the rain, which pattered down with so loud a noise that it was necessary to raise our voices to make each other hear, would at length cease. In about half an hour, the shower-bath to which we had been exposed came to an end. But still drops fell thickly from the boughs, and the darkness proved to us that the clouds had not yet cleared away.

After our unsatisfactory meeting with the natives, we were anxious not to remain longer on that part of the shore than necessary. Accordingly we once more paddled down the igarape. We soon found, however, that the wind was blowing too hard to allow us to venture out on the main stream.

On passing downwards we observed a somewhat open space on the north side, and despairing of continuing our voyage that night, we determined to encamp there. Securing our canoe, in which Ellen and Maria sat under shelter, the rest of us, with axes in our hands, set to work to clear the ground and build a couple of huts. We had become such proficients in the art that this we soon accomplished. On account of the weather we built one of them, not only with a roof, but with back and sides, in which Ellen and her attendant could be sheltered. To our own also we built a side on the quarter from which the wind came. Our difficulty was to light a fire. But hunting about, we found some dried leaves in the hollow of a tree, and there was no lack of wood, which, after chopping off the wet outside, would burn readily.

Having made all preparations, we conducted Ellen and Maria to their hut, and carried up our goods, which we placed within it, under shelter. We felt somewhat anxious at our position; but we hoped that the rain would keep any natives who might be in the neighbourhood from wandering about, and by the following morning we should be able to proceed on our voyage. Should we not meet with our father on our way down, we resolved to stop at the nearest Brazilian town on the banks, and there obtain assistance in instituting a more rigid search than we could make by ourselves. Of one thing we were certain, that had he escaped, and got thus far, he would stay there till our arrival. Still we did not abandon all hopes of finding him before that.

We had taken everything out of the canoe, with the exception of the paddles, even to the sail, which served as a carpet for Ellen's hut. We next turned our attention to cooking further portions of the animals we had killed in the morning. In spite of the storm raging outside, and our anxiety, as we sat round the blazing fire, Ellen and Maria having joined us, the smoke keeping the mosquitoes somewhat at bay, we all felt more cheerful than might have been expected. Midnight had now come on; and having cut up a further supply of wood to keep the fire burning, we slung our hammocks and turned into them, trusting to True to keep watch for us.

Chapter Eight
Adventures in the forest—
We meet with natives

The hours of the night passed slowly by. I awoke several times. Few of the usual noises of the forest were heard. The tempest seemed to have silenced its wild inhabitants. Now and then the cry of a howling baboon reached our ears from the depths of the forest. I had a feeling that something dreadful was about to occur, yet I was sufficiently awake to know that this might be mere fancy, and I did my best to go to sleep. The fire was still burning brightly. I looked down from my hammock. There was True sleeping tranquilly below me, as my companions were, around. When I looked away from the fire into the forest, I was struck by the unusual darkness. Not a ray of light appeared to come from the sky, which was still covered with a thick mantle of clouds. I succeeded at last in dropping off to sleep. How long my eyes had been closed I could not tell, when I heard True uttering a low bark. I could just see him running to the edge of the hut, and looking out towards the river. I sprang from my hammock, calling to my companions. They were on foot in a moment; but the darkness, was so great that we could see nothing beyond a few feet from where we stood. As we sprang up, True rushed forward. We heard him barking away in front of us. The fire was out, and with difficulty we found our way back. I called to True, and at last he returned, but we were still unable to discover any cause for alarm. After a time we agreed that the wisest thing we could do would be to turn into our hammocks again. I scolded True for alarming us so needlessly, and he came back and lay down in his usual place. The night passed away without any other disturbance.

When we arose in the morning the wind had ceased, the clouds had cleared away, and the weather was as fine as usual. Getting up, we prepared breakfast, and agreed to continue our voyage as soon as it was over. As we had sufficient provisions, there was no necessity to search for any. We therefore remained at our camp till our meal was over. John was the first to take up a load and proceed with it down to the canoe. I followed. When still at a little distance, I heard him utter an exclamation of dismay. He turned back, and I saw by his countenance that there was something wrong. Now he looked up the igarape, now down.

"Harry," he exclaimed, "I cannot see the canoe!"

"You must have mistaken the spot where I left it," I answered. "I secured it well."

I returned with him to the bank. In vain we searched up and down the banks of the water-path. Not a trace of the canoe did we discover.

"She must have broken adrift, then, during the night," I observed. "Perhaps she has driven up the igarape."

"I will go one way and you the other, then," said John.

I made my way as well as I could through the tangled wood from the river, while John went towards it. Wherever I could, I got down to the edge of the water. Now I climbed along a trunk which overhang it; but though I thus got a view for a considerable distance, I could see no canoe. At length I returned, hoping that John might have been more successful. I met him on the spot where we had parted.

"I cannot see her," he said. "Harry, I am afraid she has been carried off!"

The same idea had occurred to me. We now carefully examined the spot where we had left her. I found the very trunk of the tree round which I had secured the painter. It was scarcely rubbed, which it would have been, we agreed, had the canoe been torn away by the force of the wind. We were soon joined by Arthur and Domingos, who had come along with loads, surprised at our not returning. We communicated to them the alarming intelligence. Domingos was afraid that we were right in our conjectures. We returned to the camp to break the unsatisfactory news to Ellen.

"If our canoe is lost, we must build another," she remarked, in her usual quiet way, concealing her anxiety; "but it is very trying to be thus delayed."

Still it would not do to give up without a further search for the canoe. As the wind had set up the igarape, I knew that, should the canoe have broken away by herself, she must have driven before it. It was therefore settled that Arthur and I should go up still further in that direction, while John would try and make his way down to the main river, searching along the bank. Ellen and Maria, with Domingos and True to take care of them, were to remain at the camp. Arthur and I had our axes, for without them we could make no progress. I had my gun; Arthur a spear, with bow and arrows, which Naro had presented to him. Thus armed, we hoped to defend ourselves against any jaguar or boa we might meet. We had little to fear from any other wild animals. As we had seen no traces of natives, we did not expect to meet with any. We soon gained the point I had reached in the morning. After this, we had to hew a path for ourselves through the forest. Sometimes we got a few feet without impediment, and then had to cut away the sipos for several yards. Now and then we were able to crawl under them, and sometimes we were able to leap over the loops, or make our way along the wide-spreading roots of the tall trees. Thus we went on, every now and then getting down to the edge of the igarape, and climbing out on the trunk of one of the overhanging trees, whence we could obtain a view up and down for some distance.

We had just reached the bank, and were looking out along it, when I saw a troop of monkeys coming along through the forest. I kept True by my side, and whispered to Arthur not to speak. I could scarcely help laughing aloud at the odd manner in which they made their way among the branches, now swinging down by their tails, now catching another branch, and hanging on by their arms. They were extraordinarily thin creatures, with long arms and legs, and still longer tails—our old friends the spider monkeys. Those tails of theirs were never quiet, but kept whisking about in all directions. They caught hold of the branches with them, and then hung by them with their heads downwards, an instant afterwards to spring up again. Presently they came close to the water, when one of them caught hold of a branch with his fore-hands and tail, another jumped down and curled his tail round the body of the first. A third descended and slung himself in a similar manner. A fourth and fifth followed, and so on; and there they hung, a regular monkey chain. Immediately the lowest, who hung with his head downwards, gave a shove with his fore-paws, and set the chain swinging, slowly at first but increasing in rapidity, backwards and forwards over the water. I thought to myself, if an alligator were making his way up the canal, the lowest would have a poor chance of his life. The swinging increased in violence, till the lowest monkey got his paws round the slender trunk of a tree on the opposite side. Immediately he drew his companion after him; till the next above him was within reach of it. That one caught the tree in the same way, and they then dragged up their end of the chain till it hung almost horizontally across the water. A living bridge having thus been formed, the remainder of the troop, chiefly consisting of young monkeys who had been amusing themselves meantime frisking about in the branches, ran over. Two or three of the mischievous youngsters took the opportunity of giving a sly pinch to their elders, utterly unable just then to retaliate; though it was evident, from the comical glances which the latter cast at them, that the inflictors of the pinches were not unnoticed. One, who had been trying to catch some fish apparently during the interval, was nearly too late to cross. The first two who had got across now climbed still further up the trunk; and when they had got to some distance, the much-enduring monkey, who had been holding the weight of all the others, let go his hold, and now becoming the lowest in the chain, swung towards the bank. As soon as he and his companions reached it, they caught hold of the trunk either with their hands or tails. The whole troop thus got safely across.

A living bridge was thus formed.

The shouts of laughter, to which Arthur and I could no longer resist giving way, startled the monkeys. They looked about with inquisitive glances, wondering probably what sort of strange creatures we could be who had come into their territory. At length, espying us, off they set at a great rate through the forest.

They had chosen the narrowest part of the igarape to cross. Going on further, it widened considerably. We still continued making our way along its margin; but the ground at length became so swampy, that we were obliged to turn off to the left. After this we came to somewhat more open ground, which had been cleared either by fire or by the hand of man. It was, of course, overgrown with vegetation of all sorts; but not sufficiently so to prevent us making our way through it. Our intention was to go round the swamp or lake, and again reach the border of the water-path. We proceeded on for some distance, when we saw through an opening a high clay bank; it could scarcely be called a hill. But few trees grew on it. We thought that, by getting to the top, we could obtain a view of the country around. We accordingly made our way towards it. It formed apparently the eastern edge of the high country through which the Napo runs. We found, here and there, veins of that curiously-coloured clay which we had before seen. Looking eastward, a vast extent of forest was spread out before us, extending far as the eye could reach. No opening was visible except the long line of the Solimoens, at some distance from where we stood. We could look westward towards its source in the Andes; and eastward as it flowed on towards the far distant Atlantic, hundreds of miles away. The whole igarape was entirely shut out from view. We thought, however, that by continuing towards the north we might possibly again get sight of it, when we purposed to continue our search for the canoe. We had faint hopes of finding it, we could not but confess.

We had gone on some way, when, passing round a clump of trees, we saw before us two natives seated on the top of a hill, looking out, it seemed, over the country beyond them. Their bodies were tattooed or painted all over in curious devices, and their heads were decked with war-plumes, while each of them had a musket resting on his arm, as if ready for immediate use. Our first impulse was to retreat, hoping that we had not been seen; but their quick eyes had caught sight of us. They beckoned to us to approach.

"They must have had intercourse with white men, or they would not have those muskets," observed Arthur. "Perhaps they may prove to be friends."

To escape them, I saw, would be impossible. I therefore agreed with Arthur that the best way was to go forward at once in a frank manner and try to win their confidence. We climbed the hill, therefore, and as we get up to where they were waiting for us, put out our hands and shook theirs. They were accustomed, apparently, to the European style of greeting. They addressed us, and seemed to be inquiring whence we had come. We explained as well as we could by signs—pointing in the direction of the Andes, and then showing how we had glided down in the canoe. While they were speaking, I thought I detected a few words which sounded like Spanish; and listening more attentively, I found that the eldest of the two was speaking the *lingua geral*—a corrupt Portuguese, mixed with Indian words, generally used throughout the whole length of the Amazon. It was so like the language Naro and his Indians had employed when speaking to us, that I could make out, with a little difficulty, what was said. I understood the elder Indian to say that he was a friend of the whites; and that, as Arthur had supposed, he had obtained the muskets from them. Finding the natives so friendly, I invited them to our camp. They shook their heads, and pointed to the north-west, letting us understand that they were about to start away on an expedition against an enemy in that direction; but that, on their return, they would without fail come to visit us. They signified that if we would accompany them to their village, we should be hospitably received. When speaking of the enemy, they uttered the word "Majeronas" two or three times.

"Those must be the people you think attacked your father," observed Arthur. "If he and your family are prisoners, they may be the means of releasing them."

"I am afraid the Majeronas are too fierce and savage to make prisoners," I answered. "We might accompany these Indians and avenge their death, if they have been killed."

"That is not according to the Christian law," observed Arthur mildly. "I would run any risk, though, to obtain their release, should they have been made prisoners."

"I feel sure that they have not," I answered. "Had they not escaped in their canoe we should certainly have found some remains of her on the shore, or some traces of them. Oh no; I feel sure they got off, and we shall overtake them before long."

As I ceased speaking, a band of Indians appeared coming through the woods. They were—like the first two, who were evidently chiefs—decked in feathers and paint, but otherwise unencumbered by clothing. They were armed with bows and spears, but not a musket did we see among them. They were certainly the lightest of light troops. The two chiefs seemed to look upon their weapons as of immense value, as a general does his heavy guns. I saw the chief eyeing my rifle; and he then addressed us, inviting us to accompany the expedition. In spite of what I had just said, I felt greatly inclined to go, Arthur, however, urged me strongly not to do so.

"Think of your sister and brother. How anxious our absence would make them!" he observed. "You do not know what dangers they may be exposed to; and suppose we were surprised and killed by the enemy, what would become of them?"

I agreed that he was right, and explained to the chief that we could not leave our friends. He then asked me to make over my gun to him; but, of course, I could not deprive myself of our chief means of defence, and therefore turned a deaf ear to his request. The troops had halted at the foot of the hill; and we accompanied the two chiefs, who went down to meet them. The natives looked at us without much surprise, as if white men were no strangers to them. Arthur now advised that we should return, as it would be a serious matter should we be benighted in the forest. Before parting from our friends, we endeavoured to ascertain whether they had seen our canoe, but we could obtain no information from them. Still I could not help thinking that she had been carried off by some of their tribe, who might have found her on their way up the igarape. When, therefore, the chief again pressed us to pay a visit to his village, we accepted his invitation.

Several lads had accompanied the army. As they only carried blow-pipes in their hands, I suspected—as proved to be the case—that they were not to proceed further. The chief called one of them up to him; and from the way he spoke, I had little doubt that he was his son. The chief made signs to us that the lad, whom he called Duppo, would go back with us to the village, and that we should there obtain any food we might require. Duppo appeared to be about fourteen years of age, and more intelligent and better looking than most of the Indians; indeed, the two chiefs we had first seen were superior to the rest in appearance, and Duppo was very like them. We came to the conclusion that they were brothers; and that Duppo, as I have said, was the son of the eldest. This we found afterwards to be the case.

The chief, having wished us farewell, gave the signal to advance; and leading the way, the Indians set off in single file along the bottom of the hill. We, having watched them for some time, accompanied Duppo, followed by the three other lads who had come with him. We asked him his father's name, and understood him to say it was Maono, that his mother's name was Mora, and that his uncle was called Paco. Had we judged by Duppo's manner, we should not have supposed that his friends had gone on a dangerous expedition; but yet, knowing the character of the Majeronas, we could not help feeling some anxiety for the result. We found that Duppo was leading us towards the further end of the igarape, in the direction we had ourselves before proposed going. We had, however, delayed so long, that I feared we should not have time to return. Arthur suggested that we might possibly find a canoe, in which we could go back by water, or, if not, we might build a balsa, such as we had seen used on the Guayas.

"An excellent idea," I replied. "We will put it into execution should we not find a canoe."

Our young guide led the way with unerring instinct through the forest. We had gone some distance, when we heard a deep, loud, and long-sustained flute-like note. It was that of a bird. The young Indian stopped, and pointing ahead, uttered the word *nira-mimbeu*, which I afterwards ascertained meant fife-bird, evidently from the peculiar note we had just heard. The whole party stopped in the attitude of listening, and looking among the branches, we got a good view of a bird a short distance beyond us, with glossy black plumage, perched on a bough. The bird itself was about the size of a common crow. It had a remarkable ornament on its head, consisting of a crest formed of long, curved, hairy feathers at the end of bare quills which were now raised and spread out in the shape of a fringed sunshade. Round its neck was a tippet formed of glossy steel-blue feathers; and as we watched it, while it was singing it spread these out, and waved them in a curious manner, extending at the same time its umbrella-formed crest, while it bowed its head slightly forward and then raised it again. I knew at once the curious creature to be the rare umbrella-bird (*Cephalopterus ornatus*). The bird was continuing its flute-like performance, when Duppo, advancing slowly and lifting his blow-pipe, sent forth with unerring aim a tiny dart, which pierced the bird's neck. Much to my sorrow, the note ceased; but yet the bird stood on its perch as if scarcely aware of the wound it had received. We all stood watching it. For nearly a minute it remained as before, till gradually its head began to drop, and finally it fell to the ground. Duppo ran forward, and taking a pinch of white substance from a wallet which he carried at his side, placed it in the bird's mouth, and then carefully pulling out the arrow, put some into the wound, just as our Napo Indians had done when they shot our monkey, Nimble. We then went on, he carrying the apparently lifeless bird carefully in his arms. In a few minutes it began slowly to lift its head, and then to look about it as a hen does when carried in the same way. In a short time the bird seemed to be as well as if it had not received a wound, and began to peck at the bare arms of our young guide. On this he took from his bag some small pieces of fibre. On piece he wound round its bill, and another round its legs, taking great care not to hurt or injure it in any way.

We went on for some distance, our young guide keeping his sharp eyes roving round in every direction in search of some other bird or animal on which he might exercise his skill. We were naturally surprised at the wonderful way in which the bird he had shot had recovered. I could scarcely believe that the arrow had been tipped with poison, and yet I could not otherwise account for the manner in which the bird fell to the ground. I inquired of Duppo, but could not understand his reply. At last he took out of his bag some of the white stuff we had seen him apply and put it on his tongue. "Why," exclaimed Arthur, to whom he had given some to taste, "it is salt!"

Salt it undoubtedly was; and we now first learned that salt is an antidote to the wourali poison. People, indeed, who eat salt with their food are but little affected by it; while it quickly kills savages and animals who do not eat salt.

We had seen as yet no signs of habitations, when Duppo stopped and pointed through an opening in the trees. We saw, in the shade of the wide-spreading boughs, a woman kneeling before a bath, in which a little child was seated, splashing the water about with evident delight. The woman was almost as primitive a costume as the warriors we had seen. Her only ornament was a necklace, and her sole clothing consisted of a somewhat scanty petticoat. She, however, seemed in no way abashed at our presence. Duppo ran forward and said a few words to her, when, rising from her knees, and lifting up her dripping child in her arms, she advanced a few paces towards us. She seemed to be listening with great interest to what Duppo was saying, and she then signed to us to follow her. We did so, and soon came in sight of several bamboo huts. The walls, as also the roofs, were covered with a thatch of palm-leaves. On examining the thatch, I saw that it consisted of a number of leaves plaited together, and secured in a row to a long lath of bamboo. One of these laths, with a row of thatch attached to it, was hung up on pegs to the lowest part of the wall intended to be covered; another was fastened over it, the thatch covering the first lath; and so on, row after row, till the upper part was reached. The roof was formed in the same manner, secured by rope formed of aloe fibres or some similar material. Round the village were numerous fruit-trees. The most conspicuous were bananas, with their long, broad, soft, green leaf-blades; and several pupunhas, or peach-palms, with their delicious fruit, hanging down in enormous bunches from their lofty crowns, each a load for a strong man. The fruit gains its name from its colour. It is dry and mealy, of the taste of chestnuts and cheese. There were also a number of cotton and coffee trees on one side, extending down to the water, which showed that our friends were not ignorant of agriculture. We also saw melons growing in abundance, as well as mandioca and Indian corn.

The lady conducted us into her house with as much dignity as a duchess would have done into her palace. The interior of the building, however, had no great pretensions to architectural grandeur. The roof was supported by strong upright posts between which hammocks were slung, leaving space for a passage from one end to the other, as also for fires in the centre. At the further end was an elevated stage, which might be looked upon as a first floor, formed of split palm-stems. Along the walls were arranged clay jars of various sizes, very neatly made. Some, indeed, were large enough to hold twenty or more gallons; others were much smaller; and some were evidently used as cooking-pots. They were ornamented on the outside with crossed diagonal lines of various colours. There were also blow-pipes hung up, and quivers and bags made of the bromelia, very elaborately worked. In addition, there were baskets formed of the same material of a coarser description, and dressed skins of animals, with mats, and spare hammocks.

Our hostess, whom we discovered to be Duppo's mother, invited us to sit down on some mats which she spread in a clear space on the floor, a little removed from the fire. Duppo went out, and in a short time returned with a young girl, who looked timidly into the opening, and then ran off. He scampered after her, and brought her back; but it required some persuasion to induce her to enter the hut. We rose as she did so, struck by her interesting countenance and elegant form; for, although her garments were almost as scanty as those of the older woman, our impulse was to treat her with the respect we should have paid to one of her more civilised sisters. Having got over her timidity, she set to work to assist her mother in cooking some food. We asked Duppo his sister's name. He gave us to understand that it was Oria—at least, it sounded like it; and, at all events, that was the name by which we always called her. It was a pretty name, and well suited to such an interesting young creature.

Several parrots of gorgeous plumage, which had been sitting on the rafters, clambered down inquisitively to look at us; while two monkeys— tame little things—ran in and out of the hut. The most interesting creature we saw was a charming little water-fowl—a species of grebe. It seemed to be a great pet of the young girl. It was swimming about in a tub full of water, similar to the one in which we had seen our hostess bathing her baby. The girl took it out to show it to us, and it lay perfectly happy and contented in her hands. It was rather smaller than a pigeon, and had a pointed beak. The feet, unlike those of water-fowls, were furnished with several folds of skin in lieu of webs, and resembled much the feet of the gecko lizards. After exhibiting it to us, she put it back again into its tub, and it went swimming round and round, very much like those magnetic ducks which are sold in toyshops. On examining the tub I have spoken of, we found that it was formed from the spathe of the palm.

In a short time a repast was placed before us in several bowls. In one was fish, in another was a stew of meat. Arthur, without ceremony, ate some of the latter, when he came to a bone which I saw him examining curiously.

"Why, I do believe," he said, in a low voice, "it is a bit of monkey!"

"I have very little doubt about it," I answered; for I had discovered this some time before. "Try this other dish; it seems very nice."

Having eaten some of it, we bethought ourselves of inquiring of Duppo what it was; and he gave us to understand that it was a piece of snake or lizard, for we could not exactly make out which.

"I think I would rather keep to the fish," said Arthur, in a subdued voice. Indeed, with the fish and some mandioca porridge alone, we could have managed to make a very ample meal.

We had also several delicious fruits—guavas, bananas, and one, the interior of which tasted like a rich custard. A jar of a somewhat thick and violet-coloured liquor was placed before us to drink. It was made, we found, from the fruit of the assai palm, which our hostess, Illora, showed us. It was perfectly round and about the size of a cherry, consisting of a small portion of pulp lying between the skin and the hard kernel. The fruit pounded, with the addition of water, produces the beverage I have described. It was very refreshing, but stained our lips as do blackberries.

Having finished our meal, we thanked Dame Illora for it, and tried to explain that we were in search of a canoe in which to return down the igarape. For some time we could not make her comprehend what we wanted. Suddenly Duppo started up, and leading us to the water, by signs explained that all their canoes had been taken away. "Then, no doubt, the same people who took theirs, carried off ours," observed Arthur. I agreed with him. Still, I hoped that a small canoe might be found. We searched about, but I could not find one. The channel ran through the forest till it was lost to sight, and as there was a slight current in the water, we came to the conclusion that it was connected with some other river, up which the canoes had been carried.

"Then let us build a raft as we proposed," said Arthur. "If we do not return to-night, we shall alarm your sister and John. The current is in our favour, and we shall have no difficulty in descending to our camp."

At once we tried to explain to our friends what we proposed doing. Several other persons appeared, but they were mostly old men and women. The rest had evidently gone off to the war. We began by cutting down some small trees which grew at the edge of the igarape. Then we cut some sipos, and formed an oblong frame of sufficient size to support three or four people. After a little time Duppo comprehended our purpose, and we saw him explaining the matter to his people. Several of them on this set to work on a clump of bamboos which grew at a little distance, and brought them to us. Looking about, we also discovered some long reeds growing on the margin of the swamp at no great distance. Arthur and I collected as many as we could carry, and the natives, following our example, soon supplied us with what we required. Having fastened the bamboos lengthways on the frame, we secured the reeds both under and above them, till we had completely covered over the framework. The whole machine we strengthened by passing long sipos round it, and thus in a short time had a buoyant and sufficiently strong raft to carry us safely, we hoped, down the igarape. The natives had been watching our proceedings with looks of surprise, as if they had never seen a similar construction. We had cut a couple of long poles with which to push on the raft. "I think we should be the better for paddles," observed Arthur. One of the trees, we found, very easily split into boards. We soon made three paddles, agreeing that a third would be useful, in case one should break. "But perhaps Duppo would be willing to accompany us," said Arthur. "He seems a very intelligent fellow. Shall we ask him?"

We soon made our young friend comprehend our wishes. He was evidently well pleased with the proposal, though his mother at first seemed to hesitate about letting him go. We pressed her, explaining that we would reward him well for his services. Our point gained, Duppo's preparations were quickly made. He brought with him his zarabatana or blow-pipe, his bow, and a quiver full of arrows, as also a basket of farinha, apparently supposing that we might be unable to provide him with food. Seeing the curious umbrella-bird secured to a perch projecting from the wall, I asked him to bring it, as I wanted to show it to Ellen. He quickly understood me, and taking it down, again fastened up its beak, and brought it along perched on his shoulder. The whole remaining population of the village came down to the water to see us embark. We took off our hats to Oria, who scarcely seemed to understand the compliment.

Our raft was soon launched with their aid, and, greatly to our satisfaction, floated buoyantly. We got on board, and shoved off into the middle of the channel. The water was fat too deep to allow our poles to be of any use. Duppo, however, showed that he well knew the use of a paddle. Taking one in his hand, he sat down on one side of the raft, while Arthur sat on the other, and I stood astern to steer. The current was sluggish, and did not help us much. We therefore had to exert ourselves vigorously. The igarape soon widened out into a broad lake-like expanse. We could distinguish the channel, however, from its being free of reeds, which appeared in all directions in the other parts, forming thick broad clumps like islands. From amidst them numerous water-fowl rose up as we passed. Now and then an alligator poked up his ugly snout. Numerous tortoises and other water-creatures were seen swimming about. Others which rose near us, alarmed at our appearance, made off to a distance, and allowed us to proceed unimpeded.

We were delighted with the progress we made, and went paddling on as if we had been long accustomed to the work. We kept up most of the time a conversation with Duppo, although it must be owned that we could understand but little of what he said, while he had equal difficulty in comprehending us. We asked him several questions about his family. I told him that he must bring Oria down to see my sister, as I was sure she would be glad to make her acquaintance. I was, however, not very certain whether he understood me. He was evidently a quick, sagacious fellow; though his manners, like most of the Indians we had met, were subdued and quiet.

As we were paddling on, we were almost startled by hearing a sound like a bell tolling in the midst of the forest. It ceased, and we paddled on, when again it struck our ears loud and clear. Again it came within the space of a minute, and we almost expected to see some church steeple peeping forth through an opening in the primeval forest. We tried to ascertain from our young companion what it could mean, but he only nodded his head, as much as to say, "I know all about it," and then he gave a glance down at his bow and quiver which lay by his side. We went on for some minutes more, the sound of the bell reaching our ears as before, and then Duppo began to look up eagerly into the trees. Suddenly he ceased paddling, and made signs to Arthur to do the same. Gliding on a few yards further, we saw, on the topmost bough of a tree overhanging the water, a beautiful white bird, about the size of a jay. At the same time there came forth from where it stood a clear bell sound, and we saw from its head a black tube, rising up several inches above it. Duppo cautiously put his hand out and seized his bow. In an instant he had fitted an arrow to the string. Away it flew, and down fell the bird fluttering in the water. We paddled on, and quickly had it on board. I could not help feeling sorry that he had killed the beautiful creature, whose note had so astonished us.

It was, I found, a specimen of that somewhat rare and very wonderful bell-bird (*Casmarhynchos carunculata*), called *campañero* by the Spaniards. From the upper part of the bill grows a fleshy tubercle about the thickness of a quill, sparingly covered with minute feathers. It was now hanging down on one side, quite lax. It was evident, therefore, that the bird, when alive, elevated it when excited by singing or some other cause; indeed afterwards, on examining it, we found it connected with the interior of the throat, which further convinced us of this fact. I was sorry that we could not have it taken alive to Ellen, and I tried to explain to Duppo that we wished to have living creatures if possible captured, like the umbrella-bird.

We had been paddling on for some time beneath the thick overhanging boughs, almost in darkness, when a bright glow attracted our attention. "We must be near the camp," exclaimed Arthur, and we shouted out. We were replied to by True's well-known bark, and directly afterwards we could distinguish through the gloom the figure of Domingos making his way amid the wood, with True running before him, down to the bank. There they stood ready to receive us.

Chapter Nine
Lost in the Forest

"I am thankful to have you back, my young masters," exclaimed Domingos, as he helped us to land. "But what! have you not brought back the canoe? I thought it was her you had returned in, and that the third person I saw was Señor John. He set off some time back to look for you."

We briefly explained what had happened, and introduced the young Indian. Having secured the raft, we hastened to our encampment. Ellen and Maria came out to meet us.

"I am so glad you have come back," said Ellen, "for we were growing very anxious about you. I hope John will soon return. I am surprised you did not see him as you came down the igarape."

I explained to her how easily we might have passed each other. "I dare say we shall see John in a few minutes. When he found night coming on, he would certainly turn back," I added.

We now brought Duppo forward and introduced him, telling Ellen about his sister Oria.

"Oh, I should so like to see her!" she exclaimed. "Do try and make him understand that we hope he will bring her here."

Though modest and retiring in his manner, Duppo soon made himself at home, and seemed well pleased at being in our society. Ellen was delighted with the curious bird he had brought her, and Maria undertook to tame it, as she had the parrot and Nimble. John had fortunately killed a paca in the morning, and Maria had dressed part of it for supper. We were, however, unwilling to begin our meal till his return. We waited for some time, expecting him every instant to appear. We made the fire blaze brightly as a signal, and Domingos and I went to a little distance from the camp, first in one direction, then in another, shouting at the top of our voices; but we in vain listened for his in return. I then fired off my rifle, hoping that, had he lost his way, that might show him the position of the camp. We stood breathless, waiting to hear his rifle, but no sound reached our ears. We now became very anxious, but were unwilling to go further from the camp, lest we might be unable to find our way back. True, who had followed us, added his voice to our shouts.

"Hark!" said Domingos; "I hear a sound."

We listened. It was a low, deep howl. It grew louder and louder.

"That is only one of those big monkeys beginning its night music," I observed.

True, when he heard it, was darting forward, but I called him back, afraid lest he should meet with a prowling jaguar or huge boa, which might carry him off before we could go to his assistance. At length, with sad forebodings, we returned to the camp. We did our best to comfort Ellen, yet it was very difficult to account for John's non-appearance.

"He must certainly have gone further than he intended," observed Arthur; "then, not having the sun to guide him, must have taken a wrong direction. He will probably climb up into some tree to sleep, and when the sun rises in the morning he will easily find his way back."

"Oh, thank you, Arthur, for suggesting that!" said Ellen; "I am sure it must be so."

"At all events," I said, "we will start away at daybreak to look for him; and with our young Indian friend as a guide, we need have no fear in venturing into the forest."

We had none of us much appetite for supper, but Domingos persuaded us to take some. We then made up a fire, intending to keep watch during the night, hoping every moment that John might return. Domingos, however, at length persuaded Arthur and I to lie down in our hammocks; indeed, in spite of our anxiety, in consequence of the fatigue we had gone through during the day, we could with difficulty keep our eyes open. He made Duppo get into his, saying that he himself would keep watch. Every now and then I awoke, hoping to hear John's cheery voice. Each time I looked out I saw our faithful Domingos sitting before the fire, busying himself in throwing sticks on it to keep it blazing brightly. Occasionally I observed him get up, go to a little distance, and stretch out his neck into the darkness. Then he would come back again and take his seat as before, while the various tones of croaking frogs, or huge crickets, or the fearful howls of the night-monkeys, which came, now from one direction, now from another, from the far-off depths of the forest, sounded as if they were keeping up a conversation among themselves. This dismal noise continued throughout the night.

At daylight Arthur and I leaped from our hammocks, and roused up young Duppo. We tried to explain to him that one of our number had gone away, and that we wanted to go in search of him.

"Stay!" exclaimed Domingos; "you must not go without breakfast. I have been boiling the cocoa, and I will soon roast some paca."

While we were breakfasting, Ellen and Maria came out of their hut. Ellen looked very pale and anxious, as if she had passed a sleepless night; and she confessed that she had not closed her eyes for thinking of John, and what might have become of him. We were doubtful about taking True; but when he saw us preparing to start, he ran off, and would not return, for fear of being tied up: we decided, therefore, to let him go with us, thinking that he might be of assistance in finding John.

Having done my best to comfort Ellen, we set out in the direction Domingos told us John had gone. We had stored our wallets with food, that we might not run the risk of starving should we be kept out longer than we expected. Duppo had followed our example, having brought his bag of farinha on shore. He carried his bow and blow-pipe; and Arthur was armed with his bow, as well as with a long pointed staff; and I had my rifle and a good store of ammunition. Our Indian guide seemed to understand clearly our object, and led the way without hesitation through the forest. After we had gone some little distance, we saw him examining the trees on either side. Then he again went on as before. He made signs to us that the person we were searching for had gone that way. After a time he again stopped, and showed us how he had been turning about, now in one direction, now in another. Then on he went again, further and further from the camp. As we were making our way onwards, Duppo stopped, and signed to us to be silent; and then pointed to a tree a little way in front. We there saw on a bough a short-tailed animal, with white hair. After waiting a minute or two, it turned round, and a face of the most vivid scarlet hue was presented to us. It seemed unconscious of our presence for it did not move from its post. The head was nearly bald, or at most had but a short crop of thin grey hair; while round the odd-looking face was a fringe of bushy whiskers of a sandy colour, which met under the chin. A pair of reddish eyes added to its curious appearance. The body was entirely covered with long, straight, shining white hair.

Presently it moved along the branch, and began picking some fruit which grew at the further end. Duppo cautiously lifted his blow-pipe to his mouth. An arrow sped forth and struck the creature. The instant it felt itself wounded, it ran along the branch till it reached another tree. Duppo made chase, and we had no little difficulty in following him. On the creature went from tree to tree, and it seemed that there was but a slight chance of his catching it. Presently we saw it again, but moving slower than at first. Slower and slower it went, till Duppo could easily keep close under it; then down it fell, almost into his arms. True, who was ahead of us, darted forward, and, had I not called him back, would have seized the creature. The Indian, meantime, was engaged in pulling out the arrow; and having done so, he put a pinch of salt into the creature's mouth.

On examining it, we found it was a veritable monkey, one of the most curious of the race I ever saw. It was of the genera of *Cebidae*. Duppo called it a *nakári* (*Brachyurus calvus* is its scientific name). The body was about eighteen inches long, exclusive of the limbs. Its tail was very short, and apparently of no use to it in climbing; and its limbs were rather shorter and thicker than those of most monkeys. In a short time it began to show signs of life.

We soon afterwards caught sight of another, with a young one on its back, which our guide told us was a mother monkey. It, however, got away before he could bring his blow-pipe to bear on it. As soon as the little captive began to move, Duppo secured its front hands with a piece of line, and threw a small net over its head to prevent it biting. He then secured it on his shoulder; and we again pushed on through the forest as fast as we could go. We were at length obliged to stop and rest. We had taken but a slight breakfast. Arthur said he was hungry; and Duppo showed that he was by taking out a cake of farinha and some dried meat from his bag. Anxiety, however, had taken away my appetite.

While I was sitting down, I observed close to us what I took to be a seed-pod of some aerial plant, hanging straight down from a bough, at about six feet from the ground. On going up to it, I found to my surprise that it was a cocoon about the size of a sparrow's egg, woven by a caterpillar in broad meshes of a rose-coloured silky substance. It hung, suspended from the tip of an outstanding leaf, by a strong silken thread about six inches in length. On examining it carefully, I found that the glossy threads which surrounded it were thick and strong. Both above and below there was an orifice, which I concluded was to enable the moth, when changed from the chrysalis which slept tranquilly within its airy cage, to make its escape. It was so strong that it could resist evidently the peck of a bird's beak, while it would immediately swing away from one on being touched. I afterwards met with several such cocoons; and once saw a moth coming forth from one. It was of a dull, slaty colour, and belonged to the silkworm family of *Bombycidae*.

Arthur persuaded me at last to take a little food; and having rested sufficiently, we again moved on. At length Duppo came to a stand-still, and signed to me to keep back True. I could hardly hold him, however, he seemed so anxious to push forward. Duppo had slung his blow-pipe at his back, and held his bow with an arrow to shoot. Then I saw him examining the ground on every side under the boughs, many of which hung close down to it. Presently the report of a gun reached our ears.

"That is certainly your brother John!" exclaimed Arthur.

The shot came from some distance, however. Then another, and another, followed at intervals of a few minutes. We now hurried on more eagerly than ever, in spite of Duppo's signs to us to be cautious. I felt convinced that John alone could have fired those shots. Again another shot sounded close to us; and on emerging from the thicker part of the forest, we saw at a little distance the ground covered with a herd of hog-like animals—though smaller than ordinary hogs—which I guessed at once were peccaries. They were in a great state of commotion—running about in all directions, turning their long snouts up into the air. Going a few yards further on, there was John himself, seated high up on the bough of a tree, to which numerous sipos hung. His gun was pointed down towards the herd of peccaries, several of which lay dead on the ground. Some of the others kept running about, but the greater portion were standing looking up at him. There he sat, with his usual composure, regularly besieged by them. The attention of the savage creatures was so occupied with him that they did not perceive our approach.

I was somewhat surprised at the eager signs which Duppo made to us to climb up a tree by means of some sipos which hung close at hand. We were hesitating to follow his advice, when he seized Arthur by the arm and dragged him up. I thought it prudent to follow his example, as I had formed a good opinion of his sense. I lifted up True to Arthur, who caught him in his arms; and then I swung myself up to the branch after him. We had just taken our seats facing John, when the peccaries discovered us; and a number of them turning round, charged across the ground on which we had stood. Duppo had got his bow ready, and shot one as they passed. He killed another as, turning round, they charged back again, and then ran about looking up at us, as they had been watching John.

"I am very glad to see you safe!" I shouted out to John; for hitherto we had not had time to speak to him. "But why should we be afraid of these little creatures? They have more reason to be afraid of us, from the number you have killed, I should think."

"Just look into their mouths, and you will soon see that they are not so harmless as you suppose," he answered. "I have had a narrow escape of losing my life; for one of them caught me in the leg as I was climbing this tree, and had I let go my hold, the whole herd would have been upon me, and I should have been cut to pieces in a few seconds. Those tusks of theirs are as pointed as needles and as sharp as razors. I am very glad you found me out, too; for I left my wallet hanging on a branch, just before I had to run for my life from these fellows. But how did you get back?"

I briefly told him of our adventures.

"You must have been anxious about me at the camp," he observed. "But the honest truth is, I lost my way, and at this moment scarcely know where I have got to. I had, however, few fears about myself; but have been very sorry for poor dear Ellen, while I could not tell whether you were safe or not. However, we must drive away these savage little brutes."

Saying this, he knocked over another. I followed his example. Arthur and Duppo were meantime shooting their arrows at the herd. Undaunted, however, the animals stood collected below us. It was evident that they were influenced rather by dull obstinacy or ignorance of their danger than by courage. At length their obtuse senses showed them that they were getting the worst of it. The survivors began to turn their fierce little eyes towards their dead companions, and it seemed to strike them that something was the matter.

"Shout!" cried out John—"shout! and perhaps we may frighten them away."

We raised our voices, Duppo joining in with his shrill pipe. The peccaries looked at each other; and then one moved to a little distance, then another, and at last the whole herd set off scampering away through the forest. We sent reiterated shouts after them, fearing that they might otherwise stop, and perhaps come back again; but they at last discovered that discretion is the better part of valour, and the trampling of their feet became less and less distinct, till it was lost in the distance.

We now descended from our perches. I handed down True into Arthur's arms. True had been very dissatisfied with his position, and, to revenge himself, at once flew at one of the hogs which was struggling at a little distance, and quickly put it out of its pain. We shook hands with John; and, congratulating him on his escape, introduced Duppo to him, and told him how we had become acquainted.

"Here," he said, "look at these creatures, and you will see that I had good reason to be afraid of them."

On examining their long and apparently harmless snouts, we found that they were armed with short tusks, scarcely seen beyond the lips; but being acutely pointed and double-edged, and as sharp as lancets, they are capable of inflicting the most terrible wounds. Peccaries are the most formidable enemies, when met with in numbers, to be found in the forests of the Amazon. The creatures were not more than three feet long, and a whole one was but an easy load to carry. The bodies were short and compact, and thickly covered with strong, dark-coloured bristles. Round the neck was a whitish band, while the under part of the body was nearly naked. Instead of a tail, there was merely a fleshy protuberance.

"What a horrible odour!" exclaimed Arthur, as we were examining one of them.

We found that it proceeded from a glandular orifice at the lower part of the back. Duppo immediately took this out with his knife, and then began scientifically to cut up the animal. Following his example, we prepared others to carry with us, and thus each made up a load of about thirty pounds.

The learned name of the animal is *Dicotyles tajacu*. It eats anything that comes in its way,—fruits, roots, reptiles, or eggs; and it is of great service in killing snakes. It will attack the rattlesnake without fear, and easily kills it. The meat appeared perfectly destitute of fat, but we hoped to find it none the worse on that account.

John, as may be supposed, was very hungry, and thankful for some of the food we brought with us. After he had breakfasted we commenced our return to the camp, loaded with the peccary meat. Duppo carried a portion in addition to the scarlet-faced monkey. The little creature sat on his shoulder, looking far from at ease in its novel position.

"Oh, we will tame you before long, and make you perfectly contented and happy," said Arthur, going behind Duppo and addressing the monkey. "What will you like to be called, old fellow? You must have a name, you know. I have thought of one just suited to your red nose—Toby; Toby Fill-pot, eh!—only we will call you Toby. I say, Harry, don't you think that will be a capital name?"

I agreed that Toby was a very suitable name, and so we settled, with Ellen's approval, that Toby should be the name of our scarlet-faced friend.

John walked on in silence for some time. "I am very much ashamed of losing my way," he said at length when I joined him. "Setting off through the forest to meet you, I went on and on, expecting every instant to see you. I fancied that I was close to the igarape, but somehow or other had wandered from it. The gloom increasing, I had still greater difficulty in finding my way. At last I determined to go back to the camp, but instead of doing so I must have wandered further and further from it. It then grew so dark that I was afraid of proceeding, and so looked out for a tree where I could rest for the night. I saw one with wide-spreading branches at no great distance from the ground. Having cut a number of sipos, I climbed into my intended resting-place, dragging them after me. I there fastened them to the surrounding branches, making a tolerably secure nest for myself, I cannot say that I was very comfortable, for I could not help thinking that a prowling jaguar might find me out, or a boa or some other snake might climb up, and pay me a visit. I shouted several times, hoping that you might hear me, but the only answers I got were cries from howling monkeys, who seemed to be mocking me. The whole night long the creatures kept up their hideous howls. The moment one grew tired another began. So far they were of service, that they assisted to keep me awake. I can tell you I heartily wished for the return of day. As soon as it dawned I descended from my roosting-place, intending to make my way back as fast as possible. However, as the sun had not appeared, I had nothing to guide me. I tried to find the water, but must have gone directly away from it. I was walking on, when I saw the snout of an animal projecting from the hollow trunk of a large tree. Taking it for a pig of some sort, I fired, when it ran out and dropped dead, its place being immediately supplied by another. I killed that in the same way, when out came a third, and looked about it; and presently I discovered several other heads poked out from the surrounding trees. I was on the point of cutting some pork steaks out of the first I had killed, when I caught sight of the sharp little tusks projecting from its mouth. Suddenly the accounts I had heard of the dangerous character of peccaries flashed across my mind, and at the same instant I saw a number of the animals coming out of their holes. Prudence urged me to beat a quick retreat. I was making my way through the forest, and had already got to some distance from where I had first seen the creatures, when a large herd, which had apparently collected from all quarters, came scampering after me. I at once began to clamber up into a tree, where you found me. On they came at a great rate; and, as I told you, I narrowly escaped being caught by one of the savage little brutes. I must have spent a couple of hours or more besieged by them before you came up."

As we neared the camp we uttered as cheerful a shout as we could raise to give notice of our approach, and Domingos soon appeared, followed by Ellen and Maria. Ellen ran forward, and throwing her arms round John's neck, burst into tears. It showed us how anxious she had been on his account, although she had done her best, as she always did, to restrain her own feelings and keep up our spirits.

We were all of us glad, after our exertions, to get into our hammocks and rest. We found on waking that Domingos and Maria had exerted themselves to prepare a plentiful repast. While eating it we discussed our future plans.

"We must either recover our canoe or build another, that is certain," said John, "before we can continue our voyage. However, if we could be sure that this is a secure and healthy place for you to remain in, I should like to arrange with some of these Indians to make an excursion along the shores in search of our parents. Perhaps they are all this time encamped or at some village, on this or the opposite bank, not far off. It would, I think, be unwise to go further down without staying to ascertain this. What is your opinion, Harry?"

I agreed with him, but said that I would rather run the risk of the adventure, and let him remain at the camp. "Or perhaps Arthur might like to come with me," I added. "Two people might succeed better than one; and we could even manage a canoe by ourselves independently of the natives."

"Oh yes," said Arthur, "do let me go with Harry. We can take Duppo to assist us. He seems so intelligent that we should easily make him understand what we want."

"Then I propose that early to-morrow morning we set off to the village to search further for our canoe, or to purchase one, as John suggests," I said. "I am afraid we shall not be able to get up there on our raft, and we shall therefore have to make a journey round by land. With Duppo, however, as a guide, we shall have less difficulty than before in making our way to it."

It was finally settled that John, Arthur, and I should set off early the following morning to the village, guided by Duppo, while Domingos remained at the camp to take care of Ellen and Maria.

Chapter Ten
An Encounter with Savages

As there was still some daylight remaining, John took his gun to kill some parrots or other birds which might prove more palatable food than the peccary flesh.

"Take care that you do not lose yourself again," I could not help saying as he was starting.

"Do not mock me, Harry," he answered. "I wish to gain experience, and depend on it I shall be careful to take the bearings of the camp, so as easily to find my way back to it. I do not intend to go many hundred yards off."

Arthur and I were in the meantime engaged in trying to tame Master Toby and the umbrella-bird, which we called Niger. Both seemed tolerably reconciled to captivity. Ellen's little pet parrot, Poll, kept casting suspicious glances at its feathered companion, not satisfied with the appearance of the curious-headed stranger, while Nimble watched every movement of his cousin Toby.

After assisting Ellen to feed her pets, Arthur and I agreed to go out in search of John, taking Duppo with us as a guide. We had not gone far when we saw him coming limping towards us. We were afraid that he had hurt his foot. "What is the matter?" I asked, when we met.

"That is more than I can tell," he answered. "I have been for some time past feeling a curious itching sensation in my feet, and now I can scarcely bear to put them to the ground."

We helped him along to the camp, when, sitting down on a log, he took off his boots. We examined his feet, and found a few small blue spots about them.

"I suspect, Señor John, I know what it is," said Maria, who saw us. "Some chegoes have got into your feet, and if they are not taken out quickly they will cause you a great deal of suffering."

"But I can see nothing to take out," said John, looking at his feet.

"To be sure not," answered Maria, "because they have hidden themselves away under the skin. Let me see what I can do. My mother was famous for taking out chegoes, and she showed me the way she managed."

Maria, running into the hut, returned with a large needle. "Now, sit quiet, Señor John, and do not cry out, and I will soon cure you."

Maria sat down, and taking John's foot on her knee, instantly began to work away with as much skill as the most experienced surgeon. We all stood by watching her. After a little time she produced between her finger and thumb a creature considerably smaller than an ordinary flea, which she had taken out alive and uninjured. Giving it a squeeze, she threw it to the ground with an expression of anger at its having dared to molest her young master; and thus in a very short time she had extracted three or four insects from each of his feet. We had meantime begun to feel something uncomfortable in ours, and on Maria's examining them, we found that a chego had taken possession of each of our big toes. The chego is a black little creature, which makes its way quietly under the skin, where, having got to a sufficient depth, it lays its eggs, and unless removed immediately, causes annoying and dangerous ulcers. Ours were not there when we started to look for John, and by this time they had worked their way completely out of sight. After that we carefully examined our legs and feet every night before going to bed, as during the time we were asleep they would have made themselves completely at home in our flesh, with house, nursery, and children to boot.

Next morning, our feet being once more in good order, we put on thick socks, and our alpargates over them, and John and I with our guns, Arthur with his bow and spear, accompanied by True, and led by Duppo, took our way through the forest. I kept True close to me; for after the experience we had had, I was afraid of his encountering a jaguar, or peccary, or boa, knowing, however formidable the creature might be, he to a certainty would attack it. I need not again describe the forest scenery. After going on for some time we stopped to lunch, when Arthur, who was at a little distance, called out to me. "Come here, Harry," he said, "and look at this curious wooden caterpillar." On joining him, I found on a leaf the head of a caterpillar projecting out of a wooden case fully two inches long. It was secured to the leaf by several silken lines. I took it up and examined it. There could be no doubt that the case was the work of art, and not a natural growth, and that it was formed of small pieces of stick fastened together with fine silken threads. Inside this case the creature can live secure from its enemies while feeding and growing. We afterwards found several of the same description. Another sort had made itself a bag of leaves open at both ends, the inside being lined with a thick web. It put us in mind of the caddis worms which we had seen in ponds in England.

We took care when going on always to keep in sight of each other. Arthur and I were together, and Duppo a little ahead. "Hark!" exclaimed Arthur, "some one is singing in the distance." I listened, and felt sure that some native, who had climbed up a tree not far off to get fruit, was amusing himself by singing. John and Duppo stopped also, attracted by the same sounds. We looked about in every direction, but could see no one. Now the tones changed somewhat, and became more like those of a flageolet, very sweet, and we expected to hear it break into a curious native air, when presently it stopped, and instead of the flute-like notes, some clicking, unmusical sounds like the piping of a barrel-organ out of wind and tune reached our ears. Not till then had we supposed that the songster was a bird. Again it struck up in exactly the same way as before. Though we all four looked about in the direction whence the notes came, the mysterious songster could not be discovered. Duppo was evidently telling us a long story about it, but what he said we could not comprehend. I afterwards found that the bird is called by the Portuguese the realejo, or organ-bird (*Cyphorhinus cantans*). It is the chief songster of the Amazonian forests. The natives hold it in great respect, and Duppo seemed very unwilling to go on while the bird continued its notes.

At length we reached the village, and were received in a friendly way by our young guide's mother. Oria also seemed very glad to see us, and the little fat child whom Arthur called Diogenes, because he had first seen him seated in a tub, put out his hands to welcome us, in no way alarmed at what must have appeared to him our extraordinary appearance. Our hostess appeared somewhat anxious, and she had good cause to be so, for no news had been received of the war-party. Duppo explained what we had come for. She replied that she was afraid all the canoes had been carried off, though it was possible a small one might have been overlooked further up the stream, and, if such were the case, she would do her best to persuade the owner to sell it to us.

We wanted to start off immediately, but she insisted on our partaking of some food, which she and Oria set to work to prepare.

As we were anxious to know whether a canoe could be procured, we spent little time over our repast, and again set off along the bank of the igarape. We inquired at each of the huts we passed about a canoe, but Duppo invariably shook his head, to signify that he could not hear of one. Still we went on, searching in every spot where he thought a canoe might be concealed. After some time, finding a tree bending almost horizontally over the water, we climbed along it for some way, that we might get a better view up and down the channel. Arthur was the outermost of the party. "Why, what can that be?" he exclaimed. "See there!" and he pointed up the canal. There, bending over the trunk of a large tree, which hung much in the same manner as the one we were on, I saw a huge jaguar. Its claws seemed ready for immediate action. Its eyes were evidently fixed on the surface of the water.

"It is fifty yards off. It is looking out for a cow-fish, as was the one we saw the other day," whispered Arthur.

We told John, who was coming along the trunk, what we had seen.

"We will let it catch the cow-fish first, then, and perhaps we may kill both creatures," he observed.

While he was speaking, the creature darted out one of its huge paws, and drew it back again with a fish hanging to it. Instantly the fish was torn to pieces and transferred to its jaws. We waited till the jaguar had begun to watch for another, and then crawling along the tree, made our way towards it. John and I got our guns ready, hoping to kill the beast before it had discovered us. Just as we got near, however, it having caught another fish in the meantime, its eyes fell on us. Rising to its feet, it stood for a moment as if doubtful whether or not it should attack us. I lifted my rifle to fire, but at that moment the animal gave a bound and darted off through the thick foliage, amid which it was hid from sight. We looked about, expecting to see it returning, but it had probably satisfied itself that we were too formidable enemies to attack. We found some of the fish it had been eating on the trunk of the tree, and the remains of several others near it, which showed that it had been successful in its sport.

While searching round the tree Duppo gave a shout of satisfaction, and hastening up to him, we found a small canoe hid away under a thick bush. He soon discovered also two pairs of paddles, and made us understand that we were welcome to the canoe. It was, however, so small that it would barely carry all the party. It would certainly not have done so with safety, except in the very smoothest water. We launched it, and John and Arthur, using great caution, got in. One of the paddles had been left behind. Duppo ran back to get it. We saw him eagerly glancing down an open glade which extended some distance into the forest. Suddenly he turned round, his countenance exhibiting terror, and stepping into the stern of the canoe, made signs to us to shove off and paddle away. He also began paddling with all his might. We followed his example without stopping to inquire the cause of his alarm. We had got to some distance, when I happened to look round. I saw that

Duppo was doing the same. At that moment several figures appeared on the bank near the spot we had left. They were savages, with their bodies painted and decked with feathers. Bows were in their hands. They had apparently only that instant discovered us. The next a flight of arrows came whizzing after the canoe. They fell short, however, and we redoubled our efforts to urge it forward. Still, deep in the water as it was, we could scarcely hope to get beyond their reach.

"Majeronas! Majeronas!" shouted Duppo, labouring away with his paddle.

"On, boys, on!" cried John. "We must not allow them to come up with us. Active as they are, the forest is thick, and we may be able to get along the water faster than they can make their way among the trees."

Disappointed at finding that we were already beyond their reach, the savages uttered piercing shrieks and cries to intimidate us. The water bubbled and hissed as we drove our little canoe through it, coming frequently over the bows. Still on we went. I could not, however, help every now and then looking round, expecting to see the savages on the bank neat us. Their shouts had ceased.

"I am afraid our friends have been defeated," observed Arthur; "and their enemies have come to attack the village."

"If so, we must defend it," said John. "They may possibly stand in awe of our firearms. We must, however, try to get to the village before they reach it, to warn the inhabitants."

"But there are only old men, boys, and women to defend it," said Arthur. "Could we not try to come to terms with their enemies?"

"I am afraid the Majeronas, if they have been victorious, are not likely to listen to anything we have to say," said John. "We must show them our rifles. They will understand that argument better than anything else."

All this time we were paddling along as at first. Before us was a narrow part of the igarape, and I fully expected every instant to see the savages appear on the bank. Still, we had made considerable way, and it was possible that we had kept ahead of them. I said nothing, however, lest it might discourage my companions.

We were nearing the dreaded point. I saw that Duppo was keeping the canoe over to the opposite side.

"Would it not be better to get our guns ready to fire?" I said to John.

"No, no," he answered. "Keep paddling away. There is no honour nor advantage to be gained by fighting. If we reach the village, we shall meet the foe on better terms."

It was anxious work. We could not tell whether the next moment might not be our last. Then what would become of poor dear Ellen? We knew that Domingos and Maria would do their best. Still, how could they escape alone?

"Now," said John, "we must dash by that point as fast as we can! Never mind if we ship a little water. We must not let the savages kill us if we can help it."

The point was reached. I expected to see a party of the Majeronas start up from among the bushes. On we went. I held my breath as I paddled away. The point was passed. No savages appeared.

"Hurrah!" cried Arthur, who was seated in the bows. "There is the village!"

In three minutes more we were on shore. Duppo set off running, shouting at the top of his voice. The boys collected round him as he went, but instantly dispersed to their huts. Before he was out of sight they had again collected, some with bows and arrows, others with *sumpitans*. Several old men appeared also, armed with larger weapons of the same description. Altogether, fully fifty men and boys were collected. We came to the conclusion that the enemy had hoped to surprise the village, and were approaching for that object when Duppo had discovered them.

John advised that a breastwork should be thrown up, extending from the igarape across the path the Majeronas were likely to come by. After some time, our friends seemed to comprehend what we wanted. Some timbers for building a new hut were fortunately at hand. We drove several into the soft earth to form a palisade. The natives, on seeing us do this, understood what we wanted, and immediately the whole community were busy at work, bringing up posts, and placing them as we directed. They even pulled down three or four huts which stood near, the materials of which were suited to our purpose. The women worked away as well as the men; and thus, with so many willing hands, in a short time we had a fortification erected, which, though not very strong, was sufficiently so to resist the attack of a party of naked savages. We encouraged them by explaining that our guns might do good service in their defence. By degrees we had formed a complete half-circle, the ends resting on the igarape.

As there still appeared to be time, we thought it better to fortify the water side also. The people seemed clearly to understand our object.

The evening was now drawing on. I was afraid that Ellen might become anxious at our non-appearance. I saw that something was on Arthur's mind. He came up to me.

"Harry," he said, "I do not wish to alarm you unnecessarily, but it has just occurred to me that the savages may have made a circuit, and found their way to our camp. Would it not be wise to go there in the canoe; you and Duppo, for instance, and leave John and I to assist these people?"

"Oh no! I cannot desert John," I answered. "But what a dreadful thought! No; you must go, Arthur, and take them off in the canoe; or, as the canoe cannot carry you all, load the raft, and tow it out into the river. The risk is great, but anything will be better than falling into the hands of the savages."

"I will do as you wish," said Arthur; "but I do not like running away from the post of the chief danger."

"Why, Arthur, you see you could do but little with your bow," I answered; "John and I will stay with our guns. But I do not suppose the savages have gone round that way; for recollect there is the lagoon to pass, which must compel them to make a wide circuit; and I do not see how they can know anything about our camp. Still, I wish you could go to Ellen, and tell her what a strong fortification we have thrown up, and that there is really no cause to be alarmed."

I must confess, however, that all the time I was speaking I felt fearfully anxious.

At that moment, two or three bigger boys, who had gone out as scouts into the forest, came running back, and shouting out to the people. The next instant, men, women, and children rushed into the enclosure loaded with household goods and provisions; and the men set to work to block up a narrow space, which had hitherto been left open.

A few minutes only had elapsed after this was done, when, as we looked through the palisades, we caught sight of several human figures stealthily creeping among the trees. Our friends crouched down to the ground. We also carefully kept out of sight. The strangers approached nearer and nearer. Now they stopped, looking suspiciously at the fort. They evidently could not understand what it was. Several others, emerging from the depths of the forest, joined them. They seemed to be holding a consultation. Their numbers kept increasing, till they formed a formidable band. They were sufficiently near for us to distinguish their appearance, and we were thus sure that they were the same people who had shot their arrows at us from the bank of the igarape. That they came with hostile intent was very evident. After they had talked for some time, one of their number crept forward, close to the ground, keeping as much under shelter as possible; yet I could easily have picked him off had it been necessary. Having approached quite near, he again stopped, and seemed to be surveying the fortress. Presently we saw him making his way back to his companions. It was well for him that he had not come nearer, or he would have received in his body a poisoned arrow from a bow or blow-pipe. Several of our Indians were preparing to shoot. Again a long consultation was held. And now once more the savage warriors began to move towards us.

I waited for John to give the order to fire. I saw the boys dropping arrows into their blow-pipes, and the old men getting ready their bows. Even Arthur, though hating the thought of injuring a fellow-creature, was fixing an arrow to his bow. The enemy advanced slowly, extending their line on both sides. In a little time they were near enough for their arrows to reach us. Never having seen a shot fired in anger, I felt a repugnance at the thought of killing a fellow-creature. I daresay my companions felt as I did. I knew that Arthur had often expressed his horror at having to go into battle, not on account of the risk he might run of being killed, but at the thought of killing others. Still, I had persuaded him that, if people are attacked, they must use the right of defending themselves.

Again they came on; and then suddenly once more stopped, and, drawing their bows, shot a flight of arrows. Most of them stuck in the palisades, but fortunately none came through. We kept perfectly silent, hiding ourselves, as before, from the enemy. I was still in hopes they might take the alarm and go away without attacking us. Now, led by a chief, in a head-dress of feathers, with a long spear in his hand, uttering loud shouts and shrieks, like the war-whoops of North American Indians, they dashed on. As they got within twenty yards of us, our native garrison sprang up, and shot forth a shower of arrows from their bows and blow-pipes. The enemy were thrown somewhat into confusion by so unexpected a greeting, and sprang back several paces. Two or three of their people had been struck, as we saw them drawing the arrows from their breasts with looks of alarm, knowing well that though the wounds were slight they were nevertheless likely to prove fatal.

"If they come on again we must fire," said John. "It may be true mercy in the end."

We waited, expecting to see them once more rush on; but they evidently had not calculated on opposition, and seemed very unwilling to court danger. They retreated further and further off. Still we could see the chief going among them, apparently trying to induce them to renew the attack. The muzzles of our rifles were projecting through the palisades.

"I am covering the chief," said John. "I think it would be better to pick him off; and yet I am unwilling to take the life of the ignorant savage."

While John was speaking, the chief disappeared behind a tree; and the next instant his companions were hid from sight. We began to hope that, after all, they would retreat without attempting to attack our fortress. We waited for some time, when I proposed that we should send out our young scouts to try and ascertain what had become of them. Just as we were trying to explain our wishes, some of our people gave vent to loud cries, and we saw smoke rising from the furthest-off huts of the village. It grew thicker and thicker. Then we saw flames bursting forth and extending from hut to hut. It was too evident that the savages had gone round, and, to revenge themselves, had, after plundering the huts, set them on fire. Had we had a few active warrior with us, they might have rushed out and attacked the enemy while thus employed; but as our fighting men were either too old or too young, no attempt of the sort could be made. The poor natives, therefore, had to wait patiently in the fort, whilst their homes and property were being destroyed.

While most of the party were looking towards the village, I happened to cast my eyes in the other direction, from whence the enemy had come. There I saw a large body of men making their way among the trees. My heart sank within me. I was afraid that our enemies were about to be reinforced. And now, with their numbers increased, they would probably again attack us.

"It cannot be helped," I said to John. "We must allow no feelings of compunction to prevent us from firing on them. Had we shot the chief, his followers would probably not have attempted to commit this barbarous act."

At length I called Duppo, and pointed out the fresh band now approaching. Instead of being alarmed, as I had expected, his countenance brightened, and he instantly turned round and shouted out some words in a cheerful tone. The whole of the villagers on this sprang up, and a look of satisfaction, such as Indians seldom exhibit, coming over their countenances, they began to shout in cheerful tones. Then several of them rushed to the entrance last closed, and pulling down the stakes, hurried out towards the new-comers. As they drew nearer, I recognised one of the chiefs whom we had met—Maono, Duppo's father. A few words only were exchanged between the garrison and the warriors, and then the latter rushed on towards the village. In a few minutes loud cries and shouts arose, and we saw our late assailants scampering through the woods, pursued by our friends. The former did not attempt to stop and defend themselves. Several, shot by arrows or pierced by lances, lay on the ground. The remainder were soon lost to sight among the trees, pursued by the warriors who had just returned, and who seemed eager to wreak their revenge on the destroyers of their village.

No attempt was made to put out the flames; indeed, so rapidly did they extend among the combustible materials of which they were constructed, that the whole of the huts standing within reach of each other were quickly burned to the ground. We now ventured to accompany Oria and her mother out of the fort. They were met by Maono, who received them in calm Indian fashion, without giving way to any exhibition of feeling. He, indeed, seemed to have some sad intelligence to communicate. Whatever it was, they soon recovered, and now seemed to be telling him how much they owed their preservation to us—at least we supposed so by the way he took our hands and pressed them to his breast. After some time the rest of the warriors returned, and, as far as we could judge, they must have destroyed the greater number of their enemies. Maono showed more feeling when he spoke to his son, who gave him an account of what had occurred. As we hoped to learn more from our young friend than from any one else, we set to work, as soon as we could detach him from his companions, to make him give us an account of the expedition.

As far as we could understand, Maono and his brother with their followers had been unable for some time to fall in with the enemy. At length they met them in the neighbourhood of their own village, when a fierce battle had been fought according to Indian fashion. Several men had been killed on both sides, and among others who fell, pierced by a poisoned arrow, was Duppo's uncle, whose musket also had been captured. Several others had been taken prisoners, and, the lad added with a shudder, had been carried off to be eaten. In the meantime, it turned out, another party of the Majeronas, hoping to find our friend's village unprotected, had made their way through the forest to surprise it.

It was very satisfactory to us, at all events, to find that we had been the means of protecting the families of these friendly Indians. They took the burning of their village very calmly, and at once set to work to put up shelter for the night; fires were lighted, and the women began to cook the provisions they had saved. Maono invited us to partake of the meal which his wife and daughter had got ready. We would rather have set off at once to the camp, but night was now coming on, and when we proposed going, Duppo seemed very unwilling that we should do so. We understood him to say that we might encounter jaguars or huge snakes, and we should be unable to see our way through the dark avenue of trees. As Ellen did not expect us to return, we agreed at length to follow his advice. I observed that our friends sent out scouts—apparently to watch lest any of the enemy should venture to return—a precaution I was very glad to see taken.

As far as we could understand, the expedition had been far from successful, as none of the canoes had been recovered, and our friends did not even boast that they had gained a victory. From the terrible character Duppo gave of the enemy, they perhaps had good reason to be thankful that they had escaped without greater loss.

Chapter Eleven
Dangers by land and water—A new friend found

Our Indian friends, although their people are generally so undemonstrative, endeavoured by every means in their power to show their gratitude to us for the service we had rendered them. When we offered to pay for the canoe, which we were anxious to retain, Maono entreated us to accept it, intimating that he would settle with the owner. We were very glad to obtain the little craft; for, though too small for our voyage down the Amazon, it would enable us to carry out our project of searching the neighbouring shores for our parents. Though we had not preserved their village from destruction, we had certainly saved the lives of their women and children, and did not therefore hesitate about accepting the canoe as a gift.

The chiefs sat up the greater part of the night, holding a council. Next morning it was evident that they had arrived at some important determination. The inhabitants were busy collecting their scattered goods, and doing them up in portable packages. When we explained to them that we were anxious to set off immediately for our own camp, they intimated that they purposed accompanying us. As this, however, would have delayed us greatly, we got Duppo to explain that we would gladly meet them again at any spot they might appoint, but that we would go down by the igarape in the canoe.

A hurried meal having been taken, we prepared to embark. Meantime the men were employed in loading the women and children with their goods. We thought that they were reserving some of the heavier loads for themselves; but this, we soon found, was not the case, as they were placed on the backs of the stronger women. Even our hostess—the chief's wife—had to shoulder a load; and we felt very indignant when we saw that Oria had to carry one also.

"I say, Harry, don't you think we ought to save her from that?" exclaimed Arthur. "I am sure I would gladly carry it for her."

"You would somewhat astonish her if you made the offer," observed John; "and I suspect you would fall in the estimation of our warrior friends. Their creed is different from ours. They consider it derogatory to manhood to carry a load or to do more work than they can help. However, as Ellen would perhaps like to have Oria with her, we might induce her parents to let her accompany Duppo. We cannot do without him, at all events."

We tried to explain our proposal to Duppo, and after some time he comprehended us. Oria, however, seemed very unwilling to accept the offer, as she clung to her mother, and turned away her head from us. Duppo at length came back, and we all got into the canoe. Our friends insisted on our taking as many articles of food as we could possibly carry—dried fish and meat, bananas and farinha, as well as fruit and vegetables. True as usual took his seat in the bows. We were just shoving off, when Maono and his wife came down to us leading Oria. The chief addressed us and his son, but what he said we could not of course understand. However we agreed that it was all right, and Duppo seemed highly pleased when his sister stepped into the canoe and took her seat in front of him.

Bidding our friends adieu, we now began carefully to paddle down the igarape. We were some time in sight of the village, the whole inhabitants of which we saw moving off, the men stalking first, with their bows and spears in their hands and their blow-pipes at their backs, and the women following, bending under the weight of the loads they carried. Even the children, except the smallest, who sat on their mother's backs or were led by the hand, carried packages.

"I am very glad we have saved the poor girl a heavy trudge through the forest," observed Arthur; "but I cannot say much for the chivalry of these people. I was inclined to think favourably of the warriors when I saw them going forth so bravely to battle, but the example they have given us of the way they treat their women lowers them sadly in my estimation."

"Very true, Arthur," remarked John. "It is a sure sign that a people have fallen into a degraded and uncivilised condition when women do not hold an honourable position among them. But there are some savages who treat their females even worse than these do. From what I have seen, they appear in many respects kind and gentle to them. The Australian savage—who is, however, the lowest in the scale of civilisation—when he wants a wife, watches till he finds a damsel to his taste, and then knocks her down with his club, a sign to her that she is henceforth to be a submissive and dutiful wife. I am sure our friends here would not be guilty of such an act."

"No; I hope not indeed," exclaimed Arthur. "Dreadful to think that Oria should have to submit to such treatment."

We had, as may be supposed, to paddle carefully to prevent running against a bough or sunken trunk, as the least touch might have upset our frail craft. Though we might easily have scrambled out, yet we should have run the risk of losing our guns and wetting our ammunition; besides which, an alligator might have been lurking near, and seized one of us in its jaws before we could escape to land. These considerations made us very careful in our navigation. After some time, we began to feel sadly cramped from being unable to move. Oria sat quiet and silent, close to her brother, somewhat surprised, I dare say, at finding herself carried away by the three white strangers. John told us to keep our tongues steady in the middle of our mouths, lest we should make the canoe heel over; and, indeed, if we leant ever so slightly on one side the water began to ripple over the gunwale. Duppo steered very carefully; and I, having the bow paddle, kept a very bright look-out ahead for any danger which might appear under water. I could not help thinking of the big cow-fish we had seen, and dreading lest one of them coming up the igarape might give the canoe an unintentional shove with his snout, which would most inevitably have upset her.

Thus we went on. The lagoon was passed, and again we entered the channel with the thick trees arching overhead. How cool and pleasant was the shade after the heat of the sun to which we had been exposed in the more open parts! As we approached the camp our anxiety to ascertain that all was well increased. The nearer we got the more I longed to see the smiling face of our dear little sister, and I thought of the pleasure she would have when we introduced Oria to her. At length we could see in the far distance the landing-place near the camp. In our eagerness we forgot our caution, and very nearly sent the canoe under water. "Be more careful, boys," cried John, though he was paddling as hard as either of us. As we drew near I looked out for the raft at the spot we had left her moored, but could not see her. An uncomfortable misgiving came over me, yet I could not bear to think that any accident had happened. I said nothing, and on we went.

"Why, where is the raft?" exclaimed John.

"Oh, perhaps Domingos has drawn her up on the bank," observed Arthur.

"That is more than he would have strength to do," said John. "Besides, I can see the bank, and the raft is not there."

As we drew near we raised a shout to attract Domingos, True joining us with one of his cheerful barks. No one answered.

"Domingos has probably gone out shooting," observed Arthur. "We shall see your sister and Maria running down directly."

We looked eagerly towards the camp, but neither Ellen nor Maria appeared. We at length clambered out of the canoe up the bank, leaving Duppo to help out his sister, and on we ran, breathless with anxiety, to ascertain what had happened. The huts stood as we had left them, but the occupants were not there. We looked about. The goods had been carried off. Had the Indians been there—or had Ellen and her attendants fled? These were the fearful questions we asked ourselves. If the Indians had come, where had they carried our sister, and what had they done with her? We searched around in every direction. No signs of violence were to be discovered. Yet, unless the Indians had come, why should they have fled. The savage Majeronas would certainly have burned down the huts. True was running about as surprised as we were to find no one there. Now he ran into Ellen's hut, then searched about in the surrounding wood, and came back to us, as if he could not make up his mind what had happened. Duppo and Oria now arrived, having waited at the bank to secure the canoe. We tried to make Duppo understand that we wanted to know his opinion. Though very intelligent for an Indian, we could seldom judge his thoughts by the expression of his countenance. At last he comprehended us, but made no reply. After waiting an instant, he went into Ellen's hut, and then, as True had done, examined the surrounding thickets. At last he came back and had a talk with Oria. They seemed to have arrived at some conclusion. We watched them anxiously. Then we asked Duppo if the Majeronas had been there. He shook his head, and then, taking my hand, led me back to the water, narrowly examining the ground as he went. On reaching the igarape he pointed down towards the great river. I understood him.

"John! Arthur!" I shouted out, "they have gone that way on the raft. I am sure of it from Duppo's signs. Perhaps they have not got to any great distance, and we may overtake them."

"Stay," said John; "perhaps they are hiding somewhere near. We will shout out, and they may hear us."

"There is no use in doing that," I remarked. "Had the raft still been here I might have thought so, but it is evident that they have gone away on it. It would easily carry them and all our goods, and for some reason or other Domingos has persuaded them to escape on it, hoping that we should follow."

"Would not Ellen have left a note for us, or some sign, to show us where they have gone to," observed John in a desponding tone. "That she has not done so puzzles me more than anything else."

To satisfy John, we all shouted at the top of our voices again and again; but no reply came. We were going to get into the canoe, when Duppo showed us that we might prepare it with a little contrivance for encountering the rougher water of the river. Some sipos were near. These he cut down, and with Oria's assistance bound into two long bundles, which he neatly secured to the gunwale of the canoe, completely round her. By this means the sides were raised four or five inches, and would thus, I saw, greatly assist to keep out the water, and at the same time would enable her to float, even should she be partly filled. Duppo now beckoned to us to get into her. We took our seats as before, and once more we paddled down the igarape. Duppo's contrivance completely kept out the water, which would otherwise have broken on board; and we had no longer any fear of driving the canoe as fast as we could through it. We soon reached the open river.

"Which way shall we turn—up or down the stream?" I asked.

"Down, certainly," said John; "the raft could not have gone up it."

We accordingly made signs to Duppo to turn the canoe's head towards the east. Before us appeared the island on which we so narrowly escaped being wrecked during the hurricane. We steered down near the mainland, examining narrowly the shores on either side. No raft could we see, nor any one on the land. The water was smooth in the channel through which we were passing, but when we got to the end of it, we found the surface rippled over with waves, which, although small, threatened to be dangerous to our deeply-laden little craft. I proposed that we should, notwithstanding, endeavour to paddle up along the other side of the island, in case Ellen and her companions might have landed on it. We made signs to Duppo to steer in that direction; but he, instead of doing so, pointed to a spot some way down the river, signifying to as that he wished to land there. We concluded that it was the place where his father had appointed to meet him. "Perhaps he sees the raft; it may have drifted there," exclaimed Arthur. "At all events, I am sure it will be better to do as he proposes."

We accordingly paddled on under Duppo's pilotage. Now that we were exposed to the breeze blowing across the river, our heavily-laden canoe could with difficulty contend with the waves, which, in spite of the raised gunwale, every now and then broke into her. Had it not been for the young Indian's thoughtful contrivance, we should inevitably have been swamped. After going on for some distance, we reached the mouth of another igarape. Just outside it, facing the river, was a small open space, free of trees, with a fringe of rushes growing between it and the water. With some little difficulty we forced the canoe through the rushes, and we then, by scrambling up the bank, reached the spot I have described. Duppo made signs to us that it was here he wished to remain for the arrival of his father.

"We may as well do as he proposes then," said John, "and we will set off and look for the raft. If we do not find it—which Heaven forbid!—we will return and obtain the assistance of the Indians in making a more extended search."

The spot was a very beautiful one, open entirely to the river in front, while the trees behind, not growing so closely together as usual, allowed the air to circulate—a very important consideration in that hot climate. "It is just the place I should have chosen for an encampment while we are searching for our father," said John. Arthur and I agreed with him; but as we were eager to be off again, we had no time to talk about the matter. Landing the greater part of the provisions, we explained our intentions to our young friends. They understood us, but seemed unwilling to be left behind. John also proposed that Arthur should remain on shore. "I will do as you wish," he answered; "but I do not like to be separated from you." While we were speaking, standing on the bank, looking out over the river, he exclaimed, "See, see! what is that speck out there towards the other side?" We eagerly looked in the direction he pointed.

"I am afraid it is only the trunk of a tree, or a mass of grass floating down," said John.

"Oh no, no! I am nearly sure there are people on it!" cried Arthur, whose eyes, as we had found, were keener than ours.

"At all events, we will go towards it," cried John.

We hurried down and slipped into the canoe. "Yes; I know that you may go faster without me," said Arthur. "You know what I should like to do; but if it is better, I will remain on shore."

We thanked him for his self-denial, and I was about to propose leaving Truc with him, when the dog settled the point by jumping in. John and I shoved off, and paddled on with all our might. Now that we had fewer people on board, we made much better way than before, and floated buoyantly over the mimic seas which met us. We had marked the direction of the object we had seen. From the water it was at first scarcely visible. As we went on we again caught sight of it. How anxiously we watched it! One moment I thought it must be the raft, the next I was afraid it was but the trunk of a tree, or a flat island of grass. How I longed for a spy-glass to settle the point, but unfortunately we possessed none. For some minutes neither John nor I spoke.

"Harry!" he exclaimed, at length, "I see some one waving. Yes, yes; I am sure it is the raft!"

I strained my eyes to the utmost. I too thought I saw people on the object ahead of us. If people they were, they were sitting down though.

"Probably Domingos is afraid of standing up," said John. Then I remarked this to him. "I am glad the wind is across the river instead of up it, or it would be fearfully dangerous for them."

"Then you do think it is the raft?" I asked.

"I am sure of it," answered John.

We redoubled our efforts. Every instant the object grew clearer and clearer. We could scarcely be deceived.

"Heaven be praised!" exclaimed John; "I see Ellen and Maria, one on each side, and Domingos working away with his paddle at one end. They are trying to come towards us."

I saw them too, and could even make out Nimble, and Toby, and Poll, and Niger. My heart leaped with joy. In a few minutes more we were up to the raft.

"We will not stop to ask questions," exclaimed John, as we got alongside. "Here, Maria; hand me your painter, and we will secure it to ours, and tow you back to the north bank. You must tell us what has happened as we go along."

"Oh, but Arthur! why is Arthur not with you? Has anything happened to him?" exclaimed Ellen.

"No; he is all right," answered John, pointing to the shore.

While he was speaking, we transferred our painter to the stern of the canoe, and secured it as a tow-rope to the raft. We put the canoe's head the way we wished to go, and paddled on. The wind was in our favour; and Domingos, with Ellen and Maria, worked away with their paddles also on the raft. We were exerting ourselves too much to speak. Our dear sister was safe; but yet it was somewhat difficult to restrain our curiosity to know what had occurred. The wind was increasing every moment; and as we neared the shore we saw that there might be some danger of the water washing over the raft should we attempt to land under the bank. I proposed, therefore, that we should steer for the igarape. It was no easy matter, however, to get there, as the current was carrying us down. Domingos tried to urge the raft in the direction we wished to go. The wind continued to increase, and the current swept us further and further to the east. The seas rising, tossed the raft, now on the one side, now on the other; and every moment I dreaded that those on it might be thrown off or washed away. We entreated them to hold on tightly. Even the canoe, though before the wind, was tossed considerably. We could now distinguish our friends on shore watching us anxiously as we approached. Already we had drifted down below them. They were trying to make their way through the forest to follow us.

"We must drift down till we can see some place where we can get on shore with a prospect of safety," observed John.

I agreed with him that it was our only alternative; yet I knew that sometimes for miles together along the banks such a place might not be found. We turned the head of the canoe, however, down the stream, anxiously looking out for a fit spot to land. I dreaded, as I cast a look over my shoulder at the sky, that such a hurricane as we had before encountered was brewing; and if so, our prospect of being saved was small indeed. I saw that Domingos also was casting a glance back at the sky. We could see the tall trees on shore bending before the blast. Every moment our position became more and more perilous. If landing in the daylight was difficult, it would be still more so to get on shore in the dark.

Down the mighty river we floated. The last rays of the sun came horizontally over the waters, tinging the mimic waves with a bright orange hue. Then gradually they assumed a dull, leaden tint, and the topmost boughs of the more lofty trees alone caught the departing light. Still no harbour of refuge appeared. I proposed running in, as the last desperate resource, and scrambling on shore while we could still see sufficiently to find our way.

"We shall lose our goods, and the canoe, and the raft, if we make the attempt," answered John, "and perhaps our lives. We must still try to find a safe place to land at."

We were yet at some distance from the shore, though, driven by the fierce wind, we were rapidly approaching it. The storm increased. Dark clouds were gathering overhead. A bright flash of lightning darted from them, crackling and hissing as it went along the water: another, and another followed. Suddenly, as if a thick mantle had been thrown over us, it became dark, and we could scarcely have distinguished an opening in the forest had one been before us. John was more unwilling than ever to risk landing; and we therefore steered down the river, parallel with the shore, so as to prevent the raft as long as possible from being driven against it.

"Paddle on, Harry!" cried John, with his usual coolness; "we may yet find a harbour of refuge."

We could judge pretty well, by the varying outline of the leafy wall close to us, that we were making rapid way. The wind, too, had shifted more to the west, and drove us therefore still before it. Arthur and our Indian friends would, I knew, be in despair at not seeing us land; while it was certain that they could not keep pace with the raft, as they had to make their way through the tangled forest. Now that darkness had come on, they would probably be compelled to stop altogether.

The wind blew harder. The raft was tossed fearfully about. Another rattling peal of thunder and more vivid flashes of lightning burst from the clouds. Maria shrieked out with terror; while the two monkeys clung to her, their teeth chattering—as alarmed as she was, Ellen afterwards told me. Then again all was silent.

"I am afraid, Harry, we must make the attempt," said John at last. "But the risk is a fearful one. We must tell Ellen, Domingos, and Maria to be prepared.—Be ready, dear Ellen!" cried John. "Hold on tightly; and when I call to you, spring towards me. We must manage by some means to get on shore. Domingos will help Maria. Harry will try to secure the guns and ammunition; our existence may depend upon them. The animals must take care of themselves.—Domingos, are you ready?" he asked, in Spanish.

"Si, si, Señor John. But look there, master; what is that light on shore? It must come from some hut surely, where we may obtain shelter. Let us try to reach the place. Even if there are savages there, they will not refuse to help us."

As he spoke, we observed a bright light bursting forth from among the trees, at a short distance off along the bank. Now it disappeared—now it came again in sight. We paddled down towards it. It was apparently a torch held in a person's hand. We rapidly approached the light, but yet failed to discover any place where we could land with safety. We shouted loudly, hoping to attract the attention of any one who might be near. Presently a hail came off the land. We answered it. Again a voice was heard.

"Can you tell us where we can land with safety?" cried John, in Spanish.

The answer was unintelligible. Presently he asked again in English; and in a little time we saw the light moving along the bank. Then it remained stationary. We exerted ourselves to the utmost to steer for it; and we now saw a division in the wall of trees, which indicated that there was a passage between them. Again the thunder reared, the lightning flashed, and the wind blew with fearful force.

Maria shrieked loudly, "The water is washing over the raft!"

"Hold on! hold on!" cried John; "we shall soon be in safety." And in another minute we were entering the mouth of a narrow channel. "We will turn the canoe round," said John, "and let the raft go first. We may thus prevent it being dashed on the bank."

We did as he advised. Scarcely, however, had we turned the raft round when we found it had reached the shore.

"Do you, Domingos, help the señora and Maria to land!" shouted John.

By the light from the torch we saw a tall figure standing on the bank. He flung the light so that it might fall across us.

"Females!" he exclaimed. "A sorry night to be buffeting with the waves of the Amazon! Give me your hands, whoever you are. I should little have expected to find my countrymen in such a plight in this remote region."

While he was speaking he helped Ellen and Maria up the bank, the two monkeys following, while Poll and Niger clung fast to Maria's shoulders. Faithful True did not attempt to leap on shore, though he could easily have done so, but remained with me in the canoe. Domingos, meantime, was hastily throwing our goods on shore; while we continued exerting ourselves in preventing the raft being lifted by the force of the water and upset on the bank.

"All the things are safely landed," cried Domingos at length.

We then, casting off the tow-rope, paddled round, and ran the bow of the canoe on shore. Not till then did True leap out of her. Domingos and the stranger coming down, helped us to drag her out of the water.

"We may save the raft also," said the latter. "You may require it to continue your voyage; as I conclude you do not intend to locate yourselves here, and compel me to seek another home in the wilderness."

I was struck by the morose tone in which the stranger spoke. He, however, assisted us in dragging up the raft sufficiently high to prevent its being knocked about by the waves, which ran even into the comparatively smooth part of the channel in which we found ourselves.

"We heartily thank you for your assistance," said John. "We owe the preservation of our lives to you; for, with the increasing storm, we could scarcely have escaped destruction had we been driven further down the river."

"You owe me no thanks, young sir. I would have done the same for a party of benighted savages, as you call them," answered the stranger. "Your dumb companions are equally welcome. I am not ill pleased to see them. It speaks in your favour that they follow you willingly, instead of being dragged about with ropes and chains, or confined in cages, as civilised men treat the creatures they pretend to tame. I have, however, but poor shelter to offer you from the deluge which will soon be down on our heads. Follow me; there is no time to be lost."

"But we must not allow our goods to remain out," said John.

"I will assist you, then, to carry them," answered the stranger, lifting up double the number of packages which we usually carried at a time.

We then all loaded ourselves. Ellen insisted on carrying a package, and followed the stranger, who went before us with his torch. We could not even then exchange words, as we had to proceed in single file along a narrow pathway, fringed on either side with thick shrubs—apparently the after-growth of a cleared spot, soon to spring up again into tall trees. We soon found ourselves within the forest, where, so dense was the gloom, that without the torch to guide us we could not have made our way. Its ruddy flame glanced on the trunks of the tall trees, showing a canopy of wide-spreading boughs overhead, and the intricate tracery of the numberless sipos which hung in festoons, or dropped in long threadlike lines from them. Passing for a few yards through a jungle, the boughs spreading so closely above our heads that we often had to stoop, we found ourselves in an open space, in which by the light of the torch we saw a small hut with deep eaves, the gable end turned towards us. It was raised on posts several feet from the ground. A ladder led to a platform or verandah, which projected from the wall of the gable, in which was a small door.

"Here you are welcome to stow your goods and rest for the night," said the stranger. "No human being but myself has ever entered it; for I seek not the society of my fellow-men, either savage or civilised, so-called. To-morrow, if the weather clears, you will, I conclude, proceed on your way; or if you insist on remaining, I must seek another home. Let that be understood, before I make you further welcome. Now, enter, and such accommodation as my hut affords shall be yours."

There was something in the tone of the speaker which, though his dress was rough and strange, made us feel that he was a man of education.

"We cordially thank you, sir," answered John, "and accept your hospitality on the terms you propose; but as a portion of our goods still remain near the river, we would ask you to give us another torch to enable us to fetch them before the rain comes done."

"I will myself accompany you," he answered, "when I have introduced the young people to my abode."

Saying this, he stepped up the ladder, and assisted Ellen and Maria to reach the platform. He then led the way in, and lighted a lamp which stood—we could see through the open door—on a table near it.

"I am sorry I have no better accommodation to offer you," he said, looking at Ellen; "but such as it is, you are welcome to it."

He came down with another torch in his hand, and proceeded with rapid strides back to the river. We had some difficulty in following him. Again he took up a heavy load; and we, dividing the remainder of the goods between us, followed him towards the hut. Ascending the ladder as we reached it, he desired us to hand up the goods, which he carried within. As soon as we were on the platform, he drew up the ladder.

"I always secure myself thus in my fortress at night," he remarked; "and as I have taken means of preventing any snakes crawling up the posts on which it stands, I can sleep more securely than many do in the so-called civilised portion of the globe."

On entering the house, we found that it was larger than we had supposed from its appearance outside. It was divided into two rooms. The outer was fitted up, in somewhat rustic style, as a sitting-room, while we concluded that the inner one was a sleeping-room. Round the walls were arranged shelves, on one of which were a considerable number of books, with a variety of other articles. In one corner was a pile of nets and harpoons, and some spears and other weapons for the chase; in another stood an Indian mill for grinding flour, and several jars and other articles, apparently for preparing or preserving food. Against the walls stood several chests. Though the table was large enough for the whole of us to sit round it, yet there was but one stool, showing that our host, as he had told us, was unaccustomed to receive guests. He, however, pulled the chests forward, and by placing some boards between them, we all found seats.

"If you have not brought provisions, I will supply you while you stay with me," he observed; "but my own consumption is so small that I have but a limited amount to offer you."

"We would not willingly deprive you of that, sir," said John; "and we have enough to last us till we can supply ourselves with more."

"That is fortunate," remarked the recluse. "While your servant gets it ready, I will prepare my room for the young lady and her attendant. I have no cooking-place under shelter, and while the rain is pouring down, as it will begin to do presently, a fire cannot be lighted outside. You must therefore be content with a cold repast."

While the recluse—so I may call him—was absent, we for the first time had an opportunity of asking Ellen what had occurred to drive her and her attendants away from the camp.

"I was indeed unwilling to do so," she said, "till urged by Domingos. He had gone to shoot at a short distance from the hut, when he came hurrying back with a look of alarm, and told me that he had caught sight of some savages making their way through the forest. He insisted that they were trying to find us out, and that our only hope of safety was by instant flight. I pleaded that you would come back, and finding us gone, would fancy we had been carried off or killed. He argued that on your return, finding the raft gone, you would know we had embarked on it. At length he agreed, that if we would assist to carry the goods down to the raft he would again search round the camp, and should the natives appear to be going in a different direction, we might carry them back again. He had not gone long, when he returned with dismay on his countenance, asserting that they were coming towards us, and that if we did not escape we should certainly be killed. You may suppose, my dear brothers, how fearfully agitated I was. I knew how alarmed you would be on returning not to find us, and yet, if we should remain it might be still worse. Domingos and Maria settled the matter by seizing me by the arms, and dragging me to the raft before I had time to write a note or leave any signal. I scarcely thought, indeed, of doing so, till Domingos had pushed the raft off from the bank. I entreated him to go back; but he replied that it was impossible without the risk of being caught by the savages, and began paddling the raft down the channel. I looked back, and seeing no natives, again urged him to return. He replied that he was sure they would lie in ambush to catch us, and that it would be destruction to do so. Feeling that he wished to secure my safety, I could not complain. He did his best, too, to comfort me about you. He said that as you were probably with the friendly natives, you would be defended from the Majeronas; and that by the time you had come back, those he had seen would have gone away, and you would certainly guess that we were not far off. I did my utmost to arouse myself and to assist Maria and him in paddling the raft. The wind was light, the water smooth, and there appeared to be no danger in venturing out into the river. A light wind was in our favour, and he accordingly steered towards the opposite bank, saying that we should be safer there than anywhere else, and might more easily get back than by going down the stream. I looked frequently towards the shore we had left, but still saw no natives. Poor Domingos was evidently anxious about you, though he did his best not to alarm me more than he had done already. We found, after getting some way across, that the current was floating us down much faster than we had expected, and I begged Domingos therefore to return. He insisted that, having got thus far, it was better to continue our course towards the southern bank, and wait there for a favourable wind for getting back. I was thankful when at length we reached a sandy beach, where we could land without difficulty and secure our raft. Domingos fortunately shot a paca, so we had plenty of food; and Maria and I assisted him in putting up a hut. Had I not been so anxious about you, I should have had no cause to complain. They both exerted themselves to the utmost; and I do not think Domingos closed his eyes all night, for whenever I awoke I saw him, through an opening in our hut, walking about or making up the fire. We spent the morning on the bank, watching in the hope of seeing you come to look for us. As soon as the wind changed, I entreated Domingos to put off, and at last, though somewhat unwillingly, he consented to do so; but he blamed himself very much for yielding to my wishes, when the wind began to blow so violently. Had you, indeed, not arrived to assist us, I suspect that our raft would have been in great danger of being overwhelmed."

"We have reason to be thankful, dear Ellen, that you were preserved," said John. "I am very sure Domingos acted for the best. I wish for your sake that our expedition had come to a favourable end, although the rest of us may enjoy it."

"Oh, if it were not for anxiety about papa and mamma, and dear Fanny, and Aunt Martha, I should like it too," said Ellen. "When we once find them, I am sure that I shall enjoy our voyage down the river as much as any of you."

"You are a brave girl," said the stranger, who at that moment returned, "though, perhaps, you scarcely know the dangers you may have to encounter. Yet, after all, they are of a nature more easily overcome than many which your sisters in the civilised regions of the world are called to go through. Here you have only the elements and a few wild beasts to contend with; there, they have falsehood, treachery, evil example, allurements of all sorts, and other devices of Satan, to drag them to destruction."

While we were seated at supper, the rain came down in tremendous torrents, as the recluse had predicted. The strength of his roof was proved, as not a drop found its way through.

"I am protected here," he remarked, "from the heat of the summer months by the leafy bower overhead; while, raised on these poles, my habitation is above the floods in the rainy season. What can man want more? Much in the same way the natives on the Orinoco form their dwellings among the palm-trees; but they trust more to Nature, and, instead of piles, form floating rafts, sufficiently secured to the palm-trees to keep them stationary, but rising and falling as the floods increase or diminish."

I was struck with many of the remarks of our eccentric host, but the more I saw of him the more I was surprised that a man of his information should have thus secluded himself from the world. We had just time to give Ellen an account of our adventures, when he expressed his wish that we should hang up our hammocks, as it was past his usual hour for retiring to rest. This was an operation quickly performed, as we had only to secure them in the usual way to the posts which supported the roof.

"We should not part," said Ellen, somewhat timidly, "without our usual prayer; and we have cause to thank God for our preservation from danger."

The recluse looked at her fixedly. "You are in earnest, I am sure," he muttered. "Pray, young people, do not depart from your usual custom; I will wait for you."

Arthur, I should have said, though the youngest, always led us in prayer. "As he is absent," I remarked to Ellen's request, "I will do so."

"Oh, you have a young chaplain with you," said the recluse; "and what pay does he receive?"

"None at all, sir," answered Ellen. "He is only earnest and good."

"I should like to meet him," said the recluse.

"I hope you may, sir," said Ellen, "if you come with us."

A short prayer was offered up. I spoke with the earnestness I felt. Ellen then read a portion of Scripture from the Bible she had always at hand in her trunk. Our host listened attentively, his eyes fixed on our young sister. I had not observed a copy of the blessed Book on his shelves. He made no remark, however, on the subject, but I thought his tone was less morose than before.

We were soon in our hammocks, a small oil lamp, which was kept burning on the table, throwing a subdued light through the chamber. True, I should have said, from our first meeting with the stranger, had eyed him askance, having apparently some doubts as to his character. He now came and coiled himself up in his usual position under my hammock. He had kept as far off from him as he could during the evening, and did not seem satisfied till the tall figure of the recluse was stretched out in his hammock near the entrance of the hut. The rain pattering overhead, and splashing down on the soft ground round us, kept me for some time awake. It ceased at length, and soon afterwards, just as I was dropping off to sleep, a chorus of hideous sounds commenced, coming apparently from no great distance in the forest. Now they resembled the cries and groans of a number of people in distress. Now it seemed as if a whole troop of jaguars were growling and snarling over their prey. Now it seemed as if a company of Brobdignag cats were singing a serenade. Now the sounds for a moment ceased, but were instantly taken up again by other creatures at a distance. After a time, the same sounds recommenced in another quarter. Had I not already been well accustomed to similar noises, I might have fancied that we had got into some forest haunted by evil spirits bewailing their lost condition. I was sufficiently awake, however, to guess that they proceeded only from troops of howling monkeys, though we had never yet heard them so near, or in such numbers. In spite of the hideous concert, I at last fell asleep.

The voice of our host aroused us at daybreak. "As soon as you have broken your fast, I will accompany you to find your companions," he said, "unless you desire to proceed by water. In that case, you will scarcely meet them; but I would advise you to leave your canoe and raft here, as I can conduct you through the forest by the only open paths which exist, and by which alone they can make their way in this direction. I am afraid, unless they had their wits about them, they must have been exposed to the tempest last night, and may be but ill able to travel far this morning."

John at once decided to go by land, as the canoe was not large enough to convey all our party. The recluse looked at Ellen. "She will scarcely be able to undergo the fatigue of so long a walk," he remarked. "If she wishes it, she and her attendant can remain here, while we go to meet your companions; and you can then return and remove your property, or leave it till you can find the means of continuing your voyage. I did not purpose to allow my solitude to be thus broken in on; but," —and he looked again at Ellen— "she reminds me of days gone by, and I cannot permit her to be exposed to more trials than are necessary."

John thanked him for his proposal, though Ellen seemed unwilling to remain behind. We also did not like to leave her. At last John suggested that Domingos should remain also. The recluse pressed the point with more warmth than I should have expected, and at last Ellen agreed to do as was proposed. She was certainly better off in a well-built hut than she had been for some time, and strange and eccentric as the recluse appeared, still we felt that he was disposed to assist us to the best of his power.

Our early breakfast over, John and I, shouldering our rifles, followed by True, set off with the recluse. Ellen looked rather sad as we were going.

"You will find poor Arthur? I know you will," she said in a low voice to me. "I thought of him a great deal last night, out in the fierce tempest, with only two young Indians to assist him; and he is not so strong as you are, and has no gun to defend himself. I could not help thinking of fierce jaguars roaming in search of prey, or those dreadful boas, or the anacondas we have heard of."

"Oh, drive all such thoughts from your mind, Ellen," I answered. "Arthur, if not so strong, has plenty of sense and courage; and, depend upon it, the Indians will have found some hollow tree, or will have built a hut for themselves, in which they would have taken shelter during the night. I should not have minded changing places with Arthur. It is all right. We will bring him back safe enough."

With these words I hurried after John and the recluse. We had not gone far, when I saw them looking up into a tree. True darted forward and began to bark, when, in return, a chorus of terrific barks, howls, and screeches proceeded from the higher branches, and there I saw seated a group of several large monkeys with long tails and most hideous faces. Every instant they threw up their heads, and the fearful sounds I had heard issued forth from them. I could scarcely suppose that animals of such a size could make so much noise.

"You have there some of my friends who serenaded you last night," observed the recluse, when, after a few minutes, the monkeys ceased howling. "These are the *mycétes*, or ursine howlers. The creature is called in this country *araguato*, and sometimes by naturalists the *alouatte*. It is known also as 'the preacher.' If he could discourse of sin and folly, and point out to benighted man the evil of his ways, he might howl to some purpose but his preaching is lost on the denizens of the forest, who know nothing of sin, and are free from the follies of the world. Observe that with how little apparent difficulty he gives forth that terrific note. It is produced by a drum-shaped expansion of the larynx. The hyoid bone, which in man is but slightly developed, is in these monkeys very large. It gives support to the tongue, being attached to the muscles of the neck. The bony drum communicates with the wind-pipe, and enables them to utter those loud sounds."

Had Arthur been with us, I am sure we should have indulged in a hearty laugh at the curious faces of those thick-jawed creatures as they looked down upon us inquisitively to ascertain what we were about. They were considerably larger than any we had seen; indeed, the howler is the largest monkey in the New World. The fur is of a rich bay colour, and as the sun fell upon the coats of some of them above us, they shone with a golden lustre. The thick beard which hung from the chin and neck was of a deeper hue than the body. Our friend told us that those he had caught were generally about three feet long, and that their tails in addition were of even greater length. We went on without disturbing the assemblage in their aerial seat, greatly to True's disappointment, who would evidently have liked to measure his strength with one of them. Like the spider monkeys, they live entirely in trees, making good use of their long tails as they move about from branch to branch; indeed, the tail serves the howler for another hand. When by any chance he descends to the ground, he moves along very awkwardly, and can easily be caught, as we afterwards discovered.

Our new acquaintance was but little inclined to talk; indeed, had he been so, we could seldom have enjoyed much conversation, as we were compelled in most places to follow him in Indian file. Now and then he had to use his hatchet to clear the path, and we very frequently had to force our way by pressing aside the branches which met in front of us. Still he went on without wavering for a moment, or appearing doubtful of the direction he should take. After going on some way further, he again stopped, and pointed to a tree, the branch of which rose a few feet off. I knew by the way True barked that some creature was there; and looking more narrowly, I observed some animals clinging to the lower branches, but so nearly did they resemble the bark to which they were holding, that had they not been pointed out to me I should have passed them by. The animals turned listless glances at us, and seemed in no way disposed to move.

"There," observed the recluse, "are creatures in every way adapted to the mode of life which they are doomed to lead. Place them in any other, and they will be miserable. You see there the *ai*, or three-toed sloth (the *Bradypus torquatus*). Though its arms, or fore-legs more properly, are nearly twice as long as the hinder ones, it finds them exactly suited for climbing the trees on which it lives. Place it on the ground, and it cannot get along. It passes its life, not above, but under the branches. When moving along, it suspends itself beneath them; when at rest, it hangs from them; and it sleeps clutching them with its strong claws, and its back hanging downwards."

One of the creatures was hanging as our friend described; the other was on its way up the tree. It stopped on seeing us approach, and turned its round short head, with deeply sunk eyes and a large nose, to look at us. The animals had long powerful claws on all their feet. The hair was very coarse and shaggy, more like grass or moss than anything else.

"The sloth suckles its young like other quadrupeds," observed our friend; "and I have often seen the female, with her little one clinging to her, moving at a rate through the forest which shows that the sloth does not properly deserve its name. See now—give a shout—and then say if it is too sluggish to more."

John and I shouted together, and True barked loudly. The sloths gave reproachful glances at us for disturbing them, and then began to move away at a speed which an active sailor running up the rigging of a ship could scarcely equal. In a short time, slinging themselves from branch to branch, they had disappeared in the depths of the forest.

"Let them go," observed our friend. "You do not want a meal, or you would find their flesh supply you with one not to be disdained." The last remark was made as we again moved on. Once more we relapsed into silence. When, however, a bird, or moth, or any creature appeared, our guide stopped for an instant, and turning round, told us its name and habits. We passed several curious trees, one of which he pointed out rising from the ground in numerous stalks, which then united in a thick stem, and afterwards, half-way up, bulged out in a long oval, again to narrow, till at the summit six or eight branches, with palm-like formed leaves, spread forth, forming a graceful crown to the curious stem. He called it the *Iriartes ventricosa*, or bulging-stemmed palm. Again we passed through a grove of urucuri palms (*Attalea excelsa*). Their smooth columnar stems were about forty or fifty feet in height, while their broad, finely pinnated leaves interlocked above, and formed arches and woven canopies of varied and peculiarly graceful shapes. High above them rose the taller forest trees, whose giant branches formed a second canopy to shade them from the glaring rays of the sun. Many of the trees rose eighty feet without a branch, their stems perfectly straight. Huge creepers were clinging round them, sometimes stretching obliquely from their summits, like the stays of a ship's mast. Others wound round their trunks, like huge serpents ready to spring on their prey. Others, again twisted spirally round each other, forming vast cables of living wood, holding fast those mighty monarchs of the forest. Some of the trees were so covered with smaller creepers and parasitic plants that the parent stem was entirely concealed. The most curious trees were those having buttresses projecting from their bases. The lower part of some of them extended ten feet or more from the base of the tree, reaching only five or six feet up the trunk. Others again extended to the height of fully thirty feet, and could be seen running up like ribs to a still greater height. Some of these ribs were like wooden walls, several inches in thickness, extended from the stem, so as to allow room for a good-sized hut to be formed between them by merely roofing over the top. Again, I remarked other trees ribbed and furrowed for their whole height. Occasionally these furrows pierced completely through the trunks, like the narrow windows of an ancient tower. There were many whose roots were like those of the bulging palm, but rising much higher above the surface of the ground. The trees appeared to be standing on many-legged pedestals, frequently so far apart from each other that we could without difficulty walk beneath them. A multitude of pendants hung from many of the trees, some like large wild pine-apples, swinging in the air. There were climbing arums, with dark-green arrow-head shaped leaves; huge ferns shot out here and there up the stems to the topmost branches. Many of the trees had leaves as delicately cut as those of the graceful mimosa, while others had large palmate leaves, and others, again, oval glossy ones.

Now and then, as I looked upwards, I was struck with the finely-divided foliage strongly defined against the blue sky, here and there lighted up by the bright sunshine; while, in the region below through which we moved, a deep gloom prevailed, adding grandeur and solemnity to the scene. There were, however, but few flowers; while the ground on which we walked was covered with dead leaves and rotten wood, the herbage consisting chiefly of ferns and a few grasses and low creeping plants.

We stopped at last to lunch, and while John and I were seated on the branch of a fallen tree, our friend disappeared. He returned shortly, with his arms full of large bunches of a round juicy berry. "Here," he said, "these will quench your thirst, and are perfectly wholesome." We found the taste resembling that of grapes. He called it the *purumá*. We were too eager to find Arthur to rest long, and were once more on our journey.

"From the account you gave me, I hope we may soon meet with your friends," observed the recluse, "unless they have turned back in despair of finding you."

"Little fear of that," I observed. "I am sure Arthur will search for us as long as he has strength to move."

Still we went on and on, and Arthur did not appear; and we asked our companion whether he did not think it possible that our friends might have tried to make their way along the bank of the river.

"No," he answered, "the jungle is there too thick; and if we find signs of their having made the attempt, we shall speedily overtake them; for though we have made a considerable circuit, they by this time could scarcely have progressed half a mile even with the active employment of sharp axes."

This somewhat comforted me; for notwithstanding what the recluse said, I felt nearly certain that Arthur would attempt to examine the whole length of the bank, in hopes of discovering what had become of us. We went on and on till we entered a denser part of the forest, where we were compelled to use our axes before we could get through. At length I caught sight through an opening of what looked like a heap of boughs at a distance. The recluse, quickening his pace, went on towards it. We eagerly followed. It was a hut roughly built. Extinguished embers of a fire were before it. We looked in eagerly. It was empty, but there were leaves on the ground, and dry grass, as if people had slept there. It had been, there was little doubt, inhabited by Arthur and his companions. It was just such a hut as they would have built in a hurry for defence against the storm. But what had become of them?

"I believe you are right," said the recluse at last, having examined the bushes round; "they certainly attempted to make their way along the bank. I trust no accident has happened to them, for in many places it is undermined by the waters, and after rain suddenly gives way." These remarks somewhat alarmed me. "This is the way they have taken, at all events," he added; "though they have managed to creep under places we might find some difficulty in passing." Again he led the way, clearing the path occasionally with his axe. We were close to the edge of the river, though so thickly grew the tangled sipos and the underwood that we could only occasionally get glimpses of it. As we went along we shouted out frequently, in hopes that Arthur might hear us.

"Your friend and his companions have laboured hard to get through this dense jungle," he observed, "but we shall soon overtake them."

Still on and on we went, now and then having to turn aside, being unable otherwise to force our way onwards. We at length, on returning to the river, found below us a sand-bank, which extended for some distance along it.

"Here are the marks of their feet!" exclaimed John, who had leaped down on it. "See the way they are turned! We shall soon overtake them."

This discovery restored my spirits, for I had begun to fear that after all, unable to get along, they had turned back. We hastened forward along the bank, but the sand was very soft, and walking on it was almost as fatiguing as through the forest; while the heat from the sun striking down on it was intense. Climbing up the bank once more, we proceeded through the forest. We went on a short distance, when we found ourselves in more open ground—that is to say, we could get on without the use of our axes. We continued shouting out, and every now and then making our way to the bank as before.

"Hark!" said John, "I hear a cry. See! there are natives coming towards us. Yes; I believe they are the two young Indians."

"They are Indians," remarked our guide. "They are beckoning us. We will hasten on."

In another minute we saw Duppo and Oria running towards us. They kept crying out words that I did not understand. As soon as they saw the recluse they hurried to him, and took his hands, as if they knew him well.

"They tell me your young friend is ill," he remarked. "They have left him a little further on, close to the water, where, it seems, unable to proceed, he fainted. They entreat me to hasten on lest he should die. They fancy I can do everything, having occasionally cured some of their people of slight diseases."

As he said this he allowed himself to be dragged forward by Duppo and his sister, who, in their eagerness, seemed scarcely to have recognised us. The ground over which we were proceeding was somewhat swampy, and sloped down to a small lagoon or inlet of the river. John and I followed as fast as we could at the heels of our guide. Presently he stopped, and uttering an exclamation, threw aside the hands of the young Indians and dashed forward. We followed, when, what was our horror to see, under a grove of mimosa bushes, Arthur in the grasp of a huge serpent, which had wound its coils round his body. I shrieked with dismay, for I thought he was dead. He moved neither hand nor foot, seemingly unconscious of what had occurred. The recluse dashed forward. John and I followed with our axes, and True went tearing boldly on before us. It was an anaconda. Already its huge mouth was open to seize our young companion. Without a moment's hesitation the recluse sprang at the monster, and seizing its jaws with a power I should scarcely have supposed he possessed, wrenched them back, and held them fast in spite of the creature's efforts to free itself. "Draw him out!" shouted the recluse; and John, seizing Arthur, drew him forth from amid the vast coils, while I with my axe struck blow after blow at its body and tail. The recluse did not let go his hold, although the creature, unwinding its tail, threatened to encircle him in its coils. Now it seemed as if it would drag him to the ground, but he recovered his feet, still bending back the head till I could hear the bones cracking. I meantime had been hacking at its tail, and at length a fortunate blow cut it off. John, placing Arthur at a little distance, came back to our assistance, and in another minute the reptile lay dead at our feet, when True flew at it and tore away furiously at its body.

"Your young friend has had a narrow escape," said the recluse, as he knelt down and took Arthur's hand; "he breathes, though, and is not aware of what has happened, for the anaconda must have seized him while he was unconscious."

We ran to the river. The dry shells of several large nuts lay near. In these we brought some water, and bathed Arthur's brow and face. "He seems unhurt by the embrace of the anaconda," remarked the recluse, "but probably suffered from the heat of the sun."

After this he lifted Arthur in his arms, and bore him up the bank. John and I followed with a shell of water. The contrast between the hot sandy bank and the shady wood was very great. As we again applied the water, Arthur opened his eyes. They fell on the recluse, on whom he kept them steadily fixed with a look of surprise.

"I thought John and Harry were with me," he murmured out. "I heard their voices calling as I lay fainting on the bank."

"Yes; we are here," John and I said, coming forward. "Duppo and his sister met us, and brought us to you."

"I am so glad," he said in a low voice. "I began to fear that you were really lost, we wandered on so far without finding you. I felt ready to die too, I was so sick at heart. And your sister—is she safe?" he asked. "Oh yes; I am sure you would look more sad if she were not."

"Yes, she is safe and well, Arthur," I said; "and we must take you there to be nursed, or, if it is too far to carry you, we must build a hut somewhere near here, where we can join you."

The stranger looked at Arthur, and murmured something we did not hear.

"It is a long way to carry the lad," he said; "though if I had him in my hut I would watch over him."

"Perhaps it may be better to build a hut at the spot we proposed, and bring our sister and goods to it," I said.

"No; I will take the lad to mine," answered the recluse. "You can build a hut as you proposed, and when he has recovered I will bring him to you."

I was very glad to hear this, because I was afraid that Arthur might suffer unless we could get him soon placed in a comfortable hammock, and give him better food than we should be able to prepare without our cooking apparatus.

"I am ready to go on whenever you wish it," observed Arthur, who heard the discussion; "but I am afraid I cannot walk very fast."

"I will carry you then," said the recluse; "but it will be better to form a litter, on which you can rest more at your ease. We will soon get one ready."

Duppo and Oria stood by watching us eagerly while we spoke, as if they were anxious to know what we were saying.

"You stay with your young friend, while your brother and I prepare the litter," said the recluse to me, replacing Arthur on the ground.

I sat down by his side, supporting him. He did not allude to the anaconda, and, I suspected, was totally unconscious of the danger he had been in. While the recluse and John were cutting down some poles to form the litter, Duppo and his sister collected a number of long thin sipos, showing that they understood what we proposed doing. In a short time the litter was completed. John and I insisted on carrying it, though we had some difficulty in persuading the recluse to allow us to do so. He spoke for some time to Duppo and his sister, who looked greatly disconcerted and sad.

"I was telling them that they must go and find their people," he said, "and that they must build a house for you on the spot you selected. They will be true friends to you, as they have ever been to me. I advise you to cultivate their friendship by treating them with kindness and respect."

The young Indians seemed very unwilling to take their departure, and lingered some time after we had wished them good-bye. John and I took up the litter, on which Arthur had been placed. As we had already cut a road for ourselves, we were able to proceed faster than we did when before passing through the forest. We hurried on, for the sun had begun to sink towards the west, and we might be benighted before we could reach the hermit's abode.

We proceeded by the way we had come. After we had gone some distance, Arthur begged that he might be put down and allowed to walk. "I am sure I have strength enough, and I do not like to see you carry me," he said. Of this, however, we would not hear, and continued on.

At last we sat down to rest. The spot we had chosen was a pleasant one. Though shaded, it was sufficiently open to allow the breeze to circulate through it. Round us, in most directions, was a thick jungle. We had brought some water in a shell of one of the large nuts, and after Arthur had drunk some, we induced him to take a little food, which seemed greatly to revive him. We were seated round the contents of our wallets, John and I, at all events, feeling in much better spirits than we had been in the morning; even the recluse threw off some of his reserve. We took the opportunity of telling him of our anxiety about our parents, and of the uncertainty we felt whether they had passed down the river. He in return asked us further questions, and seemed interested in our account.

"I may be of use to you," he said at length, "by being able to make inquiries among the Indians on the river, who would probably have observed them should they have passed; but promises are so often broken, that I am ever unwilling to make them. Therefore, I advise you to trust to your own exertions," he added.

We were on the point of again taking up Arthur to proceed, when a loud sound of crashing branches was heard in the distance. It seemed as if a hurricane was sweeping through the forest. It came nearer and nearer.

"Oh I what can it be?" cried Arthur. "Leave me and save yourselves. It seems as if the whole forest was falling."

The crashing increased. Boughs seemed broken off, shrubs trampled under foot. Presently we saw, bearing down upon as, a large dark-skinned creature, though its form could scarcely be distinguished amid the foliage.

"Stand fast!" said the recluse. "It will not harm you. See! it has an enemy to contend with."

As the creature drew nearer, I saw that it bore on its back a huge jaguar, distinguished by its spotted hide and its fierce glaring eyes. Its jaws were fixed in the creature's neck, to which it clung also with its sharp claws.

"The animal is a tapir," said the recluse. "I am not certain yet though whether the jaguar will conquer it. See, the back of the latter is bleeding and torn from the rough branches beneath which the tapir has carried it."

As he spoke, the animals came close to us, the tapir making for the thick branch of a fallen tree kept up by a network of sipos, which hung like a beam almost horizontally a few feet from the ground. The tapir dashed under it, and we could hear the crash of the jaguar's head as it came in contact with the hard wood. Still it clung on, but its eyes had lost their fierce glare. Blood covered the backs of the animals, and the next moment the jaguar fell to the ground, where it lay struggling faintly. Twice it tried to rise, but fell back, and lay apparently dead.

John had lifted his rifle to fire at the tapir. "Hold!" said the recluse; "let the victor go; he deserves his liberty for having thus sagaciously liberated himself from his tormentor. Would that we could as easily get rid of ours! How eagerly we should seek the lower branches of the trees!" He gave one of those peculiar, sarcastic laughs, which I observed he was apt to indulge in.

We cautiously approached the jaguar, feeling uncertain whether it might not yet rise up and spring at us. John and I kept our rifles at its head, while True went boldly up towards it. He had been an excited spectator of the scene, and I had some difficulty in keeping him from following the tapir. The jaguar did not move. Even a poke with the muzzle of my rifle failed to arouse it. True began to tear away at its neck; and at length we were convinced that the savage creature was really dead. "There let him lie," said the recluse. "Strong as he was a few moments ago, he will be food for the armadillos before morning."

We again lifted up Arthur, and proceeded onwards, the recluse leading and clearing away the branches which might have injured Arthur as we passed between them. Of course we now required a broader passage than when we came through ourselves. We took exactly the same route; our guide never faltering for a moment, though in many places I should have had difficulty, where the marks of our axes were not to be seen, in finding the road. Several times he offered to take my place, observing that I might be tired; but John and I begged him to allow us to carry our young friend, as we did not like to impose the task on him. Thus we went on till my arms and shoulders began to ache, but I determined not to give in. Arthur had not spoken for some time. I looked at his face. It was very pale, and his eyes were closed. I was afraid he had received more injury from the fearful serpent than we had at first supposed. We hurried on, for it was evidently very important that he should as soon as possible be attended to. We did not stop, therefore, a moment to rest. Thinking that he would not hear me, I expressed my fears to John. "Oh no, no," said Arthur; "I do not feel so very ill. I wish you would put me down, for I am sure you must be tired."

I was greatly relieved when I heard him speak; at the same time his voice was so weak, that we were unwilling to do as he begged us. It was getting late, too, as we could judge by the increasing gloom in the forest. Looking up through the occasional openings in the dark-green canopy above our heads, we could see the sky, which had now become of the intensest shade of blue. A troop of allouattes commenced a concert, their unmusical howlings echoing through the forest. Numerous macaws passed above us, giving vent to strange harsh cries; while whole families of parrots screamed in various notes. Cicadas set up the most piercing chirp, becoming shriller and shriller, till it ended in a sharp screeching whistle. Other creatures— birds, beasts, and insects—added their voices to the concert, till the whole forest seemed in an uproar. As the sky grew darker, and the shades of night came thickly round us, the noises gradually ceased, but were soon succeeded by the drumming, hoohooing, and the croaking of the tree-frogs, joined occasionally by the melancholy cries of the night-jar. "Follow me closely," said the recluse, "and step as high as you can, not to catch your feet in the tangled roots. My eyes are well accustomed to this forest-gloom, and I will lead you safely."

At length we found ourselves passing through a narrow passage between thick bushes, which reminded us of the approach to the recluse's hut. Emerging from it, we saw light ahead, and now reached the steps which led to the verandah.

"You have come on well," he observed. "I will carry up your young friend. Leave the litter on the ground."

I had to stop and assist up True, for although he made several attempts to mount the ladder by himself, it was somewhat too high for him to succeed. On entering the hut I found Ellen, in a state of agitation, leaning over Arthur.

"Oh! what has happened?" she asked. "Will he die? Will he die?"

"I trust not, young lady," remarked our host. "He wants rest and careful nursing, and I hope in a few days will have recovered. I will now attend to him, and afterwards leave him under your care."

"Do not be alarmed, Miss Ellen," whispered Arthur. "I only fainted from the hot sun and anxiety about you all. Now I am with you, I shall soon get well."

"As I have by me a store of medicines, with which I have doctored occasionally the poor natives, I can find, I hope, some remedies which may help to restore your friend," observed the recluse. "Rest is what he chiefly now requires."

Arthur was put into his hammock, and after he had taken a mess which Maria had prepared, fell asleep.

Chapter Twelve
The Recluse—More Adventures in the Forest

Three days passed away, and Arthur had almost recovered. We none of us had liked to ask the recluse any questions about himself, and he had given us no information as to who he was, where he had come from, or how long he had lived in that secluded spot. He had merely told us that he was English, and he certainly seemed from his conversation to be a man of education. He made no inquiries about us, though he listened from politeness, apparently, rather than from any interest he took in the matter, to the account we gave him of our adventures. One thing was very evident, that, though he bore with our society, he would rather be left alone to his usual solitude.

I awoke early the following morning, and found John already on foot. He proposed going down to the igarape to bathe, and asked me to accompany him. Our host, we found, had already left the hut. Arthur was asleep, so we would not disturb him. Domingos also had gone out, and we concluded had accompanied the recluse to obtain provisions, as he had taken with him a couple of baskets which usually hung on the wall at the entrance of the hut. At all events, they were not there when we looked for them. Taking our guns, we proceeded as we proposed. The rays of the rising sun came through the few openings among the tall trees, their light flashing on the wings of the gorgeous butterflies and still more brilliant plumage of several humming-birds, which flitted here and there amid the opening in the forest.

There was a sandy spot where we thought that we could venture into the water, without the risk of being seized by an alligator or anaconda. We were making our way towards it, when we caught sight of a small canoe, in which a man, whom we at once recognised as the recluse, was seated. He was paddling slowly up the igarape. We watched him for some time, till he was lost to sight among the thick foliage which lined the banks. We naturally concluded that he was merely taking a morning excursion, perhaps to fish or bathe, and expected to see him again at breakfast.

While John took a bath, I stood by and beat the water with a long pole, to frighten away any alligator which might be near, and he performed the same office for me—a very necessary precaution, from the number of the huge reptiles which swarm in all the rivers.

Much refreshed, we returned to the hut. We waited for the recluse some time before beginning breakfast, which Maria had prepared; but he did not appear, nor did Domingos. We all agreed that we ought no longer to impose our society on our strange friend. The first thing to be done was to build a canoe, but we had not found a tree in the neighbourhood of the hut exactly suited to our purpose.

"We may perhaps discover one near the place at which we landed the other day, and we may get our Indian friends to help us to build a canoe," I observed. "Or it is possible that they may have recovered some of theirs, and be ready to sell one of them to us."

"Then the sooner we find them out the better," observed John.

"I wonder Duppo and his sister, or some of the other Indians, have not come here to look for us," said Arthur. "I thought Duppo, at all events, would have shown more regard for us."

"Perhaps the recluse has taught them not to visit his hut without his leave," I remarked. "They seem to hold him in great respect."

While I was speaking Domingos appeared at the door, with his baskets loaded with fruit, vegetables, and birds—chiefly parrots and toucans of gay plumage. He gave a note to John, which he had received, he said, from the strange señor early in the morning.

"I will not conceal from you that I have departed greatly from my accustomed habits in affording you an asylum," it ran. "If you wish it you can remain, but I desire to be once more alone, and can find a home elsewhere till you take your departure. I have communicated with your Indian friends, and they will assist you in building a lodge more suitable for you than this, in the situation you first selected. A party of them will appear shortly to convey your goods; and they will also construct a montaria of a size sufficient for you to continue your voyage. I will, in the meantime, institute inquiries about your missing friends, and, should I hear tidings of them, will send you word. I beg that you will return me no thanks, nor expect to see me. The life of solitude upon which your appearance has broken I desire to resume, and it will therefore cause me annoyance should you attempt to seek me. Accept such good wishes as a wretched outcast can venture to end."

This strange note caused us much regret. "He is so kind and gentle, in spite of the strange way he sometimes expresses himself, that I should grieve not to see him again, and thank him," said Arthur. "Do you not think we could leave a note, asking him to let us come and visit him before we go away altogether? Surely he would not refuse that."

"I am afraid, from the tenor of his note, it would be of no use," said John; "but if you wish it you can do so; and it will show him, at all events, that we are not ungrateful for his kindness."

We waited all day in expectation of the arrival of the Indians, but no one appeared. John went out, and shot some birds and a couple of monkeys. In our rambles, which were further than we had yet been, we came upon a cleared space containing a plantation of bananas, maize, and several edible roots; and, from the neat and scientific way in which the ground was cultivated, we had little doubt it belonged to the stranger; indeed, from the supplies he had brought us, notwithstanding his first remark, we had suspected that he was not without the means of supporting himself with vegetable food. Although he had allowed us to cook the animals we killed, we had remarked that he did not touch any of the meat himself.

Early next morning, as I was standing on the verandah, True poked his nose forward and began to bark. I thought he had seen some animal in the woods, and got my gun ready to fire at it, when I caught sight of a figure emerging from the narrow path of which I have spoken, and, greatly to my satisfaction, I recognised Duppo. As soon as he saw us he ran forward. I went down to meet him. He took my hand, and, by his action, and the gleam of satisfaction which passed over his impassive countenance, showed the satisfaction he felt at again being with us. He then made signs that others were coming, and soon afterwards a party of eight Indians, with his father at their head, made their appearance. Maono gravely saluted John and I, and signified that his men had come to convey our property to another place. Duppo asked whether any of us would like to return in the canoe. We agreed that it would be a good plan for Arthur and Ellen to do so.

"Oh, let me go through the woods," exclaimed Ellen; "I should like to see the country."

"But then, who is to look after Arthur? He is not fit to walk so far yet," said John.

"Oh, then I will go and take care of him," answered Ellen.

It was finally arranged that Maono and Duppo should paddle the canoe, and look after Ellen and Arthur. They formed a sufficiently large freight for the little craft. The Indians now shouldered our goods, each man taking a load twice as heavy as any one of us could have carried, although much less than our Napo peons had conveyed down to the river. Before starting, Arthur wrote the note he had proposed to the recluse, and left it on the table. We could not help feeling sorry at leaving that shady little retreat. At the same time, there was no chance while remaining there of obtaining tidings of our family. Having handed Ellen and Arthur into the canoe, with Nimble, and Ellen's other pets, we watched her for some minutes as Maono paddled her along the shore, which presented as far as we could see one wall of tall trees of varied forms rising almost from the water. "We shall meet again soon," exclaimed Ellen as she waved an adieu. "Who knows what adventures we shall have to recount to each other!" We could not tear ourselves from the spot while the canoe remained in sight. As soon as she disappeared we hurried after the Indians. Domingos and Maria had gone on with them. We walked on rapidly, fully expecting, as they had loads, that we should quickly overtake them. John was a little ahead of me, when suddenly I saw him take a tremendous leap along the path. I was wondering what sudden impulse had seized him, when I heard him exclaim, "Look out, Harry I see that creature;" and there I observed stretched across the path, a big ugly-looking serpent. I sprang back, holding True, who would have unhesitatingly dashed at the dangerous reptile. It was nearly six feet in length, almost as thick as a man's leg, of a deep brown above, pale yellow streaks forming a continued series of lozenge-shaped marks down the back, growing less and less distinct as they descended the sides, while it had a thin neck, and a huge flat head, covered with small scales.

As we had our guns ready, we did not fear it. It seemed disinclined to move, and, had it not lifted up its tail, we might have supposed it dead. We soon recognised, by the shape of the point, the fearful rattlesnake;— fearful it would be from its venomous bite, had not the rattle been fixed to it to give notice of its approach. We threw sticks at it, but still it did not seem inclined to move. Again it lifted up its horny tail, and shook its rattle. "Take care," cried John; "keep away." The serpent had begun to glide over the ground, now looking at one of us, now at the other, as if undecided at which it should dart. I took John's advice, and quickly retreated. He fired, and shattered the reptile's head. As it still moved slowly, I finished it with a blow of my stick.

As it would have been inconvenient to drag after us, we cut off the tail, that we might examine it at leisure. We found that the rattle was placed with the broad part perpendicular to the body. The last joint was fastened to the last vertebra of the tail by means of a thick muscle, as well as by the membranes which united it to the skin. The remaining joints were so many extraneous bodies, as it were, unconnected with the tail, except by the curious way in which they were fitted into each other. It is said that these bony rings or rattles increase in number with the age of the animal, and on each casting of the skin it acquires an additional one. The tip of every uppermost bone runs within two of the bones below it. By this means they not only move together, but also multiply the sound, as each bone hit against two others at the same time.

They are said only to bite when provoked or when they kill their prey. For this purpose they are provided with two kinds of teeth,—the smaller, which are placed in each jaw, and serve to catch and retain their food: and the fangs, or poisonous teeth, which are placed without the upper jaw. They live chiefly upon birds and small animals. It is said that when the piercing eye of the rattlesnake is fixed on an animal or bird they are so terrified and astonished that they are unable to escape. Birds, as if entranced, unwillingly keeping their eyes fixed on those of the reptile, have been seen to drop into its mouth. Smaller animals fall from the trees and actually run into the jaws open to receive them. Fatal as is the bite of the rattlesnake to most creatures, the peccary attacks and eats the reptile without the slightest hesitation; as, indeed, do ordinary hogs,—and even when bitten they do not suffer in the slightest degree.

This encounter with the rattlesnake having delayed us for a little time, we hurried on as rapidly as we could to overtake our companions. We had gone some distance, and still had not come up with them. I began to be afraid that we had turned aside from the right path. In some places even our eyes had distinguished the marks of those who had gone before us. We had now lost sight of them altogether, and as the wood was tolerably open, and the axes had not been used, we could only judge by the direction of the sun how to proceed.

We went on for some time, still believing ourselves in the right direction; but at last, when we expected to find the marks of the axes which we had before made, we could discover none. We searched about—now on one side, now on the other. The forest, though dense, was yet sufficiently open to enable us to make our way in a tolerably direct line. Now and then we had to turn aside to avoid the thick mass of creepers or the fallen trunk of some huge tree. We shouted frequently, hoping that Domingos and the Indians might hear us. Then John suggested that they, finding it an easy matter to follow the right track, did not suppose we could lose it. At last we grew tired of shouting, and agreed that we should probably fall in with the proper track by inclining somewhat to the right; and I had so much faith also in True's sagacity that I had hopes he would find it. However, I gave him more credit than he deserved. He was always happy in the woods, like a knight-errant in search of adventures, plenty of which he was indeed likely to meet with.

Still in the belief that we were not far wrong in our course, we walked briskly forward. We had gone some distance, when True made towards the decayed trunk of a huge tree, and began barking violently. While we were still at a considerable distance, a large hairy creature rose up before us. True stood his ground bravely, rushing now on one side, now on the other, of the animal. It had an enormous bushy tail, curled up something like that of a squirrel, but with a great deal more hair, and looked fully eight feet in length. As we drew nearer we saw that it had also an extraordinary long snout. It seemed in no degree afraid of True, and he evidently considered it a formidable antagonist. Presently it lifted itself up on its hind legs, when True sprang back just in time to avoid a gripe of its claws. Still the creature, undaunted by our appearance, made at him, when, seeing that he was really in danger, John and I rushed forward. We then discovered the creature to be a huge ant-eater, which, though it had no teeth, was armed with formidable claws, with which it would inevitably have killed my brave dog had it caught him. A shot in the head from John's rifle laid it dead.

It was covered with long hair, the prevailing colour being that of dark grey, with a broad band of black running from the neck downwards on each side of the body. It lives entirely on ants; and on opening its mouth we found that it could not provide itself with other food, as it was entirely destitute of teeth. Its claws, which were long, sharp, pointed, and trenchant, were its only implements of defence. Its hinder claws were short and weak; but the front ones were powerful, and so formed that anything at which it seizes can never hope to escape. The object of its powerful crooked claws is to enable it to open the ant-hills, on the inhabitants of which it feeds. It then draws its long, flexible tongue, covered with a glutinous saliva, over the swarms of insects who hurry forth to defend their dwelling.

The scientific name of this great ant-eater is *Myrmecophaga jubata*. There are, however, several smaller ant-eaters, which are arboreal — that is, have their habitations in trees. Some are only ten inches long. One species is clothed with a greyish-yellow silky hair; another is of a dingy brown colour. They are somewhat similar in their habits to the sloth; and as they are seen clinging with their claws to the trees, or moving sluggishly along, they are easily mistaken for that animal, to which, indeed, they are allied. Some are nocturnal, others are seen moving about in the daytime.

True seemed to be aware of the narrow escape he had had from the formidable talons of the ant-eater, for after this encounter he kept close behind my heels. I hoped that he had received a useful lesson, and would attack no animal unless at my command, or he might do so some day when no friend was at hand to come to his rescue.

We had been walking on after this occurrence for some time in silence, when True pricked up his ears and began to steal forward. I could, however, see nothing. The undergrowth and masses of sipos were here of considerable denseness. Still, as he advanced, we followed him. Presently the forest became a little more open, when we caught sight of a creature with a long tail and a tawny hide with dark marks. "It is a jaguar," I whispered to John. "It is watching some animal. In a moment we shall see it make its spring." It was so intent on some object before it, that it did not discover our approach. On it went with the stealthy pace of a cat about to pounce on an unwary bird or mouse. It did not make the slightest noise, carefully avoiding every branch in its way. True, after his late adventure with the ant-eater, was less disposed than usual to seek an encounter, and I was therefore able to keep him from dashing forward as he otherwise would have done.

"The creature is about to pounce on some deer he sees feeding in the thicket," whispered John; "or perhaps he espies a tapir, and hopes to bring it to the ground."

Unconscious of our approach, the savage animal crept on and on, now putting one foot slowly forward, now the other. Now it stopped, then advanced more quickly. At length it stopped for a moment, and then made one rapid bound forward. A cry reached our ears. "That is a human voice!" exclaimed John; "some unfortunate native caught sleeping." He fired as he spoke, for we could still see the back of the animal through the thick underwood. The jaguar bounded up as it received the wound, and the next moment the tall figure of the recluse appeared, bleeding at the shoulder, but otherwise apparently uninjured.

"What, my young friends," he exclaimed, "brought you here? You have saved my life, at all events."

"We chanced to lose our way, and are thankful we came up in time to save you from that savage brute."

"Chance!" exclaimed the recluse. "It is the very point I was considering at the moment;" and he showed us a book in his hand. "Your arrival proves to me that there is no such thing as chance. I was reading at the moment, lost in thought, or I should not have been so easily surprised."

John then told him how we had waited to see Ellen and our young friend off; and then, in attempting to follow our companions, had lost our way.

"We should have got thus far sooner had we not been delayed by an attack which a great ant-eater made on our dog."

"If you have lost your way, you will wish to find it," said the recluse. "I will put you right, and as we go along, we can speak on the point I mentioned. You have some distance to go, for you should know that you have come almost at right angles to the route you intended to take. No matter; I know this forest, and can lead you by a direct course to the point you wish to gain. But I must ask you before we move forward to bind up my shoulder. Here, take this handkerchief. You need not be afraid of hurting me."

Saying this, he resumed his seat on the log, and John, under his directions, secured the handkerchief over the lacerated limb. He bore the process with perfect composure, deep as were the wounds formed by the jaguar's claws.

"What has occurred has convinced me that chance does not exist," he said, resuming his remarks as we walked along. "You delayed some time, you tell me, in watching your friends embark; then, losing your way, you were detained by the ant-eater, and thus arrived at the very moment to save my life. There was no chance in that. Had you been sooner you would have passed me by, for I sat so occupied in reading, and ensconced among the roots of the trees, that I should not have heard you. Had you delayed longer, the fierce jaguar would have seized me, and my life would have been sacrificed. No, I say again, there is no such thing as chance. He who rules the world ordered each event which has occurred, and directed your steps hither. It is a happy and comforting creed to know that One more powerful than ourselves takes care of us. Till the moment the jaguar's sharp claw touched my shoulder, I had doubted this. The author whose book I hold doubts it also, and I was arguing the point with him. Your arrival decided the question."

While he was speaking I missed True, and now heard him bark violently. I ran back, and found the jaguar we thought had been killed rising to its feet. It was snarling fiercely at the brave dog, and in another moment would have sprung upon him. True stood prepared for the encounter, watching the creature's glaring eyes. I saw the danger of my faithful friend and fired at the head of the savage animal. My shot was more effectual than John's. It fell back dead. John and the recluse came hurrying up.

"We should never leave a treacherous foe behind us," observed the latter. "However, he is harmless now. Come on. You have a long walk before you; though, for myself, I can find a lodging in the forest, suited to my taste, whenever I please."

The recluse, as in our former walk, led the way. For a considerable distance he went on without again speaking. There was much that was strange about him, yet his mind seemed perfectly clear, and I could not help hoping that we might be the means of persuading him to return to civilised society. He walked forward so rapidly that we sometimes had difficulty in keeping up with him; and I remarked, more than I had done before, his strange appearance, as he flourished his sharp axe, now striking on one side, now on the other, at the sipos and vines which interfered with his progress. He was dressed merely in a coarse cotton shirt and light trousers secured round the waist by a sash, while a broad-brimmed straw hat sheltered his head. His complexion was burned almost red; his features were thin, and his eyes sunken; but no tinge of grey could be perceived in his hair, which hung wild and streaming over his shoulders.

True, after going on for some time patiently, began to hunt about on either side according to his custom. Presently he gave forth one of his loud cheery barks, and off he bounded after a creature which had come out of the hollow of a tree. Calling to John, I made chase, getting my gun ready to fire. The ground just there was bare, and I caught sight of an animal the size of a small pig, but its whole back and head were covered with scales. In spite of its awkward appearance, it made good play over the ground, and even True, with all his activity, could scarcely keep up with it. It turned its head here and there, looking apparently for a hole in which to seek shelter. He, however, made desperate efforts to overtake it. The base of a large tree impeded its progress, when, just as he was about to spring on it, it suddenly coiled itself up into a round ball. True kept springing round and round it, wishing to get hold of the creature, but evidently finding no vulnerable part. I ran forward and seized it, when, just as I got hold of the ball, I received so severe a dig in my legs from a pair of powerful claws which it suddenly projected, that I was glad to throw it down again.

"You have got hold of an armadillo," said the recluse, who with John at that moment arrived. "If you want a dinner, or wish to make an acceptable present to your Indian friends, you may kill and carry it with you; but if not, let the creature go. For my part, I delight to allow the beasts of the forest to roam at large, and enjoy the existence which their Maker has given them. The productions of the ground afford me sufficient food to support life, and more I do not require. Yet I acknowledge that unless animals were allowed to prey on each other, the species would soon become so numerous that the teeming earth itself could no longer support them: therefore man, as he has the power, so, I own, he has the right to supply himself with food which suits his taste. I speak, therefore, only as regards my own feelings."

While he was speaking he seemed to forget that he had just before been in a hurry to proceed on our way, and stood with his arms folded, gazing at the armadillo. The creature, finding itself unmolested, for even True stood at a respectful distance, uncoiled itself, and I then had an opportunity of observing its curious construction. Its whole back was covered with a coat of scaly armour of a bony-looking substance, in several parts. On the head was an oval plate, beneath which could be seen a pair of small eyes, winking, as if annoyed by the sunlight. Over the shoulders was a large buckler, and a similar one covered the haunches; while between these solid portions could be seen a series of shelly zones, arranged in such a manner as to accommodate this coat of mail to the back and body. The entire tail was shielded by a series of calcareous rings, which made it perfectly flexible. The interior surface, as well as the lower part of the body, was covered with coarse scattered hairs, of which some were seen to issue forth between the joints of the armour. It had a pointed snout, long ears, short, thick limbs, and stout claws.

"There are several species of the armadillo," observed our friend. "The creature before us is the *Dasypus sexcinctus*. It is a burrowing animal, and so rapidly can it dig a hole, that when chased it has often its way made under ground before the hunter can reach it. Its food consists of roots, fruits, and every variety of soft vegetable substances; but it also devours carrion and flesh of all sorts, as well as worms, lizards, ants, and birds which build their nests on the ground. In some parts of the continent the natives cook it in its shell, and esteem it a great delicacy."

Whilst our friend was giving us this account, the armadillo, suddenly starting forward, ran off at a great rate into the forest, True made chase, but I called him back, and he came willingly, apparently convinced that he should be unable to overtake the creature, or overpower it if he did.

We were once more proceeding on our way. The day was drawing to a close, and yet we had not overtaken our companions. "You are scarcely aware of the distance you were from the right road," observed the recluse. "When once a person gets from the direct path, he knows not whither he may wander. It may be a lesson to you. I have learned it from bitter experience." He sighed deeply as he spoke. At length we saw the bright glare of a fire between the trees. "You will find your friends there," said the recluse, "and, directed by that, can now go on."

"But surely you are going with us to the camp?" said John.

"No; I shall seek a resting-place in the forest," he answered. "I am too much accustomed to solitude to object to be alone, even though I have no sheltering roof over my head. Farewell! I know not whether we shall meet again, but I would once more give you the assurance that I do not forget that you were the means of saving my life; and yet I know not why I should set value upon it."

In vain John and I entreated him to come on. Not another step further would he advance; and he cut us short by turning hastily round and stalking off into the depths of the forest, while we hurried on towards the camp.

"Oh, there they are! there they are!" exclaimed Ellen, running forward to meet us as we appeared. "I have been so anxious about you, and so has Arthur! Domingos told us he was sure you would come up soon, but I could not help dreading that some accident had happened."

We had to confess that we had lost our way, and that, had it not been for the stranger, we should still be wandering in the forest.

"And why would he not come to the camp?" she asked. "Arthur is longing to see him again. Duppo has been telling him of the way in which he rescued him from the anaconda. I was at last obliged to tell him what occurred."

Arthur now came up. "I must thank him!" he exclaimed. "I will run and overtake him."

We had great difficulty in persuading Arthur of the hopelessness of finding him, and that he would be more likely to lose his own way in the forest.

The Indians had been busily employed in putting up huts for our accommodation. Ellen and Maria, with their pets, had already possession of theirs. We hung up our hammocks in the more open shed which had been prepared for us.

Chapter Thirteen
Our new resting-place, and the
Adventures which befel us there

Next morning Maono and his people began erecting a more substantial habitation for us, signifying that his white friend, meaning the recluse, had desired him to do so. It was built on the spot we had previously selected near the igarape, and overlooking the main river. A number of stout poles were first driven into the ground, and to their tops others were joined and united in the centre, forming a conical roof, the eaves projecting below to a considerable distance. Palm-leaves were then fastened, much in the fashion I have before described, over the roof, layer above layer, till a considerable thickness was attained. The walls were formed by interweaving sipos between the uprights, a space being left for ventilation. We had thus a substantial hut erected, which it would have taken us, unaided, many days to build. While the Indians were working outside, John and I, with Domingos, formed a partition in the interior, to serve as a room for Ellen and Maria. "We must manufacture a table and some stools, and then our abode will be complete," said John. Some small palms which grew near were split with wedges into planks. Out of these we formed, with the assistance of Domingos, a table, and as many rough stools as we required.

When all was complete, Maono begged by signs to know whether we were satisfied. We assured him that we were better accommodated than we expected to be. He seemed highly pleased, and still more so when we presented him and his men each with a piece of cloth, he having three times as much as the others. We gave him also an axe, a knife, and several other articles, besides a number of beads, which we let him understand were for his wife and daughter. He, however, seemed rather to scorn the idea of their being thus adorned in a way superior to himself, it being, as we observed, the custom of most Amazonian tribes for the men to wear more ornaments than the women. We understood that his tribe had settled a short way off, in a secluded part of the forest, where they might be less likely to be attacked by their enemies the Majeronas.

We now tried to make Maono understand that we were anxious to have a large canoe built, in which we might proceed down the river. He replied that he would gladly help us, but that he must return to his own people, as they had first to be settled in their new location. To this, of course, we could not object, but we begged him to return as soon as possible to assist us in our work. As soon as he was gone we agreed to hold a consultation as to what we should next do. We took our seats under the verandah in front of our new abode, John acting as president, Ellen, Arthur, Domingos, and I ranging ourselves round him. True, Nimble, and Toby stood by the side of Maria, as spectators, the latter almost as much interested apparently as she was in the discussion, while Poll and Niger stood perched on the eaves above us. The question was whether we should devote all our energies to constructing a large canoe, or make excursions in the small one we already possessed, as we before proposed? We requested Ellen, not only as the lady, but the youngest of the party, to speak first. She was decidedly of opinion that it would be better to build the large canoe, as she was sure that our parents had already proceeded further down the river.

"But what reasons have you for so thinking?" asked John.

Ellen was silent. "Pray do not insist upon my giving my reasons," she said at last. "I can only say that I feel sure they have gone further down. If they had not, I think we should have found them before this; indeed, my heart tells me that we shall find them before long if we continue our course down the river."

John smiled. "Those are indeed very lady-like reasons," he observed. "However, we will record your opinion; and now wish we to know what Arthur has to say."

"I should like to agree with Miss Ellen, but at the same time cannot feel sure of a matter of which we have no evidence," said Arthur. "We have not examined the banks up the stream or on the opposite side. Although we have good reasons for supposing that, after quitting their first location, your family proceeded downwards, as the labour of paddling against the current is very great, yet, as they may have stopped at some intermediate spot, I advise that we examine the banks on both sides of the river between this place and that where we expected to find them."

"Now, Harry, what do you say?" asked John.

"I agree with Arthur," I replied. "As we came down a considerable distance at night, I say we should examine the shores we then passed. As the greater part of our voyage was performed by daylight, I do not think it at all likely we could have missed them had they been sailing up to meet us. I also advise that we make the excursion we proposed in the small canoe in the first place, while our Indian friends are constructing the larger one."

Domingos had been standing with his arms folded, as was his custom, watching our countenances. He had perfectly understood what was said. Taking off his hat, he made a bow to Ellen, saying, "I agree with the señora. I feel sure that my honoured master would desire to place his family in safety at a distance from the savage tribe who attacked him, and that, therefore, he has moved further down the river, probably to one of the nearest Portuguese settlements on the banks. But knowing his affection for you, his children, I believe he would have sent back messengers to meet us should he have been unable to return himself. It is they, in my opinion, we should look out for; probably, indeed, they have already passed us. I am sorry that we did not leave some signals at our stopping-places, which might show them where we have been, and lead them to us. Then, again, as Señor Fiel might not have been able to procure messengers at once, and as the voyage up the stream is laborious, they may not have got as far as this. Thus we are right in remaining at this spot, whence we can see them should they approach. I therefore hold to the opinion that the large canoe should be constructed without delay, in which we might continue our voyage, but that we should keep a look-out both by day and night, lest our friends might pass by without observing us."

"It becomes, then, my duty as president to give the casting vote in this important matter," observed John, "as the members of the council are divided in opinion. Although the opinion expressed by Ellen and Domingos has probability on its side, yet it must be considered theoretical; while that given by Arthur and Harry is undoubtedly of a more practical character. Should we on exploring the shores higher up find no traces of our relatives, we shall then proceed with more confidence on our voyage, buoyed up with the hope of overtaking them. In the other ease we might be sailing on with the depressing consciousness that, not having searched for them thoroughly, we might be leaving them behind. I therefore decide that, while our Indian friends are engaged in building a canoe, in which work, from our inexperience, we cannot render them any effectual aid, we employ the interval in making the exploring expeditions we proposed. The point to be settled is, how are we to carry out that plan?"

"The small canoe will not convey more than three people at the utmost," I observed. "I should like to go with Arthur and Duppo, as I at first suggested; while you, John, stay to take care of Ellen, and superintend the building of the canoe. You will be better able than any of us to keep the Indians to their work, and guard Ellen, should any danger occur from hostile Indians, or of any other description."

"I should certainly have liked to have gone myself," said John. "But your argument is a strong one. I am sure I can trust you and Arthur, and Duppo, from his acuteness, will be of great assistance to you; and yet I do not like you to run the risk of the dangers to which you may be exposed."

"It would not be worse for us than for you," remarked Arthur. "I would willingly stay to defend Miss Ellen; but I am afraid I should not manage the Indians, or act as you would do in an emergency."

I saw that John put considerable restraint on himself when he finally agreed to let us go. Yet as we were as well able to manage the canoe as he was, and much lighter, we were better suited to form its crew. At the same time, it seemed evident that Ellen would be safer under the protection of two grown-up men, than of lads like Arthur and I. It was necessary, however, to wait to arrange provisions for our expedition, and obtain also the advice of Maono on the subject. We much regretted that we could not communicate with the recluse, as he would have interpreted for us, and would also have given us his advice.

While taking a paddle in our canoe, we agreed that she required considerable alterations to fit her for our intended expedition. Our first task was to haul her up, and strengthen her bulwarks; for it will be remembered that they were before put up in a hurried manner, and were already almost torn off.

We were thus engaged in front of the hut when we heard Ellen exclaim, "There is some one coming." And looking through an opening in the forest, I saw Duppo and his sister approaching, carrying baskets on their backs. Arthur and I ran forward to meet them. They made signs that they had brought a present of farinha to the young white lady, as they designated Ellen; not by words, however, but by putting a piece of white bark on their own brown cheeks. We then conducted them to Ellen.

"I am so glad to see you," she said, taking Oria's hand; and though the Indian girl could not understand the words, she clearly comprehended the expression of my young sister's countenance, which beamed with pleasure. Maria grinned from ear to ear, not at all jealous of the attention her young mistress paid the pretty native; and all three were soon seated in front of the hut, talking together in the universal language of signs. It was extraordinary how well they seemed to understand each other. Oria's garments were certainly somewhat scanty; but in a short time Maria ran into the hut, and quickly returned with a petticoat and scarf, part of Ellen's wardrobe. Nothing could exceed the delight of the young savage (for so I may properly call her) when her white and black sisters robed her in these garments. Pretty as was her countenance, it usually wanted animation; but on this occasion it brightened up with pleasure. The clothes seemed at once to put her more on an equality with her companions. When they had talked for a time, Ellen called out her pets to introduce them to Oria, who signified that if it would gratify her new friend she would undertake to obtain many more.

"Oh, yes, yes!" exclaimed Ellen. "I should so like to have some of those beautiful little humming-birds which have been flying about here lately, feeding on the gay-coloured flowers growing on the open ground around, or hanging by their long tendrils from the trees."

Neither Duppo nor Oria could understand these remarks, but they did the signs which accompanied them; and they both answered that they hoped soon to obtain for her what she wished.

We then took Duppo down to the canoe, and I tried to explain to him our intention of making a voyage in her. This he understood very clearly; indeed, the recluse had, we suspected, already intimated to the Indians our anxiety about our missing friends. Duppo was of great assistance to us in repairing the canoe and putting on fresh bulwarks. We determined, in addition to the paddles, to have a mast and sail. We had some light cotton among our goods, which would answer the purpose of the sail, and could be more easily handled, and would therefore be less dangerous, than a mat sail.

We found that Oria had taken the invitation as it was intended, and had come to remain with Ellen.

"I am so glad," said our sister, when she discovered this. "I shall now be able to teach her English; and, I am sure, we shall be great friends."

"But would you not also be able to teach her about the God of the English?" said Arthur, in a low voice. "That is of more consequence. She now knows nothing of the God of mercy, love, and truth. From what I can learn, these poor savages are fearfully ignorant."

"Oh yes," said Ellen, looking up. "I shall indeed be glad to do that. I am so thankful to you, Arthur, for reminding me."

"We should remember that that Saviour who died for us died for them also," said Arthur; "and it is our duty to make known that glorious truth to them."

"It will be a hard task though, I fear," remarked Ellen, "as Oria does not yet know a word of English; and though we may make signs to show her what we want her to do, I do not see how we can speak of religion until she understands our language."

"The more necessity then for teaching her without delay," observed Arthur. "She seems very intelligent; and if we lose no opportunity of instructing her, I hope she may soon acquire sufficient knowledge to receive the more simple truths, which, after all, are the most important."

"Then I will begin at once," said Ellen. "She has already been trying to repeat words after me; and I hope before the end of the day to have taught her some more."

Ellen was in earnest. Our dear little sister, though very quiet and gentle, had a determined, energetic spirit. It was very interesting to see her labouring patiently to teach the young Indian girl. Duppo had already learned a good many words, and seemed to understand many things we said to him. We scarcely ever had to repeat the name of a thing more than two or three times for him to remember it; and he would run with alacrity to fetch whatever we asked for.

We had much more trouble in teaching manners to our dumb companions; for in spite of Master Nimble's general docility, he was constantly playing some trick, or getting into scrapes of all sorts. One day he was seen by Duppo trying to pull the feathers out of Niger's head; and on another occasion he was discovered in an attempt to pluck poor Poll, in spite of her determined efforts to escape from his paws. He often sorely tried True's good-temper; while if a pot or pan was left uncovered, he was sure to have his fingers in it, to examine whether its contents were to his liking.

We were working at the canoe one morning when I heard Maria's voice calling to us.

"See what it is she wants, Harry," said John, who was busily employed.

I ran up to the hut.

"O Señor Harry!" exclaimed Maria, "Nimble has scampered off into the woods, and enticed Toby to go with him; and Señora Ellen has run after them, and I do not know what may happen if there is no one near to protect her."

I took up my gun on hearing this, and followed Ellen, whose dress I caught a glimpse of among the trees. Presently I saw her, as I got nearer, throw up her hands, as if she had seen some object which had alarmed her. I hurried on.

"What is it, Ellen?" I shouted out.

"Oh, look there, Harry!" she exclaimed. "They will catch Nimble and Toby."

I sprang to her side, and then saw, just beyond a thicket of ferns, two huge pumas, which were on the point of springing up a tree, among whose branches were clinging our two pets, Nimble and Toby, their teeth chattering with terror, while their alarm seemed almost to have paralysed them. In another instant they would have been in the clutches of the pumas. I was more concerned about my dear little sister's safety than for that of her monkeys. At first I thought of telling her to run back to the hut; but then it flashed across me that the pumas might see her and follow. So I exclaimed, "Get behind me, Ellen; and we will shout together, and try and frighten the beasts. That will, at all events, bring John to our help."

We shouted at the top of our voices. I certainly never shouted louder. Meantime I raised my gun, to be ready to fire should the pumas threaten to attack us or persist in following our pets. Scarcely had our voices ceased, when I heard True's bark, as he came dashing through the wood. The pumas had not till then discovered us, so eagerly had they been watching the monkeys. They turned their heads for a moment. Nimble took the opportunity of swinging himself out of their reach. Ellen shrieked, for she thought they were going to spring at us. I fired at the nearest, while True dashed boldly up towards the other. My bullet took effect, and the powerful brute rolled over, dead. The sound of the shot startled its companion; and, fortunately for gallant little True, it turned tail, and bounded away through the forest,—John, who had been hurrying up, getting a distant shot as it disappeared among the trees. Arthur and the two Indians followed John, greatly alarmed at our shouts and the sound of the firearms.

Nimble and Toby, still chattering with fear, came down from their lofty retreat when we called them, and, looking very humble and penitent, followed Ellen to the hut; while we, calling Domingos to our assistance, set to work to skin the puma. The meat we cooked and found very like veal, and Domingos managed to dress the skin sufficiently to preserve it.

Duppo had clearly understood Ellen's wish to have some humming-birds caught alive. We were always up at daybreak, to enjoy the cool air of the morning. He had gone out when the first streaks of dawn appeared in the eastern sky, over the cold grey line of the river. When we could do so with safety, we never failed to take a bath. We had just come out of the water, and were dressing, when Duppo ran up, and signed to us to follow him. We called Ellen as we passed the hut, and all together went towards the igarape, where, in a more open space than usual, a number of graceful fuschia-looking flowers, as well as others of different forms, hung suspended from long tendrils, intertwined with the branches of the trees. Into this spot the rising sun poured its glorious beams with full brilliancy. We cautiously advanced, when the space before us seemed suddenly filled with the most beautiful sparking gems of varied colours, floating here and there in the bright sunlight. I could scarcely believe that the creatures before us belonged to the feathered tribes, so brilliant were their hues, so rapid their movements. Sometimes they vanished from sight, as they darted with inconceivable rapidity from branch to branch. Now one might be seen for an instant hovering over a flower, its wings looking like two grey filmy fans expanded at its sides. Then we could see another dip its long slender bill into the cup of an upright flower. Now one would come beneath a suspended blossom. Sometimes one of the little creatures would dart off into the air, to catch some insect invisible to the eye; and we could only judge of what it was about by its peculiar movements. As we watched, a tiny bird would perch on a slender twig, and rest there for a few seconds, thus giving us an opportunity of examining its beauties. Ellen could scarcely restrain her delight and admiration at the spectacle; for though we had often seen humming-birds before, we had never beheld them to such advantage. The little creature we saw had a crest on the top of its head of a peculiarly rich chestnut, or ruddy tint. The upper surface of the body was of a bronzed green hue, and a broad band of white crossed the lower part, but the wings were purple-black. The chief part of the tail was chestnut. The forehead and throat were also of the same rich hue. On either side of the neck projected a snow-white plume, tipped with the most resplendent metallic green. The effect of these beautiful colours may be imagined as the birds flew rapidly to and fro, or perched on a spray, like the one I have described. Another little creature, very similar to it, was to be seen flying about above the heads of the others. It also had a crest, which was of the same colour as the others, but of a somewhat lighter tint; while at the base of each feather, as we afterwards observed, was a round spot of bronzed green, looking like a gem in a dark setting. The crest, which was constantly spread out, appeared very like that of a peacock's tail, though, as Ellen observed, it would be a very little peacock to have such a tail. On searching in our book, we found that the first of these humming-birds we had remarked was a tufted coquette (*Lophornis ornatus*), while the other, which we seldom saw afterwards, was the spangled coquette. These birds, with several others of similar habits and formation, are classed separately from the *Trochilidae*, and belong to the genus *Phaëthornis*. They are remarkable for the long pointed feathers of their tails, the two central ones being far longer than the rest. We met with a greater number of them than of any other genus on the banks of the Amazon.

After we had enjoyed the spectacle for some time, Duppo begged us to come a little further, when he showed us a beautiful little nest, secured to the innermost point of a palm-leaf. On the top of the leaf a little spangled coquette was watching her eggs within. Unlike the nests of the *Trochilidae*, which are saucer-shaped, it was of a long, funnel-like form, broad at the top and tapering towards the lower part. The outside, which was composed of small leaves and moss, had a somewhat rugged appearance; but the inside, as we had reason to know, was soft and delicate in the extreme, being thickly lined with silk-cotton from the fruit of the sumaúma-tree. Below the first was perched a tufted coquette, looking as boldly at us as any town sparrow. The little creatures, indeed, kept hovering about; and one came within a few feet of our faces, as much as to ask how we dared to intrude on its domains. More pugnacious or brave little beings do not exist among the feathered tribes.

I cannot hope to describe with any degree of accuracy the numbers of beautiful humming-birds we met with in different places; for though some are migratory, the larger proportion strictly inhabit certain localities, and are seldom met with, we were told, in any other. The humming-birds of the Andes, of which there are a great variety, never descend into the plains; nor do those of the plains attempt to intrude on the domains of their mountain relatives. Although they may live on the nectar of flowers, they have no objection to the tiny insects they find among their petals, or which fly through the air, while many devour as titbits the minute spiders which weave their gossamer webs among the tall grass or shrubs.

"I should not think that any human being could catch one of those little creatures," said Ellen, as we returned homewards. "The sharpest-eyed sportsman would find it difficult to hit one with his fowling-piece."

"He would certainly blow it to pieces," observed John, "if he made the attempt. They are shot, however, with sand; and perhaps our young Indian friend himself will find the means of shooting one, if he cannot capture it in some other way."

"Oh, I would not have one shot for the world!" exclaimed Ellen. "Pray let him understand that he must do nothing of the sort for my sake."

While we were at breakfast, Duppo, who had disappeared, came running up with one of the beautiful little creatures which we had seen in his hand. It seemed much less alarmed than birds usually are in the grasp of a boy. Perhaps that was owing to the careful way in which Duppo held it.

"Oh, you lovely little gem!" exclaimed Ellen; "but I am sure I shall never be able to take proper care of it."

Duppo, who seemed to understand her, signified that Oria would do so for her. Oria, who had been watching us taking sugar with our tea, and had by this time discovered its qualities, mixed a little in a spoon, which she at once put before the bill of the little humming-bird. At first it was far too much alarmed to taste the sweet mess. At length, growing accustomed to the gentle handling of the Indian girl, it poked out its beak and took a sip. "Ho, ho!" it seemed to say, "that is nice stuff!" and then it took another sip, and very soon seemed perfectly satisfied that it was not going to be so badly off, in spite of its imprisonment. Oria intimated that she would in time make the little stranger quite tame.

"But we must keep it out of the way of Master Nimble's paws, for otherwise he would be very likely to treat it with small ceremony," observed John. "Why, Ellen, you will have a perfect menagerie before long."

"Yes, I hope so," she answered; "I am not nearly contented yet. I should like to have one of those beautiful little ducks you were telling me of, and as many humming-birds as I can obtain."

"Perhaps you would like to have a jaguar or puma," said John. "If caught young, I dare say they can be tamed as well as any other animal."

"I am afraid they would quarrel with my more harmless pets," answered Ellen. "And yet a fine large puma would be a good defence against all enemies."

"Not against an Indian with a poisoned arrow. He would be inconvenient, too, to transport in our canoe. I hope therefore you will confine yourself to small animals, which will not occupy much space. You may have as many humming-birds as you like, and half-a-dozen monkeys, provided they and Nimble do not quarrel."

"Except some pretty little monkeys, I do not wish for any others besides those I already have," said Ellen.

Duppo and Oria understood Ellen's wish to obtain living creatures, and they were constantly seeking about, and coming back sometimes with a beautiful butterfly or moth, sometimes with parrots and other birds.

While we were getting the canoe ready, Ellen and Maria, with the assistance of Oria, had been preparing food for us—baking cakes, and drying the meat of several birds and animals which John had killed. We had hoped to see the large canoe begun before we took our departure, but as the Indians had not arrived, we agreed that it would be better to lose no more time, and to start at once.

We took an experimental trip in the canoe before finally starting. We could have wished her considerably lighter than she was; at the same time, what she wanted in speed, she possessed in stability.

Early in the morning we bade Ellen and John, with our faithful attendants, good-bye. Oria, we thought, exhibited a good deal of anxiety when we were about to shove off, and she came down to the water and had a long talk with her brother, evidently charging him to keep his wits about him, and to take good care of us. Dear Ellen could scarcely restrain her tears. "Oh, do be careful where you venture, Harry!" she said. "I dread your falling into the power of those dreadful savages." John also gave us sundry exhortations, to which we promised to attend.

We were just in the mouth of the igarape, when we saw in the distance a small canoe coming down it. We therefore waited for her arrival. She drew nearer. We saw that only two people were in her, and we then recognised our friend Maono and his wife Illora. They were bringing a quantity of plantains and other fruits, with which the centre of the canoe was filled. Among others were several crowns of young palm-trees, which, when boiled, are more delicate than cabbages, and are frequently used by the natives. Maono was dressed in his usual ornaments of feathers on his arms and head, his hair being separated neatly in the centre, and hanging down on either side. Round his neck was a necklace, and his legs were also adorned like his arms.

"I have been thinking a good deal lately about the account of the early voyagers, who declared that they met a nation of warrior-women on the banks of this river," observed Arthur; "and looking at Maono, it strikes me that we have an explanation of the extraordinary circumstance. If a party of strangers were to see a band of such men, with shields on their arms, guarding the shores, they would very likely suppose them, from their appearance, to be females, and consequently, not having had any closer view of them, they would sail away, declaring that they had met a party of Amazons, who had prevented their landing. It was thus this mighty river obtained the name of the Amazon. The idea would have been confirmed, had they seen in the distance a band of people, without ornaments of any description, carrying burdens on their backs. These the strangers would naturally have supposed to be slaves, taken in war, and employed to carry the baggage of the fighting ladies." I agreed with him that it was very likely to have been the case.

As our friends drew near, Duppo spoke to them, and told them where we were going. He then explained to us that if we would wait a little longer, they would accompany us and assist us in our search. On reaching the shore, they carried up their present to Ellen, Illora, I must confess, bearing the larger portion. Some of the plantains and fruits they put into our canoe as they passed. They had another long talk, by the usual means of signs, with John and Domingos, who managed tolerably well to comprehend their meaning. We asked Duppo how it was they came to have a canoe. He replied that they had found one which had been left behind by the Majeronas, and, as we understood, they had brought it down through the igarape, which communicated with another river to the north of us, running into the main stream. When I heard this, the idea struck me that we were not yet altogether free from the danger of being attacked by the Majeronas, who, having possessed themselves of our canoe and those of our friends, might some night come down and take us by surprise.

I jumped on shore and took John aside, so that Ellen could not hear me, that I might tell him my fears. "You are right to mention them to me," he answered; "at the same time, I do not think we need be alarmed. I will, however, try and explain your idea to the Indians, and get them to place scouts on the watch for such an occurrence. I certainly wish we were further off; but yet, as we are now at a considerable distance from their territory, we shall be able to hear of their approach, should they come, in time to escape. We must make our way through the woods to the hut of the recluse, and I am very sure that he will be able to afford us protection. From what he said, he is well-known among all the surrounding tribes, who appear to treat him with great respect. Though we may lose such of our property as we cannot carry off, that will be of minor importance if we save our lives. For my part, however, I am under no apprehension of the sort; and I am very glad you did not mention your fears in the presence of Ellen."

Though I hoped I might be wrong in supposing an attack possible, I was satisfied at having warned John before going away. Arthur and I tried to make Duppo understand our plans, that he might describe them to his father and mother. They, in return, signified that they would proceed part of the way with us, and make inquiries as they went along, having been requested to do so by their white friend—meaning the recluse.

John, Ellen, Domingos, and Maria came down to the edge of the water once more to see us off, accompanied by Nimble and Toby—Toby placed on the shoulders of Domingos, while Nimble perched himself on John's arm, holding him affectionately round the neck with his tail. Poll and Niger always accompanied Ellen. "We shall soon be back!" I exclaimed, as I shoved off; "and who knows but that we may be accompanied by papa, mamma, Fanny, and Aunt Martha! Ellen, you must get out your books, for she will be shocked at finding that you have been so long idle." With these and other cheerful remarks we backed away from the shore, then, turning the canoe's head round, proceeded after our Indian friends. By keeping close to the banks we were out of the current, and thus made good way. Sometimes I steered, sometimes Duppo. Arthur always begged that he might keep at his paddle, saying he did not like to take the place of those who had more experience than himself. A light wind at length coming from the eastward, we hoisted our sail, and got ahead of Maono and his wife. The wind increasing, we ran the other canoe out of sight; but Duppo assured us that his father and mother would soon catch us up, and that we need not therefore wait for them. We looked into every opening in the forest which lined the bank, in the faint hope of seeing the habitation of our friends; but not a hut of any description was visible; indeed, the shores were mostly lined with so dense a vegetation, that in but few places could we even have landed, while often for leagues together there was not a spot on which a hut could have been built. The wind again falling, we were obliged once more to lower our sail and to take to our paddles, when we were quickly rejoined by our Indian friends. As it was important to examine every part of the shore carefully, we had agreed, if we could find an island, to land early in the evening on it.

Chapter Fourteen
Our exploring expedition—fearful danger

A week had passed away. We had crossed the stream several times to examine the southern bank of the river, and every inch of the northern bank had been explored. Sometimes we met Maono and his wife to compare notes, and then we again separated to continue our explorations. We were now once more proceeding up the Napo, with high clay banks surmounted by lofty forest trees above our heads. "I see some people moving on the shore there. O Harry! can it be them?" exclaimed Arthur. Several persons appeared coming through an opening in the forest, at a spot where the ground sloped down to the water. We could, however, see no habitation.

"It is possible," I answered. We passed this part of the river in the dark, and might thus have missed them.

Having been exploring the western bank, we were crossing the river at that moment. As we paddled on, my heart beat with excitement. If it should be them after all! The people stopped, and seemed to be observing us. We paddled on with all our might, and they came down closer to the water. Suddenly Duppo lifted up his paddle and exclaimed, "Majeronas!" We looked and looked again, still hoping that Duppo might have been mistaken; but his eyes were keener than ours. Approaching a little nearer, we were convinced that he was right. To go closer to the shore, therefore, would be useless and dangerous. We accordingly paddled back to the side we had just left, where we once more continued our upward course.

We had parted two days before this from Maono and Illora, who were to explore part of the bank we had left unvisited, and to meet us again at the island where we had been so nearly wrecked at the mouth of the igarape. We had almost reached the spot where we had expected to find my father and the rest of our family. The shores of the river were occasionally visited, as we had learned by experience, by the Majeronas, though not usually inhabited by them. It was therefore necessary to use great caution when going on shore. We landed, however, whenever we saw a spot where we thought it possible our friends might have touched on their voyage, in the hope that they might there have left some signal or note for us. The banks were here very different from those lower down. In many places they were composed of sand or clay cliffs of considerable height, often completely overhanging the river, as if the water had washed away their bases—indeed, such was undoubtedly the case. Frequently the trees grew to the very edge of these cliffs, their branches forming a thick shade over the stream. To avoid the hot sun we were tempted to keep our canoe close under them, as it was very pleasant to be able to paddle on in the comparatively cool air. Thus we proceeded, till we arrived at the spot where we had been so bitterly disappointed at not finding my family. No one was to be seen, but we landed, that we might again examine it more carefully. The ground on which the hut had stood still remained undisturbed, though vegetation had almost obliterated all the traces of fire. After hunting about in vain for some time, we took our way back to the canoe. We had nearly reached the water's edge, when Arthur exclaimed that he saw something white hanging to the lower branch of a tree, amid the thick undergrowth which grew around. We had some difficulty in cutting our way up to it. We then saw a handkerchief tied up in the shape of a ball.

"Why, it is only full of dried leaves!" exclaimed Arthur, as we opened it.

"Stay a moment," I answered. "I think there is something within them though."

Unrolling the leaves, I found a small piece of paper, torn apparently from a pocket-book. On it were written a few lines. They were: "Dear Brothers,—I trust you will see this. Enemies are approaching, and our father has resolved to quit this spot and proceed down the river. We hope to send a messenger up to warn you not to land here, but I leave this in case you should miss him, and do so. Where we shall stop, I cannot say; but our father wishes, for our mother's sake and mine, and Aunt Martha's, not again to settle till we reach a part of the river inhabited by friendly natives. That will, I fear, not be till we get some way down the Amazon. I am warned to finish and do this up. The natives are seen in the distance coming towards us."

This note, the first assurance we had received that our family had escaped, greatly raised our spirits. We had now only to make the best of our way back to John and Ellen with the satisfactory intelligence. We accordingly hurried back to the canoe, and began our downward voyage. We had gone some distance when we saw a small opening in the river, where, on the shore, two or three canoes were hauled up. They might belong to friendly natives, from whom we might obtain some fish or other fresh provisions, of which we were somewhat in want. We were about to paddle in, when we caught sight of several fierce-looking men with bows in their hands, rushing down towards the bank. Their appearance and gestures were so hostile that we immediately turned the head of our canoe down the stream again, and paddled away as fast as we could. We had not, however, got far, when, looking back, we saw that they had entered one of the larger canoes, and were shoring off, apparently to pursue us. We did our best to make way, in the hope of keeping ahead of them. I should have said the weather at this time had been somewhat changeable. Clouds had been gathering in the sky, and there was every sign of a storm. As I have already described two we encountered, I need not enter into the particulars of the one which now broke over us. Under other circumstances we should have been glad to land to escape its fury, but as it was, we were compelled to paddle on as fast as we could go. On looking back, we saw that the Indians were actually pursuing us. "Never fear," cried Arthur. "We shall be able to keep ahead of them!" The lightning flashed vividly, the rain came down in torrents, but through the thick wall of water we could still see our enemies coming rapidly after us. Although the current, had we stood out into the middle of the stream, might have carried us faster, the shortest route was by keeping near the bank. The Indians followed the same course. True rushed to the stern, and stood up barking defiance at them, as he saw them drawing nearer. I dreaded lest they should begin to shoot with their poisoned arrows. Should they get near enough for those fearful weapons to reach us, our fate would be sealed. Only for an instant could we afford time to glance over our shoulders at our foes. Nearer and nearer they drew. Duppo courageously kept his post, steering the canoe, and paddling with all his might. Every moment I expected to see them start up and let fly a shower of arrows at us. I might, of course, have fired at them; but this would have delayed us, and probably not have stopped them. Our only hope of escape therefore depended upon our being able to distance them. Yet they were evidently coming up with us. We strained every nerve; but, try as we might, we could not drive our little canoe faster than we were going.

My heart sank within me when, looking back once more, I saw how near they were. In a few minutes more we might expect to have a shower of arrows whizzing by us, and then we knew too well that, though we might receive comparatively slight wounds, the deadly poison in them would soon have effect. This did not make us slacken our exertions, though scarcely any hope of escape remained. Still we knew that something unforeseen might intervene for our preservation. I do hold, and always have held, that it is the duty of a man to struggle to the last. "Never say die!" is a capital motto in a good cause.

The rain poured down in torrents, the lightning flashed, the thunder roared, and gusts of wind swept down the river. We were, however, greatly protected by the bank above us. The storm blew more furiously. We could see overhead branches torn from the trees and carried into the stream. Still the Indians, with unaccountable pertinacity, followed us. We scarcely now dared look behind us, as all our energies were required to keep ahead; yet once more I turned round. Several of our pursuers were standing up and drawing their bows. The arrows flew by us. "Oh, I am hit!" cried Arthur. "But I wish I had not said that. Paddle on! paddle on! I may still have strength to go on for some time." Now, indeed, I felt ready to give way to despair; still, encouraged by Arthur, I persevered. For a moment only he ceased paddling. It was to pull the arrow from the wound in his shoulder; then again he worked away as if nothing had occurred. The next flight of arrows, I knew, might be fatal to all of us. I could not resist glancing round. Once more the Indians were drawing their bows; but at that instant a fearful rumbling noise was heard, followed by a terrific crashing sound. The trees above our heads bent forward. "Paddle out into the middle of the stream!" cried Arthur. Duppo seemed to have understood him, and turned the canoe's head away from the shore. The whole cliff above us was giving way. Down it came, crash succeeding crash, the water lashed into foam. The spot where the canoe of our savage pursuers had last been seen was now one mass of falling cliff and tangled forest. Trees were ahead of us, trees on every side. The next instant I found myself clinging to the branch of a tree. True had leaped up to my ride. Duppo was close to me grasping the tree with one hand, while he held my gun above his head in the other. I took it from him and placed it in a cleft of the trunk. Without my aid he quickly climbed up out of the water. The canoe had disappeared, and where was Arthur? The masses of foam, the thick, down-pouring rain, the leaves and dust whirled by the wind round us, concealed everything from our sight.

"Arthur!—Arthur!—where are you?" I cried out. There was no answer. Again I shouted at the top of my voice, "Arthur!—Arthur!" The tree, detached from the bank, now floated down the stream. I could only hope that it would not turn over in the eddying waters. Still the loud crashing sounds of the falling cliff continued, as each huge mass came sliding down into the river. The current, increased in rapidity by the rain, which had probably been falling much heavier higher up the stream, bore us onward. Oh, what would I have given to know that my friend had escaped! I could scarcely feel as thankful as I ought to have done for my own preservation, when I thought that he had been lost.

The whole river seemed filled with uprooted trees; in some places bound together by the sipos, they formed vast masses—complete islands. On several we could see creatures moving about. Here and there several terrified monkeys, which had taken shelter from the storm in a hollow trunk, were now running about, looking out in vain for some means of reaching the shore. Ahead of us we distinguished some large animal on a floating mass, but whether jaguar, puma, or tapir, at that distance I could not make out. No trace of the Indians or their canoe could we discover. It was evident that they had been entirely overwhelmed; indeed, as far as we could judge, the landslip had commenced close to the spot where we had last seen them, and they could not have had the warning which we received before the cliff was upon them. Not for a moment, however, notwithstanding all the terrifying circumstances surrounding me, were my thoughts taken off Arthur. Wounded as he had been by the poisoned dart, I feared that, even had he not been struck by the bough of a falling tree, he would have sunk through weakness produced by the poison. It made me very sad. Duppo was trying to comfort me, but what he said I could not understand. Our own position was indeed dangerous in the extreme. Any moment the tree might roll over, as we saw others doing round us: we might be unable to regain a position on the upper part. Should we escape that danger, and be driven on the bank inhabited by the hostile Majeronas, they would very probably put us to death. I had, however, providentially my ammunition-belt round my waist, and my gun had been preserved; I might, therefore, fight for life, and if we escaped, kill some animals for our support. Should we not reach the land, and once enter the main river, we might be carried down for hundreds of miles, day after day, and, unable to procure any food, be starved to death. Ellen and John would be very anxious at our non-appearance. These and many similar thoughts crossed my mind. I fancied that had Arthur been with me I should have felt very differently, but his loss made my spirits sink, and I could hardly keep up the courage which I had always wished to maintain under difficulties. Duppo's calmness put me to shame. True looked up in my face, and endeavoured to comfort me by licking my hand, and showing other marks of affection. Poor fellow! if we were likely to starve, so was he; but then he did not know that, and was better able to endure hunger than either Duppo or me.

The rain continued pouring down, hiding all objects, except in the immediate vicinity, from our view. I judged, however, that the falling cliff had sent us some distance from the shore into the more rapid part of the current. Providentially it was so, for we could still see the indistinct forms of the trees come sliding down, while the constant loud crashes told us that the destruction of the banks had not yet ceased. Thus we floated on till darkness came down upon us, adding to the horror of our position. The rain had by that time stopped. The thunder no longer roared, and the lightning ceased flashing. The storm was over, but I feared, from the time of the year, that we might soon be visited by another. We had climbed up into a broad part of the trunk, where, among the projecting branches, we could sit or lie down securely without danger of falling off. My chief fear arose from what I have already mentioned,—the possibility of the tree turning over. This made me unwilling either to secure myself to the branches, or indeed even to venture to go to sleep.

Hour after hour slowly passed by. Had Arthur been saved, I could have kept up my spirits; but every now and then, when the recollection of his loss came across me, I could not help bursting into tears. Poor, dear fellow! I had scarcely thought how much I had cared for him. Duppo spoke but little; indeed, finding himself tolerably secure, he probably thought little of the future. He expected, I dare say, to get on shore somewhere or other, and it mattered little to him where that was. True coiled himself up by my side, continuing his efforts to comfort me. In spite of my unwillingness to go to sleep, I found myself frequently dropping off; and at last, in spite of my dread of what might occur, my eyes remained closed, and my senses wandered away into the land of dreams. Duppo also went to sleep, and, I suspect, so did True.

I was awoke by the rays of the sun striking my eyes; when, opening them, I looked about me, wondering where I was. Very soon I recollected all that had occurred. Then came the sad recollection that Arthur had been lost. Our tree appeared to be in the position in which it had been when we went to sleep. Numerous other trees and masses of wood, some of considerable size, floated around us on either hand. The banks were further off than I had expected to find them. True, pressing his head against me, looked up affectionately in my face, as much as to ask, "What are we to do next, master?" It was a question I was puzzled to answer. I had to call loudly to Duppo to arouse him. After looking about for some time, I was convinced that the tree had been drifted into the main stream. On and on it floated. I began to feel very hungry; as did my companions. We were better off than we should have been at sea on a raft, because we could, by scrambling down the branches, quench our thirst. I brought some water up in my cap for True, as I was afraid of letting him go down, lest he should be washed off. I was holding it for him to drink, when Duppo pointed, with an expression of terror in his countenance, to the upper end of the tree, and there I saw, working its way towards us along the branches, a huge serpent, which had probably remained concealed in some hollow, or among the forked boughs, during the night. A second glance convinced me that it was a boa. To escape from it was impossible. If we should attempt to swim to the other trees it might follow us, or we might be snapped up by alligators on our way. I might kill it, but if I missed, it would certainly seize one of us. It stopped, and seemed to be watching us. Its eye was fixed on True, who showed none of his usual bravery. Instinct probably told him the power of his antagonist. Instead of rushing forward as he would probably have done even had a jaguar appeared, he kept crouching down by my side. Unacquainted with the habits of the boa, I could not tell whether it might not spring upon us. I knelt down on the tree and lifted my rifle; I did not, however, wish to fire till it was near enough to receive the full charge in its body. Again it advanced along the boughs. It was within five yards of us. I fired, aiming at its head. As the smoke cleared away, I saw the huge body twisting and turning violently, the tail circling the branch on which it was crawling. Duppo uttered a shout of triumph, and, rushing forward with a paddle which he had saved from the canoe, dealt the already mangled head numberless blows with all his might. The creature's struggles were at length over.

Pointing to the boa, Duppo now made signs that we should not be in want of food; but I felt that I must be more hungry than I then was, before I could be tempted to eat a piece of the hideous monster. When I told him so, he smiled, enough to say, "Wait a little till you have seen it roasted." I had my axe in my belt. He asked me for it, and taking it in his hand cut away a number of chips from the drier part of the tree, and also some of the smaller branches. Having piled them up on a broad part of the trunk near the water, he came back to ask me for a light. I told him that if I had tinder I could get it with the help of the pan of my gun. Away he went, scrambling along the branches, and in a short time returned with a bird's nest, which he held up in triumph. It was perfectly dry, and I saw would burn easily. In another minute he had a fire blazing away. I was afraid that the tree itself might ignite. Duppo pointed to the water to show that we might easily put it out if it burned too rapidly. He next cut off some slices from the body of the boa, and stuck them on skewers in the Indian fashion over the fire. Though I had before fancied that I could not touch it, no sooner had I smelt the roasting flesh than my appetite returned. When it was done, Duppo ate a piece, and made signs that it was very good. I, at length, could resist no longer; and though it was rather coarse and tough, I was glad enough to get something to stop the pangs of hunger. True ate up the portion we gave him without hesitation. Duppo then cut several slices, which, instead of roasting, he hung up on sticks over the fire to dry, throwing the remainder into the water.

He tried his best to amuse me by an account of a combat his father once witnessed in the depths of the forest between two huge boas, probably of different species. One lay coiled on the ground, the other had taken post on the branch of a tree. It ended by the former seizing the head of its opponent with its wide open jaws, sucking in a part of its huge body, gradually unwinding it from the tree. It had attempted, however, a dangerous operation. Suddenly down came the tail, throwing its coils round the victor, and the two monsters lay twisting and writhing in the most terrific manner, till both were dead. I have given the account as well as I could make it out, but of course I could not understand it very clearly.

The clouds had cleared away completely, and the sun's rays struck down with even more than their usual heat. Still, from the storms we had had of late, I suspected that the rainy season was about to begin. I could only hope, therefore, that we might reach the shore before the waters descended with their full force. Slowly we floated down with the current. On either side of us were several masses of trees, and single trees, such as I have before described. The rate at which we moved differed considerably from many of them. Now we drifted towards one; now we seemed to be carried away again from it. This, I concluded, was owing partly to the different sizes of the floating masses, and to the depth they were sunk in the water; and partly to the irregularity of the current. The wind also affected them, those highest out of the water of course feeling it most.

Chapter Fifteen
Voyage down the Amazon on a Tree

All day and another night we drifted on. The flesh of the boa was consumed. Unless a strong breeze should get up which might drive us on shore, we must go on for many days without being able to obtain food. I again became anxious on that point, and was sorry we had not saved more of the boa's flesh, unpalatable as I had found it. Again the sun rose and found us floating on in the middle of the stream. Duppo, although his countenance did not show much animation, was keeping, I saw, a look-out on the water, to get hold of anything that might drift near us. Presently I observed the small trunk of a rough-looking tree come floating down directly towards us. As it floated on the surface, being apparently very light, it came at a more rapid rate than we were moving. At length it almost touched the trunk, and Duppo, signing to me to come to his assistance, scrambled down towards it. He seized it eagerly, and dragged it up by means of a quantity of rough fibre which hung round it. He then asked me to help him in tearing off the fibre. This I did, and after we had procured a quantity of it, he let the trunk go. When I inquired what he was going to do with it, he made signs that he intended to manufacture some fishing-lines.

"But where are the hooks? and where the bait?" I asked, doubling up my finger to show what I meant.

"By-and-by make," he answered; and immediately on regaining our usual seat, he set to work splitting the fibre and twisting it with great neatness.

I watched him, feeling, however, that I could be of little assistance. He seemed to work so confidently that I hoped he would manage to manufacture some hooks, though of what material I was puzzled to guess. The kind of tree which had so opportunely reached us I afterwards saw growing on shore. It reaches to about the height of thirty feet. The leaves are large, pinnate, shining, and very smooth and irregular. They grow out of the trunk, the whole of which is covered with a coating of fibres hanging down like coarse hair. It is called by the natives *piassaba*. This fibre is manufactured into cables and small ropes. It is also used for brooms and brushes; while out of the finer portions are manufactured artificial flowers, baskets, and a variety of delicate articles.

While Duppo was working away at the fishing-lines, I was watching the various masses of trees floating near us. One especially I had observed for some time a little ahead of us, and we now appeared to be nearing it. As I watched it I saw something moving about, and at length I discovered that it was a monkey. He kept jumping about from branch to branch, very much astonished at finding himself floating down the river. He was evidently longing to get back to his woods, but how to manage it was beyond his conception. I pointed him out to Duppo. "He do," he said, nodding his head. It was a great question, however, whether we should reach the floating island. Even when close to it the current might sweep us off in another direction. Still, as we had drawn so near, I was in hopes that we should be drifted up to it. Had I not been hungry, I should have been very unwilling to shoot the monkey but now, I confess, I longed to get to the island for that very object. The creature would supply us and True with food for a couple of days, at all events. By that time Duppo might have finished his fishing-lines, and we might be able to catch some fish. Had we been on a raft, we might have impelled it towards an island; but we had no control over the huge tree which supported us. All we could do therefore was to sit quiet and watch its progress. Sometimes I doubted whether it was getting nearer, and my hopes of obtaining a dinner off the poor monkey grew less and less. Then it received a new impulse, and gradually we approached the island. Again for an hour or more we went drifting on, and seemed not to have drawn a foot nearer all the time. Duppo every now and then looked up from his work and nodded his head, to signify that he was satisfied with the progress we were making. He certainly had more patience than I possessed. At length I lay down, True by my side, determined not to watch any longer. I fell asleep. Duppo shouting awoke me, and looking up I found that our tree had drifted up to the floating mass; that the branches were interlocked, and as far as we could judge we were secured alongside. The monkey, who had been for a brief time monarch of the floating island, now found his dominions invaded by suspicious-looking strangers. For some time, however, I did not like to venture across the boughs; but at length the trunk drove against a solid part of the mass, and Duppo leading the way, True and I followed him on to the island. "Ocoki! ocoki!" he exclaimed, and ran along the trunk of a tall, prostrate tree of well-nigh one hundred feet in length. On the boughs at the further end grew a quantity of pear-shaped fruit, which he began to pick off eagerly. I did the same, though its appearance was not tempting, as it was covered with an outer skin of a woody texture. As he seemed eager to get it, I did not stop to make inquiries, but collected as much as I could carry in my wallet and pockets. He meantime had filled his arms full, and running back, placed them in a secure place on the trunk of the tree we had left.

The monkey had meantime climbed to a bough which rose higher than the rest out of the tangled mass. Hunger made me eager to kill the creature. I took good aim, hoping at once to put it out of pain. I hit it, but in falling it caught a bough with its tail, and hung on high up in the air. Duppo immediately scrambled away, and before long had mounted the tree. Though the monkey was dead, its tail still circled the bough, and he had to use some force to unwind it. He brought it down with evident satisfaction, and now proposed that we should return to our tree and light another fire. We first collected as much dry wood and as many leaves as we could find. Duppo quickly had the monkey's skin off. True came in for a portion of his dinner before ours was cooked. I saw Duppo examining the smaller bones, which he extracted carefully, as well as a number of sinews, which he put aside. He then stuck some of the meat on to thin spits, and placed it to roast in the usual fashion over the fire. While this operation was going on, he peeled some of the fruit we had collected. Inside the rind was a quantity of pulpy matter, surrounding a large black oval stone. I found the pulpy matter very sweet and luscious. I ate a couple, and while engaged in eating a third I felt a burning sensation in my mouth and throat, and, hungry as I was, I was afraid of going on. Duppo, however, consumed half-a-dozen with impunity. I may as well say here that this fruit is of a peculiarly acrid character. When, however, the juice is boiled it loses this property, and we frequently employed it mixed with tapioca, when it is called *mingau* by the natives. It takes, however, a large portion of the fruit to give even a small cup of the mingau. It grows on the top of one of the highest trees of the forest, and as soon as it is ripe it falls to the ground, when its hard woody coating preserves it from injury. The natives then go out in large parties to collect it, as it is a great favourite among them.

As may be supposed, we were too hungry to wait till the monkey was very much done. I found that I could eat a little ocoki fruit as a sweet sauce with the somewhat dry flesh.

Although the island was of some size, yet, as we scrambled about it, we saw that its portions were not firmly knit together, and I thought it very likely, should a storm come on, and should it be exposed to the agitation of the water, it might separate. I therefore resolved to remain on our former tree, that, at all events, having proved itself to be tolerably stable.

We were engaged in eating our meal when my ears caught that peculiar sound once heard not easily forgotten—that of a rattlesnake. Duppo heard it too, and so did True, who started up and looked eagerly about. At length we distinguished a creature crawling along the boughs of a tree about a dozen yards off. It had possibly been attracted by the smell of the roasting monkey, so I thought. It seemed to be making its way towards us. Perhaps it had long before espied the monkey, which it had been unable when alive to get hold of. At all events, it was a dangerous neighbour. I had no wish for it to crawl on to our tree, where it might conceal itself, and keep us constantly on the watch till we had killed it. Now I caught sight of it for a moment; now it was hidden among the tangled mass of boughs. Still I could hear that ominous rattle as it shook its tail while moving along. Though its bite is generally fatal, it is easily avoided on shore, and seldom or never, I have heard, springs on a human being, or bites unless trodden on, or suddenly met with and attacked. In vain I looked for it. It kept moving about under the boughs, as I could tell by the sound of its rattle. Now it stopped, then went on again, now stopped again, and I dreaded every instant to see it spring out from its leafy covert toward us. I kept my gun ready to fire on it should I see it coming. I was so engaged in watching for the snake, that I did not observe that the island was turning slowly round. Presently there was a rustling and a slightly crashing sound of the boughs, and I found that our tree was once more separated from the island, and just then I saw not only one but several snakes moving about. One of the creatures came along the bough, and lifting its head, hissed as if it would like to spring at us, but by that time we were too far off. Again we went floating down with greater speed than the floating island, and, judging from the inhabitants we had seen on it, we had reason to be thankful that we had escaped so soon.

Duppo, since he had finished eating, had been busy scraping away at some of the monkey bones, and he now produced several, with which he intimated he should soon be able to manufacture some hooks. Having put out our fire lest it should ignite the whole tree, we once more scrambled back to our former resting-place. Duppo, having got a couple of lines ready, worked away most perseveringly with the monkey bones, till he had manufactured a couple of serviceable-looking hooks. These he bound on with the sinews to the lines. He was going to fasten on some of the knuckle-bones as weights, but I having some large shot in my pocket, they answered the purpose much better. The hooks, baited with the monkey flesh, were now ready for use. Duppo, however, before putting them into the water, warned me that I must be very quick in striking, lest the fish should bite the lines through before we hauled them up. As we were floating downwards we cast the lines up the current, taking our seat on a stout bough projecting over the water. There we sat, eagerly waiting for a bite, True looking on with great gravity, as if he understood all about the matter. I almost trembled with eagerness, when before long I felt a tug at my line. I struck at once, but up it came without a fish. Again, in a short time, I felt another bite. It seemed a good strong pull, and I hoped that I had caught a fish which would give us a dinner. I hauled it up, but as it rose above the water I saw that it was not many inches in length. Still, it was better than nothing. It was of a beautiful grey hue. On getting it into my hand to take it off the hook, what was my surprise to see it swell out till it became a perfect ball. "*Mamayacu!*" exclaimed Duppo. "No good eat." I thought he was right, for I certainly should not have liked attempting to feed on so odd-looking a creature. When going to unhook it I found that its small mouth was fixed in the meat. When left alone it gradually resumed its former proportions.

I soon had another bite, and this time I hoped I should get something worth having. Again I hauled in, when up came a fish as long as the other was short and round, with a curious pointed snout. This, too, had been caught by the tough monkey meat, and promised to be of little more service than my first prize. I caught two or three other curious but useless fish, though, if very much pressed for food, we might have managed to scrape a little flesh off them. Duppo sat patiently fishing on. Though he had got no bites, he escaped being tantalised as I was by the nibbling little creatures which attacked my bait. Perhaps he sank his lower down. I could not exactly make it out, but so it was; and at length I saw his line pulled violently. His eyes glistened with eagerness. He had evidently, he thought, got a large fish hooked. He first allowed his line to run to its full length, then gradually he hauled it in, making a sign to me to come to his assistance. He then handed me the line. I felt from the tugging that a fish of a considerable size was hooked. He meantime got an arrow from his quiver and fitted it to his bow. Then he signed to me to haul in gently. I did so, dreading every instant that our prize would escape, for I could scarcely suppose that a bone hook could withstand so strong a pull. Kneeling down on the trunk, he waited till we could see the dark form of the fish below the surface. At that moment the arrow flew from his bow, and the next all resistance ceased; and now without difficulty I hauled the fish to the surface. Stooping down, he got hold of it by the gills, and with my assistance hauled it up to the trunk. It was nearly three feet long, with a flat spoon-shaped head, and beautifully spotted striped skin. From each side of its head trailed thin feelers, half the length of the fish itself. I felt very sure that with such tackle as we had that I should never have been able to secure so fine a fish. We had now food to last us as long as the fish remained good. We had just time to light a fire and cook a portion, as we had dressed the monkey flesh, before darkness came on.

The night passed quietly away, and the morning light showed us the same scene as that on which the evening had closed, of the far-off forest, and the wide expanse of water, with single trees and tangled masses of underwood floating on it. After we had lighted a fire, and cooked some more fish for breakfast, Duppo put out his lines to try and catch a further supply. Not a bite, however, did he get. He hoped, he said, to be more successful in the evening. We therefore hauled in the lines, and I employed the time in teaching him English. I was sure that Ellen would be greatly pleased, should we ever return, to find that he had improved.

Another day was passing by. The wind had been moderate and the river smooth. Again it came on to blow, and our tree was so violently agitated that I was afraid it would be thrown over, and that we should be washed off it. As we looked round we saw the other masses with which we had kept company tossed about in the same way, and frequently moving their positions. Now we drove on before the wind faster than we had hitherto gone. There was one mass ahead which I had remarked from the first, though at a considerable distance. We were now drifting nearer to it. I had watched it for some hours, when I fancied I saw an object moving about on the upper part. "It must be another monkey," I said to myself. I pointed it out to Duppo. He remarked that it moved too slowly for a monkey; that it was more probably a sloth. Then again it stopped moving, and I could scarcely distinguish it among the branches of the trees. I hoped that we might drift near enough to get it. It would probably afford us more substantial fare than our fish. After a time I saw Duppo eagerly watching the island. Suddenly he started up, and waved his hand. I looked as keenly as I could. Yes; it seemed to me that the figure on the island was again moving, and waving also. It was a human being; and if so, who else but Arthur? My heart bounded at the thought. Yet, how could he have escaped? How had he not before been seen by us? Again I waved, this time with a handkerchief in my hand. The figure held out a handkerchief also. There was now no doubt about the matter. It was very doubtful, however, whether we should drift much nearer the floating island. The wind increased; a drizzling rain came down and almost concealed it from sight, so that we could not tell whether or not we were continuing to approach it. This increased my anxiety. Yet the hope of seeing my friend safe, once kindled, was not to be extinguished; even should we not drive close enough to the island to join each other, we still might meet elsewhere. All we could do, therefore, was to sit quietly on the tree, and wait the course of events.

One of the most difficult things to do, I have found, is to wait patiently. Hour after hour passed by. The wind blew hard, and often so high did the waves rise that I was afraid we might be swept off. What would become of us during the long, dreary night? I felt the cold, too, more than I had done since we began our voyage. How much more must poor Duppo have suffered, with less clothing! I should have liked to have lighted a fire; but with the rain falling, and the tree tossing about, that was impracticable. We all three—Duppo, True, and I—sat crouching together in the most sheltered part of the tree. Thus the hours of darkness approached, and crept slowly on. Did I say my prayers? it may be asked. Yes, I did; I may honestly say that I never forgot to do so. I was reminded, too, to ask for protection, from feeling how little able I was, by my own unaided arm, to escape the dangers by which I was surrounded. I tried to get Duppo to join me. I thought he understood me; but yet he could scarcely have had the slightest conception of the great Being to whom I was addressing my prayers. I hoped, however, when he knew more of our language, that I should be able to impart somewhat of the truth to his hitherto uncultivated mind.

In spite of the rain, the darkness, and the movements of our tree, I at length fell asleep, and so, I believe, did Duppo and True. I was awoke, after some time, by a crashing sound, similar to that which had occurred when we drove against the floating island. I started up. True uttered a sharp bark. It awoke Duppo. Presently I heard a voice at no great distance exclaiming, "What is that? Who is there?"

"Who are you?" I shouted out.

"I am Arthur! And oh, Harry! is it you?"

"Yes," I answered. "How thankful I am that you have escaped!"

"And so am I that you have been saved," answered Arthur. "But where are you? I cannot find my way among the bough. Have you come off to me in the canoe?" I told him in reply how we were situated. "Can you join me?" he asked. "I have hurt my foot, and am afraid of falling."

"Stay where you are," I answered; "we will try to reach you."

I made Duppo understand that I wished to get to where Arthur was. It was necessary to move very cautiously, for fear of slipping off into the water. We could not tell, indeed, whether the butt-end or the boughs of our tree had caught in the floating island; all we could see was a dark mass near us, and a few branches rising up towards the sky. I was afraid, however, that if we did not make haste we might be again separated from it as we had been from the other island. We scrambled first some way along the boughs; but as we looked down we could see the dark water below us, and I was afraid should we get on to the outer ends that they might break and let us fall into it. I thought also of True, for though we might possibly have swung ourselves across the boughs, he would have been unable to follow us. I turned back, and once more made my way towards the root-end, which, by the experience we had before had, I hoped might have driven in closer to the mass we wished to reach. We had to crawl carefully on our hands and knees, for the rain had made the trunk slippery, and we might easily have fallen off. As I got towards the end, I began to hope that it was touching the island. I again called out to Arthur. His voice sounded clearer than before. When I got to the end among the tangled mass of roots, I stopped once more to ascertain what Duppo advised we should do.

I sat some time trying to pierce the gloom. At length I thought I saw a thick bough projecting over the extreme end of our tree. If I could once catch hold of it I might swing myself on to the island. There was one fear, however, that it might give way with my weight. Still I saw no other mode of getting to Arthur. True, I hoped, might leap along the roots, which were sufficiently buoyant to bear his weight, at all events. Having given my rifle to Duppo to hold, I cautiously went on. I got nearer and nearer the bough. With one strong effort I might catch hold of it. I sprang up, and seized it with both hands. It seemed firmly fixed in a mass of floating wood. After clambering along for a short distance I let myself down and found footing below me. I now called to Duppo, and holding on to the bough above my head with one hand, stepped back till at last I was able to reach the rifle which he held out towards me. True sprang forward, and was in an instant by my side. Duppo followed more carefully, and at length we were all three upon the island.

I made my way up the branch.

"We shall soon find our way to you," I cried out to Arthur.

"Oh, thank you, thank you!" he answered.

It was no easy matter, however, to make our way among the tangled mass of trunks and roots and boughs without slipping down into the crevices which yawned at our feet. I could judge pretty well by his voice where Arthur was. Duppo pulled at my arm. He wished that I would let him go first. This I was glad to do, as I had great confidence in his judgment and activity. Following close behind him, we at length got directly under where Arthur was perched.

"Here we are," I cried out, "on a firm trunk. Could you not manage to come down?"

"I am afraid not," he answered.

"Stay, then; I will climb up and assist you," I said.

Putting my gun down, I made my way up the branch. Most thankful I was again to press his hand.

"I am somewhat sick and hungry," he said; "but now you have come, I shall soon be all right."

"Well, let me help you down first," I replied. "We have brought some food, and when you have eaten it we will talk more about what has happened to us. I hope we shall manage somehow or other to reach the shore before this island is carried out to sea."

"Oh yes, I hope so indeed," he said. "I have never thought that likely."

I now set to work to help Arthur down. Duppo stood under the branch and assisted me in placing him at length in a more secure position.

"Oh, I am so thankful you have come!" he kept repeating; "my only anxiety was about you. Still I hoped, as I had so wonderfully escaped, that you might also be safe. All I know is, that I was in the water, and then that I found myself clinging to a bough, and that I gradually pulled myself up out of the water. I believe I fainted, for I found myself lying among a mass of boughs; and when I managed at last to sit up, I discovered that I was floating down the river. Not for some time did I feel any sense of hunger. At length, when I did so, I found, greatly to my satisfaction, that I had my wallet over my shoulders, well stored with provisions. They were, to be sure, wet through; but I ate enough to satisfy the cravings of hunger. In the morning I looked about me, hoping to see you on one of the masses of trees which were floating down the stream round me. You may fancy how sad I felt when I could nowhere distinguish you. I knew, however, that it was wrong to give way to despair, so when the sun came forth I dried the remainder of the food, which has supported me hitherto."

"But did you feel any pain from your wound?" I asked. "That has been one great anxiety to me. I thought you were truck by a poisoned arrow."

"No," he answered. "I pulled it out at once, and had forgotten it, till I felt a pain in my shoulder. Then the dreadful thought that it was poisoned came across me, and I expected, for some time, to feel it working within my system. It was perhaps that which made me faint; but as I did not feel any other ill effects, I began to hope that, either in passing through my jacket the poison had been scraped off, or that it has, as I have heard, but slight noxious effects on salt-eating Europeans."

I agreed with him that this must be the case; indeed, he complained of only a slight pain in the shoulder where the arrow had struck him. In the darkness which surrounded us, I could do no more than give him some of the food we had brought with us. The remainder of the night we sat on the trunk of the tree, Duppo and I supporting Arthur in our arms, while True crouched down by my side. We could hear the water washing round us, and the wind howling among the branches over our heads. The rain at length ceased, but I felt chilled and cold; and Arthur and Duppo were, I feared, suffering still more. Thus we sat on, doing our best to cheer each other. So long a time had passed since Arthur had been struck by the arrow, that I no longer apprehended any dangerous effects from it. Still, he was very weak from the long exposure and the want of food, and I became more anxious to get him safe on shore, where, at all events, he might obtain shelter and sufficient nourishment. Wherever we might be cast, we should, in all probability, be able to build a hut; and I hoped that with my gun, and Duppo's bow, we should obtain an ample supply of game.

"Now we have found each other, I am afraid of nothing," said Arthur.

"Neither am I," I answered. "Still I fear that Ellen and John will be very unhappy when they do not see us."

We had been talking for some time, when we felt a violent shock. The water hissed and bubbled up below us, and the mass of trees on which we floated seemed as if they were being torn asunder. Such, indeed, was the case. Duppo uttered a cry of alarm.

"What shall we do?" exclaimed Arthur. "O Harry, do try and save yourself. Never mind me. What can have happened?"

"We have driven ashore," I answered. "I am nearly certain of it. All we can do till daylight is to cling on to this trunk; or, if you will stay here with Duppo, I will try and make my way to the other side, to ascertain where we are."

"Oh, do not leave me, Harry," he said. "I am afraid something may happen to you."

We sat on for a few minutes. Still the crashing and rending of the boughs and sipos continued. At length I was afraid that we might be swept away by the current, and be prevented from reaching the shore. I therefore told Duppo what I wanted to do. He taking Arthur by one arm, I supported him by the other, and thus holding him up we tried to force our way among the tangled mass. Now we had to hang on by our hands, finding no firm footing for our feet. In vain we tried to force our way onwards. In the darkness I soon saw that it was impossible. A thick wall of sipos impeded our progress. It was not without the greatest difficulty that at length we got back to the trunk we had left. Even that was violently tossed about, and I was even now afraid that we might be thrown off it. Once more we sat down on the only spot which afforded us any safety. Gradually objects became more clear, and then I saw, rising up against the sky, the tall upright stems of trees. They could not be growing on our floating island. I now became aware that the mass on which we sat had swung round. It seemed once more to be moving on. There was no time to be lost. Duppo and I again lifted up Arthur, and made our way towards the end of the trunk. Not till then did I discover that it was in actual contact with the shore. We hurried along. A few feet only intervened between us and the dry land. "Stay, I will go first," I exclaimed, and made a sign to Duppo to support Arthur. I let myself down. How thankful I was to find my feet on the ground, though the water was up to my middle. "Here, Arthur, get on my back," I cried out. Duppo helped him, and in another minute I was scrambling up the bank on the dry ground. Duppo let himself down as I had done, and True leaped after us. Scarcely were we on shore when the trunk we had left floated off, and we could see the mass, with several detached portions, gliding down the river. Where we were we could not tell, but daylight coming on would soon reveal that to us. We sat ourselves down on the bank, thankful that we had escaped from the dangers to which we should have been exposed had we remained longer on the floating island.

Chapter Sixteen
Our Return

Where we had been cast we could not tell. Daylight was increasing. The clouds had cleared off. We should soon, we hoped, be able to see our way through the forest, and ascertain our position. We all remained silent for some time, True lying down by my side, and placing his head upon my arm. While thus half between sleeping and waking, I heard a rustling sound, and opening my eyes, half expecting to see a snake wriggling through the grass, they fell on a beautiful little lizard making its way down to the water. At that moment a pile of dry leaves, near which it was passing, was violently agitated, and from beneath them sprung a hairy monster, with long legs and a huge pair of forceps, and seized the lizard by the back of its neck, holding it at the same time with its front feet, while the others were firmly planted in the ground to stop its progress. In vain the lizard struggled to free itself. The monster spider held it fast, digging its forceps deeper and deeper into its neck. I was inclined to go to the rescue of the little saurian, but curiosity prevented me, as I wished to see the result of the attack, while I knew that it had already, in all probability, received its death-wound. The struggles of the lizard grew feebler and feebler. Its long tail, which it had kept whisking about, sank to the ground, and the spider began its meal off the yet quivering flesh. I touched Arthur, and pointed out what was taking place. "The horrid monster," he exclaimed. "I must punish it for killing that pretty little lizard." Before I could prevent him, he had jumped up and dealt the spider a blow on the head.

On examining it I found that it was a great crab-spider, one of the formidable *arachnida*, which are said to eat young birds and other small vertebrates, though they generally, like other spiders, live upon insects. This spider—the *mygagle avicularia*—will attack humming-birds, and, indeed, other small specimens of the feathered tribe. When unable to procure its usual food of ants, it lies concealed under leaves as this one had done, and darts out on any passing prey which it believes it can manage; or if not, it climbs trees and seizes the smaller birds when at roost, or takes the younger ones out of their nests. It does not spin a web, but either burrows in the ground, or seeks a cavity in a rock, or in any hollow suited to its taste.

I had never seen any creature of the spider tribe so monstrous or formidable. Under other circumstances I should have liked to have carried the creature with us to show to my companions. As soon as Arthur had killed it, Duppo jumped up and cut off the two forceps, which were as hard and strong as those of a crab; and I have since seen such set in metal and used as toothpicks, under the belief that they contain some hidden virtue for curing the toothache.

The rest had almost completely cured Arthur's sprained ankle, and on examining his shoulder, I found that the arrow had inflicted but a slight wound, it having merely grazed the upper part after passing through his clothes. This, of course accounted for the little inconvenience he had felt. Still, I believe, even had the wound been deeper, the poison would not have affected him. I was indeed very thankful to see him so much himself again.

We were now aroused, and, getting on our feet, looked about as to settle in which direction we should proceed. We soon found that we were at the western end of an island, and as the distant features of the landscape came into view, we felt sure that it was the very one, near the entrance of the igarape, where we had first landed. We had supposed that we had floated much further down the river.

"The first thing we have to do is to build a raft, and to get back to our friends," I said to Arthur. "We shall have little difficulty, I hope, in doing that. We must lose no time, and we shall be able to reach them before night."

This discovery raised our spirits. We had first, however, to look out for a bed of rushes to form the chief part of the intended construction. The experience we had gained gave us confidence. We explained to Duppo what we proposed doing, and set forward along the northern shore of the island. We were more likely to find on that side, in its little bays and inlets, the materials we required. The axe which Duppo had saved was of great importance. We had made our way for a quarter of a mile along the beach, when the increasing density of the underwood threatened to impede our further progress. Still we had not found what we required. "I think I see the entrance of an inlet, and we shall probably find reeds growing on its banks," said Arthur. "We can still, I think, push our way across these fern-like leaves."

We pressed forward, though so enormous were the leaves of which he spoke, that a single one was sufficient to hide him from my sight as he made his way among them. Duppo and True followed close behind me, but True could only get on by making a succession of leaps, and sometimes Duppo had to stop and help him through the forked branches, by which he ran a risk every instant of being caught as in a trap.

"I think I see the mouth of the inlet close ahead," said Arthur. "If we push on a few yards more we shall reach it. Get the axe from Duppo and hand it to me; I must cut away some sipos and bushes, and then we shall get there."

I did as he requested. I had broken down the vast leaves which intervened between us, when I saw him beginning to use his axe. He had made but a few strokes when a loud savage roar, which came from a short distance off, echoed through the wood. His axe remained uplifted, and directly afterwards a sharp cry reached our ears. "That is a woman's voice," I exclaimed. "Where can it come from?" Duppo, as I spoke, sprang forward, and endeavoured to scramble through the underwood, as did True.

"Cut, Arthur, cut," I exclaimed. "Unless we clear away those sipos we shall be unable to get there."

Arthur needed no second bidding, and so actively did he wield his axe, that in a few seconds we were able to push onwards. Again the savage roar sounded close to us, but the cry was not repeated. "Oh, I am afraid the brute has killed the poor creature, for surely that must have been a human being who cried out," exclaimed Arthur.

We dashed on, when, reaching the water, we saw, scarcely twenty yards off, on the opposite bank, a canoe, in which were two persons. One lay with his head over the gunwale; the other, whom I at once recognised as our friend Illora, was standing up, no longer the somewhat retiring, quiet-looking matron, but more like a warrior Amazonian—her hair streaming in the wind, her countenance stern, her eyes glaring, and with a sharp spear upraised in her hands, pointed towards a savage jaguar, which, with its paws on the gunwale, seemed about to spring into the canoe. It was too evident that her husband had been seized, and to all appearance killed. What hope could she have of resisting the savage creature with so slight a weapon. That very instant I dreaded it would spring on her. Poor Duppo shrieked out with terror; but though his mother's ears must have caught the sound, she did not withdraw her glance from the jaguar. She well knew that to do so would be fatal. Duppo made signs to me to fire, but I feared that in so doing I might miss the jaguar and wound one of his parents. Yet not a moment was to be lost. My rifle, fortunately, was loaded with ball. I examined the priming, and prayed that my arm might be nerved to take good aim. Again the brute uttered a savage growl, and seemed on the point of springing forward, when I fired. It rose in the air and fell back among the foliage, while Illora thrust her spear at it with all her force. Not till then did she seem to be aware of our presence. Then waving to us, she seized the paddle and brought the canoe over to where we were standing. Duppo leaped in and lifted up his father. The blood had forsaken his dark countenance; his eyes were closed, his head was fearfully torn—the greater part of the hair having been carried away. Illora knelt down by his side, resting his head upon her arm. Arthur and I felt his pulse. It still beat. We made signs to his wife that he was alive, for she had evidently thought him dead. I fortunately had a large handkerchief in my pocket, and dipping it in water, bound up his head. He appeared to revive slightly. Illora then made signs to us that she wished to go down the river. We did not even stop to look what had become of the jaguar, convinced that he was killed. No time was to be lost. Having placed Maono on some leaves in the stern of the canoe, she seized one of the paddles and urged it out into the main stream. Duppo took another paddle. Fortunately there were two spare ones at the bottom of the canoe. Arthur and I seized them. Illora paddled away, knowing well that the life of her husband depended on her exertions. However callous may be the feelings of Indians generally, both she and Duppo showed that they possessed the same which might have animated the breasts of white people. Every now and then I saw her casting looks of anxiety down on her husband's face. He remained unconscious, but still I had hopes that if attended to at once he might recover.

"I am thankful a jaguar did not spring out on us as we were passing through that thick underwood," observed Arthur. "How utterly unable we should have been to defend ourselves."

"Yes, indeed; and still more so that we did not take up our abode there," I remarked. "Probably the island is infested with jaguars, and we should have run a great chance of being picked off by them."

"I doubt if more than one or two would find support there," he remarked. "How that one, indeed, came there is surprising."

"Possibly he was carried there on a floating island," I answered. "I doubt whether intentionally he would have crossed from the mainland; for though jaguars can swim, I suppose, like other animals, they do not willingly take to the water." This, I suspect, was the case.

We tried to learn from Illora how her husband had been attacked. She gave us to understand that, after looking about for us, they had put in there for the night, and were still asleep when the savage brute had sprung out of the thicket and seized Maono. She heard him cry out, and had sprung to her feet and seized her lance just at the moment we had found them.

"We should be doubly thankful that we were cast on the island and arrived in time to rescue our friend," I observed to Arthur.

As may be supposed, however, we did not speak much, as we had to exert ourselves to the utmost to impel the canoe through the water. I was, however, thankful when at last we saw the roof of our hut in the distance. We shouted as we approached, "Ellen! Maria!" Great was our delight to see Ellen and Maria, with Domingos, come down to the edge of the water to receive us. As I jumped out, my affectionate little sister threw her arms round my neck and burst into tears.

"Oh, we have been so anxious about you!" she exclaimed; "but you have come at last. And what has happened to the poor Indian? Have you been attacked again by the Majeronas?"

I told her briefly what had occurred, and set her anxiety at rest with regard to our parents by giving her Fanny's note, and telling her how we had found it. I need not repeat her expressions of joy and thankfulness. I then asked for John, as he understood more about doctoring than any of us. He had gone away with his gun to shoot only just before, and might not be back for some time. The Indians were at their own settlement, a couple of miles off.

"What can we do with him!" I exclaimed.

"Why not take him to the recluse?" said Ellen. "He will know how to treat him."

I made Illora comprehend what Ellen proposed. She signified that that was what she herself wished to do.

"Then, Ellen, we must leave you again," I said. "We must do our best to save the life of our friend."

Arthur agreed with me, and entreating Ellen to keep up her spirits till our return, we again, greatly to Illora's satisfaction, jumped into the canoe. "We hope to be back to-morrow morning!" I cried out, as we shoved off.

Though somewhat fatigued, we exerted ourselves as much as before, and having the current in our favour, made good progress. Examining the banks as we went along, I saw how almost impossible it would have been to have effected a landing on that dreadful night of the storm, when we had the raft in tow, for one dense mass of foliage fringed the whole extent, with the exception of a short distance, where I recognised the sand-bank on which Arthur had been nearly killed by the anaconda. Maono every now and then uttered a low groan when his wife bathed his head with water—the best remedy, I thought, she could apply.

The voyage was longer than I had expected, for nearly two hours had passed before we reached the mouth of the igarape, near which the hut of the recluse stood. Having secured the canoe, Illora lifted up her husband by the shoulders, while we put the paddles under his body, and his son carried his feet. We then hastened on towards the hut. As we came in sight of it, Duppo shouted out to announce our approach to the recluse. No one appeared. The door, I saw, was closed, but the ladder was down. We stopped as we got up to it, when Duppo, springing up the steps, knocked at the door. My heart misgave me. The recluse might be ill. Then I thought of the ladder being down, and concluded that he was absent from home. Again Duppo knocked, and obtaining no reply, opened the door and cautiously looked in. No one was within. What were we to do? Were we to wait for the return of the owner, or go back to our settlement? I advised that Maono should be carried within, and proposed waiting till he appeared. We lifted him up and placed him under the shade of the verandah. Meantime Duppo collected a number of dried leaves, with which to form a bed, as he was not in a fit state to be placed in a hammock. I then advised Illora to send Duppo for water, while Arthur and I went out and searched for the recluse, in the hope that he might be in the neighbourhood. We first went to his plantation, thinking that he might be there, but could nowhere find him. It appeared, indeed, as if it had not been lately visited, as it was in a far more disordered state than when we had before seen it. We were afraid of going into the forest, lest we should lose our way; we therefore turned back and proceeded up the igarape, which would serve as a guide to us. It grew wilder and wilder as we went on. At length we reached a spot which we could not possibly pass. The trunks of the mighty trees grew close to the water, their roots striking down into it, while thousands of sipos and air-plants hung in tangled masses overhead, and huge ferns with vast leaves formed a dense fringe along the banks. Near us the trunk of an aged tree, bending over the water, covered with parasitic plants, had been seized by the sipos from the opposite side, and hung, as it were, caught in their embrace, forming a complete bridge across the igarape. I have already described these wonderful air-plants. They here appeared in greater numbers and more varied form than any we had yet seen. Flights of macaws and parroquets flew here and there through the openings, or climbed up and down, cawing and chattering in various tones. Although I should have liked to have obtained some, I saw that, should I kill any, they would have fallen where it would be impossible to get at them, for even True could not have made his way through the wood; and I was afraid that if they fell into the water, he might be snapped up by an alligator who might be lurking near.

We were on the point of turning away, when Arthur exclaimed, "I see something moving high up the igarape, among those huge leaves." I scrambled down to where he was standing, and presently, amid the dim light, a human figure came into view. At first it seemed as if he was standing on the water, but as he slowly approached we saw that a raft of some sort was beneath his feet. He was hauling himself along by the branches, which hung low down, or the tall reeds or leaves fringing the banks.

"I do believe it is the recluse," whispered Arthur to me. "What can have happened to him?" We waited till he came nearer. He looked even wilder and more careworn than usual. He had no covering on his head except his long hair, while he had thrown off his coat, which lay on the raft. Slowly and not without difficulty he worked his way on. He did not perceive us till he was close to where we stood.

"Can we help you, sir?" I said. "We came to look for you."

"What induced you to do that?" he asked. "I thought no human being would care for me."

"But we do, sir," said Arthur, almost involuntarily. "You can be of service to one of your friends, a poor Indian, who has been severely hurt."

"Ah! there is something to live for then!" he exclaimed, looking up at us. "But I must have your assistance too. I have injured my leg; and had I not been able to reach the igarape and construct this raft, I must have perished in the forest. I have with difficulty come thus far, and should have had to crawl to my hut, as I purposed doing, had you not appeared to assist me. My canoe I had left a league or two further away, and could not reach it."

"Oh, we will gladly help you, sir," exclaimed Arthur; "and if you will let us, we will tow the raft down nearer to the hut."

"It is strange that you should have come; and I accept your offer," answered the recluse.

We soon cut some long sipos, and fastening them together we secured one end to the raft. The recluse sat down, evidently much exhausted by his previous exertions; and while we towed the raft along, he kept it off the bank with a long pole. When we got down opposite the hut, we assisted him to land. He could not move, however, without great difficulty.

"Let me go and call Mora and Duppo, that we may carry you in the litter on which I was brought to your hut," said Arthur. "No, no; I can get on, with your assistance, without that," answered the recluse, placing his arms on our shoulders. He groaned several times, showing the pain he suffered;

but still he persevered, and at length we reached the hut. We had great difficulty in getting him up the ladder. When he saw Maono, he seemed to forget all about himself.

"My hurt can wait," he observed. "We must attend to this poor fellow." Having examined the Indian's head, he produced a salve, which he spread on a cloth, and again bound it up. "A European would have died with such a wound," he observed; "but with his temperate blood, he will, I hope, escape fever."

Having attended to his guest, he allowed Arthur and I to assist him in binding up his leg, and in preparing a couch for him in his own room, instead of the hammock in which he usually slept. He explained to Illora how she was to treat her husband, and gave her a cooling draught which he was to take at intervals during the night. Having slung his hammock in the outside room, Arthur and I lay down, one at each end; while the Indian woman sat up to keep watch, and Duppo coiled himself away on one of the chests.

At daybreak, Arthur, hearing the recluse move, got up and asked him if he could be of any service.

"Yes, my good lad," answered our host; "you can help me to bind this limb of mine afresh. Bring me yonder jar of ointment!" I heard what was said, though I could not see what was going forward. "Thank you, my lad," said the recluse. "No woman's hand could have done it better. Now go and see how the Indian has passed the night."

Arthur came out, and having looked at Maono, reported that he was still sleeping quietly.

"He must not be disturbed then," was the answer. "When he wakes I will attend to him. Now, go and see what food you can obtain. My plantations will afford you some; or if not, your brother will be able to shoot some birds. He will find troops of toucans and parrots not far off. Some farinha will be sufficient for me."

"Harry will, I am sure, do his best to kill some game," said Arthur; "but you called him my brother. Though he is a dear friend, we are not related. He has father, and mother, and sisters; and the gentleman you saw is his brother; but I have no relations—none to care for me except these kind friends."

"I know not if you are to be pitied then," said the recluse. "If you have none to care for you, you are free to take your own way."

"Oh, but I do care for the kind friends who brought me out here," exclaimed Arthur. "And I feel that I care for you; and I ought to do so, as you took care of me and nursed me when I was ill." The recluse was silent, and Arthur came into the larger apartment.

The recluse was sufficiently recovered during the day to be placed in his more airy hammock in the outer room. His eyes, I observed, were constantly following Arthur. "It is strange," I heard him whispering to himself. "There is a resemblance, and yet, it is so unlikely."

Maono was going on favourably; and the recluse was able to crawl from his hammock to attend to him as often as was necessary. I was very anxious to get back to Ellen and John; especially to assist in finishing the canoe, that we might at soon as possible recommence our voyage down the river. I proposed, therefore, that Arthur and I should set off at once, as I thought we could find our way through the forest without difficulty. The recluse seemed far from pleased at my proposal.

"I would not deprive you of the society of your friend," he said, "but he will be of great assistance to me if he can remain; and you can call for him when you come down the river. Instead of him, take the boy Duppo with you. He may be of more use in guiding you through the forest. The Indian woman will probably wish to remain with her husband."

I found that Arthur was ready to stay with the recluse. "Poor man," he said, "I may, I think, be of some service in soothing his mind, as well as assisting him as he wishes. I do not like to leave you, Harry; but if you do not object, I will remain. I wish, however, that you would go in the canoe."

"She is too heavy, I fear, to paddle against the stream," I answered; "and if I have Duppo as a guide, I would rather return through the forest."

I explained this to the Indians, who at once consented that Duppo should return with me; while Illora remained to nurse her husband. As there was time to reach our location before dark, I begged to set off at once. Duppo and I stored our wallets with fresh farinha; and I hoped to kill a toucan, or a brace of parrots, on our way, which would afford us sufficient food. As no time was to be lost, we set off at once. Duppo showed some affection when parting from his mother. She was certainly less demonstrative, however, than a European would have been. He was evidently very proud of being allowed to attend on me.

He led the way with unerring instinct through the forest; and I felt that there was no danger of losing the path, as John and I had done when travelling in the same direction. I kept my eyes about me as we proceeded, hoping to shoot some game, as we had but a limited supply of food. I got a shot at a toucan, which was climbing with bill and claws up a tree above our heads. It hung on to the branch for an instant, and I was afraid I should lose it. Its claws and beak, however, soon let go, and down it came, its beautiful plumage shining in the sun as it fell. I could scarcely bring myself to kill it; but I had to confess that necessity has no laws, and should as willingly at that moment have shot the most gaily-coloured macaw or parroquet. It would, however, afford Duppo and I, and True, but a scanty meal; I therefore kept my gun ready for another shot.

Going on a little further, directly in front of us a beautiful deer started up from behind a thicket. True darted forward, and flew at the creature, which turned round and round to defend itself. I thus had the opportunity of having a good aim, and wounded the deer in the neck. Duppo started off in pursuit. He had brought his father's blow-pipe instead of his own, which he had lost. It was too heavy, however, for him to manage. I thought we should have lost the deer; but kneeling down, he raised it on a hanging sipo, and let fly an arrow, which struck the animal. He had time to send another shaft before the deer got out of sight. Then calling to me, he urged me to pursue it. Away we went through the forest, True at the heels of the deer, and I following Duppo as closely as I could. Still, notwithstanding its wounded condition, there seemed every probability of its escaping. Duppo thought otherwise, and continued the pursuit; though I could not perceive either the animal or its track. He was right, however; for in ten minutes we again caught sight of it, moving slowly. Just as we reached it, it sank to the ground. It was the first deer we had killed; though I had seen several scampering in the distance through the more open parts of the forest, and I believe they are numerous along the banks of the Amazon and its tributaries. We packed up as much of the flesh as we could carry, and hung the remainder on the branch of a tree.

We were walking on with our loads, when a loud crashing sound echoed through the forest. I had never seen Duppo show any sign of fear before, but he now came close up to me, trembling all over. "What is the matter?" I asked. All was again silent for some minutes. Then came from the far distance the melancholy howl, which had often kept us awake at night—the cries, I felt sure, of howling monkeys. They again ceased; and a loud clang sounded through the forest, such as I had read of in that wonderful romance, "The Castle of Otranto." Duppo grew more and more alarmed; and now caught hold of my jacket, as if I could protect him. I was puzzled to account for the sound; but still I saw nothing very alarming in it. When, however, a loud piercing cry rent the air, coming, I could not tell from whence, I confess that I felt somewhat uncomfortable. Poor Duppo trembled all over, and clung to my arm, exclaiming, "*Curupíra! curupíra!*" True pricked up his ears, and barked in return. "Do not be afraid, Duppo," I said, trying to encourage him. "It may have been only the shriek of a monkey, caught by a jaguar or puma." He, however, seemed in no way disposed to be satisfied by any explanations which I could suggest of the noises we had heard.

As we proceeded, he tried to explain to me that he was sure that that part of the forest was haunted by a spirit, which made the noises. It was like a huge monkey, covered with long shaggy hair. He committed, he said, all sorts of mischief. He had a wife and family, whom he taught to do as much harm as himself; and that, if they caught us, they would certainly play us some trick. I tried to laugh away his fears, but not with much success.

At last he gained a little more confidence, and walked on ahead to show the way. No other sound was heard. He looked back anxiously to see that I was close to him.

Among the fruits I observed numbers of a curious bean-like description. Several species had pods fully a yard long hanging to delicate stalks, and, of course, very slender. Others were four inches wide, and short. While I was looking down to pick up some of the curious beans I have mentioned, I saw the big head of a creature projecting from a hole. For a moment I thought it was a large serpent, but presently out hopped a huge toad in pursuit of some little animal which had incautiously ventured near its den. Presently it gave sound to a most extraordinary loud snoring kind of bellow, when True dashed forward and caught it. I rescued the creature before his teeth had crushed it. On recovering its liberty, it croaked away as lustily as before. On measuring it, I found it fully seven inches long, and as many broad. It had a considerable enlargement of the bone over the eyes, while the glands behind the head were of great size. I knew it thus to be the agua toad — *Bufa agua*. I had no doubt that he and his brothers produced some of the hideous noises we had heard at night. I have since read that these toads will kill rats, and that a number of them were carried to Jamaica for the purpose of keeping down the swarms of rats which devastated the plantations of that island. I found, indeed, the bones of several rodent animals near its den. It was somewhat remarkable, but a few minutes afterwards I saw another toad lying quietly on the ground. I kept True back, not wishing to let him hurt the creature. I saw some small animals moving on its back, and stooping down, what was my surprise to see a number of little toads scrambling out of holes apparently in its skin. First out came one, and slipping down the fat sides of the big toad, hopped along on the ground. Another little head directly afterwards burst its way through the skin, and imitated the example of its small brother. Several others followed. Even Duppo, in spite of his late fright, could not help bursting out laughing. The colour of the big toad was a brownish-olive and white below; but the head was most extraordinary, as it had a snout almost pointed, the nostrils forming a kind of leathery tube. The creature was, I at once guessed, the Surinam toad—*Pipa Americana*—which I knew was found, not only in Surinam, but in other parts of this region. It is, though one of the ugliest of its race, one of the most interesting. The male toad, as soon as the eggs are laid, takes them in its paws, and places them on the back of the female. Here, by means of a glutinous secretion, they adhere, and are imbedded, as it were, in a number of cells formed for them in the skin. Ultimately a membrane grows over the cells and closes them up. The eggs are here hatched, and the young remain in them till their limbs have grown and they can manage to take care of themselves. The skin of the back is very thick, and allows room for the formation of the cells, each of which is sufficiently large to contain a small-sized bean placed in it edgeways. As soon as the brood have left the cells, they are again closed, giving a very wrinkled appearance to the back. Duppo made signs to me that the creature was good to eat; but I must say, I should have been very hard pressed for food before I should have been tempted to try it. I succeeded in dragging True away, and prevented him interfering with the family arrangements of the wonderful *batrachian*.

We met with several other curious frogs and toads, but the creatures which abounded everywhere, and unfortunately surpassed all others in numbers, were the ants—*termites*. The termites, I should remark, differ from the true ants by appearing out of the egg with their limbs formed, and in the same shape they bear through life. Some we met with in our walk were an inch and a quarter in length, and stout in proportion. The creatures were marching in single file, coming out from a hole formed in the roots of a small tree. I took up one to examine it, and received a sting for my pains, but the pain soon went off. We all suffered much more from the stings of several smaller ants, especially the fire-ants, by which we had on more than one occasion been attacked.

Although I had twice before made the trip through the forest, I still felt certain that we were far from the hut, when Duppo signified to me that we should soon reach it. Just then I heard a shot, and a magnificent macaw fell down a short distance ahead of us. True dashed forward, and directly afterwards I heard John's voice. I hurried on.

"Yes, we are all well," answered John to my inquiries, as he took my load of venison and slung it over his more sturdy shoulders. "The canoe is finished, and we were only waiting for your return to set out. No positive news about our parents; but the Indians describe having seen a canoe with white people, women among them, pass down the river several weeks ago Ellen feels sure it was they who were seen; though, as is sometimes the case with her, dear girl, she can give no other reason than her own feelings. I am disappointed at not seeing Arthur; but we must put in to take him on board, and save him the journey through the forest."

Of course John wanted to know all about our adventures, and I briefly recounted them as we walked homewards.

"It is, indeed, a mercy that your life was saved," he observed. "I would almost advise you not to tell Ellen all the fearful dangers you went through; it will make her nervous, for she even now sometimes dreads that the Majeronas will again attack us."

"They will certainly not come so far by water," I remarked; "and our friends will give us warning should they venture by land. Still, as the canoe is ready, we ought not to delay in commencing our voyage."

As soon as we emerged from the thick part of the forest, we caught sight of Ellen watching for us in front of the hut. She came running forward, followed by Maria and Oria, and not only by Nimble and Toby, but a whole troop of other creatures. John laughed. "There comes our little sister," he said, "with her happy family. She and her young companions have not been idle. It is wonderful how they have contrived to tame all those creatures."

In another minute Ellen and I were in each other's arms. She looked very well, and glad to see me, but her eye roved about in quest of Arthur. She was satisfied, however, when I told her that he had remained behind to attend to the recluse.

"I am not surprised at it," she said; "for I could not help fancying that there was some relationship between the two. Our strange friend was evidently more interested in Arthur than in any of us. In spite of his cold and repelling manner, Arthur, too, took greatly to him. However, perhaps I am wrong."

"Yes; I suspect, Ellen, it is but one of your fancies. You would like it to be the case; it would be so interesting and romantic, and so you cannot help thinking that it must be so," observed John.

Ellen was eager at once to introduce me to her pets. Nimble and Toby knew me immediately, and climbed up my back without hesitation.

"Here," said Ellen, "is a dear little bird." It was a small heron of a very graceful shape. The plumage was variegated with bars and spots of several colours, as are the wings of certain moths. She called it, and it immediately came up to her with a peculiarly dainty, careful gait. An insect was crawling along the ground. It immediately afterwards pierced it with its slender beak, and gobbled it up. It was the *ardea helias*. John said he had seen the birds perched on the lower branches of trees in shady spots: their note is a soft, long-drawn whistle; they build their nests in trees, of clay, very beautifully constructed.

"Now I must introduce my *curassow* turkey," she said, calling another very handsome bird, almost as large as an ordinary turkey. It was of a dark-violet colour, with a purplish-green gloss on the back and breast. The lower part was of the purest white, while the crest was of a bright golden-yellow, greatly increasing the beauty of the bird. John called it the crested curassow—the *crax alector*.

"See," she said, "I have greatly increased the number of my feathered friends. Look at this beautiful marianna."

It was a small parrot, with a black head, a white breast, and orange neck and thighs—a most lovely little creature. As soon as she called it, it came down from its perch and sprang upon her wrist. When she again let it go, off it went, poking its head into the various articles on the verandah, examining a basket of fruits which Oria had just brought in, and the pots of which Domingos had charge; now pecking at one thing, now another. Our Indian friend had brought her another parrot called an *anaca*. This was also a beautiful bird, its breast and belly banded with blue and red, while the back of the neck and head were covered with long bright-red feathers margined with blue. True approaching it, up went the crest, looking remarkably handsome. From this crest it obtains the name of the hawk-head parrot. It came when called, but quickly retired in rather a solemn fashion to its perch.

"Do you know," said Ellen, "Oria has brought me that beautiful little duck you described. I would rather take that home with me than all the other pets, and yet I should be sorry to lose any of them."

"I tell Ellen that her menagerie is a mere bait to jaguars or boas, or other prowling animals of the forest," observed John. "What a nice breakfast one of them would make if it found its way into our settlement!"

"You shall not frighten me with any such ideas," she answered; "and I hope before we leave the country that I may add many more to my collection. But I have not shown you my humming-bird yet," she said. "I keep it in a cage in the house for fear the others should get at it; but it takes a flight by itself every day, and comes back again when it wants a sip of sirrup, or wishes to go to roost. I must show you some nests of the beautiful little birds which have built not far off. Would you like to go and see them at once?"

Knowing it would please her, while Domingos and Maria were preparing our evening meal, I accompanied her to a little distance, where, hanging to some long, pendant leaves, she pointed out two little purse-shaped nests, composed, apparently, of some cottony material bound together with spider-web. A graceful little bird was sitting in each of them, with tails having long, pointed feathers. The upper part of their bodies were of a green bronze, except the tail-coverts, which were of a somewhat rusty red; while the tails themselves were of a bronzed tint, broadly tipped with white. I knew them by the shape of their bills and their nests to belong to the genus *Phaëthornis*.

"They are quite accustomed to me now," she said, "and will not fly away even when I go near them."

While we were looking, the mate of one of the birds came up and perched close above the nest. As we were going away I saw two others pass by us, of the same size, it seemed to me. Another settled on a flower near at hand, when the idea seized me that I could catch it. I struck it with my hat, and down it fell. Ellen uttered a cry of sorrow; but stooping down, what was my surprise to find, instead of a humming-bird, a moth so exactly in shape and appearance like the humming-birds, that it was no wonder I had been deceived.

"You would not have killed a humming-bird so easily," said Ellen; "but I am sorry for the poor moth."

The moth, however, though stunned, was not killed. On taking it to the hut I compared it with her tame pet, and was struck by the remarkable similarity in the shape of the head and position of the eye. The extended proboscis represented the long beak of the bird, while at the end of the moth's body was a brush of long hairs, which, as it flew along, being expanded, looked very much like the feathers of the bird's tail. Oria, when she saw the moth, told Ellen that it would some day turn into a bird; and Ellen, I believe, did not succeed in persuading her that such would certainly never happen. The resemblance, of course, is merely superficial, their internal construction being totally different. I have not as yet described nearly all Ellen's new pets; but just then, as I was very hungry, I had something else to think of.

Chapter Seventeen
Our Voyage Recommenced

I was awoke the following morning by an unusual commotion among our four-footed and feathered friends. The monkeys were chattering away and running along the rafters, up and down the posts; the parrots were talking energetically together; while True every now and then ran to the door and gave a peculiar bark, coming back again under my hammock. John and Domingos were quickly aroused by his barks. "What can be the matter!" I exclaimed. "Some animal is outside," answered John, springing out of his hammock. "It has probably been trying to find an entrance into our hut. If a puma or jaguar, we will soon settle him."

"Oria thinks it is some big serpent, from the way the animals are frightened," said Ellen, from her room.

"Whether big serpent or savage beast, we need not fear it, my sister," answered John, going to the door, which we always kept closed at night for safety's sake.

What was our dismay to see a huge serpent coiled round the post of the verandah, with its head moving about as if in March of prey. Duppo sprang forward and shut to the door, exclaiming, "*Boiguaeu!*" Even True ran behind us, not liking to face the monster. From the glimpse we got of it, it seemed of enormous size, and might readily have crushed two or three people together in the folds of its huge body. John and I went back and got our guns ready, while Domingos and Duppo kept guard at the door.

"I said those pets of Ellen's would serve as baits some day for one of those creatures!" exclaimed John. "However, if we can hit it in the head, we need not fear its doing us any harm."

Having carefully examined the loading of our firearms, we told Domingos again to open the door. He seemed, however, very unwilling to do so, alleging that the serpent might dart in and seize some one before we could kill it. Not till John had insisted upon it would he consent. "Oh, my dear young masters, do take care!" he exclaimed. "If you would but wait, perhaps the creature would crawl away. Suppose you miss it, you do not know what may happen."

"Now," cried John, "calm your fears, and open the door."

Domingos on this pulled open the door, springing back himself at the same time, while John and I stepped forward with our rifles, ready to fire. The serpent was gone. We looked about in every direction. It was not pleasant to know that so dangerous a monster was in our neighbourhood. Domingos said he was sure it was hid away somewhere, and Duppo agreed with him. We hunted about anxiously, but nowhere could we discover it. Believing that it had altogether gone away, we told Ellen and her companions that they might venture out. Ellen came fearlessly, but Maria and the Indian girl were evidently far from satisfied, and I saw them glancing round anxiously in every direction. However, as the snake did not appear, we had breakfast, and then went down to work at the canoe. John told me that he had engaged four Indians to paddle her, and that he expected them that morning. We were working away, when we heard a low cry, and Oria was seen running towards us with looks of terror in her countenance. She uttered a few hurried words to her brother, the meaning of which we could not understand; but he soon showed us by signs that something had happened at the hut. On getting near—for it was concealed where we were at work—we saw, to our dismay, the boa-constrictor coiled as before round one of the outer supports, and evidently intent on making an entrance into the hut. The door was closed. We heard Ellen's and Maria's voices calling from within. We had unfortunately left our guns in the verandah, and could not get at them without approaching dangerously near to the huge reptile. Every moment I dreaded to see it break through the slight door. John and Domingos had hatchets in their belts, but we were possessed of no other weapons. How to get rid of the creature was the question. We shouted at the top of our voices, hoping to frighten it away, but our cries had no effect. Every moment we knew, too, that it might come down and attack us. Ellen and Maria were naturally in a great state of alarm. They had secured all their pets, though John suggested that by sacrificing some of them they might possibly satisfy the boa. He shouted out to them a recommendation to that effect. "No, Señor John, no!" answered Maria from within. "Señora Ellen says she would remain here for a week, rather than give up one to the horrid monster."

As we stood at a respectful distance, the serpent now and then turned his head, as if he would dart at us, when Domingos cried out, "Oh, my young masters! fly! fly! The boiguaeu is coming!"

"We must cut its head off if it does!" exclaimed John, "I have a great mind to dash in and get hold of my gun."

I entreated him not to attempt so rash an experiment. While we were watching the serpent, the Indians we had been expecting appeared, emerging from the thick part of the forest, Duppo and Oria ran towards them. They seemed to be telling them about the boa. Instead of coming on to our assistance, however, away they started back into the forest.

"The cowards!" exclaimed John; "they have run off and left us to fight the battle by ourselves."

"I am not quite so certain of that," I answered.

We waited. Still the boa did not move, but continued watching the door. Probably through one of the chinks its eye had caught sight of Nimble or True, who had also fortunately been inside. After waiting till our patience was nearly exhausted, the Indians re-appeared, carrying between them a young peccary, while others carried long coils of sipos. At some little distance from the hut they stopped, when one of them climbed a tree, to which he secured a loop of sipos, passing through it another long line. At the end of this a loop was formed. With a stake they secured the peccary close to the loop, so that to get at it the serpent must run its head through the noose. The peccary, having its snout tied up, was unable to squeak. As soon as the arrangement was made, they retired to a distance, holding the other end of the line. One of them then unloosed the peccary's muzzle, when the creature instantly began to grunt. At that instant the serpent turned its head, and, unwinding its huge body, made its way towards the animal. In another moment almost the peccary was struck, and the huge serpent began to fold its body round it. Its own head, however, was meantime caught in the noose, but this it apparently did not feel, and opening its wide jaws, began to suck in the animal. As it did so the Indians pulled the noose tighter and tighter. The teeth of the reptile are so formed that it could not again force the peccary out of its mouth, while the noose prevented it swallowing it. John and I eagerly sprang forward and seized our guns, but Duppo now coming up, told us that there was no necessity to use them, as in a short time the boa would be dead.

As the boa lay on the ground John boldly rushed up and gave it a blow with his axe. The natives now without fear forced their spears into the creature's mouth, and dragged out the mangled body of the peccary. This done, they hoisted the serpent up by the neck to the branch of the tree, whence it hung down, showing us its full length, which could not have been much less than twenty-five feet. To make sure that it would not come to life again, one of them climbed up, and with his knife split open the body. Even during the short time it had coiled itself round the peccary it had broken every bone in the creature's body. I observed that it placed coil above coil, as if to increase the force of the pressure, and it had instantly begun to swallow its prey without first lubricating it, as it is erroneously described as doing. The part of the peccary which had entered the mouth was, however, covered with saliva, but this had only been poured upon it in the act of swallowing.

We thanked the Indians for the assistance they had given us in killing our enemy. They had come, they said, to finish the canoe, and also to inquire about Maono and Illora, whose absence had caused the tribe great alarm. They had also brought us some mandioca-flour and a supply of fruits. Farinha or flour, I should say, is produced from the same root—cassava, or manioc—as is tapioca, and is like it in appearance, only of a yellower colour, caused by the woody fibre mixed with the pure starch which forms the tapioca. There were also several cabbage-palms, always a welcome addition to our vegetables. Among the fruit were some pine-apples, which had been procured in a dry treeless district—so we understood—some miles in the interior.

Ellen begged that they would remove the body of the serpent to a distance, as she did not at all like seeing it hanging up to the tree near us. Fastening sipos to it, they accordingly dragged it away. By the following morning not a particle of it remained, it having furnished a feast to several armadillos, vultures, and other birds of prey.

The last evening of our stay had arrived. Our provision were ready for embarking, and all our goods packed up. I was awoke by hearing Domingos cry out—

"Some rats, or other creatures, have got into the hut, and are eating up the farinha."

On striking a light, we hurried to the corner in which our provisions were stored, intending to drive out the intruders, when, instead of rats, we found a column of ants passing to and fro between the door and our baskets of food. Each of them carried a grain of a tapioca-like substance as big as itself. In vain we tried to drive them off. Though hundreds were killed, others came on in a most determined manner, as if they had resolved to rob us at all cost. At last John proposed that we should blow them up. We called out to Ellen not to be alarmed, and then spread a train of powder across the column, when we set it on fire. This seemed to stagger them, but others still came on. Not till we had performed the operation three times did they seem to discover their danger, when the first coming on turned round and warned those behind, and the whole took their departure. The next morning we traced them to a spot at a considerable distance, where we came upon a mound of earth between two or three feet high, and nearly eleven yards in circumference. This we found was the dome which protected the entrance to the abode of our visitors of the previous night. It was a wonder they had not found us out before. It was of a different colour to the surrounding ground. This was owing to its being composed of the under-soil brought up from below. We perceived a number of small holes in the sides—the commencement of galleries. We discovered, on digging into it, that each led to a broad gallery four feet in diameter. This again led down into the centre of the wonderful habitation.

"Hilloa!" cried Arthur; "here comes Birnam Wood in miniature."

He was at some distance from us. On going up to him we found what looked like a vast number of leaves moving along over the ground. On examining them, we discovered that each was of the size and shape of a small coin, and carried by an ant. On tracing them back we found the tree at which they were at work. It was covered by vast multitudes. Each ant was working away at a leaf, cutting out a circle with its sharp scissor-like jaws. As soon as the operation was complete, it lifted it up vertically and marched away towards the mound. As one lot of labourers descended, others ascended and took their places, so that in a short time the tree was denuded of leaves. These leaves were used, we discovered, to thatch the domes of their galleries and halls to keep them dry, and protect the young broods in the nests beneath them. One body of workers was employed in bringing the leaves which they cast down on the hillock, while another placed them so as to form the roof, covering them with a layer of earth brought up in single grains with prodigious labour from the soil below. There appeared to be three different classes of workers—some employed entirely below, others acting as masons or tilers, and others entirely engaged in bringing the materials from a distance. There were, besides, soldiers armed with powerful mandibles, who accompanied the workers for defence, and walked backwards and forwards near them without doing anything. They have also a queen-ant, who dwells in the centre of their castle, and is engaged in laying the eggs, not only to furnish broods for the colony, but to send forth vast numbers of winged ants to form new ones. At the commencement of the year the workers can be seen clearing the galleries, and evidently preparing for some important event. Soon afterwards a vast number of winged males and females issue forth, the females measuring two and a quarter inches in expanse of wing, though the males are much smaller. Few of them, however, escape to enjoy existence, for they are immediately set upon by numbers of insectivorous animals and devoured. The few females who escape become the mothers of new colonies.

While digging, we came upon a snake-like creature about a foot long. Directly Duppo saw it he entreated us not to touch it, as it was fearfully poisonous, and called it the mother of the saubas. We, however, knew it to be perfectly harmless. He declared that it had a head at each end of its body. We convinced him, however, that he was wrong, by showing him the head and tail. The body was covered with small scales, the eyes were scarcely perceptible, and the mouth was like that of a lizard. He asserted that the sauba-ants are very much attached to the snake, and that, if we took it away, they would all desert the spot. In reality, the snake found a convenient hiding-place in the galleries of the ants, while, when in want of food, it could at all times make a substantial meal off them. When the ant-eater opens one of these galleries, the workers immediately run off and hide themselves, while the soldier-ants rush forth to attack the intruder, and, of course, immediately fall victims; thus preserving, by the sacrifice of their own lives, the rest of the community. The peculiar motion of the snake we found, scientifically called *amphisbaenae*, wriggling as it does backwards and forwards, has given rise to the idea of its having two heads. Duppo told us many other stories about it, which I have no space to mention. These ants sometimes form mounds from thirty to forty yards in circumference, and have been known to burrow even under rivers. As they attack fruit-trees, they are a great pest to the inhabitants of the settled parts of the country, and are sometimes destroyed by forcing fumes of sulphur through their galleries. Their chief use in the economy of Nature seems to be the consumption of decayed vegetable matter, as they are exclusively vegetarians.

While the Indians were getting the boat down to the water, and Ellen and her attendants, assisted by Domingos, were packing up, John, Duppo, and I took a ramble into the woods to kill some more game, as we were not likely to have anything but fish for some time to come. As we were going along, I heard the twittering of some dull-plumaged birds in the bushes, and was trying to get a shot at them, when I saw John, who was a little way ahead, jumping about in the most extraordinary manner. Duppo cried out, on seeing him, "Tauoca!" and made a sign to us to run off, himself setting the example. John followed. "I have been attacked by an army of ants," he exclaimed. "See, here are hundreds sticking to me." Duppo and I went to his assistance, and we found his legs covered with ants with enormous jaws, holding on so tight to the flesh that, in pulling them off, the heads of many were left sticking in the wounds they had made. We caught sight of the column which was advancing, about six deep, with thinner columns foraging on either side of the main army. Creatures of all sorts were getting out of their way with good cause, for whenever they came upon a maggot, caterpillar, or any larvae, they instantly set upon it and tore it to pieces, each ant loading itself with as much as it could carry. A little in front of them was a wasp's nest, on a low shrub. They mounted the twigs, and, gnawing away at the papery covering, quickly got at the larvae and the newly-hatched wasps. These they carried off in spite of the efforts of the enraged parents, who kept flying about them. They were ecitons, or foraging ants, of which there are numerous species. They also came upon a bank, in their course, in which was a nest belonging to a large species of white ant. They forced their way in, attacked them, and dragged out the bodies of the slain. These were cut into three or four pieces, each of which was lifted up by an eciton and carried off.

However, a volume could be filled with accounts of the numberless ants and termites of South America, and their curious and varied habits. One species is quite blind; others tunnel as they go, or form ways to enable them to make their attacks in secret. For this purpose the little creatures will form miles of covered ways. Some build their nests of clay in trees, and others hollow out abodes under the bark. They vary, too, in size and form. Some are half an inch long; some white, others red and black; some sting furiously. The ants inhabiting trees are those which commit depredations in houses chiefly. The most annoying of the species is the fire-ant—a little creature of a shining reddish colour. They live in the sand, where they form subterranean galleries covered by a sandy dome. They enter houses, and attack eatables of all sorts. When they attack human beings they fix their jaws in the flesh, and, doubling up their tails, sting with all their might; and a very fearful sting it is. When we met with them we were obliged to smear the ropes of our hammocks with balsam of *copaüba*. Eatables are suspended in baskets by ropes covered with the same balsam, and the legs of chairs and footstools are also covered to prevent their climbing up and stinging those sitting on them. Villages have sometimes been deserted in consequence of the attacks of these fierce little insects. However, they are only found on the sandy banks of the river and drier parts of the country.

After this digression I must continue my narrative. We shot only two or three birds, and then had to hurry back to prepare for our departure. Our new canoe floated well, but was smaller than we could have wished. Over the centre was an awning of palm-leaves, under which was seated Ellen, with her black and brown attendants and her numerous pets, surrounded by our goods and chattels. Four Indians sat in the bows to paddle, while John and Domingos took it by turns to steer. Duppo had especial charge of the various pets, while I was glad to be relieved from the labour of paddling. I had my gun ready for a shot, and we kept out our books of natural history, which I wished to search through, and two or three others for reading. We were thankful to be once more on our voyage, but still we could not help looking with some interest and regret at the beautiful spot in which we had spent the last few weeks. "All on board?" cried Domingos. "On, boys, on!" and giving a shove with his pole, we left the bank and glided down the stream, our dark-skinned crew keeping time with their paddles to the monotonous song which they struck up. Although the wet season was commencing, the weather promised to be fair for a time; and we hoped soon to have Arthur on board, and to continue our voyage without interruption till we should at length fall in with those dear ones of whom we were in search.

I have already described the broad river, and the wall of strangely varied and lofty trees which border it. We kept along the left bank, not to run the risk of missing the entrance to the igarape of the recluse, as we called it.

"Do you think we shall persuade him to come with us?" asked Ellen. "I should be so delighted if we could draw him out of his strange way of life and restore him to society."

John thought there was little chance of our doing so.

"If anybody can, I think Arthur may," I observed.

"Then you agree with me in my notion?" said Ellen.

"It is possible you may be right," I answered; "but yet it would be very strange."

The recluse formed the chief subject of our conversation during the day's voyage. At length we approached his igarape. I almost expected to see him and Arthur standing on the bank, but looked out in vain. To give them notice of our approach, I fired off my rifle. We had already made the canoe fast at our former landing-place. Ellen, John, and I were going towards the hut when Arthur appeared. "O Arthur will he come—will he come?" cried out Ellen.

Arthur shook his head. "I am very glad to see you," he said; "but if you had delayed a few days longer perhaps he would have made up his mind. However, you must come and try what you can do."

"And how is Maono?" I asked.

"He is wonderfully recovered, but is still unable to move."

"I hope he and his wife will not insist on Oria remaining with them!" said Ellen.

"I think not," answered Arthur. "Were it not for their other children, they would like to come themselves, I suspect, were Maono better. But you must come and see our friend; he has been so kind and gentle, and talked a great deal to me. I have been greatly puzzled to know the meaning of some of his questions. Sometimes he spoke as if he would like me to remain with him; but when I told him that I could not leave you, my old friends, he agreed that I ought not."

As we entered the open space before the hut of the recluse he advanced to meet us, and courteously invited us to remain till the next day. We had wished to push on, as we had still some hours of daylight; but Arthur begged us so earnestly to remain, that at last John agreed to do so. The Indians built themselves a hut near the canoe, in which Domingos remained to watch over our goods; while we passed the night at the hermitage. Ellen tried her utmost to persuade our host to accompany us; but he declined, saying that he could not abandon his present mode of life, and would not desert his patient Maono till he had recovered. Maono and Illora showed more pleasure at seeing us than is usually exhibited by Indians. His head was still bound up, and both he and his wife appeared clothed in light garments, which, though not so picturesque as their savage want of attire, made them look much more civilised.

The next morning we were on foot before daybreak, and having breakfasted, and bid farewell to the chief and his wife, repaired at early dawn to the canoe, attended by the recluse. Again Arthur entreated him to accompany us, observing that Maono had so far recovered that Illora might attend to him without his aid. He seemed to hesitate, but finally shook his head, saying, "It cannot be; no, it cannot be!"

"Then do you wish me to remain with you?" asked Arthur, looking up in his face.

The recluse seemed to be agitated with contending feelings. "No, boy, no!" he answered. "I cannot allow you to leave friends who have shown that they are interested in your welfare. But take this packet, and do not open it till you have rejoined Mr Faithful's family. You will, I doubt not, ere long find them, for from the information I have obtained they some time ago proceeded down the river. Where they are settled I cannot tell, but two if not more messengers have been despatched by them in search of you, some of whom have either gone higher up the river, or have fallen victims to the treacherous savages."

Arthur took the packet from the recluse with a look of surprise.

"It will explain all," said the latter. "Put it by now, and keep it carefully. I have acted for the best, and you will acknowledge that when you come to notice the contents."

Saying this, he pressed Arthur's hand, and assisting Ellen into the canoe, waved an adieu, and turning hastily round, with long hasty strides hurried back towards his abode. The Indians stood up and saluted him with signs of respect, and then, at the command of Domingos, began to ply their paddles, and we once more recommenced our voyage. Arthur watched the recluse till he disappeared among the trees.

"It is very, very strange," I heard him say to himself; "I cannot understand it." Several times he pulled out the packet and looked at it wistfully. "I must not disobey him," he added aloud, "and yet I long to know what he meant by giving me this."

"So do I," said Ellen; "but I am sure you ought to obey him."

Arthur started; he seemed not to be aware that he had been speaking aloud.

John looked at Ellen. "Sister," he said rather gravely, "do not utter your ideas; whatever they may be, you are likely to be wrong."

Ellen was silent. Arthur replaced the packet in his wallet, and the subject was not again alluded to. For several hours we glided down the stream without interruption. In the middle of the day we landed to give our crew rest and to cook our dinner. While the men were resting, we rambled through the forest with Duppo. We took Duppo that we might not run the risk of losing our way. We had gone on for some distance, when he exclaimed, "*Jacaré tinga!*" I called True close to me, knowing that the words meant alligator. Duppo crept cautiously on. Every moment we expected to come up with the monster, though on dry ground we knew we had little cause to fear it. "What is that?" exclaimed John, and he fired his rifle at a creature which went bounding through the forest. For a moment I caught sight of a jaguar, and directly afterwards we came on an alligator which had evidently just been killed by the jaguar. I should have liked to have seen the combat in which the fierce mammal had come off victorious. What mighty strength it must have put forth to kill the huge reptile which lay mangled before us, a considerable portion of the interior devoured. Duppo, on seeing it, began to search about in the neighbourhood, and came before long on a conical pile of dead leaves, from among which he dug out upwards of twenty eggs. They were nearly twice the size of those of a duck, and of an elliptical shape. The shells were very hard, of the texture of porcelain, and extremely rough on the outside. Duppo rubbed them together, producing a loud sound. Then he shook his head, as much as to say, "If the mother were alive that would bring her, but there she lies;" and he then told us that it was the way his people had of attracting alligators when they found a nest, knowing that the female is sure to be near, and will come to see what is the matter with her eggs. We carried them on board as a present to our crew, knowing that they would be acceptable, as the natives are very fond of them. At night we landed on an island, and built our huts in the same style that we had done on descending the Napo. And thus, with various incidents which I have not space to recount, we proceeded on our voyage for several days without interruption.

Chapter Eighteen
Joyful News

Day after day we sailed down the mighty Amazon, often the opposite shore appearing like a blue line in the distance, and yet we were upwards of twelve hundred miles from the mouth. Now it again narrowed into more river-like proportions. Sometimes we found ourselves navigating between numerous islands, cut off from the mainland by the rush of waters; but along the whole extent, often for a hundred miles together, not a hut was to be seen, not a sign of a human habitation. Whenever we came near the abode of man we landed, and Domingos or John and one of the natives approached cautiously to make inquiries; but hitherto without success. Here and there we came to a mission establishment of the Portuguese. They consisted generally of the priest's house, a larger building for the church, and a few huts scattered about, inhabited by natives. As far as we could judge, these so-called Christian natives were but little raised above their still heathen countrymen, while the effect of the religion they had assumed was to make them more idolatrous and superstitious than before. The priests, however, were very civil, but there was nothing to tempt us to remain at their stations; we therefore, after gaining the information we required, pushed on and camped in our usual way. We agreed that our father had probably acted in the same way, for we could gain no certain news of him. We heard, however, what gave us some anxiety—that the country was in a greatly disturbed state, and that the natives had, in several places, risen against the Portuguese, and driven them from their settlements. The poor priests, indeed, seemed unhappy about themselves, and not at all confident that their flocks might not rise and treat them in the same way. One, indeed, gave out strong hints that he would like to accompany us, and would undertake to pilot us down the river; but our canoe had already as many on board as she could carry, while our provisions were so greatly diminished that they would not hold out much longer.

We frequently avoided the main channel, the navigation of which in bad weather is dangerous, and made our way through some of the numerous channels filled by the rising waters on either side. Thus we paddled on through channels sometimes so narrow that the boughs arched almost overhead, at other times spreading out into lake-like expanses. I have already so frequently described the vegetation, the numberless palms and other trees, some of enormous size, with their festoons of air-plants and climbers of all sorts, that I need not again draw the picture. Emerging from a narrow path, we entered a calm and beautiful lake, when there appeared before us, floating on the water, a number of vast circular leaves, amid which grow up the most gigantic and beautiful water-lilies.

"Oh, what flowers!" exclaimed Ellen; "do gather some."

"Surely those cannot be leaves!" exclaimed Arthur. "See, a bird with long legs is walking over them!"

John fired, and the bird fell in the centre of the leaf on which it was standing, and which still supported it in the water; and taking it off the leaf, alongside which we paddled, we found it to be a jacana, remarkable for the great length of its toes, especially the hinder one, and their spine-like claws. It was a wonderfully light bird also, and these peculiarities enable it to walk over the leaves of the water-plants and procure its food, which consists of worms. The beak was orange colour, but the greater part of the body black, with the back and wing-coverts of a bright chestnut, with a few yellow touches here and there, and the legs of a greenish-ash colour. We heard the shrill and noisy notes of its fellows in the trees near us. "Ah, that is a *piosoca*!" said Duppo, "and that leaf is its oven;" and so it was in shape like the pans in which the natives roast their mandioca meal.

Ellen had, in the meantime, been examining one of the beautiful flowers which the boatmen picked for her. The outside of the leaves was of a delicate white, deepening in colour through every shade of rose to the deepest crimson, and then fading again to a creamy-yellowish tint at the heart. Many of the leaves were five feet and upwards in diameter, and perfectly smooth on the upper surface, with an upright edge of an inch to two inches all the way round. We managed, though not without difficulty, to pull up some stalks, and found them covered with long sharp spines. The construction of the leaf was very curious, it being supported below by a number of ribs projecting from the stalk, and giving it greater buoyancy and strength. One of the boatmen, plunging down, brought up a young leaf from the bottom. It had the form of a deep cup or vase, and on examining it we discovered the embryo ribs, and could see how, as they grew, their ramifications stretched out in every direction, the leaf letting out one by one its little folds to fill the ever-widening spaces. At last, when it reaches the surface of the water, its pan-like form rests horizontally above it without a wrinkle. This beautiful lily, then unknown to science, has since been called the Victoria Regia.

Nothing could exceed the beauty of this calm lake, covered for a considerable distance with these magnificent flowers. Among the lilies appeared a variety of other water-plants, some gracefully bending over like bamboos, others with large deep serrated leaves, while the different forest trees in varied forms rose round us, fringed by a broad band of feathery grass. Several trees floated on the borders covered with water-fowl, among which were many ducks and ciganas, while amid the lofty branches of the living forest flew numerous macaws of a red, green, and yellow species, and one of the small flock of the still more beautiful blue macaw, appeared to add their lovely tints to the landscape. Such was the scenery through which we passed during the greater part of the day. Had we felt sure about the safety of our family, how much more should we have enjoyed it. Our anxiety again increased. We had good reason to be anxious about ourselves. Our stock of provisions was almost exhausted; all our luxuries except coffee had come to an end, and of that we had very little, while we had only a small supply of farinha remaining.

We encamped at the end of our day's voyage through that labyrinth of canals on the only spot we could find free from trees, the rising waters having covered nearly all the ground. While looking for some poles for our hut, I saw on the branch of a tree overhanging the water, gazing down upon us, a hideous monster, fully five feet long, which at the first glance I took to be a species of alligator with which I was unacquainted. Presently, as I gazed at it, it filled out a large bag under its throat, and opened its hideous mouth. It was covered with scales, had a long tail, the point of which was hid among the branches, and enormous claws at the end of its legs. I beat a quick retreat, calling to John to come to my assistance with his gun, for I fully believed that the creature would leap off and attack me. The Indians, hearing my voice, came towards me, and cut down some long thin sipos, at the end of which they formed a running noose. Thus prepared, they boldly advanced towards the creature, and one of them throwing up the noose, adroitly caught it round the neck. The others, taking the end, gave it a sudden jerk, and down it came to the ground. As soon as it regained its feet it boldly made at them, but they nimbly leaped out of its way; and as its movements were slow, there seemed but little risk of its catching them.

"Why, that must be an iguana!" exclaimed John.

While some kept hauling at the creature's neck, turning it when it tried to get away, others ran to the canoe and brought their spears, with which they ran it through the neck, and quickly killed it. It was an iguana (*Iguana tuberculata*). Though the head was very different from that of the alligator, being blunt, yet, from having a number of sharp teeth, it could evidently have given a severe bite. Its head was somewhat large, and covered with large scales. It had an enormous wide mouth, while under its chin was a sort of big dew-lap, which, as it had shown me, it could inflate when angry. At the sides of the neck were a number of tubercles, while the tail was very long, thin, and tapering. It was of a dark olive-green, but the tail was marked with brown and green in alternate rings. The creature was nearly six feet long. The Indians seemed highly delighted with their prize, and as soon as our huts were built, commenced skinning and cutting it up. Domingos assured us that it was very good to eat, and produced a fricassee for supper, which we could not help acknowledging was excellent. A part also was roasted.

Shortly afterwards I saw another iguana on the ground. True darted at it, and I shouted to him to come back. Fortunately for itself, my shouts startled the iguana, which took to the water, and swam away, sculling itself forward by meant of its long tail at a rapid rate.

Arthur had manufactured a net for catching insects. As soon as we were seated in front of our hut, enjoying the cool air after the sun had set, Ellen exclaimed, "Oh, see what beautiful fireworks!" At a short distance from us there appeared suddenly to rise thousands of sparks of great brilliancy. Arthur ran forward with his net, and quickly returned, placed the hoop on the ground, and lifted up the end, when so bright was the light which came from the interior that we could without difficulty read a page of the book on natural history we had been examining a short time before. On taking out some of the insects he had caught to look at them more narrowly, Arthur placed one on its back, when it sprang up with a curious click and pitched again on its feet. On examining it we found that this was produced by the strong spine placed beneath the thorax, fitting into a small cavity on the upper part of the abdomen. It brings this over its head, and striking the ground with great force, can thus regain its natural position. The creature was about an inch and a half long, and of a brown colour. The light proceeded from a smooth, yellow, semi-transparent spot on each side of the thorax. We found that even with a single one passed over the page we could see the letters clearly. Ellen ran and brought a vial, into which we put a dozen, when it literally gave forth the light of a bright lamp, sufficient to write by. It is known in the country as the cocuja. It is the elater, or still more scientifically, the *Pyrophorus noctilucus*. The forest behind the hut was literally filled at times with brilliant sparks of light, now vanishing, now bursting forth with greater brightness than at first. The Brazilian ladies wear these beetles alive secured in their hair, and sometimes on their dresses, which thus glitter brightly as they move about in the dusk.

The next morning at daylight Duppo was busily employed hunting about in the neighbourhood, and at length shouted to us to bring a basket. We found he had just discovered the nest of an iguana, filled with eggs.

He assured us that they were excellent. On boiling some for breakfast, we agreed with him. Like those of the turtle, they did not harden by boiling, but only became somewhat thicker, and were filled almost entirely with yellow, having very little albumen. We all set to work to hunt for more, and were fortunate in finding another nest, the eggs being a welcome addition to our scanty supply of food. The Indians meantime, while we were finishing breakfast, set off into the forest, and just as we were ready to start came back with another iguana.

We were constantly employed in trying to teach Duppo English. Arthur was explaining to him the animals of our country, and was mentioning the cow, and describing its milk. He seemed much interested, and then gave us to understand that they also had cows in their land, which, instead of walking about on four legs, grew in the ground, and were of great size. After this he was constantly looking out along the banks, and at length he shouted out to the men, "Massaranduba!" and they at once paddled in for the bank. One of them accompanied us with an axe. As we passed along we found on the ground a number of woody vessels, which had evidently contained seeds. Duppo picked up one of them, and found another piece close by which fitted on to it, and then told us that they were called monkeys' drinking-cups; the Portuguese call them *cuyas de macaco*. These shells had contained nuts. When falling off the tree—the sapucaya—the tops split off, and the nuts are scattered on the ground. Duppo made us understand that these cups would serve well to collect the milk from the cow he promised to show us.

I may observe that the trees which bear the monkey drinking-cups are closely allied to the Brazil-nut tree, the fruit of which we had often seen sold in England under that name. Its seeds are also enclosed in large woody vessels, but they, having no lid, fall entire to the ground, and are thus easily collected by the natives.

Supplied with these vessels, we went on a few yards further, when we stopped under an enormous tree, one of the giants of the forest. Its trunk was covered with deeply scored reddish and rugged bark. Duppo patted it, saying, "This my cow." Another tree of the same species, but much smaller, grew near. He ran to it, and saying, "Small cow give better milk," began to attack it with his axe. After making a few strokes, out flowed a perfectly white liquid, which John, kneeling down, caught in the monkey-cup. As soon as it was filled I handed him another, the milk continuing to flow in great abundance, so that we soon had four cups filled full of the tempting liquid. On tasting it we found it sweet, and of a not unpleasant flavour, and wonderfully like milk.

We returned to the boat with our prize. Domingos had meantime been boiling some coffee; as we had now no sugar, the fresh milk proved a most valuable acquisition. The Indians, however, recommended us not to take much of it. We kept it, intending to use it again in the evening, but on taking off the lid of one of the monkey-cups, we found that our milk had thickened into a stiff and excessively tenacious glue. "My cow good?" asked Duppo, as he saw us tasting the liquid. When we showed him the gluey substance in the evening, he inquired sagaciously whether the milk of our cow would keep so long, and we confessed that, in that climate, it would be very likely to turn sour. After this, on several occasions we obtained fresh milk from the cow-tree for our breakfasts and suppers.

We encamped at night on a bank, and found two sorts of tiger-beetles, with very large heads, running about on the sand. It was extraordinary how rapidly they moved. Arthur and I tried to catch them, but each time they baffled us. One was very similar in hue to the sand over which it runs, the other was of a brilliant copper colour. Arthur, who was very acute in his remarks, observed that the white species ran far more swiftly than the copper-coloured one. As they only appear in the gloom or night, the white is far more easily seen than the darker one; and this has by the Creator greater means afforded it of escaping from its enemies. The dark-coloured one, however, he discovered, is not left without means of defence; for when at last Duppo caught one for him, he found that on touching it it emitted a strong, peculiar, and offensive putrid odour, which is not the case with the whiter one.

"How delightful it is!" he exclaimed, "to examine the habits of God's creatures, and see how admirably adapted they are to the life they are destined to lead."

I must not, however, attempt to describe the numberless insects and creatures of all sorts we met with on our voyage. Duppo brought us a large wood-cricket, called the *Tanana*, the wonderfully loud and not unmusical notes of which we had often heard. These sounds, we found, were produced by the overlapping edges of the wing-cases, which they rub together. In each wing-case the inner edge, near the lower part, has a horny expansion. On one wing this horny expansion is furnished with a sharp raised margin; on the other, the strong nervure which traverses it on the other side is crossed by a number of short, sharp furrows, like those of a file. When, therefore, the insect rapidly moves its wings, the file of one expansion scrapes sharply across the horny margin of the other, thus producing the curious sounds. The wing-cases, which are of a parchment-like nature, and the hollow drum-formed space which they enclose, assists to give resonance to the tones. The music they make is employed undoubtedly to serenade their mates, for the same object which induces the feathered tribe to utter their varied notes in the forest.

We had once more entered the main stream, which, after the confined navigation of the last few days, appeared to our eyes almost like the wide ocean. We landed rather earlier than usual, as a favourable spot appeared, and we could not tell how far off another might be found. We had formed huts as usual, our camp-fire was lighted, and Domingos and Maria were engaged in cooking our evening meal, making the most of the scanty fare we had remaining. A point was near from which we believed we could get an uninterrupted view for a great distance down the river. As we found we could make our way to it without much difficulty, we begged Ellen and Oria to accompany us.

On reaching the point we sat down on a bank. A small object appeared in the distance on the water. Arthur was the first to espy it. I thought it was but a log of wood. We pointed it out to Oria. She at once declared that it was a canoe. It was certainly approaching, and at length we made out a small canoe gliding over the smooth water; and as it came near we saw a white man in the stern steering, and ten natives urging her on with rapid strokes. "What if those people should be able to give us news of our father!" exclaimed Ellen. "Do call them, lest they should pass by." John hailed the canoe. Presently we saw the white man stand up and look towards us. Instantly the head of the canoe was turned in our direction. We hastened down to the point where they would land, and the white man stepped on shore. He gazed first at one, then at the other, with an inquiring glance.

"Can you tell me, my friend," asked John, "if an English family are stopping anywhere on the banks down the river?"

"Indeed I can, señor," answered the white man; "for I have been sent up by the master to look out for some part of his family who ought long since to have arrived. He has already sent two messengers to inquire for them; and his heart, and those of the señora and señorita, are well-nigh worn out with anxiety on their account. At last I begged that he would let me go; and I promised not to return without gaining tidings of them."

"Why, then you must be Antonio, and we are those you are looking for!" said John.

"Heaven be praised!" exclaimed Antonio, our father's old servant, who, rushing forward, seized John in his arms, and gave him a warm embrace. He then turned to me, and gave me the same affectionate yet respectful greeting. "And this is the señorita!" he exclaimed, turning to Ellen. "Oh, it does my old heart good to see you. How little did I think that before the sun set I should behold those I so longed to find. And Domingos and Maria; surely they have come with you!"

"Oh yes," said John; "they are at the camp. Send your montaria round the point, and come with us. We shall soon be there."

As may be supposed, we had numberless questions to ask about our father and family; how far off they were from us, and all that had happened.

"Oh, señor, I should like to have a dozen tongues in my head to reply to you," answered Antonio. "They are well and safe now, though the times are perilous. And, Heaven be praised, they have passed numberless dangers unharmed. It has taken me two weary weeks to come thus far, but I hope that we may descend the river to them in far less time. How could I have expected to meet with you when others, we had cause to fear, had failed. First, a Brazilian trader, who was proceeding up in his montaria, undertook the task, promising without fail to find you, and speedily to send down notice; but after waiting and waiting some weary weeks, no news came, and my master, your father, was resolved to go himself, though unwilling to leave the señoras without his protection, when, just then, two young Englishmen arrived from Para, and made themselves known to your father as friends of yours; and hearing that you were missing, agreed to go up in search of you."

"Why, those must be our two school-fellows, Houlston and Tony Nyass!" I exclaimed.

From the description which Antonio had given of them, we had no doubt that this was the case. But what had become of them? A few minutes before I had thought all our anxieties were over, but now they were again aroused on account of our friends. What if they had fallen into the hands of the Majeronas, or been exposed to some of the storms we had so narrowly escaped! "You forget how easily they may have passed us," observed Arthur. "We might have been not a quarter of a mile apart, and yet have passed without seeing or hearing each other."

Dear Ellen was so agitated with the thoughts of meeting those we loved so soon, that she could scarcely speak. She overheard, however, the remarks between Arthur and myself. "And why do you doubt that all will come right in the end?" she exclaimed. "Think of the many dangers we have gone through, and how we have been preserved from them all. Let us hope the same for our friends."

Domingos was standing over the fire with his frying-pan when we came round the point with Antonio. At that moment he happened to look up, when, forgetting what he was about, he let the frying-pan and its contents fall into the middle of the fire, thereby spoiling a delicious fricassee of iguana, and sprang forward to welcome his fellow-servant, and to make inquiries for their master. The two rushed into each other's arms, and the tears fell from the black man's eyes when he heard that our father was well.

We spent the evening at our encampment, hearing from Antonio all that had occurred: how our father had received information of the intended attack of the Majeronas, and had embarked just in time to escape them. He would have waited for us higher up the river had he not been compelled, for the sake of obtaining assistance for our mother, to proceed downwards. They had all been hospitably received at the farm of a Brazilian family, where she having recovered, he determined to wait for our arrival. The first messengers he had despatched not having been heard of, on the arrival of Houlston and Tony Nyass, they had insisted on proceeding upward. As they also had not returned, Antonio, with the party we had met, had been sent to search for us.

It was the happiest evening we had spent since the commencement of our journey. Anxiety about our friends did not damp our spirits, as we hoped that they would hear of us at some of the places at which we had called; and that we should soon all meet, and continue our adventures in company. "Fancy Tony and I, and old Houlston, after all, sailing together on the Amazon, just as we used to talk about at school!" I acclaimed. "It will be jolly, will it not, Arthur?"

Chapter Nineteen
A Happy Meeting

A week had passed away. The two canoes keeping in company, we no longer felt the solitude which had oppressed us as we navigated that vast stream, or the intricate labyrinth of channels, often far away from the main shore. Several times we had inquired of Antonio whether we were approaching the farm of Senhor Pimento, where our family were living. "Paciencia; logo, logo," was his answer—"Patience; soon, soon we shall be there." We turned off from the main stream, and ascended an igarape thickly shrouded by palms and other trees, completely shutting out the sky above us. At the end of the vista the bright sunlight shone on an open space, where appeared a small lake, on the opposite side of which we could distinguish several buildings raised on piles—a large one in the centre with a deep verandah, the palm-thatched roof of which extended beyond the walls; the whole surrounded by plantations of mandioca, cacao, peach-palms, and other trees.

"Is that where we are going?" asked Ellen eagerly of Antonio. "We shall see—we shall see, señorita!" he answered. Rounding a point, we observed a hut beneath a grove of inaja palms; their leaves springing almost from the ground, and spreading slightly out from the slender stem, so as to form an open vase of the most graceful shape. Few objects of the vegetable kingdom are more beautiful. "Oh, what lovely trees!" exclaimed Ellen. "And see! there is some one coming out from among them."

As she spoke, a person emerged from the wood, engaged apparently in reading. As his back was towards us, he did not observe the approach of the canoes. "Oh, it is papa!" exclaimed Ellen; "I am sure of it." And in another instant we were on shore, and Ellen flying over the ground.

It was indeed a happiness to see her in our father's arms. "And my boys too, safe after all your dangers!" he exclaimed, as he embraced us. "And your young friend too!"

Maria and Domingos came running up to kiss his hand, pleasure beaming in their dark countenances. We hurried forward to the house, and in a few minutes had the happiness of seeing our mother and Fanny.

Even Aunt Martha, I thought, looked far more kindly than she used to do, and was as gentle and affectionate to Ellen as she could be. It was indeed a happy meeting.

We, of course, had to recount all our adventures; and thus most of the talking was on our side, as Antonio had already told us all that had happened to them. Our Brazilian friend, Senhor Pimento, was a fine burly old gentleman, habited in light nankeen jacket and trousers, with a broad-brimmed hat. He was of a somewhat dark hue, and his wife, who was a slight, active old lady, was considerably darker. Their family consisted of a son, who was away hunting at the time, and two daughters. I cannot call them fair, but they were attractive, lively girls, who had lived in that remote district all their lives, and knew nothing of the world beyond, believing Para, next to Rio, to be its largest city. Fanny and her Portuguese friends were much pleased with Oria and Duppo, and delighted when they found that they could speak a little English, a language the two latter were trying to learn. The house was of considerable size, built of palm-trees, thatched with palm-leaves; and even the doors and windows were composed of palm-leaves, not opening on hinges, but being hooked up or taken down like mats. There were open galleries round on either side, and several of the rooms were open also; and in these the hammocks of the men of the party were hung up. The floors were also of split palm-trees, and were raised about ten feet above the ground, so as to be at a sufficient elevation during the higher floods which occasionally inundate the larger portion of that region. None of the inmates of the house were idle. Senhor Pimento was constantly out, superintending his labourers; while Donna Joséfa, his wife, was engaged in household matters. The young ladies, it must be owned, were the least industrious of the family.

Arthur had said nothing of the packet he had received from the recluse, yet I was sure that he would not lose a moment in opening it after the time had arrived when he had permission to do so. Ellen came running to me the following morning, I having gone out before breakfast to look round the farm. I saw by her beaming countenance that she was full of some matter of importance.

"It is as I told you, Harry!" she exclaimed. "The recluse is Arthur's father—I knew it—I was sure of it. Arthur read to me last night some of the letter he gave him. Poor fellow, he is in a great state of agitation, and blames himself for having come away and left him. The recluse—that is to say, Mr Mallet—speaks somewhat vaguely of a fearful event which compelled him to leave England; and he says that, though yearning to have his son by his side, he will not take him out of the path which Providence has placed him in, and from the protection of kind friends—that he himself, long an outcast from his fellow-men, cannot help him, and that by starting alone in life he will have a far better prospect of success than should it be known whose son he is. These remarks, though Arthur is thankful to have found his father, have made him very unhappy. He will talk to you by-and-by, when he has thought the matter over; and do you know, the recluse—I mean, Mr Mallet—says that papa is an old friend of his, and that Arthur may tell him so, as he is sure that though papa may not desire to meet him, he will not in consequence withdraw his protection from his son."

"That I am sure papa will not," I exclaimed. "Poor Arthur! I do not know whether to be sorry or glad at what you have told me. Had he spoken to me I might have been better able to advise him."

Ellen looked into my face. Perhaps she thought that I felt a little jealous that Arthur had not first consulted me. We agreed not to say anything about the matter, but to let Arthur speak to our father himself, being assured that he would do what was kind and generous, and act as he judged for the best.

Arthur during the day was, I observed, more silent than usual. He was waiting, I suspected, to become more acquainted with our father before venturing to speak to him. I was not present when he did so.

The day after our arrival Duppo came to me with a countenance of alarm. "We get among witches!" he exclaimed, looking round cautiously. I asked him what he could mean; and he then told me that he had seen the two young ladies in a wood close to the house, amusing themselves by playing with venomous snakes, which he was sure they could not do if they were like other human beings. "Come, you see them," he said, wishing to prove his assertion correct; and he led me round the house, through the grove of palms, where, sure enough, seated on a bench, from whence there was a lovely view of the lake, were the two daughters of our host. I confess I was almost startled on seeing them with a number of brilliant looking snakes. One was round each of their necks, while others they had twisted like bracelets, encircling their arms; and one of the girls was holding another in her hand, allowing its forked tongue to dart out towards her face. They were of a bright grass-green colour, with remarkably thin bodies; and it was curious to see the graceful way in which the lithe, active creatures crawled about, or lay coiled up perfectly at home in their laps. Unwilling to be an eavesdropper, I was retiring, when I met Fanny and Ellen, and told them what I had seen, and Duppo's suspicions. Fanny laughed, saying they were perfectly harmless, and had been tamed by their friends, and returned with me to where the girls were seated. Duppo, however, beat a retreat, evidently unwilling to be in such a dangerous neighbourhood. They were highly amused at hearing of Duppo's alarm, and showed me that the snakes were perfectly harmless. I took one in my hand, when the creature coiled itself round my arm, and I could admire at leisure its colour, and the beautiful topaz yellow of its eyes. The snakes were between two and three feet long. They were so thoroughly tamed, that though placed on the ground they did not attempt to escape, but came back immediately they were called by their young mistresses. So slender were their bodies, that when coiled completely up I could place one on the palm of my hand.

Though I told Duppo afterwards that I had actually handled the snakes, he was not convinced of their harmless character, and insisted that it was another proof that they had been charmed by the white witches, which he still evidently considered our Brazilian friends. Oria, however, was far braver; for when she saw Fanny and Ellen play with the creatures, she without hesitation took one of them up, and allowed it to coil itself round her neck, where it made a pretty ornament on her dark skin.

Pedro, the son of our host, returned the next day with a boat-load of turtle and fish which he had caught; as well as a number of birds, some of them of exquisite plumage. John, Arthur, and I begged to accompany him the next time he set out on a similar expedition; and we found that he proposed starting again the following day. Meantime Senhora Joséfa, with the assistance of her slaves, was employed in salting and drying the fish and fowl she had just received.

We started in the morning with two canoes, equipped with nets, spears, and lines, bows and arrows, and blow-pipes as well as guns.

The lower portion of the banks of the Amazon were at this time covered with water on either side, varying in height from one to ten feet, and in some places reaching twenty. This district, known as the Gapo, extends from the Napo upwards of seventeen hundred miles, to the very borders of Peru. It thus becomes a region of countless islands, separated by expanses of water—but not open water, as forest trees appear growing out of it in all directions; while in other parts there are numbers of lakes of all sizes— some many miles in extent, others mere pools, dry in summer, but all abounding in fish of various sorts, in turtles and alligators. We could often, in consequence of the flooded state of the country, make short cuts in our canoe directly through the forest, in some places with a depth of five to ten feet below our keels.

As we were paddling on through a scene such as I have described, we passed near a raft secured to the trunks of four trees, on which was an Indian family, with a small fire burning on it. The mother was cooking fish, while the father lay in his hammock suspended between the trees. A small, crazy looking canoe was moored to it. The family appeared perfectly contented and unconcerned, and accustomed to the curious mode of life. Pedro told us they were Muras Indians. During the dry season they live on the sand-banks, employed in catching turtle in the large river; and when the rainy season sets in they retire to these solitudes, whence they sally forth in their canoes to catch manatees and turtle, and fish of many sorts. We were proceeding away from the main stream by a broad water-path, with numberless narrower paths leading off in all directions. During the first part of our voyage we could see for a considerable distance through the irregular colonnade of trees; but as we progressed the path became narrower, and the trees grew closer together, their boughs frequently stretching forth over our heads. From many of them beautiful bright yellow flowers hung down, the stems several feet in length, while ferns and numerous air-plants thickly covered the trunks of the palms or drooped over from their summits. Now and then we passed through a thicket of bamboos, their slender foliage and gracefully-curving stems having arranged themselves in the most elegant feathery bowers. Crossing through the forest, we passed a grove of small palms, their summits being but a few feet above us. They bore bunches of fruit, which our Indians cut off with their knives. We found it of an agreeable flavour. The birds feeding overhead now and then sent down showers of fruit, which splashed into the water round us. Frequently we heard a rustling in the leaves, and caught sight in many places of troops of monkeys peeping down from among the dense foliage. Then off they would go, leaping from bough to bough through the forest. Here a flock of paroquets appeared in sight for a few moments. Now one of the light-blue chatterers, then a lovely trogon, would seize a fruit as it darted by; or the delicate white wing and claret-coloured plumage of a lovely pompadour would glance from the foliage; or a huge-billed toucan would pitch down on a bough above us, and shake off a fruit into the water. Gay flowers, too, were not wanting, of the orchid tribe: some with white and spotted and purple blossoms; the most magnificent of a brilliant purple colour, called by the natives Saint Ann's flower, four inches across. We plucked some, which emitted a most delightful odour. At last we came out once more into the bright sunshine, at a small lake, the surface of which was adorned in many parts with numberless beautiful water-plants—graceful lilies, yellow bladder-worts, and numbers of a bright blue flower, which contrasted with the green leaves. The whole track, indeed, consisted, we found, of igarapes, lakes, and gapo; here and there patches of high and dry land so mingled together that we could not have told whether we were on the main shore or on an island.

At length we reached another lake with higher banks, where Pedro told us we would encamp and commence fishing. The little lake extended over an area of about ten acres, and was surrounded by the forest. The borders were somewhat swampy, and covered with a fine grass. On these borders the hunters erected little stages, consisting of long poles, with cross-pieces secured by lianas. The pool abounded with turtle. Our hunters mounted the stages, armed with bow and arrow. The arrow was so formed that the head when it struck the animal remained in its body, while the shaft floated to the surface, though remaining attached to it by a long line. We remained in a larger canoe to watch proceedings, while Pedro and two Indians entered a smaller one. The Indians did not even wait for the turtles to come to the surface; but the moment they saw a ripple in the water, the man nearest shot his arrow with unerring aim, and it never failed to pierce the shell. As soon as one was shot, Pedro paddled towards it, and, taking the shaft and line in his hand, humoured the creature as a fisherman does a salmon, till, exhausted, it rose to the surface, when it was further secured by another arrow shot at it, and then with the two lines easily hauled into the canoe. John and I tried our skill; but our arrows missed their aim, and I very nearly shot our friend Pedro instead of the turtle.

Another small canoe had been sent for, which now arrived. So rapidly were the turtle shot that both canoes were actively engaged in picking them up. Fully forty were thus killed in a short time. The net was then spread at one end of the pool, while the rest of the party began beating the water from the opposite side with long poles, some along the edges and others in the canoes. We could see the backs of the turtles as they swam forward. When they got close to the net the two ends were rapidly drawn together, surrounding a large number of them; and then all hands uniting at the ropes, quickly dragged it towards the shore. As they appeared above the water, the men seized them, and threw them into the canoes, which came up to the spot. Many, however, managed to scramble out again before they were turned on their backs. Arthur and I rushed in with the rest to assist in their capture, when suddenly I felt an extraordinary sensation in my foot.

"Oh, I have been bitten by a water-snake!" I exclaimed, leaping up.

"And so have I!" cried Arthur. And we rushed on shore, both of us looking anxiously down at our legs. No wounds, however, were to be seen.

When the net was finally drawn on shore, after a vast number of small turtle had been taken out of it, several curious fish were seen, and among them five or six eel-looking creatures, with large heads. The Indians cried out something; but not understanding them, I took up one of the creatures to examine it, when instantly I felt the sensation I had experienced in the water, and now discovered that they were electric eels. To prove it yet further, I took out my knife, and Pedro, Arthur, and I, with several Indians, joined hands, when instantly the rest, greatly to their astonishment, felt the shock as if they had touched the fish itself. We persuaded the other Indians to try the experiment; and they were greatly amused and astonished at finding the electric spark pass through their systems.

Altogether we caught upwards of a hundred turtle. We then moved on to another lake with a sandy shore, where the net was again drawn for the sake of obtaining fish. I had never seen so many and various fish taken together. It would be impossible to describe them. Among them was a beautiful oval-shaped fish, which the natives call *acara*. There are numerous species, we heard: some of them deposit their eggs in the sand, and hover over them until the young are hatched; but there are others which take still greater care of them, and have a cavity near the gills, in which the male takes up the eggs and carries them there, not only till they are hatched, but actually keeps the young fry in safety within them. When able to swim they go out and take exercise; but on the approach of danger they rush back into their parents' mouths for protection. This cavity is in the upper part of the bronchial arches. I should scarcely have believed the fact from the report of the natives, had I not actually seen both the eggs and the young fry in their parents' head. There are several species of fish in the waters of the Amazon which are thus wonderfully supplied with the means of protecting their young.

"You shall now see another way we have of taking fish," said our friend Pedro.

We paddled off to a still part of the lake. He then poured out of a calabash some coloured liquid.

"And now let us land," he said, "and while we take our dinner, watch the result."

The liquid, he told us, was produced from a poisonous liana called *tambo*. This is cut up into lengths, washed, and soaked in water, which becomes thus impregnated with the juice.

Before dinner was over, as we looked out on the pool we saw the surface covered with fish floating on their sides, with their gills wide open. The canoe then pushed off, and collected them in great numbers. The poison appeared to have suffocated the fish, although only a small quantity had been poured into the water.

We were as successful in shooting birds, monkeys, and other game, as we were in fishing. One of the Indians used his bow in a curious way, which we had not before seen employed. Throwing himself on his back, he placed his feet lifted up above his body against the bow, and drew the string to his head with both his hands. It was surprising what a correct aim he could thus take. He quickly brought down several birds on the wing at a great height. He showed us also that he could shoot up in the air, and make the arrow fall wherever he pleased. Several times it descended within a few inches of his own head or feet, where it stuck quivering in the ground. We dreaded that it might stick into him; but he laughed at our fears, assuring us that there was not the slightest danger, as he had practised the art from his boyhood, and could perform still more difficult feats. Darkness coming on prevented him from exhibiting them. We spent the night on the driest spot we could find on the banks of the lake. Blazing fires were lighted to keep jaguars, pumas, and boas at a distance.

Next morning, loaded with the spoils of the chase, we commenced our voyage homewards. We were passing a dry, thickly-wooded island, when we caught sight of a number of people among the trees, while fires were burning in the centre of several open spots. We asked Pedro what they were about.

"They are my father's labourers," he said. "You shall come on shore, and we will see how they are employed."

We found a number of Indians and a few blacks busily engaged in various ways; some in making gashes in the stems of trees, under each of which they placed a little clay cup or a shell, into which trickled the sap issuing from the wound. This sap we found was of the consistency of cream. And now we saw for the first time the india-rubber with which we had only before been acquainted when using it to rub out our pencil strokes when drawing at school. The trees which were thus treated had a bark and foliage not unlike that of the European ash; but the trunks were of great size, and shot up to an immense height before throwing off their branches. People with large bowls were going about from tree to tree, and emptying the contents of the little cups into them. From thence they were carried to their camp. Here we found large bowls full of the cream-like sap. The labourers were provided with a number of clay moulds of various shapes, though most of them were in the form of round bottles. These moulds were dipped into the liquid, and then hung up to dry. As soon as one layer was dry the mould was again dipped in, and thus coat after coat was put on. Pedro told us it took several days before the coating was considered sufficiently thick. It was then hard and white. This operation being finished, it was passed several times through a thick, black smoke which issued from fires. We found that this smoke was produced by burning the nuts of the inaja and other palm-trees, by which means the dark colour and softness are obtained. The process is now complete; and the moulds being broken, the clay is emptied out, and the rubber is fit for sale.

The Brazilian india-rubber tree—the *Siphonia elastico* (*caoutchouc*)—differs from the *ficus* which furnishes the india-rubber of Africa and the East Indies. It bears a small flower and circular fruit, with strongly-marked divisions in the rind.

Having left some of our game for provisioning the camp of the india-rubber collectors, we made the best of our way homewards. Evening was coming on. We were still at some distance from home. The sky had become overcast, and rain had begun to fall. It seemed impossible that we should find our way through the forest in the darkness. We entered at length a channel, the land on one side of which was elevated some feet above the water. As we were paddling along it, Pedro proposed that we should land and camp. Just then we caught sight of a fire burning in a shed at some distance from the bank.

"We may there find shelter," said Pedro, "without having the trouble of building huts, which, after all, would not keep out the rain."

We three accompanied him towards the fire. We found two Indians standing near it, both busily employed in concocting some mixture in a large pot simmering over the flames. They were evidently, by the manner in which they received us, displeased at our coming. Pedro, however, told them that we proposed spending the night at their hut; and sent to the canoe for some game, which put them in better humour. He inquired what they were about.

"I see what it is. They are making the wourali poison for tipping the arrows for their bows and blow-pipes. See! we will make them show us the process."

After a little talk with the Indians, they consented to do as he wished. First they showed us some long sticks of a thin vine—the wourali itself. This, with the root of a plant of a very bitter nature, they scraped together into thin shavings. They were then placed in a sieve, and water poured over them into an earthen pot, the liquid coming through having the appearance of coffee. Into this the juice of some bulbous plants of a glutinous nature was squeezed, apparently to serve the purpose of glue. While the pot was simmering, other ingredients were added. Among them were some black, venomous ants, and also a little red ant, which stings severely. They seemed to set great value also on the fangs of two snakes, which, when pounded, were added with much ceremony. One, Pedro told us, was the venomous *labarri*;

and another, the largest among the venomous reptiles in America, known as the *curucu*, or bushmaster (*Lâchesis mutus*). The Indians, however, call it the *couana couchi*. It is of the most beautiful colour. Its body is brightly tinted with all the prismatic colours; and sometimes it is to be seen coiled round the branches of a tree, ready to strike its prey. It is allied, I should say, to the fearful *fer de lance*, which strikes its prey with so rapid and straight a stroke that it is impossible to escape it. A quantity of the strongest Indian red pepper was lastly added; and as the ingredients boiled, more of the juice of the wourali was poured in as was required. The scum having been taken off, the compound remained on the fire till it assumed the appearance of a thick syrup of a deep brown colour. Whether all these ingredients are necessary, I cannot say. Others also, I believe, are occasionally used.

I should have observed that we, as well as the other Indians, were desired to keep at a respectful distance during the operation, as it is considered that even the vapour ascending from the pot is injurious to health. Having been pronounced perfectly made, the syrup was poured into a number of little pots, and carefully covered over with skin and leaves. We observed that the two Indians who manufactured it washed their hands and faces frequently. Pedro purchased several pots which had thus been manufactured, as the poison is an article of commerce throughout the country.

The Indians' hut was at some distance from the shed. After supper we hung up our hammocks, and after turning into them, went to sleep. Little did we think of the fearful danger we ran that night.

Chapter Twenty
Another Flight

Early the next day we arrived at Senhor Pimento's farm. The turtles were turned into a large tank near the house, staked round so as to prevent the creatures from getting out. Here they would live for many months. Most of the Brazilian, as well as many of the natives' houses, have similar reservoirs attached to them, in which turtle are kept alive, to be taken out as required for use.

We found our two sisters seated by the bank of the lake, and little Oria with them. They seemed somewhat agitated. Oria had been out the previous day, they told me, in the forest to gather fruit, and had unwisely wandered on, without waiting for Duppo, who was to follow her. Unaccustomed to that part of the country, she had lost her way. As evening approached, she found an Indian hut, when, the rain coming down, she crept into it for shelter. No one was there. She had thrown a mat over her, and had dropped off to sleep, when she was awakened by hearing several persons talking. Although their dialect was very different from her own, she could understand them. As she listened she became more and more interested. They were speaking of a plot to surprise the whites, and put them to death, so that not a Portuguese should remain in the country. This plan, Oria understood, was very soon to be carried into execution. Fanny and Ellen cross-questioned Oria, and seemed satisfied that they clearly understood her. They then begged me to go and call our father, that we might have his opinion before alarming our host and hostess. I fortunately found him near the spot. He came to the conclusion that Oria's opinion was to be relied on, and at once determined to warn Senhor Pimento.

Soon afterwards I met Duppo. He drew me aside, with a mysterious look. He, too, evidently had something which he wished to communicate. He in vain, however, tried to find words to explain himself. Just then we caught sight of the daughters of our host in the distance. He shook his head at them, and then made signs that no good could come from living with a family who could play with poisonous snakes with impunity; and then pointed to the canoe, and urged us to go away from so dangerous a neighbourhood. I felt sure, however, that he had some other reason, which he was afraid to communicate. I told him so, and I asked him if he did not believe that the natives in the neighbourhood were about to attack the plantation. He looked surprised, evidently not being aware that Oria had already warned my sisters. At last he confessed that such was the case, and implored me earnestly to induce my family to fly. On this I went in search of John, who had talked of going out to shoot. I persuaded him, though not without difficulty, to remain at home, and come and consult with our father. He had, in the meantime, found Senhor Pimento.

"I am afraid that I shall be unable to persuade our Portuguese friend to take precautions against an attack of the natives. He declares that they have always been on good terms with him, and he sees no reason to be alarmed," he observed.

"What, then, do you mean to do, father?" I asked.

"To take the wisest course," he answered. "I have directed Domingos and Antonio to get the montarias ready, and to ascertain the feeling of the Tucuna Indians who came with you. They are, however, anxious to return homewards; and I have promised them one of the canoes, and additional payment, if they will accompany us in our flight to a place of safety. There is an uninhabited island some way down the river, where, I hope, we may remain concealed, should what we apprehend take place. As delay may be dangerous, I have told Senhor Pimento that I purpose starting this evening; and I have urged him to have his own montarias ready, and manned by negroes in whom he can place confidence. I shall be very glad if I can, at all events, induce him to take this precaution, so that, should he see any likelihood of his being attacked, he may, at all events, get on board, and save the lives of his family and himself. We will, as soon as the canoes are ready, carry our own property down to them. But we must take care that we are not observed by the natives, who might attempt to stop us, or watch the direction we take. Your mother and sisters are engaged in packing up, and I hope that soon all will be ready."

Though Senhor Pimento appeared to be incredulous as to the sinister intentions of the natives, I thought that possibly Pedro might be induced to believe them. I therefore went in search of him. I told him what we had heard.

"It may be," he answered. "I have had many black looks of late from those who used at one time to be ready to kiss my feet. I am, therefore, inclined to agree with you that some mischief is intended. I will try and persuade my father to act prudently; but he has been so long accustomed to look down upon the natives, it will be difficult to persuade him that they will dare to injure a white skin. I think your father is very right to escape from hence, though we shall be sorry to part from you."

I thanked Pedro for his kind feelings, and urged him to try and induce his father to act with caution. As all the natives on the estate were absent gathering caoutchouc, our operations were conducted with less difficulty than would otherwise have been the case. Our own Indians had fortunately remained behind. It was settled that two should go in our canoe. John should act as captain of our father's, and Domingos of ours. Our goods were quickly conveyed on board. We found that Senhor Pimento had sent a supply of farinha, as well as several turtles and other provisions, on board each of them, as a mark, he said, of his good-will.

We bade him and Senhora Joséfa and their two daughters farewell. Pedro accompanied us down to the canoe.

"Do not fear," he said, "about us. I suspect we shall soon be following you. But should nothing happen to us, forget not those who held you in affectionate esteem."

I am, of course, only translating his words.

The canoes shoved off, and working our paddles, we glided across the lake. It was nearly dark before we reached the entrance to the igarape down which we were to proceed. It was a perfect calm. The tall trees were reflected in the mirror-like expanse of the lake, sprinkled, as it were, with the myriads of stars which shone forth from the clear sky. Here and there a night-bird darted from its covert in search of its insect prey. The tree-crickets had begun to utter their evening notes, and from far and near came forth from the forest the numberless sounds which often to the solitary traveller make the night hideous.

"Oh, what can that be?" we heard Ellen exclaim from the other canoe. "See! see!"

We looked astern, towards the plantation we had left. Bright flames were darting up from among the buildings very instant growing higher, while dreadful cries, coming across the water, struck our ears.

"Oh, I am afraid our friends have delayed too long to escape," exclaimed Arthur. "Could we not go back to help them?"

I asked our father if he would allow us to do so.

He hesitated. "They have their montarias; and should they have been attacked, you can render them no assistance."

Still, I did not like the thought of deserting our friends, and promised, should we not meet with them, to return at once. At last he consented to our going; and turning the head of our canoe, we paddled back towards the shore we had left. We had nearly reached it, when we saw a boat approaching. It might have our friends on board, or might be manned by natives. We approached cautiously, ready to turn round at a moment's notice.

"Who goes there?" I asked.

I was greatly relieved by hearing Senhor Pimento's voice.

"Turn round!" he exclaimed. "Fly! fly! I fear we may soon be pursued. We are all on board. I wish we had followed your advice."

Back we paddled, as fast as we could urge our canoe through the water. Meantime the whole plantation appeared in a blaze—not only the buildings, but the fields and groves of fruit-trees seemed to have been set on fire. We made for the mouth of the igarape, where we found our father's canoe waiting for us. Away we all went together. The cries and shouts of the Indians, as they searched about for the proprietor, reached our ears. We had too much reason to believe that we should be followed. There was sufficient light to enable us to keep in the centre of the water-path. We anxiously looked astern, expecting every moment to see the canoes of our enemies in our wake. In some places the igarape was so narrow, and the trees so completely joined overhead, that we could with difficulty discover our way, and were compelled to paddle at less speed to avoid running among the bushes at its borders. And now, from every side, those sounds which I have so often mentioned burst forth from the forest; yet, though so frequently before heard, their effect was wonderfully depressing. Sometimes, indeed, they sounded so exactly like the cries of natives, that we felt sure we were pursued, and expected every moment to discover our enemies close astern of us.

We continued our night voyage, paddling as fast as we could venture to move through the darkness. Now and then the light penetrated into the centre of the igarape, and allowed us to move faster. Ever and anon flights of magnificent fireflies flitted across the igarape, revealing the foliage on either side, amid which sometimes it seemed as if gigantic figures were stalking about, to seize us as we passed. They were, however, only the stems of decayed trees, or distorted branches bending over the waters.

Thus we went on, hour after hour, not venturing to stop even to rest the weary arms of the paddlers; for we had received too clear a warning of what would be our fate should we fall into the power of the hitherto submissive, but now savage and vindictive natives. It was no slight cause probably which had induced them to revolt. The cruelty and tyranny, the exactions and treachery of the white man had at length raised their phlegmatic natures, and they were about to exact a bitter revenge for long years of oppression and wrong. As in many similar instances, the innocent were doomed to suffer with the guilty; and as far as we had been able to judge, our friend Senhor Pimento had treated those around him with all kindness and consideration.

At length a pale light appeared ahead; and emerging from the dark shades of the igarape, we entered the wide expanse of the Amazon, across which at that instant the moon, rising above the line of forest, cast the silvery light of her bright beams. My sisters, and even the Brazilian girls, uttered exclamations of admiration. We made our way across the lake-like expanse, which was now just rippled with a light breeze; and after an hour's progress, found ourselves approaching a lofty wall of forest. Coasting along it, we entered a narrow channel similar to the one we had quitted. Here and there the moonbeams, penetrating amid the branches, enabled us to find our way till we reached an open spot on the shores of a small lake.

"Here," said our father, "is the place I have selected for our retreat; and as the Indians will believe that we have continued down the stream, there is little probability, I think, of their coming here to search for us. If they do, we may escape through the opposite side, and take one of several channels which will again conduct us into the main stream."

There was sufficient light to enable us to erect rude huts for the accommodation of the ladies of the party. As there was no fear of the glare of the fires shining through the forest, and thus betraying our position, we could venture to light a sufficient number for the protection of the camp against wild beasts.

The next morning found us quietly settled in our new location. My father and mother did their best to comfort Senhor Pimento and his family for the loss of their property.

"Think how much worse it would have been," said my father, "had you, and your wife, and daughters, and son been deprived of your lives! We should be thankful for the blessings we receive."

"See, it is true—it is true," answered our Portuguese friend. "But—"

"Oh, utter not any 'buts,'" observed my father. "'But' is an ungrateful word. It should be discharged from human language."

Ellen had saved all her pets, even her humming-bird; and she and Fanny, with the assistance of their Brazilian friends, had plenty of occupation in arranging accommodation for them.

My father was anxious to have a larger vessel built, fit to navigate the lower part of the river, over whose sea-like expanse strong winds occasionally blow, which our smaller canoes were but ill-calculated to encounter. The first thing, however, to be done, was to erect huts, in which the party might live till the vessel could be got ready, or till they received information that the voyage could be accomplished without risk of being attacked by the rebels.

"I have been thinking, Harry," said Arthur, "that if Houlston and Nyass should come down, and make for Senhor Pimento's farm, would there not be a great risk of their falling into the hands of the rebels, and being killed?"

"Indeed there would," I answered. "I did not think of that. I wish we could send and stop them."

"Would it not be better to go ourselves?" asked Arthur.

"Indeed it would," I exclaimed. "We will see what my father says to it."

I told John, who agreed with me; and we at once determined to proceed up the stream with our Tucuna Indians. We promised them that on finding our friends they should have our canoe in which to perform their homeward voyage. They seemed perfectly satisfied, and we congratulated ourselves on the arrangement we had made. As there might not be room to return in their canoe, John, Arthur, and I determined to go alone. We would not even take Duppo, as he could do little, compared with the other Indians, in working our vessel. Fanny and Ellen were very unhappy at the thoughts of our going. We begged them to look after Duppo, and to give him his lessons in English till we should return.

We started early in the morning, paddling vigorously up the stream, which we found a very different thing to going down with it. At first we kept along the shore, opposite Senhor Pimento's sitio, and then crossed over, that we might have a better chance of seeing our friends, should they be coming down. For some time, when the wind was fair, we rigged a sail, and were thus able to run up with ease against the current. At night we always chose a spot where we could command a view of the river, which had so much fallen by this time that we hoped our friends would keep in it instead of branching off among the channels at the side.

For several days we continued our voyage, till we began to fear that some accident might have happened, or that, not hearing of us, they might have pushed onwards, with the intention of sailing up the Napo. Sometimes we slept under the awning in the montaria; sometimes we built huts, according to our usual custom, on the shore.

One morning, just as we were embarking, John shot a fine paca, which we took on board, and agreed we would roast during our noon-day meal, when our Indians generally lay down to sleep. At the hour we intended, we found a bank, which afforded us a tempting resting-place. Arthur and I agreed to act as cooks; while John, who had been up before daybreak with his gun in the forest, said he would rest till dinner was ready. The chief Indian, Tono, meantime took his blow-pipe and bow, saying he would go into the forest and shoot some more game for supper, our stock having become somewhat scanty; while his companions lay down to sleep in the canoe. John lay down on the grass, away from the fire, though near enough for the smoke to keep the flies at a distance. We had the paca scientifically trussed and spitted, and placed over the fire on two forked sticks. Sometime! Arthur, sometimes I turned the spit. It was my turn to attend to it, and Arthur was sitting near me, when I felt the ground shake, as if some large object had pitched down on it at my side; and what was my horror, on turning my head, to see Arthur, in the claws of an enormous puma, being dragged over the ground. We had imprudently left our guns in the montaria. At the same time John awoke, and quickly sprang into the canoe. I felt for my knife—the only weapon I possessed—when I found that I had left it on the other side of the fire, where John had been lying. As I turned my head for an instant, intending to seize it, I saw another puma stealthily approaching. Arthur did not cry out, but lay with his face on the ground, the better to avoid the stroke of the puma's paw. Horror kept me from moving. The savage beast was dragging Arthur away. Despair seized me. His death seemed inevitable. All passed in a moment. Then I saw John standing up in the montaria, with his rifle pointed at the puma's head. My tongue clove to my mouth. I could not shout out to awake the Indians. The second puma was drawing near. I might be its victim. Just then John's rifle echoed through the forest: the puma which had seized Arthur sprang up in the air, and then down it fell, its claws only a few inches from Arthur's body. I now rushed up to him, and dragged him out of the way of its dying struggles, calling to John to look after the other puma. The Indians had now started to their feet, uttering loud shrieks. The puma stopped just as I fancied it was about to spring at me, and turning round, bounded into the forest. They then, running up to where the puma lay, quickly despatched it with their spears; while John and I lifted up Arthur and carried him to the side of the fire. He was insensible, but groaned heavily. His arm and shoulder were fearfully torn, while his head had received a blow, though comparatively a slight one, or it would inevitably have killed him.

"O John, do you think he will recover?" I exclaimed, as we examined his hurts.

"If we knew how to treat him, he might," answered John; "but I am a very bad doctor, and I am afraid our Indians are not better ones."

"Then, John, we must go back to the island," I exclaimed; "it would be impossible to continue our voyage with Arthur in this state; and though we have been many days coming up, we may hope to get back again in two or three."

John agreed with me, and we explained our intentions to the Indian boatmen. They looked very dissatisfied, especially Tono, who just then returned from his shooting excursion. I had not from the first liked his countenance, and I saw by his gestures that he was endeavouring to incite his companions to disregard our orders.

Though on their side they mustered four stout, athletic fellows, yet John and I had our rifles, and we agreed, for Arthur's sake, to make them do as we thought best. John at once reloaded his rifle; and as soon as he had done so, he told me to hurry down to the boat and seize mine. I got hold of it before the Indians were aware of my intention, and quickly rejoined him. Our first care was to wash and dress Arthur's wounds as well as we could. John covered me with his rifle, while I went down to get the water.

"Now, Harry," he said, "as we do not know when we shall be able to dress another paca, we had better make a good dinner off the portion which has escaped burning during the time you were unable to turn the spit."

Having finished our meal, and secured a portion for Arthur—in the hope he might recover sufficiently to eat it—we handed the rest to our crew. They took it sulkily enough, and returned with it to the montaria.

"We must keep a sharp look-out on these fellows; for, depend upon it, they intend to play us a trick," observed John.

Our chief difficulty was now how to get Arthur into the montaria; for while we were occupied in so doing, they might suddenly attack us.

"You must guard me, Harry, while I lift him up. He is a good weight, but still I can carry him as far as the montaria," observed John.

He did so; while I walked by his side, with my rifle ready for action. When the Indians saw how much Arthur was hurt, they appeared to feel compassion for him, and expressed their sorrow by signs. When we ordered them to shove off, they obeyed at once, and willingly paddled on down the river again.

"I really think, after all, we must have been mistaken in our opinion of those men," said John. "I never like to think harm of our fellow-creatures. Perhaps, after all, they did not understand us."

I was not quite so certain of this. A strong breeze came up the river, and prevented us making as much progress as we had expected. As evening drew on it increased greatly, and signs of a storm appeared in the sky. We were over on the southern shore, and had passed an island near the mainland similar to the one on which our family had lately taken refuge. Just then the tempest burst on us. I had observed an opening in the forest, apparently the mouth of a channel, and towards it we now steered. It was not without difficulty, however, that we could keep the canoe before the fast rising seas. Had we fallen into the trough, we should instantly have been upset.

The Indians seemed well aware of our danger, and paddled steadily. I was thankful when at length we found ourselves is calm water, though the wind still whistled and howled through the trees, which bent their tall boughs over our heads, as if they would come down and crush our bark. We paddled on, therefore, for some distance, till we reached a sheltered spot, where we agreed to land and build a hut, that Arthur might sleep more comfortably than he could in the canoe.

When we told the Indians what we wanted, they immediately set to work, with apparent good-will; and in a short time had erected a neat and comfortable hut, with a bed-place of bamboos. On this, having spread several mats brought from the canoe, we placed Arthur.

"Oh, how kind you are," he whispered.

I was rejoiced to hear him speak.

"I know all about it," he added; "I saw the puma, but had not time to cry out."

The Indians had consumed the remainder of the paca; and as there was still an hour or more of daylight, they proposed going out to catch some fish. I thought of accompanying them, but I did not like to leave Arthur. John then said he would go; but when he got down to the water, the Indians had already shoved off.

"I dare say I may find some game in the woods, and that may be better for Arthur than fish," he observed, coming back.

We saw the canoe at a little distance, the Indians standing ready, some with their harpoons and others with their bows, to strike any fish which might be passing. Now they came nearer to us, and I saw they had struck several fish. With these they returned to the shore, and called to me to come and receive them. Tono then made signs that he would go and get some more, and again they paddled off. I became quite vexed at having entertained unjust suspicions of them. After they had got to a little distance,

I saw them strike another fish—evidently a large one, by the time they took to haul it in. Now they went further and further off. At length I lost sight of them.

John had in the meantime gone into the woods with his gun. He returned, just as it was growing dusk, with a couple of birds, which he immediately plucked and prepared for roasting at the fire which I had made up. Our pot for boiling fish had been left in the canoe. We could, therefore, only roast a portion of those just caught by the Indians.

"They ought to be back by this time," observed John, as the shades of night fell over the river.

"The fish seemed to be plentiful, and probably they have been tempted to go further off than they proposed," I observed.

Still we waited and waited, and they did not return. John went a little way along the bank, and shouted loudly; but no answer came to his hail. At length we hung up our hammocks; and having attended to Arthur, added fuel to our fire, and placed True at the entrance of our hut to watch, we lay down to rest. Still, neither John nor I felt much inclined to sleep.

"I am afraid that Tono and his people, after all, have gone off in the canoe," I said at last.

"I suspect so too," he answered; "but yet they were behaving so well, that I did not think they would play us so treacherous a trick."

"We shall soon see, however. I cannot help expecting to hear them return every moment."

We waited and waited, anxiety keeping us awake. Several times I got up to give Arthur a little water, which was all he appeared inclined to take. He was much less feverish than I expected. Towards morning, however, he began to ramble in his speech, and talked about his mother and father, and a young sister who had died. "I thought I should find him," I heard him say. "Oh, that my mother could have lived to have seen him again! Oh, that I could once more be with him! If he were here now, I am sure that I should soon get well." These words were said at intervals, between other less coherent remarks.

Daylight broke before I had closed my eyes. We again looked out, in the faint hope that the Indians might have landed at some spot near us, and encamped for the night; but we could nowhere see them. We were at length convinced that they had made off with our canoe, and deserted us. Had we been by ourselves, our position would have been bad enough; but with poor Arthur in his wounded state, requiring immediate help, it was still worse. The Indians had so long behaved well and faithfully, that we had not supposed them capable of such conduct, although they had showed such discontent on the previous day.

"What must we do?" I asked of John.

"We must either build a canoe or a raft, or wait till we can hail some passing craft, and get taken off," he answered. "Our father will certainly send and look for us by-and-by, when he finds that we do not return; but in the meantime they will all be very anxious, and think that we have been cut off by the rebels."

John and I had fortunately brought our guns and ammunition; so that we were better off than we might have been had the Indians overpowered us, and put us on shore by force. We were, indeed, able to supply ourselves amply with food, but it was not well suited for Arthur. By the end of the day he appeared to have grown worse instead of better. I sat up with him part of the night, forgetting how little sleep I had had for some time. He rambled more than ever. It was painful sometimes to hear him. When he at last dropped to sleep, I began to doze also, till I slipped off my seat, and lay utterly overcome with fatigue on the ground. It was daylight, and I found John lifting me up. I had never seen him look so anxious.

"I thought you had swooned, Harry," he said; "and poor Arthur seems no better. What can we do for him?"

I looked at Arthur. He was in a troubled sleep, was very pale, and uttering incoherent expressions. I would have given anything to have known what to do; but except moistening his lips with water, there was nothing I could think of likely to benefit him. All day long he remained in that state. I sat by his side, while John occasionally went out with his gun. He was never long absent, as he said he could not bear the thought of being away from Arthur, fearing he might be worse. Now and then I got up and added fresh fuel to our fire, that I might make some broth with some of the game John had brought in; thinking that might possibly do good to my poor patient. I was thus employed, when I heard John shout out. Taking a glance at Arthur, I ran forward, when I caught sight of John near the bank, waving his hat, while just beyond him was a montaria, with a number of people in her, among whom I distinguished the tall figure of the recluse standing up and waving in return. The canoe approached the bank just as I reached it; and directly afterwards two other persons jumped up and waved to us, while a dog put his paws on the gunwale and uttered a loud bark. True, who had followed me, barked in return. What was my joy to recognise my two old school-fellows Houlston and Tony. In a couple of minutes they were on shore, and we were warmly shaking hands; while True and Faithful were rubbing noses with equal cordiality.

"Where is my boy?" exclaimed the recluse—or rather Mr Mallet, for so I should properly call him.

"He is with us. He has been sadly hurt. If any one can do him good, I am sure you can, sir," I said.

"Oh, take me to him—show me where he is!" exclaimed Mr Mallet, in an anxious tone. "Hand me out that box there! It contains the few medicines I possess—it may be of use."

"Is it Arthur Mallet he is speaking of?" asked Houlston, following with the chest. "What is the matter with him?"

I told him briefly what had occurred. There were several other persons in the canoe, but I was too much interested in my friends to observe them. We hurried back to the hut where Arthur was lying. The recluse had hastened on before us, and was now kneeling by the side of his young son. He was perfectly calm, but I saw how much he felt, by the expression of his anxious countenance. Arthur opened his eyes and recognised his father.

"This is what I was praying for," he whispered. "I have been very ill, and was afraid of leaving the world without once again seeing you. I am so thankful. If it is God's will, I am now ready to die."

"Oh, but I pray it may not be his will, my boy," said Mr Mallet. "You must live for my sake, to be a comfort and support to me."

"You will not go back, then, and live in the woods by yourself, my dear father?" said Arthur.

"No; I hope to live wherever you do, my boy," he answered.

Arthur's pale countenance brightened, and he pressed his father's hand.

"You must not talk, however, Arthur," said Mr Mallet. "You require rest, and I may find some remedies which may benefit you."

He eagerly looked over the contents of his medicine-chest; and desiring to have some fresh-water brought him, he quickly compounded a draught, which he gave to Arthur. We left the father and son together, while we returned to the canoe. On our way Houlston and Tony recounted to me briefly what had occurred. They had made their way nearly up to the mouth of the Napo, when, not finding us, they had determined to visit every spot on the shore where we were likely to have stopped. They had at length put into the creek, near the abode of the recluse.

"Much to our surprise," said Houlston, "we were accosted in English by a tall white man. On telling him our errand, he informed us that you had long since gone down the stream, and seemed very much surprised and grieved to find that we had not encountered you. He at once volunteered to accompany us, saying that he was greatly interested in your welfare, and could not rest satisfied without assisting in our search for you. We were, of course, very glad to have his company; and going back to his hut, he soon returned with two Indians—a man and his wife—who also wished to come with us. They are there," and Houlston pointed to the canoe.

Just then one of the Indians landed; and though dressed in a shirt and trousers, I recognised him as our friend Maono. He was followed by Illora, also habited in more civilised costume than when we had at first seen her. They greeted me kindly, and inquired, with more warmth than Indians generally exhibit, for their son and daughter. I assured them of their welfare, and of the esteem in which they were held by my family. They appeared to be gratified, and then inquired for the Indians who had accompanied us. Maono was excessively indignant when we told him of the trick they had played us, and threatened to put them to death when he got back to his people. We entreated him, however, for our sakes, not to punish them so severely; indeed, we told him we would rather he pardoned them altogether, as they had been influenced by a desire to return to their people, and perhaps supposed that we might prevent them from so doing. They had till that moment been faithful and obedient, and we assured him that we had had no cause to complain of them.

Some time was spent in talking to Tony and Houlston. On our return to the hut we found Mr Mallet standing in front of it. He said Arthur was improving, but begged that we would remain where we were, as he was unwilling to move him at present. We of course willingly agreed to do what he wished, and forthwith set to work to put up huts for the time we might have to remain on the island. We gave up our hut to Mr Mallet and Arthur, and made a large fire in front of it, while we had another, at which we cooked our suppers. Not for a moment, I believe, did the recluse close his eyes during that night, though most of our party slept soundly. Whenever I awoke I saw him moving to and fro. Once I could not help getting out of my hammock and asking him whether Arthur was improving. "I trust he may be," was the answer. "I shall know to-morrow."

In the morning Arthur certainly appeared better, his wounds having been dressed by the skilful hands of his father. Arthur's state, however, was still too precarious to allow of his removal without risk. Anxious as we were to get back to our friends, we remained, therefore, three days longer on the island. Occasionally John, Houlston, Tony, and I made excursions to the mainland, finding it inhabited, to shoot; while Maono and Illora were very successful in their fishing expeditions.

"Oh, I wish Arthur was well!" exclaimed Tony. "This is just the sort of fun we were looking forward to; and I say, Harry, I hope it is only the beginning of our adventures. Our employers, I know, will very gladly send us up the river to purchase produce, and I dare say you can make arrangements to come with us."

I of course said I should be very glad to do so, though I could not then say what my father intended to do after reaching Para.

We shot a good deal of game—quadruped, four-handed, and feathered. Among the latter, by-the-by, was a curious bird, which we found feeding on the marshy banks of a lake, to which we made our way, attracted by its loud and peculiar cry. Creeping on, we caught sight of it as it stood on the shore. Houlston, who first saw it, declared that it was a large crane. It was about the size of a swan, and getting nearer, I saw that it had an extraordinary horn on the top of its head, surrounded by black and white feathers, while the upper part of its wings had two sharp horns projecting from them—formidable weapons of attack or defence. Houlston fired, but missed. He had not improved as a sportsman since we parted. John at that moment came up, and sent a ball into the bird's neck. On this True and Faithful dashed forward, but still the bird, though unable to run, showed fight with its wings and kept them at bay. It soon, however, sunk down lifeless on the ground. Its plumage was very handsome. The head and neck were of a greenish-brown colour, covered with soft feathers. The breast and thighs were of silvery white, and the back was black, with the exception of the upper part, which was brown, with yellow spots. It was, we found, the anhima of the Brazils, known also as the horned kamichi, or, more learnedly, *Palamedea*. It is sometimes called the horned screamer, from its loud and wild cry. We laughingly told Houlston that, as he had missed it, he should have the honour of carrying it; which he very good-naturedly did, though it was a considerable load to bear through the forest.

Chapter Twenty One
Conclusion

Next morning Mr Mallet gave us the satisfactory intelligence that Arthur was sufficiently well to bear moving. We therefore at once proceeded on our voyage. Each day after that he improved; and at length we came in sight of the island where we had left our family. We had some, difficulty in finding our way up the narrow channel which led to their camp. As we approached the spot, we saw a good-sized vessel on the stocks, surrounded by a number of persons. One of them, discovering us as we turned the point, shouted to his companions, when, suddenly leaving their work, they advanced towards us with guns in their hands in a threatening attitude. We shouted out to them, when they, perceiving that we were friends, came forward to meet us. Our father was among the first we saw. After he had received us affectionately, and warmly greeted Houlston and Tony, we told him that Mr Mallet had come with us. No sooner did my father see him, than, taking his hand, he exclaimed, "What, my old friend and school-fellow! I little expected to find you out here! Where have you come from?"

"From the wilderness, where I have spent long years of banishment, and from whence my young son succeeded in thus too far dragging me forth. I could not make him lead the life I have so long lived, and I cannot bear the thought of parting from him."

"And what could make you wish to think of doing anything of the sort?" exclaimed my father. "You surprised all your friends by leaving England—so my brother long since wrote me word—and no one has been able to account for it."

"Not account for it!" exclaimed Mr Mallet. "Surely my friends would not have wished me to remain, dishonoured or disgraced, or doomed to a felon's death?"

He looked round as he spoke, and seeing that I was nearer than he had supposed, led my father to a distance. Meantime our mother, Fanny, and Ellen, had come down.

I need not describe our meeting, or the concern Ellen exhibited at hearing of Arthur's accident, and saw his still, pale face as we lifted him out of the canoe. He was, however, able to walk with our assistance. We found the whole party very anxious, as information had reached them that the natives had discovered their retreat and intended attacking them. They had therefore been hurrying on the large montaria with all speed, in hopes of getting away before the arrival of the enemy.

In a short time our father and Mr Mallet arrived. A wonderful change had taken place in the countenance of the latter. He now looked bright and cheerful, and a smile played over his features such as I had never before seen them wear. After being introduced to my mother and sisters, and Senhor Pimento's family, he hurried up to Arthur, and as he threw his arms round his neck tears burst from his eyes, but they were evidently tears of joy.

"But we must not lose time," said my father, pointing to the vessel, at which Domingos and Antonio and the other men were still busily working. We soon had occupation given us—ample to employ our minds as well as our hands. Arthur was taken good care of by my mother and sisters, and I was glad to see him play with Nimble and Toby, who at once knew him. We worked away till dark. The fires were lighted, and by their bright blaze we were still able to continue our labours. Thus we hoped in a couple of days to have our craft ready for launching. It was decked over astern and forward, so as to afford a cabin to the ladies and shelter for our stores, which required protection from the weather. We had large mat-sails and long oars, so that she was well fitted, we hoped, to encounter the heavy seas we were likely to meet with towards the mouth of the mighty river. John suggested that we should erect a stockade near the vessel, behind which we might defend ourselves, and prevent her from being burned, should the rebels make the threatened attack. This we all set to work to do; and as we had an abundance of materials at hand, a fort was soon erected, of sufficient strength, if defended by firearms, to repel any attack the natives were likely to make against it.

"I hope the fellows will come on!" exclaimed Tony, who, with Houlston, was among the most active in the work. "I should like to be engaged in a skirmish. We have had but a tame life of it. I thought we might have seen some of the fun going forward at Santarem; but the whites had all escaped out of the place before we passed by, and the red-skins had possession of it."

"I rather think we were fortunate in escaping those same red-skins!" exclaimed Houlston. "They murdered all the whites they could find, and they would probably have treated us in the same way if we had fallen in with them. If those fellows had attacked us, depend upon it we should have had to fight hard for our lives."

"Perhaps, my friend, we can find some better means of keeping the enemy at bay than those you are taking," observed the recluse. "However, follow your own plan. I trust, for the sake of humanity that it may be labour lost."

I did not hear John's reply, but he continued the work. Scouts were sent out at night to watch the entrance of the channel, lest the rebels might attempt to steal upon us during the hours of darkness; while we all slept with our arms ready for instant use.

I was awakened by hearing a shot fired. Another followed. "The rebels are coming!" I heard my father shouting out. "To your posts, my friends!"

In less than a minute our whole party had assembled, and with my father at our head, we advanced in the direction whence the shots had proceeded. Before we had gone many paces, our two scouts came running up with the announcement that several canoes were approaching the mouth of the igarape. Daylight was just then breaking, though it had not penetrated into the forest. The two Indians were again sent back to watch the further movements of the rebels. We meantime held a council of war, and having conveyed all our stores and provisions within the stockade, retired to it, there to await the enemy. In a short time the scouts came back, reporting that the Indians had landed, and were advancing through the forest.

"Let me now try, my friends, what I can do with these people," said the recluse, standing up in our midst. "I resided among them for some time. They know me, and I trust will be more ready to listen to my arguments than to those with which you are prepared to receive them."

"Pray do as you judge best," said my father.

Senhor Pimento appeared to have little confidence in his success, and addressing his people, entreated them to fight bravely, as the rebels would certainly give them no quarter.

The recluse, without further delay, taking not even a stick in his hand, went forth from the fort, and was soon lost to sight among the shades of the forest. Our Portuguese friends were in a great state of agitation; but my sisters, especially Ellen, remained perfectly calm. I complimented her on her courage. "Oh, I am sure Arthur's father will accomplish what he undertakes," she answered. "I have therefore no fear of an attack."

We, however, could not help looking anxiously for the return of the recluse. The time went slowly by. "I am afraid the wretches will shoot him before he has time to speak to them," observed Senhor Pimento. Pedro, who was of a generous, warm-hearted disposition, proposed that some of us should sally out, and try and overtake him before he reached the enemy.

This was overruled by my father. "Our friend does not act without judgment," he observed. "He knows the character of the people better perhaps than we do. Hark! what is that?" The sound of many voices shouting came faintly through the forest, as from a distance.

"Hurrah! they are coming on to attack us!" cried Tony; "we will give them a warm reception."

"I hope rather that those sounds betoken that the Indians have recognised our friend," observed my father.

Still we waited, many of our party looking out, as if they expected to see the rebels approaching in battle array. At length a single figure appeared emerging from the forest. It was the recluse. He hurried forward towards us, and on entering the fort, took my father, John, and I aside.

"I have not been so successful as I should wish," he said. "They are perfectly ready to let the English, with whom they have no cause of quarrel, go free, but they insist that the Portuguese gentleman and his son should be delivered up to them, though they consent to allow the rest of his family to accompany you if you wish it."

"We cannot accept such terms," said my father at once. "We are resolved to defend our friends with our lives!"

"I thought as much," said Mr Mallet. "I promised, however, to convey their message, in order to gain time. Is there no way by which your friends can escape by the other end of the igarape?"

"There may be, but the Indians know it as well as we do," observed my father, "and would probably lie in wait to catch them. I must ask you to return and inform them that we cannot give up our friends who have hospitably entertained us, and that if they insist on attacking the fort, they must take the consequences."

The recluse once more went back to the insurgent Indians. Pedro, on hearing the message, tried to persuade his father to escape with him in one of the small canoes; but the old gentleman declared at once that he would not make the attempt, as he was sure he should thus only fall into the hands of his enemies.

We now anxiously awaited the return of our friend. An hour passed by, when we saw among the trees a large number of natives approaching the fort, some armed with muskets, but the greater number with bows and arrows.

"We shall have no difficulty in beating back that rabble!" exclaimed Tony. "We must first pick off the fellows with firearms, and the others will soon take to flight."

I did not feel so confident as my friend. The enemy from their numbers alone were formidable, and if well led, might, I feared, easily overpower us. Their numbers increased, and they seemed on the point of making a dash at the fort, when a loud shout was raised behind them. They turned round, looking eagerly in the direction from whence it came. Presently three persons came out from among them. One I recognised as the recluse; but the other two I looked at again and again, and at length was convinced that one was Don José, and the other his attendant Isoro. Don José, turning to the natives, addressed them in the Lingua Geral, which they all probably understood. They were sufficiently near for us to hear what was said.

"My friends," he exclaimed, "what is it you require? Do you seek the blood of these white people? What will that benefit you? Listen to Pumacagua—a Peruvian cacique—who regards with affection the whole Indian race; who would wish to see them united as one tribe, prosperous and happy, enjoying all the benefits of our magnificent country. If you destroy these people, you will but bring down the vengeance of the powerful whites on your heads. Some among them are my friends. They have never harmed you. They wish you well, I know, and are even now sufferers for the cause of liberty. Be advised by me. Return to your homes, and seek not by force to obtain your rights. It will, I know too well by bitter experience, be in vain. Trust to me and my English friends, who will not rest till we have gained for you the justice you demand."

We saw the leaders among the Indians consulting together. The recluse now went among them, and addressed them earnestly. His and Don José's words seemed to have a powerful effect. Greatly to our relief, they began to retire through the forest. Our friends accompanied them to their canoes, while Arthur and I followed at a distance to watch what would next take place. The canoes were launched, and the natives, bidding an affectionate farewell to the recluse, and a respectful one to Pumacagua, leaped into them, and took their departure to the opposite bank of the river. We hurried on to meet our friends, and soon afterwards my father came out of the fort to welcome Don José. They greeted each other warmly.

"Finding that I could no longer render service to my countrymen, and that my own life was in constant danger," Don José said, "I was on my way down the river to join you, when I saw a large number of canoes drawn up on the beach, a few people only remaining with them. From them I learned what was taking place, and I at once suspected, from what they told me, who it was they were about to attack. I instantly landed, and overtook the main body of insurgents. The rest you know."

Our friends then returned to the fort, and all hands at once set to work to complete our vessel. Tony alone was somewhat disappointed at so pacific a termination to the affair. The additional hands whom Don José had brought with him were of great assistance, as they were all expert boat-builders; and in less than a couple of days our craft was launched, and ready to proceed on her voyage. Don José and our father had, of course, much to talk about. The former seemed greatly out of spirits at the turn affairs had taken, and in despair of the establishment of true liberty in his country. His affection for my father had induced him to follow us, and he purposed to remain with him at Para till a change of affairs in Peru might enable him to return.

The rainy season was now completely over; though the heat was very great, the weather was fine. At length our new vessel, which we called the *Manatee*, with the canoes of Don José and Houlston in company, emerging from the igarape, made sail to the eastward.

I have not space to describe the voyage. Sometimes we navigated a wide expanse of water, where the river's banks were several miles apart; sometimes we passed amid an archipelago, through narrow channels where the branches of the giant trees almost joined overhead. Sometimes we sailed on with a favourable breeze, and at other times had to lower our sails and take to the oars. For some hundred miles we had the green forest alone in sight on either side, and here and there long extending sand-banks, in which turtles are wont to lay their eggs. As we passed near the shore, vast numbers of wild fowl were seen on the banks, while the river swarmed with living creatures. Dolphins came swimming by, showing their heads above the surface, again to plunge down as they advanced up the stream. Now and then we caught sight of a huge manatee, and we saw alligators everywhere basking on the shores or showing their ugly snouts above the surface. At length a high, flat-topped range of hills appeared on our left hand—the spurs, I believe, of the mountains of Guiana. The river was now for some distance fully ten miles in width; so wide, indeed, that it looked more like an inland sea or the ocean itself than a fresh-water stream. At length we entered one end of the Tajapurú, which is a curious natural canal, extending for one hundred miles or more from the main stream towards the city of Para. It is of great depth in some places, and one hundred yards in width; but in others so narrow that the topmost boughs of the trees almost met over our heads. Often as we sailed along we were hemmed in by two green walls, eighty feet in height, which made it seem as if we were sailing through a deep gorge. Emerging from it, we entered the Para river, and sailing on, were soon in a magnificent sea-like expanse, the only shore visible being that of the island of Marajo, presenting a narrow blue line far away on our left. We passed a number of curious boats and rafts of various shapes and rigs, bringing produce from the villages and farms scattered along the banks of the many vast rivers which pour their waters into the Atlantic. Still, all this time, we were navigating merely one of the branches of the mighty Amazon; for, though we had long felt the influence of the tide, yet the water, even when it was flowing, was but slightly brackish.

At length, entering the sheltered bay of Goajara, we, with thankful hearts, saw the city of Para stretching out before us along the shore, and our vessel was soon moored in safety alongside the quay. Houlston and Tony hurried off to their friends, who came down to welcome us and take us to their house. In most places we should have attracted no small amount of curiosity as we proceeded through the streets. Each of the ladies, as well as Maria and the Indian girl, with two or more parrots and other birds on their shoulders; Nimble sitting on mine with his tail round my neck; Arthur carrying Toby; while Tony and Houlston had a couple of monkeys apiece, which they had obtained on their voyage. Such a spectacle, however, was too common in Para to attract much attention.

I must now, as briefly as possible, bring my journal to a conclusion. My father here resolved to establish a house of business, of which Mr Mallet was to be made chief manager, with Arthur as his assistant. Maono and Illora, after remaining some time with us, considerably, I hope, to their benefit, returned to their people with the intention of showing them the advantages of civilisation, and imparting a knowledge of the true God and his plan of salvation, which they themselves had obtained. We were thankful that they consented to leave Duppo and Oria with us. The two young Indians made rapid progress in English, besides learning Portuguese; and Ellen and Arthur spared no pains in their endeavours to instruct them in the more important truths of religion. Don José and his faithful Isoro returned at length to Ecuador, when peace was once more established in that long distracted province; and the cacique wrote whenever an opportunity occurred for sending a letter down the Amazon. Senhor Pimento and his family after a time returned to their estate, and we never failed to pay them a visit when we went up the river. The rebellion of the natives was at length happily quelled, with less bloodshed than often occurs under similar circumstances.

Houlston, Arthur, Tony, and I made not only one, but several excursions up the mighty river, and throughout many parts of that wonderful region embraced by the Brazils. I might give a long account of our adventures, which were not less interesting than those I have already described. Perhaps I may some day have an opportunity of doing so.

Nimble and Toby lived to the extreme end of monkey existence—the patriarchs of Ellen's ever-increasing menagerie, which was superintended by Domingos when she had more important duties to attend to, and guarded, I may add, by the two attached canine brethren, Faithful and True.

I made two trips to England, each time on board the *Inca*, still commanded by Captain Byles. The first time Sam was on board, but on our return to Para he obtained his discharge, and settled down in that city, where I often had the pleasure of a long talk with him. "Ah, Massa Harry!" he used to say, "I chose de good part, and God take care of me as he promise; and his promise neber fail. He gib me good t'ings here, and I know him gib me better when I go up dere;" and he pointed to the blue sky, seen through the front of the provision store of which he was the owner.

I am thankful to say that the rest of my friends also, as Sam had done, chose "the good part." Arthur had the happiness of being the means of bringing his father to a knowledge of the truth. His great wish was to make the simple gospel known among the long benighted natives of that magnificent region in which we met with the adventures I have recorded, and, though hitherto opposed by difficulties which have appeared insurmountable, he still cherishes the hope that they may be overcome, and that missionaries with the Bible in their hand may, ere long, be found traversing the mighty Amazon and its tributaries, now ploughed by numerous steamers up to the very foot of the Andes, engaged in opening up to commerce the unmeasured resources of the Brazils. I should indeed be thankful if my tale contributes to draw the attention of the Christian philanthropist to the unhappy condition of the numerous tribes of that interesting country which I have attempted to describe.